Critics praise Andrew Taylor's Lydmouth mysteries:

An Air that Kills

'Captures perfectly the drab atmosphere and cloying morality of the 1950s, when surface respectability masked nasty social and sexual undercurrents. Taylor is an excellent writer. He plots with care and intelligence and the solution to the mystery is satisfyingly chilling'

The Times

'There is no denying Taylor's talent, his almost Victorian prose exudes a quality uncommon among his contemporaries . . . his eye for detail and an enviable ability to dissect relationships and communal habits make for a pleasurable read'

Time Out

The Mortal Sickness

'The reader sees inside the pressure-cooker of village life and how it leads to murder and then, as inexorably, to exposure. Very enjoyable'

Spectator

'A fine, atmospheric thriller'

Daily Mail

'Taylor's remarkable talent shows in his language and his skilful plotting . . . Wicked and wonderful'

Yorkshire Post

The Lover of the Grave

'The tensions, both emotional and sexual, that run through this deftly plotted novel stretch the reader's nerves almost to breaking point'

Val McDermid, *Manchester Evening News*

'Andrew Taylor was given the thumbs up long ago for beautifully crafted, well written narratives combining subtlety, depth and that vital "Oh my God what the hell is going to happen next" factor, which is the driving force of the storyteller . . . *The Lover of the Grave* . . . makes you long to read the next tale'

Frances Fyfield, *Express on Sunday*

The Suffocating Night

'As usual with Taylor's stories, there is no more to the puzzle than is immediately apparent. It's another satisfying read, in which the characters are as important as the events and tension develops naturally, without contrivance'

Susanna Yager, *Sunday Telegraph*

'Andrew Taylor does not fall into the trap of mistaking drama for melodrama. Nor does he suffer from the insecure urge to say too much . . . Taylor is the master of small lives writ large and, in the phrase coined in this era of surley pubs and poor food, he has carved a detective story which is deceptively calm and cool, but really smashing'

Frances Fyfield, *Express*

Where Roses Fade

'Taylor is an excellent writer'

The Times

'Andrew Taylor is a writer who constantly surprises'

Spectator

Also by Andrew Taylor

THE LYDMOUTH NOVELS

An Air that Kills
The Mortal Sickness
The Lover of the Grave
The Suffocating Night

About the author

Andrew Taylor has worked as a boatbuilder, wages clerk, librarian, labourer and publisher's reader. He has written many crime novels as well as children's books, and lives with his wife and their two children in the Forest of Dean, on the borders of England and Wales.

Where Roses Fade

Andrew Taylor

NEW ENGLISH LIBRARY
Hodder & Stoughton

First published in Great Britain in 1998
by Hodder and Stoughton
First published in paperback in 1999
by Hodder and Stoughton
A division of Hodder Headline

A New English Library Paperback

10 9 8 7 6 5 4 3 2 1

A CIP catalogue record for this title
is available from the British Library.

ISBN 0 340 69600 1

Printed and bound in Great Britain by
Clays Ltd, St Ives plc

Hodder and Stoughton
A division of Hodder Headline
338 Euston Road
London NW1 3BH

With rue my heart is laden
 For golden friends I had,
For many a rose-lipt maiden
 And many a lightfoot lad.

By brooks too broad for leaping
 The lightfoot boys are laid;
The rose-lipt girls are sleeping
 In fields where roses fade.

A. E. Housman, *A Shropshire Lad*, LIV

The Principal Characters

JOAN AILSMORE – WPC, Lydmouth Division

BERNIE BROADBENT– County Councillor; cousin of Edith Thornhill

MRS BROWNING – manageress of the Gardenia Café

MINNIE CALDER – a retired nurse; aunt of Jimmy Leigh

VIOLET EVANS – a secretary; and her parents TED and JUNE EVANS

JILL FRANCIS – deputy editor of the *Lydmouth Gazette*

MATTIE HARRIS – a waitress; and her parents MR and MRS HARRIS of Eastbury

BRIAN KIRBY – Detective Sergeant, Lydmouth Division

JIMMY LEIGH – nephew of Minnie Calder

GERALD PEMBRIDGE – County Director of Planning; EDNA, his wife; and BILL, his son

ROBERT SEDBURY – estate agent and auctioneer, and his wife; MALCOLM, his son

RICHARD THORNHILL – Detective Inspector, Lydmouth Division; EDITH, his wife; DAVID and ELIZABETH, their children

CHARLOTTE WEMYSS-BROWN – owner of the *Lydmouth Gazette*; and PHILIP her husband, editor of the newspaper

RAYMOND WILLIAMSON – Detective Superintendent; and BUNTY, his wife

SWIMMING DANGER

Councillor Warns Young Swimmers

Once again the Town Council has asked police to keep a close eye on children swimming in the Lyd during the summer. Some members felt the practice should be banned altogether for the duration of the War because police resources were so stretched.

'There was too much dangerous horseplay last year.' said Councillor Bryant. 'I urge boys to act responsibly, especially when diving or jumping from New Bridge. Someone could have a very nasty accident indeed.'

Lydmouth Gazette, Friday, 28 May, 1943

Threats are dark prayers.

'Jimmy Leigh,' he said, so softly only he could hear, 'Jimmy Leigh, I'll kill you, Jimmy Leigh.'

He felt his lips move, his tongue flicking against the top of his mouth, the feather-like touch of his breath slipping away from him and into the warmth of the summer night. He imagined the words swooping through the high-ceilinged room, then hovering like buzzards above their prey.

'Jimmy Leigh, I'll kill you, Jimmy Leigh.'

Down the words went, dark prayers, down to the sleeping mind of Jimmy Leigh.

Not buzzards now: the words would work their way like burrowing worms into what his father called the old grey matter.

Perhaps Jimmy Leigh didn't have grey matter. Everyone knew he wasn't all there.

The boy in the next bed whimpered in his sleep. It was never silent here, never entirely dark either. Someone else stirred and springs creaked. A teaspoon clattered in the little office at the end of the ward. Nurse Calder was playing cards with Nurse Jones, and sometimes he heard them say 'spades' or 'your deal', the soft click as a card went down on the table, and the rustle as the pack was shuffled.

Nurse Calder hated him. Nurse Calder was Jimmy Leigh's aunt.

'You dirty boy, Malcolm Sedbury, the next time you do that in your bed, I'll make you eat it.'

He cringed at the memory, his stomach contracting. Now she left it as long as possible when he asked for the bedpan, hoping he would have another accident, so that she would have the excuse that she needed.

'Why haven't you finished your porridge, Malcolm Sedbury? Think yourself too smart for it, do you?' Nurse Calder haunted his mealtimes too, and encouraged her colleagues to do likewise. 'Well, I know one little boy who's not going to see his mummy and daddy this afternoon.'

He stared up at the ceiling far above his head. It looked as remote as the sky. Like everything else in the ward, the scale was wrong for him. The beds were too big, too far from the floor. The meals too large, the blankets too heavy. They were in Lydmouth Cottage Hospital, a building which before he had known only from the outside. He remembered his father once saying that the place looked like a lunatic asylum. It had pointed windows and battlements like a castle. It was built of local stone, a murky purple streaked with soot. Inside was worse. It did not look like a lunatic asylum, it was one.

Usually this was where old men came to die – Malcolm had heard Nurse Calder muttering about it to one of the parents. Now it was the boys' long-term orthopaedic ward. There were twenty-four of them here, twelve a side, from a four-year-old boy who slept or whined like a puppy, to a seventeen-year-old who was almost a man and had a soft black moustache. Once there had been a three-year-old boy who called endlessly for his mother. But they must have moved him out of the fever ward before they should have done, or perhaps there was something else the matter with him. In any case, one day they'd put the curtains around his bed and, in the morning, the curtains were gone and the bed was empty, waiting for the next patient.

Everyone told Malcolm he was lucky to be alive. They had told him it had been much worse in the fever ward, where he had so nearly died. He had jumbled dreamlike memories of that time, of terrible pains, especially in his head, of the doctors and the nurses moving slowly between the beds with long, sad faces as if they too were in a dream. They hadn't even allowed his parents to come in. Once or twice, a nurse had pointed out their faces bobbing like white fish in goldfish bowls behind the porthole windows of the ward doors.

But this ward was worse. This ward had Nurse Calder and Jimmy Leigh. He almost wished the fever and the pain would come back again, just so they would have to move him. Here, in this ward, was another fear. He saw it in the pity in the faces of his parents and his sisters. He saw it in the expensive presents they brought him, the toys, the soldiers, the books, most of which never felt truly his, or not for very long.

'You won't mind if Jimmy borrows this for five minutes, will you?' Nurse Calder would say. 'It's only right. He's not got anyone to give him expensive presents, after all. He's not a lucky little boy like you.'

After Jimmy had played with a toy, it was never the same. Lead soldiers had come back without their weapons or even entire limbs. Cars lost wheels and sometimes had the unmistakable marks of teeth scarring the paint work. Jimmy was as old as Malcolm, but he chewed toys.

'You mustn't mind, dear,' Malcolm's mother told him in a

whisper when he complained to her. 'The poor little boy's not quite right in his head. He's very sweet, though, isn't he?'

Jimmy was one of the more mobile patients. He could drag himself around the ward on crutches. Once he came over to Malcolm's bed while Malcolm slept, and woke him by poking him in the eye with a finger. Malcolm had screamed his way into consciousness. Nurse Calder had slapped his palm with a ruler for disturbing everyone.

If only they would let Bill come and see him. Bill was his best friend. If he knew what Jimmy was doing to Malcolm when the nurses weren't looking, Bill would soon sort him out. Bill was big, and good with his fists.

Yet another night stretched itself out as if time had become infinitely elastic. No raids tonight, unfortunately. He welcomed the raids because the sirens and distant drone of the engines punctuated the great desert of the night. They gave him something to think about, something normal to be afraid of. They stopped him thinking of the last day.

The last day. Over and over again he remembered it until he wished he could drown his memories, drown himself. He remembered the Whit weekend, with the sun shining from a sky the colour of his elder sister's new dress, with the river swollen with recent rain, cool and inviting.

That afternoon he and Bill went down to New Bridge. This was where people often fished, and when the weather was hot young men and boys climbed on the broad stone parapet on the downstream side and leapt into the brown water below. Most of them came from Templefields, were what his mother would call 'vulgar'. That added an element of danger to the excitement. Malcolm and Bill were in their last year at the prep department of Ashbridge School, and therefore would often be considered natural prey by the boys who went to elementary schools and lived in Templefields.

Not that afternoon, however. Perhaps it was the sunshine, or the thrill of plummeting into the water, but there had been a carnival spirit in the air. Bill and Malcolm sauntered on to the bridge, hands in pockets, nerves as taut as violin strings. They paused to look down at the Lyd flowing between the massive piers. Jimmy Leigh was nearby, swinging his legs over the river, staring foolishly at the water.

A deep voice said, 'You kids going to jump or just get in everyone else's way?'

It was one of the bigger boys, cigarette dangling from the corner of his mouth, still good humoured. He looked in turn at the three of them, Bill and Malcolm leaning on the parapet, and Jimmy Leigh sitting a few feet beyond them.

'Jump,' Jimmy said, nodding his head slowly as if he had suddenly and unexpectedly understood something. *Jump?*

Malcolm had thought, why not? He didn't answer the boy but he unstrapped his sandals and kicked them off his feet. He pulled his green Aertex shirt over his head. His mother might kick up a bit of a stink, he didn't think she would really mind if his old khaki shorts were a little damp when he got home. Besides, it was such a hot day that with a bit of luck they would be dry by the time he saw her.

Fear fluttered in his stomach. He glanced at Bill, who was pulling off his shirt, following Malcolm's lead, as usual. Why did Bill always follow, never lead?

'Jump,' Jimmy Leigh said, beaming at the older boy. 'I knows how to jump.'

He was wearing a shirt and shorts, shoes and socks. He didn't take off any of them. With his hands he pushed himself up from the parapet and launched himself into space. A scream hung in the air where he had been. He belly-flopped into the river, sending up silver wings of water on either side of his body.

'Bet that hurt,' said the older boy with quiet satisfaction. 'Who's next? Not yellow, are you? Afraid the Drowner's going to get you?'

He moved a little nearer Malcolm as he spoke and there was something in the movement which was a threat, which gave

Malcolm the sense that if he didn't jump he would very soon be lifted and thrown. He had his pride to consider, too. He climbed up onto the parapet – right up until he was standing, arms outstretched over the void, just as he'd seen the older boys and the young men do. He tried to suppress the memory of that scream, of the great splash that Jimmy Leigh's body had made.

'Come on, Bill,' he said as coolly as he could. 'Last one in's a sissy.'

When he jumped, he tightened the muscles of his stomach and squeezed his buttocks together, as if trying to make his body as small as possible. No time even to feel afraid. Then the cool, brown water sucked him into itself. His arms and legs moved automatically. He swallowed a mouthful of the Lyd, felt himself choking, drowning.

His head broke the surface of the water and he opened his eyes. Drops of water flew through the air like broken glass. Everything was unbearably bright. He gasped for air. Joy as fierce as anger filled him. He had never seen anyone as small as him jump off New Bridge. No one could say he was yellow, not now. He floated on his back and swam a few strokes upstream. He squinted up through the sunlight.

Bill was still on the parapet of the bridge, tall and blond like a Greek god in the encyclopaedia in the school library, looking down at him in the water.

'Come on,' Malcolm croaked because his mouth was watery. 'It's—'

Something hard collided with his forehead and forced his head underwater. He swallowed another mouthful of the Lyd. A second later he resurfaced, coughing. Jimmy Leigh was a few yards away, his arms flailing in a grossly violent doggy paddle, the hands balled into fists, swimming towards the bank.

You did it on purpose, Malcolm thought, you bloody oik.

Later that day, in the warmth of a glimmering early summer evening, when the pains began and when his temperature began to rise, he was convinced that the dagger-like centre of the headache was at the precise spot where Jimmy Leigh's fist had hit him when they were both in the River Lyd.

On purpose.

Chapter One

―――∞∞∞――――

Another warm evening between another spring and another summer.

The rivers were high. There had been much rain in the previous week and now the water was draining down from the hills upstream. The Lyd rustled and surged between the piers of New Bridge. The water slid like a brown, whispering snake down the Minnow, the broad tributary which joined the Lyd a few hundred yards north of New Bridge.

The girl saw nothing of this. Her head swam as she sat up in the bath and turned on the hot tap. The Ascot heater above the bath belched and gave out a subdued roar. It was almost dark now outside, and the bluey orange flames of the gas swamped the soft grey twilight. She adjusted the tap, gradually turning down the flow to increase the heat of the water. The temperature rose. She raised her right arm. The glistening skin was already rosy with the heat.

'Christ,' she muttered, 'why are they so long?'

Loneliness was the one thing she really feared. She lay back in the long bath, and tried not to think about the fact that an old man had died in this house. He must have lain here, time after time.

The heat stung her skin like nettle rash. She lifted her leg away from the stream of water coming from the hot tap. That was the trouble with baths, you were either too hot or too cold. She needed it as hot as possible, as hot as she could bear. A few seconds later, she hooked her big toe around the tap and turned off the flow. The roaring stopped, the flames died, and in the darkening silence she felt more lonely than ever.

If only they hadn't run out of cigarettes. She put out her hand in the darkness, fingers outstretched, until she felt the tips brush against the glass. Not quite alone. She picked up her glass. The raw spirit had made the inside of her mouth numb. It was no longer hard to swallow. She felt suddenly superhuman, as though she could go on drinking and drinking. Perhaps that was the way to deal with the loneliness, to deal with everything. She put down the glass and let the fingers of her right hand slide through the water and trail down her body.

Just skin and flesh and bone, after all. Why do men want it? Wouldn't it be simpler if we none of us had bodies? They only get in the way.

'Come on,' she whispered, afraid to speak more loudly. 'Come on, you stupid buggers, where are you?'

The sky beyond the window was almost black. She saw half a dozen pinpricks of light, the stars. The window was open a few inches because she had not wanted to run the risk of condensation. She thought she heard movement outside. It was almost like slow stealthy footfalls. Perhaps they were coming back. But the bathroom was at the back of the house, overlooking the lawn which sloped down to the Minnow, and they would come to the front. Perhaps she had imagined the noise. Shivering despite the heat, she hugged herself and listened. No sound now, apart from a faint rustling which might have been the leaves of the chestnut tree near the river.

She was imagining things. She had always had too much imagination for her own good, everyone said so. What she needed was a drink.

She stretched out her hands to the glass again, then remembered it was empty. She should have told them to leave the bottle up here. *Need to settle my nerves.* She sat up in the bath, clasping her arms around her knees. The evening air was cooler now and she felt a chill across her shoulders.

The thought of that squat green bottle glowed in her mind like a vision of the Holy Grail. It would be in the morning room at the back of the house. They had sat there when they had first arrived because there was less risk of being seen. She moistened her lips, running her tongue over the slight tackiness of the lipstick. She would need to repair her make-up. Later, though.

First things first. And the first thing of all was another drink. She should have had the bottle upstairs. It was bloody stupid leaving it downstairs. She wasn't going to put up with it.

She clung to the side of the bath and slowly hauled herself to her feet. Suddenly it was much colder. The night air lapped around her body like a tide. She seemed to have become much heavier, too, and when she tried to lift her right leg over the side of the bath, it was as though the air had turned to treacle. She leant against the wall for a moment, gathering strength. Then, with a huge effort, she climbed out of the bath, pushing through the invisible treacle. She staggered, saved herself from falling by gripping the back of the chair and at last stood triumphantly on her own feet.

'I'll do it,' she said aloud. 'I'll bloody show them.'

Part of her mind, the part that was still sober, registered the fact that she had slopped water on the floor, made a mental note that something would have to be done about it. *Settle my nerves first.* She pulled a towel from the wooden rail near the basin – the house was almost fully furnished still, and she had found towels and bed linen, faintly musty but dry, neatly folded on the slatted shelves of a large cupboard on the landing. She dried her feet and then draped the towel around her. It clung to her body like a second skin and made her think of the cocktail dress she had seen in Madame Ghislaine's window the other day. Mid calf-length cream satin, embroidered with sprays of flowers, with a strapless bodice and a fitted straight skirt. Perhaps she could persuade one of the men to buy it for her.

She took a deep breath and opened the bathroom door.

Silly to feel scared of shadows, she told herself. But the landing was darker than the bathroom and the head of the stairs was a black pit. What was there to be frightened of? She laughed to show herself she wasn't scared. The sound that emerged was high and nervous, not like her usual laugh at all. Like someone else's laugh. She walked down the landing towards the stairs as briskly as the tightness of the towel and the surrounding gloom would let her.

Carpeting ran along the middle of the landing and flowed on down the stairs. Its warmth was comforting. She followed it down to the hall, where she peeped out of the window by the front door. No sign of anybody on the drive. Not that she could see properly. There were no street lights here so it was hard to disentangle shapes from the twilight. The white gates glimmered faintly at the end of the drive.

She turned and went into the morning room. There was a round table near the door to the kitchen, and nearer the window several armchairs where they had sat before she came upstairs for the bath. The bottle was still on the table. She had forgotten to bring her glass, but it didn't matter. She would take the bottle to the glass, she thought with a giggle, rather than the other way round. Not straightaway, though. The mouth of the bottle clattered against her teeth and some of the gin ran over her chin and rolled into the valley between her breasts. She was warmer now, braver. What she needed was a cigarette, and then everything would be bearable.

She walked to the armchairs by the window, banging her hip against the sideboard. They had left the ashtray on the little table by the French windows. With a bit of luck there would be something left on at least one of the stubs. People were very wasteful with their cigarettes, especially those who didn't have to worry about the price of another packet.

She sat down heavily and not entirely intentionally in one of the armchairs and prodded the contents of the ashtray with her forefinger. Just as she'd hoped — one of the butts was more than an inch long. There were matches on the table and a moment later the cigarette was in her mouth and a match was in her hand.

It was in that moment, just as the match scraped along the side of the box, just before the flame burst out of the match head, that she sensed movement on the other side of the glass. The flame flared. She lit the cigarette automatically, despite the panic welling up inside her.

Someone tapped on the window.

Lost the front door key?

A face swam into focus, the features pushed against the window. The panic dwindled, pushed away by relief as she recognised who it was.

The lips moved soundlessly. Once again there was a tapping on the glass.

Well, why not?

She struggled out of the chair, unbolted the French window, top and bottom, and pulled one leaf open. Night air flowed into the room.

'Don't just stand there,' she said. 'Come in before I catch my death of cold.'

Swaying like a leaf in the breeze, she smiled. The familiar sense of power flooded through her, blanketing all the things she did not want to think about. She beckoned with the cigarette, its tip a fiery line.

'Come on. I've not got all night, you know.'

This time she swayed too far. She stepped backwards hurriedly to regain her balance. Her calves collided with something yielding. She collapsed into the seat of the armchair behind her, so neatly that the move might have been planned. The towel slackened its grip on her body.

Well, why not?

The idea amused her and she began to laugh. She noticed

with pride that the sound did not come out as a nervous giggle as it had in the bathroom. She was no longer scared – she was herself again. No, this was her usual laugh, husky, and full of promise.

People liked it when she laughed.

Chapter Two

───◆◆◆───

Jimmy Leigh was down in Templefields, holding the engine as if it were a baby and watching the blood in the water.

The red streaks were clearly visible at this point because the Minnow ran clear over a gravelled bed. Further down, where it joined the Lyd, the streaks vanished, merging with the reddish brown water.

Jimmy heard footsteps on the towpath, He ducked back and waited, trembling, praying he hadn't been seen. The footsteps continued in the same even rhythm. When it was safe again, Jimmy could not help peeping. He saw the back of a man in khaki overalls streaked with what looked like rust. Jimmy thought he probably worked at the slaughterhouse a little further upstream at the end of Mincing Lane. Earlier in the afternoon, Jimmy had heard the high, senseless protests of the animals coming under the knife.

He leant back against the wall, trying to quieten his breathing. He stroked the smooth tin of the engine's boiler. The man on the towpath hadn't seen him. He was safe here. This was Mattie's special place, and he remembered her saying you could spend all day in Fenner's, and no one would know. When she worked at the slaughterhouse, she and Violet used to come here most lunchtimes in the summer. Sometimes they'd share their sandwiches with Jimmy. No one else ever came.

Violet said that sooner or later they were going to pull the place down and build something else there. But for now Fenner's stood empty, safe behind iron gates and a high wall topped with broken glass. It wasn't big – just a cobbled yard, surrounded on three sides by buildings. Most recently it had been used as a timber mill. Directly in front of the gates was what had once been the main shed where they stacked and cut the timber, now a roofless shell. To the right was a block of stone offices, single-storied, the lower halves of their windows covered in gauze screens with G W & H Fenner Limited printed across each one in gilt lettering. And on the left was the row of storehouses and stables which backed on to the towpath.

At the back of one of the stables was a wooden ladder which was safe enough if you avoided the centres of the rungs. It led to a loft with a narrow window looking over the path and the river Minnow beyond. That was where Mattie, Violet and Jimmy came. Violet worked for an estate agent's. She had found a spare key for the wicket set in the iron gates at her office. They had hidden it under a stone in the lane leading down from Mincing Lane. The key had been their secret.

But Mattie didn't come here any more, and nor did Violet, not since Mattie got the job at the Gardenia Café. But Violet had forgotten about the key. It was still under the stone. So Jimmy could still come. But it wasn't the same without Mattie. At least he was safe here. For the time being.

He rested his back against the wall and slid down until he was squatting on his haunches. He hugged the engine. It was green and black, with the letters GWR stencilled in gold on the tender. Luckily the key had been in the engine when he took it.

Now he wished he hadn't. He didn't even have any rails. Besides, Aunt Minnie would ask where he had found the money to buy it. She would start telling him off again, which in a way was why he had taken the engine in the first place.

No. He was getting muddled. Everything was so confusing.

By now everyone — the police, Aunt Minnie — would know he had stolen the engine. The trouble was, the man in the shop had seen him. He had shouted as Jimmy sidled out of the shop with the little locomotive tucked under his jersey. Jimmy had started running, and the man had come after him.

'Stop, thief,' the man had shouted. 'Police, police.'

Now they'd all be looking for him, Jimmy thought, the police, the shop man and Aunt Minnie. He didn't know who terrified him more. They would never understand that he hadn't meant to steal the engine. But Aunt Minnie had upset him so much that he hadn't really known what he was doing. Until he'd done it. He'd wanted something to cheer himself up. Then he saw the engine, so he took it. He hadn't meant to steal it. He was only trying to make himself happy, that was all.

He wondered what would happen when they caught him. He thought probably Aunt Minnie would cane his right hand with the ruler and then send him to bed without supper. Then, later, when he was even hungrier than he was now, the police would come and put him in prison.

Jimmy wound up the engine, pulled the lever that made it go forward, and set it on the floor. The engine careered madly across the dusty boards. Then one of the wheels slipped into a crack and the engine fell whirring onto its side. Jimmy watched the wheels turn round and round until the spring ran down. Even the engine failed to give him pleasure now.

He screwed his eyes shut, trying to hide from the fear and the hunger. Time trickled by. Soon he dozed off — he had always been good at sleeping, the one reliable refuge, the one place where no one could harm him.

When he woke he was colder and hungrier than before. He saw at once that the light had changed. He guessed it was past nine, which meant it was after his bedtime. Sometimes Auntie Minnie let him stay up longer but never when she was cross with him. Now she was going to be even crosser.

He scrambled up and stretched. He was faint with hunger.

No point in going home for food because Auntie Minnie wouldn't give him any, not in the state she'd be in.

He picked up the engine and stroked its cool tin boiler. Aunt Minnie would make him give it back if he took it home. He pulled the forward lever and the wheels whirred and the pistons slid in and out. The thought of losing it was unbearable. Jimmy stood on tiptoe and tucked the engine on the wall plate under the angle of the roof

He clambered down the ladder and edged into the yard. He cocked his head, listening. Then he unlocked the wicket, slipped into the alley and locked the gate behind him.

There was a burst of laughter on his right from the direction of Mincing Lane. It was Friday evening. The King's Head would be busy.

He turned left, following the line of the factory wall. The alley narrowed and ahead of him glinted the river, golden in the evening sunlight. He came out onto the towpath and looked up and down. Nobody was in sight. If he turned left, he would be back in River Gardens in five minutes, back to Aunt Minnie. He turned right. Anything was better than Aunt Minnie.

The towpath beside the Minnow curved in a great arc around the northern boundary of Templefields. They'd told them at school that Templefields was one of the oldest parts of Lydmouth. Jimmy thought that was why it was so tatty and nasty. It was a network of alleys and lanes linking yards and workshops, tenements and houses. The buildings huddled together like refugees from another time. The Council was tearing them down, stage by stage, and putting up nice new houses for the people who used to live there, houses like the one where Jimmy lived, and smart new factories. Most of the old shops and businesses had gone, so apart from a few streets like Mincing Lane the area was almost empty, full of places waiting to be demolished. Aunt Minnie said it was especially dangerous at night-time and he wasn't to go there.

Jimmy hurried down the towpath, remembering that the

evening was when the ghosts came out in Templefields. He spent much of his life in a state of fear, but being afraid of ghosts was worst of all, because you couldn't touch and see ghosts so you never knew where they were or what they were about to do.

At last the Minnow broadened and slid into the broader waters of the Lyd. Suddenly everything was brighter. The evening sun shone on the forested hills on the other side of the river. To the left were the allotments which bordered the broad green swathe of the playing fields. To the right was the soft pink stonework of New Bridge. On either side of the bridge, the Council had put seats where people sat for picnics and, almost equally interesting, lovers for a cuddle. Once, Jimmy remembered, he had found a half-eaten packet of sandwiches in one of the litter bins. Perhaps he would be lucky again.

He wandered towards the bridge. This was where the Drowner lived. Aunt Minnie said the Drowner would come and get you if you were naughty, would drag you down into the depths of the water and there you'd stay until he had sucked the life out of you. The Drowner lived between the Minnow and New Bridge. That was why, Jimmy thought, when people jumped off the New Bridge, they always jumped off the other side, the downstream side.

He gave one litter bin a wide berth because it was next to a bench with a courting couple. He would have liked to look more closely at what they were doing, as well as at the bin, but he was afraid the man would shout at him. Was his hand really underneath the lady's skirt?

The next bin contained nothing edible. Jimmy drifted on to the bridge itself. He saw the railway line and heard the whistle of a train as it drew into the station. The stone parapet was still warm from the day's sun. He peered over the edge. The water slid underneath the bridge. This was where the Drowner lived. Lucky old Drowner. Jimmy liked water. He felt less clumsy when he was in the water, and he was proud that he could swim because he knew many boys couldn't.

The ache in his belly grew stronger and he straightened up.

'Hey! Jimmy! Jimmy Leigh!'

Walking briskly towards him along the opposite side of the bridge was a large police officer. Jimmy turned to flee. But someone else was coming towards him from the other direction. It was another man in uniform, one of the porters from the railway station, and Jimmy knew from bitter experience that men in uniforms tended to stick together.

Behind him the police officer blew his whistle.

'Stop!'

Heavy footsteps tramped across the bridge. The porter, a burly man, would be on top of him in a moment.

'Come on, son,' the policeman called behind him. 'No need to make this worse than it is.'

There was only one way to go, and that was where Jimmy went. He scrambled onto the parapet of the bridge, rolled across it and over the edge. As he fell, he scraped his elbow on the stonework. He heard himself scream. Simultaneously, in a searing mental flash, he wondered if the reason why people never jumped off the upstream side of the bridge was because the water was too shallow. Perhaps you hit your head on the bottom, and that was how the Drowner got you.

Then his body crashed into the water. It was much colder than he had expected. The shock of it shook him awake, gave him extra energy. He struck out blindly. When he opened his eyes, a few seconds later, he discovered that he was swimming away from the bridge, his arms thrashing the water as though trying to punish it.

Someone was shouting, but he couldn't hear the words, didn't want to hear them. Everything was simple now. All he had to do was swim and swim. He would leave them all behind.

Slowly, he churned through the water, fighting the current, which was pushing him back to the bridge. A couple of meadows ran along the eastern bank of the Lyd, fringed by willows which trailed their branches into the river. He was feeling tired now, so he struck out for the shelter of the nearest tree to get his breath. It would take them time to get round by the bridge and down through the meadows. If he heard them coming he would simply swim across the river.

He clung to a branch and sucked in huge mouthfuls of air. It was dark in the shelter of the trees. His feet touched the bottom here, and he kicked off his shoes, which had been making it harder to swim. He knew Auntie would be furious, but for once the thought of her anger failed to worry him. Things were different in the water. He could do anything. He was free.

Parting the branches, he peered out. The police constable and the porter were still leaning over the bridge. The porter must have seen him because he raised his arm and pointed directly at Jimmy.

'Can't catch me,' Jimmy chanted quietly between ragged breaths. 'Can't catch me.'

He turned his head. A little further upstream was the Minnow. The towpath along the Minnow would take him home.

Except he didn't want to go home. He hauled himself round, using the branches to gain momentum. The bank was only four or five feet away. He could scramble up it and run away into the forest and live on nuts and berries like outlaws did in stories. It was nice under the willows, a cool green cave.

If only he wasn't so cold and hungry. Then he could stay here all by himself forever, safe and sound.

The only thing was, he wasn't alone after all.

Someone else had been swimming this evening. Someone else had found this secret place under the willow.

He stared at the woman, whose face in the gloom was a pale green blur half-covered by a sodden sheet of newspaper. She was lying in the water, moving slowly to and fro as though swinging lazily in a hammock on a summer afternoon.

She was lying *under* the water.

Jimmy stretched out his hand, wanting to give her a shake to wake her up, and say, 'You mustn't go to sleep now.

Don't you know you can't breathe when your head's underwater?'

When his fingertip touched the skin below the left eye, it was as if a spark of understanding passed across from her to him. Now he knew what had happened. He retched, and a trickle of saliva dribbled into the water.

The two men on the bridge heard Jimmy's scream. They saw his face appear between the branches of the willows, though they were too far away to see the tears which were already running down his cheeks.

'It's the Drowner!' Jimmy Leigh shouted across the water. 'Drowner's got another one!'

Chapter Three

Why did nothing turn out as you expected? Even Trollope.

Book in hand, Jill Francis was sitting in the wicker armchair by the bedroom window and looking down at the polished pewter ribbon of the Lyd Estuary. Her eyes strayed for a moment from the window to the bed. For an instant, she felt so happy she wanted to cry and so sad she wanted to howl.

The book was *The Vicar of Bullhampton*. She had bought it second-hand in a bookshop on Charing Cross Road during the last year of the War. She had been looking forward to reading it ever since. Now here she was with a nine-day holiday in front of her and the book in her hand, only to find out that she couldn't concentrate on Trollope or anything else.

She was meant to be resting. The trouble with resting was that it gave you too much time to think. Not that Jill seemed to be capable of rational thought at present. The nearest she came to thinking was a mental process that seesawed violently and unpredictably between joyous excitement and complete despair. In the background was a constant, niggling worry like static marring a concert on the radio. She had been running a slight temperature for several days, and her body felt as if it were no longer entirely hers but shared with a stranger.

Not exactly a stranger.

She smiled, laid the book on the windowsill and stood up.

She wanted a cup of tea, and she had an even more pressing need to visit that unpleasant cubicle at the foot of the overgrown garden. She stretched, glad of her body as she had not been for years. She was wearing a faded dressing gown made of Shantung silk that had once belonged to her mother, and nothing else. She tightened the belt, glanced once more at the bed and tiptoed on bare feet out of the room and down the steep staircase.

There were two small rooms downstairs, one no more than a cubby-hole, with a lean-to kitchen that also served as a bath-room. The living room smelled of last night's cigarette smoke. Jill opened the window. She was about to go through to the kitchen when she heard the sound of a car.

The moment of peace shattered. Cars were unusual on Eastbury Hill. The grassy lane, twenty yards away from the side of the cottage, led only to a small house occupied by an elderly retired couple. Then it dwindled to a footpath and dawdled down the hill to the village. So there was at least a fifty-per-cent chance that the car was coming to Walnut Tree Cottage.

Jill conducted a rapid inventory of the entire ground floor. Then she heard footsteps on the path outside the door. She rushed to the sink and began to fill the kettle.

Nothing to worry about, please God? Nothing that shouldn't be here?

There was a tap on the glass. She twitched, artistically miming surprise, and turned to see Charlotte's face framed in the little window. Jill smiled, waved and went to unbolt the door.

'So glad I didn't wake you.' Charlotte stood on the doorstep, uncharacteristically hesitant, a shopping bag on her arm. 'I hap-pened to be passing . . .'

'I'm afraid I've only just got up. You make me feel quite ashamed.'

'Oh no, dear.' Charlotte's eyes were darting to and fro, taking in the dressing gown and no doubt speculating on what was underneath it. 'You're on holiday. Yes, I happened to be passing, and I thought you might be low on bread.'

She produced a loaf of white bread from the bag, sidled through the door and put it on the table.

'I'll just light the Primus,' Jill said, knowing that the last thing she must do was advertise her reluctance to provide hospitality. 'You will stay for tea, won't you?'

Charlotte shook her head. 'I'd better not. I'm on my way to Chepstow. Sophie Ruispidge says that Herbert Lewis have got some new curtain material in stock, and the ones in the dining room are practically rags. And then I promised Madge I'd buy her some Brashers Mint Imperials. For some reason no one in Lydmouth stocks them, and they're her secret weakness. Chepstow's the nearest place, and she finds it so hard to get away in term time. When I saw her at the governors' meeting on Thursday night, she looked quite haggard. "You need an early bed, my girl," I told her. "If you're not careful you'll end up in an early grave."'

Charlotte was talking rather fast, and while she talked she moved restlessly about the little room, her great legs nudging against the furniture, her eyes never still. Despite the anxiety Jill felt – and every second Charlotte lingered increased the anxiety – she felt unwilling admiration. Madge was Dr Margaret Hilly, the headmistress of Lydmouth High School for Girls. It was unlikely that anyone other than Charlotte would dare to tell her what to do.

'And how are you finding the Elsan?'

'Wonderful, thank you,' Jill said, trying to ignore the pressure of her bladder.

'We had to make do with an earth closet when we were children. Splendid things, chemical lavatories. Makes me feel frightfully modern when I'm in there, just like being in an RAF bomber. But I draw the line at electricity. One can manage perfectly well without it.'

'It's very kind of you to let me stay here.'

'Not at all. It's just standing empty most of the time.' Charlotte shrugged. 'The cottage was wonderful when we were children. We used to spend half the summer here. But I must confess it seems rather primitive now. All those sheep – not exactly stimulating. Still, it's very restful. You must stay as long as you like, dear. You've been working far too hard recently. Philip and I both think you've been looking peaky.'

A noise upstairs? A soft thud, a bare foot landing on a rug?

Jill smiled as if trying to split her face in two. She strained to hear what might be happening above their heads.

Just imagination?

She realised that Charlotte was still talking, saying something about the river.

'So there's no need for you to worry. Philip's got it all under control.'

'Sorry – what was that?'

'No need for you to hurry back. Philip doesn't want to see you in the office until Monday week. You need a complete break.' She paused, and something in the hesitation drew Jill's attention. 'A complete break from everything.'

And everyone?

'Anyway,' Charlotte was saying, 'the odds are it was an accident. Just a silly girl falling in the water and not being able to swim. Very sad, of course.'

Jill wondered why Charlotte had thought that the news of a girl's accidental death might persuade her to cut short her holiday and rush back to Lydmouth. She was conscientious about her job, but not fanatical.

'Have you sorted out the provisions yet? You've met Mrs Harper down the hill, I expect, the one with a garden full of rusting motor cars? She normally has some eggs to spare. The baker in the village won't deliver but the butcher will. And if he likes you, he can be very obliging and he'll bring up anything you order from the village shop as well. But not until the following morning, which can be a little inconvenient.'

Charlotte was now in the doorway of the kitchen. With a lurch of her stomach, Jill realised that she had forgotten to dry up last night. Charlotte's eyes strayed towards the sink — and the draining board.

Two cups, two saucers, two plates.

'Who exactly was this girl?' Jill asked, more loudly than necessary.

'Didn't I say? Her name's Mattie Harris. You've probably seen her around. She worked as a waitress at the Gardenia. Little redhaired girl. I've a feeling her parents live in Eastbury now.'

Jill nodded, briefly distracted from her own problems. She knew whom Charlotte meant. A girl with a triangular face, like a cat's, with little green eyes. Usually, she'd looked rather sullen. But there had been another side to her — Jill had seen her serving a couple of salesmen once, and she remembered how the girl's face lit up at something one of the men had said, how her laugh had filled the café making the other customers turn towards her, smiling involuntarily. It was the sort of laugh that made you want to join in. She couldn't have been more than twenty-one or two, Jill thought, poor kid. The sort of girl men liked.

'How did it happen?' Jill asked.

'Fowles didn't know. He told Philip that it looked like an accident.'

Apart from Charlotte, Jill was the only other person in the world who knew that Sergeant Fowles at Police Headquarters was in the habit of feeding snippets of information to Philip Wemyss-Brown at the *Gazette*.

'Still, I mustn't stay here chattering.' Charlotte opened the door, which opened directly from the living room on to the path outside the cottage. 'I'm sure you've got things you want to do.'

From upstairs there came a creak. Then another.

'It really is a lovely morning—' Charlotte began.

Simultaneously, Jill said, 'Thank you so much for the loaf.'

The two women stopped talking at the same time, too. For an instant they looked at each other and then both smiled. Theirs was a complicated friendship, Jill thought, and she never knew where it began and where it ended. Or how far she could trust it.

'Time and tide wait for no man,' said Charlotte, who was apt to take refuge in quotations in times of stress. 'I hope you enjoy the cottage. Bye.'

She strode down the path, her thick-soled shoes thudding on the uneven flagstones, one heel decapitating a primrose that had thrust itself out of a crack. Jill waited in the doorway. Charlotte settled herself in the Rover, which was parked just outside the gate. She looked at Jill through the open window.

'The poor girl was found in the river by New Bridge, apparently.' Charlotte started the engine and raised her voice to be heard above the roar. 'Ten to one they'll say it's all the Drowner's fault. People can be so credulous, can't they, even in this day and age.'

With a wave, Charlotte let out the clutch. The car ground its way up the lane, brushing against the hedgerow and driving two startled sheep before it. As Jill was walking back to the cottage, she heard a valedictory blast of the Rover's horn.

Chapter Four

———◦◦◦◦———

The sun was shining on Saturday morning but Violet Evans thought it might as well have been raining. When she woke up, she slipped down to the kitchen for tea and a few slices of toast, and then went back upstairs to feed Grace.

She could hear her parents snoring on the other side of the wall. This new house in Broadwell Crescent was meant to be so wonderful, and they were so lucky that Mr George had let them have it on such favourable terms. But Violet didn't like it. It might have all the mod cons but you couldn't get away from people as you'd been able to do in the old house. She heard her father, and her father heard the baby.

Grace had made Violet's nipples sore. The baby did everything with total concentration. Now she guzzled milk. Next, when she was full, she wept because of the wind. Once the wind was dealt with, she needed changing, and that was a long and tedious job because Violet had put the nappy on rather than her mother, and Violet was not as yet very skilled at it.

'Stop wriggling,' Violet hissed. 'Oh darling, please stop wriggling.'

When at last she had Grace dry and changed, Violet wept softly, her mind awash with tiredness, frustration and fear. She had always thought of herself as a placid person. Now she was adrift on a sea of emotions. Enormous waves came at her. One day soon, she knew, she would drown.

Grace dribbled on Violet's shoulder and fell asleep. Violet waited until the baby's breathing was heavy and regular, till the little body grew hot and heavy, before laying her down in the cot. Grace was a tyrant, though only three weeks old and totally helpless.

Violet was hungry again so she dried her eyes and went downstairs. Her father came out of her parents' bedroom as she crossed the landing. He looked through her as if she wasn't there and went into the bathroom, ramming the bolt home as if he hated it. Violet bit her lip to keep herself from crying and went into the kitchen. Rab came over to her as soon as she reached the kitchen, his tail wagging furiously and his eyes pleading. Like Grace, he wanted food.

'Go away, Rab,' Violet said, unbolting the back door. 'Please go away.'

With her foot she edged Rab into the small wilderness of mud and builders' rubbish that her father called a garden. She watched the dog squeezing through the hedge at the bottom and running into the meadow beyond. Broadwell Crescent was Mr George's new development, ten houses squeezed together on what had once been a small field at the back of Broadwell Drive. Theirs was the only one which had been finished.

She poured herself a large bowl of cereal and added milk and a thick layer of white sugar. Still in her dressing gown, she sat at the table to eat it. Her jaws moved faster and faster, as if they were in a race. When she had finished the first bowl, she poured herself another. There were eggs in the larder, and she wondered how her mother planned to cook them for breakfast.

Violet had nearly finished her second helping of cereal when her parents came downstairs. Her father sat at the table drinking tea and reading last night's newspaper while her mother began to cook breakfast.

'Looks like the weather will hold for the match, doesn't it, Ted?' Violet's mother said.

Her father grunted.

'What have you got planned for this morning, then? You said you might be able to put the shelves in the pantry this weekend.'

Ted raised his head. He was a broad-shouldered man, not tall but powerfully built. He had cropped grey hair and a heavy jaw. 'I'm going down the allotment after breakfast.'

'If you want to be outside, there's enough work to be done in the garden here.'

'I'm going down the allotment, all right, June?'

There was a silence, then June tried again. 'You'll be wanting an early lunch, I expect, with the match, I mean.'

Ted shook his head. 'I'll have something at the Ferryman. No point in coming back all the way here.'

'What about your bag?'

'I'll take my bag with me – I can change at the ground.'

'But Ted—'

'Don't fuss,' he snapped, and went back to yesterday's newspaper.

None of them spoke again until breakfast was on the table. Violet screwed her hands into tight little fists on her lap. She was waiting for the outburst. She knew it was coming. She and her father had been close, and they were very alike. She could still sense his moods.

He mopped up the last of his egg with a square of fried bread and popped it in his mouth. Still chewing, he said, 'That baby kept me awake half the night with its wailing.'

'She's got a name,' Violet said. 'Why won't you ever call her Grace?'

He chewed for a moment, staring out of the window at the muddy wasteland, swallowed, and went on, 'Saw Doctor Bayswater the other day. He said there's an agency that handles adoptions. Something to do with the Church of England.'

Tears pricked at her eyelids. Her hands were shaking, the nails digging into the palms. 'Grace is my baby. I'm not giving her away.'

'Not just yours, is she? Seems to me someone else has got a responsibility to help out. Are you going to tell us who the father is?'

She stared at her empty plate.

'I bet that Harris girl knows,' Ted went on. 'Anyway, I don't want a little bastard in my house. And even if I did, what makes you think I can afford it?'

'It won't cost much to buy her food and a few clothes, Dad, and anyway—'

'It's not just her, though, is it? It's you. You eat like a horse, in case you haven't noticed.'

Tears, fat and heavy just like herself, slid down her cheeks.

Her mother put a hand on her father's arm. 'Ted, don't you think—'

He shook off the hand as if it were a fly. 'Listen, it's not cheap having a mortgage. Do you think we'd have taken it on if you hadn't got that job at Sedbury's?'

'But – but I'll go back to work—'

'If they'll have you. Have you thought of that? Everyone will know by now. You can't fool people, not in Lydmouth. And anyway, even if you do go back to work, who's going to look after the baby? Your mother goes out to work now. There's no one else.'

He glared at her and threw down his knife and fork. The two women sat in silence while he gathered up his newspaper and cigarettes and went outside to the lavatory. He would be in there for five or ten minutes; he always was – regular as clockwork.

Violet pushed back her chair and stumbled out of the kitchen and up the stairs. She sat on her bed and looked at the baby in the cot. Grace was lying on her stomach with her bottom in the air. She had black spiky hair. One of her little booties had come off revealing a little pink foot with curling toes, a miracle of perfection.

Time passed. Violet was too miserable even to cry. She heard her father getting his bicycle out of the shed, and looked out of the window to see him negotiating the potholes of Broadwell

Crescent. His cricket bag was strapped to the crossbar. With luck they wouldn't see him again until the middle of the evening, because he'd probably go back to the Ferryman for a few drinks after the match. It wasn't so long ago that she'd loved her father more than anyone in the world. But that was before he had discovered she was pregnant.

Her mother came upstairs, tapped on the door and poked her head into the room. When she saw that Grace was asleep, she came to peer down at the baby. Her lined face softened.

'Does he mean it?'

June nodded. 'You know what he's like when he's made his mind up.'

Violet felt the tears gathering once again. She had not known she had so many tears inside her until this last few weeks. 'I'm sorry.'

'What can't be cured must be endured. But I wish you'd say who the father was.'

'There's no point.'

'So he won't marry you?'

Violet shrugged.

'It's not just the baby,' June went on. 'It's the money side.'

'This house?'

'It's a lovely house,' June said, automatically loyal. 'When the Crescent's finished, it's going to be perfect. And after the mortgage is paid off, we'll be sitting pretty.'

All the old arguments, all the old reasons.

'Of course, there's no denying that having your own house has a lot of other unexpected expenses, especially when it's new. But it will be worth it in the end.'

Violet muttered, 'Not for me and Grace it won't.'

'Why don't you get out? Get a bit of fresh air? I'll look after Baby.'

Violet shook her head.

'It's not good for you, moping at home. Anyway, you can make yourself useful. I've got a shopping list ready.'

Violet opened her mouth, ready to object, then closed it again.

'Don't go looking for that Mattie Harris, though,' June said. 'You know what your father thinks.'

Grace slept on while Violet got ready. Since coming back from hospital, she had hardly been out. Usually she took Rab for a walk in the early evening, which was how she and Mattie had managed to meet. Mattie hadn't been welcome at the house even before Grace was born. Violet's father thought she was fast.

Violet collected the list from her mother and went outside. The sunlight hurt her eyes. She picked her way through the mud of Broadwell Crescent and into Broadwell Drive beyond. She waited at the bus stop on Chepstow Road, feeling exposed. It was like one of those nightmares when she suddenly realised that she was in public but only partly dressed. She imagined everyone must have heard about Grace. She knew several of the women standing in the queue, though only slightly.

One of them said to her, 'Nice to see a bit of sunshine at last. Worst May we've had for years.'

Violet automatically agreed. Then the bus came. She found a seat, but though the bus was crowded nobody came to sit beside her. Maybe everyone's ashamed to be seen with me, she thought, or maybe there simply isn't room. She glanced down at her broad thighs. She did not like looking at her body. It overflowed across one and a half seats. How she hated it. The only good thing you could say about it was that it had concealed the fact of her pregnancy until the very last moment. She wished she was slim and delicate like Mattie.

She got off the bus in the High Street. Instead of doing the shopping, she went straight to the Gardenia, hoping to beat the mid-morning rush. She found a vacant table near the back and squeezed herself into a corner seat. A tall and slender waitress called Myra — why was everyone else thin? — took her order. Myra was pleasant enough, but it was hard to tell. She must have heard about Grace.

'One coffee and a toasted tea cake,' Myra said, admiring her reflection in the mirror behind Violet's table. 'Shan't be long.'

'Is Mattie in?'

Myra grimaced. 'Wish she was. We'll be rushed off our feet in an hour or so.'

'I thought she was meant to be in today.'

'She was. Had the day off yesterday, special favour, and now she's not turned up this morning. Ma Browning's going round the bend.' The bell on the door pinged and more customers came in. Myra's interest slipped away from Violet. 'Cup of coffee and a tea cake, wasn't it?'

'Two tea cakes,' Violet said. 'Missed my breakfast.'

When the order came, Violet ate the tea cakes slowly, just to show anyone who might be watching that she wasn't the sort of person who wolfed her food. She drank the coffee with her little finger crooked. But she wondered if the other customers were talking about her. She paid her bill as quickly as possible.

The day was growing warmer. She drifted up the High Street in the direction of the Bull Hotel. She knew she should do the shopping, that the longer she left it the more tedious it would be. Although the sun was out, it had a wan, weary quality. The air was muggy. Prickles of perspiration broke out in the crannies of her body, as though moist insects were exploring her innermost recesses.

There was a telephone box on the corner by the public lavatories. Violet squeezed inside and fumbled for her purse. She knew she shouldn't do this, but she no longer cared what anyone would say or think.

The phone rang in her ear. She imagined it ringing on and on in the big, new house with the picture windows. She had never been inside but she had walked past it many times. She knew by heart the tarmac drive, the two big trees at the front, the grey rectangle of the tennis court and the shrubs and flowerbeds set at regular intervals in the lawn like a green desert.

It was a woman who answered the phone, a slight Lydmouth accent, sounded cross and middle-aged.

'Can I speak to Bill please?'

'Who is it?'

Violet has been dreading this, praying that it would be Bill himself who answered. Bill said his mother was as nosy as an aardvark, which was why, he said, he had told her never to ring him at home. Violet looked across the road and saw the steps leading up to the public library.

'This is the library. We've got a query about a book he reserved.'

The woman went away, and a moment later she heard footsteps which must be Bill's approaching the phone. He said hello, and it seemed to her that his voice was wary and no longer familiar.

'Bill, it's me.'

'Wait a moment.' The voice had changed, still wary but now harder.

She heard his footsteps again and the click of a door closing. Then he returned to the phone.

'I thought we'd agreed—'

'Bill, I'm worried.'

'What's wrong? It's not the baby?'

'Her name's Grace,' said Violet automatically, blinking at his sudden change of tone. 'No. It's Mattie. What happened?'

'Nothing. Nothing at all. Didn't turn up.'

'She was going to come round yesterday evening. But she didn't.'

'Maybe she wasn't well.'

'I've just been round to the Gardenia. She's not come into work, either.'

'There you are,' Bill said. 'She's ill.'

'But she would have let Ma Browning know. Their next-door neighbour's got a phone, and she always uses that if there's a problem.'

'I'm sure she's fine, love.' The words were kind, but the voice was impatient now.

Violet said nothing.

Bill cleared his throat. 'Anyway, I thought your dad didn't approve of Mattie. Perhaps she thought she wouldn't be welcome at the house.'

'We were going to meet at the field behind when I took Rab for a walk. That's where we always meet.'

Violet stared through the glass at the busy street hoping to see Mattie, late as usual, half running, half walking towards the Gardenia. She thought about the wariness in Bill's voice. She closed her eyes, and everywhere she looked in her mind there were problems. They all had faces. There was Grace, demanding. Her mother, worried, her father angry, Mr Sedbury disapproving, Bill – Bill of all people – wary. The only face that was warm and welcoming was Mattie's. And Mattie wasn't there.

So Mattie was a problem, too.

'Darling?' Bill was saying. 'Darling, are you there?'

Violet looked at the black, Bakelite receiver and saw that her fingers had left smudges of perspiration on its surface.

'Darling?' said Bill's tinny voice, now eighteen inches away from her ear.

She put down the receiver, pushed open the door and went out into the muggy sunshine of the Whit weekend Saturday morning.

You can't trust anyone, she thought, not Bill, not Mattie.

Chapter Five

'I tried to phone last night when the news came in, Guv.' Sergeant Kirby smoothed his tie, which was silk, with large red polka dots on the navy-blue background. 'So it's lucky you dropped in this morning.'

Thornhill nodded, knowing silence was the best policy. The lobby smelled of disinfectant and Kirby's cigarettes. It was already very hot. Despite the rain, it had been a warm spring, and people said that everything was early this year. The hare-lipped clerk who had fetched Kirby had retreated to his little office. He was watching them surreptitiously through the half-glazed door marked ALL VISITORS MUST REPORT HERE.

'I knew you'd want to be informed,' Kirby went on, still fishing. 'Even though you're off duty.'

Thornhill had taken the whole of the Whit weekend off, planning to go down to Bournemouth with Edith and the children. They were going to stay with Edith's sister and her children. It was not a weekend he had been looking forward to. Then the miracle had happened. The landlady had taken more bookings than she had beds. With a little improvisation, however, she could find somewhere to sleep for all the party except one. She offered to ask around her friends and neighbours, but at this point Thornhill had suggested that the long weekend might be a golden opportunity for him to repaint the dining room. Brian

39

Kirby knew all that, which was why he had expected to find Thornhill at home when he phoned.

'Doctor Bayswater's having a look at her now,' Kirby said. 'She worked at the Gardenia. Funny when it's someone you know, isn't it?'

'Very funny.'

Kirby shot him a suspicious glance. 'That little redhead. I was in at the end of last week, and she brought me sardines on toast. Makes you think, doesn't it?'

'What was she like?'

'Youngish. Rather attractive, actually. But a bit skinny for my taste. Not that that's either here or there.'

'I'll take a look now.'

'You can leave this to me, sir, if you want. No need for you to bother — you're off duty, and I somehow doubt we'll be calling in the Yard on this one.'

Thornhill shook his head. *I am never off duty.* That is what he'd said to Jill Francis. It sounded pompous then and it sounded pompous in memory. She'd looked at him as if he'd said something stupid or childish. He shouldered open the swing doors leading into the mortuary itself. Kirby followed him into the long, cool room with its permanent smell of antiseptics and putrefaction. Dr Bayswater was bending over the slab. He looked up as they came into the room.

'Ah – Thornhill. Thought you weren't meant to be here.'

'Couldn't keep away, Doctor.'

'Well, we're nearly done.' Smiling wolfishly, he turned to his assistant, whose gleaming hair and pressed white coat made Bayswater look even seedier than ever. 'They won't always be as nice as this one, so you'd better make the most of it.'

There was a flush like a shameful stain on the younger man's sallow face. Thornhill wondered if this was his first time, if the sight of a body had turned his stomach. Bayswater's sense of humour seemed to have stopped growing at the banana-skin stage.

'All quite straightforward?' Thornhill said, partly to distract attention from the blushing young man.

'Yes and no.' Bayswater bared yellow teeth and smiled. 'Not quite as simple as you might wish. I'm not sure what the pathologist will make of it.'

Thornhill raised his eyebrows. 'You've not taken her clothes off. So is there something obvious? Something we've missed?'

The question implied that there might be something Brian Kirby had missed. Thornhill sensed his sergeant's attention sharpening.

Bayswater chuckled. 'Not really. Depends if you've got any necrophiles on the strength, any officers with a prurient interest in dead flesh. Come and have a look, gentlemen. Don't be shy.'

The woman was lying on her back. There was still a smear of lipstick on her pale face. The mouth was open, showing blackened teeth with cheap fillings. The hair had dried into ragged dark-red spikes. The colour seemed to go down to the roots, Thornhill noticed, so it was probably natural. She had a sharp face with a pointed chin and a hint of freckles.

Death had robbed her of individuality. It was impossible to tell what she would have looked like in life. Thornhill thought that if she had been reckoned attractive, it was the sort of attractiveness that comes from movement and personality, rather than from features. Except perhaps for that hair.

He ran his eyes down the body. She had been small, barely larger than a child. No wedding ring or other jewellery. The fingernails had been chewed to the quick and the skin around the tips of the fingers was still grubby. The skin he could see was like dull grey marble, suggesting she'd been in the water for a good few hours. She wore a blouse of some shiny material, probably satin, and a tight skirt which was rucked up above her knees.

He looked at Bayswater, who was waiting, his face expectant. 'All right, Doctor, I give up.'

Bayswater winked. 'You policemen are too nice. You should try lifting ladies' skirts sometimes. It can be very instructive.'

The combination of the wink and the cultivated voice was like a bishop farting in church.

'Suppose you show us.'

Bayswater pushed up the hem of the skirt, which wasn't easy because the material was wet. He had to turn the body to and fro and work the skirt higher and higher towards the hips. When he came to the tops of the stockings, he pushed the body onto its side and said triumphantly, 'Look!'

'A suspender's undone,' Kirby said. 'Is that it? So what? Could have happened when—'

Bayswater flapped his hand. 'Not that. Look at the way they're twisted. The seam on the left leg is practically doing a corkscrew. The stocking on the right leg is inside out. And look at that suspender there. It's on back to front.'

'So what do you think—' Thornhill began.

'And there's more.' Bayswater smiled proudly, like a conjuror who has saved his best trick until last. 'Just look at this.'

He pushed the skirt still higher, revealing the base of the girdle and the knickers beneath. In a gesture that could have been obscene but was instead ludicrous, he pointed at the crotch.

'See that? They're inside out too.'

Kirby shrugged. 'It could just mean that the last time she got dressed, it was in a hurry and in the darkness.'

'Either way,' Bayswater said, 'it suggests she may not have been alone.'

'Shoes?' Thornhill said. 'Coat, hat, handbag?'

'Nothing else has turned up yet, sir,' Kirby said.

Thornhill turned away from the body. 'Thank you, Doctor. We'll talk later.'

He went out of the building, followed by Kirby, and climbed into the car.

'Where to, sir?'

'The river.'

Thornhill felt out of place in the back of the marked police car, like a member of the public, not a police officer. Even in plain clothes, he dressed for the job, usually in a suit and hat. Now he was wearing a shirt open at the neck, a battered tweed jacket, a pair of grey flannels which had seen better days, and a pair of brown brogues. He didn't feel like a police officer any more. He knew why, too. It was nothing to do with his clothes, really. It was everything to do with the reason why he was wearing them. And the reason was called Jill Francis.

The High Street was crowded, so the car moved slowly. Kirby nursed an affronted silence. Thornhill broke the silence, partly to avoid thinking about Jill, and partly because there was no point in upsetting a good sergeant without good cause.

'Where exactly did she turn up?'

'Floating under a willow on the other side of New Bridge. One of those trees along the water meadows. You heard how she was found?'

'They told me when I called in at the station before coming to the mortuary.'

Kirby shrugged. 'It was a queer business in its own right. We'll need to talk to Jimmy Leigh again. Anyway, she wasn't identified as Mattie Harris till this morning—'

'Who identified her?'

'WPC Ailsmore, sir.' Kirby's eyes flickered. 'She often goes to the Gardenia. She'd talked to the girl a few times. She'd actually seen Harris in the café on Thursday afternoon. Off the cuff, Bayswater reckoned that she'd been in the water a few hours. So the odds are she went in some time on Thursday night.'

'She was all dressed up.'

'So maybe she went out for the evening, had a few drinks and fell in. It happens. Or maybe there was a boyfriend and they had a quarrel.'

They were running down the hill towards the river now. They passed the approach road up to the station, crossed New Bridge and turned left. Their driver braked sharply almost at once and swung the car into a gateway leading into a field. By the gate, a uniformed officer straightened himself and dropped the cigarette which had been cupped in his hand. The car bumped over ruts and came to a halt, gently rocking.

'It gets muddy nearer the river, sir,' Kirby said. 'Simpler to walk from here.'

Thornhill was already feeling for the door handle. He got out of the car and stretched. The riverbank had been cordoned off. There were screens around one area of the bank, which he presumed was around the immediate area where the body had been found. A team of men, some in uniform and some plainclothed were working their way methodically down the riverbank in a line abreast.

'The softness of the ground makes things a bit tricky,' Kirby said. 'But at least if there's been a struggle or something, we should find some sign.'

'You've done well,' Thornhill said quietly. 'Who uses the meadow at present?'

'The farmer next door puts cows in occasionally.' Kirby had turned away, pretending he hadn't heard the compliment. 'You get a lot of anglers, though. Especially at the weekend. We've been turning them away in droves.'

'Fishing rights?'

'Ruispidge owns them. Surprise, surprise. But the estate hasn't leased out the rights since the 1920s, and the idea's grown up that this patch of the river is open to anyone who lives in Lydmouth.'

While they talked, they walked slowly down the gently sloping field towards the river bank. Their shoes squelched in the mud. The brown brogues had been a wise choice after all. They found Joan Ailsmore behind the screen on her hands and knees. Her skirt was muddy and her hair had come adrift. She turned a flushed face up to them.

'Where was the body?' Thornhill asked.

'Just there.' Kirby pointed to the base of the willow. 'Rubbing up against it.'

'Any traces of footprints?' Thornhill scanned the ground, now an unreadable morass.

Kirby looked at Ailsmore, giving her the chance to speak.

She said, 'When we got here it was already quite a mess. PC Hemlett had come over with the porter from the station. They dragged the body out. And then Hemlett waited here while the porter and Leigh went to phone for help. There was a chance she was alive, so they called out an ambulance team. Even so, we don't think we've found any fresh prints which belong to anyone else. It's hard to be sure, of course.'

'So what's the alternative?' Thornhill said. 'That she was washed here by the river?'

Kirby nodded. 'It's quite feasible. The water's high and the currents are strong.' As he spoke, he unfolded a map. 'You've got the Lyd coming down there – see that bend – and things tend to get washed up on this bank, because it's the outside edge of the curve. And then you've got the Minnow coming in there' – his finger jabbed the map – 'and sweeping another lot of water right across on to this bank. Then it ricochets off and goes under New Bridge.'

'We'll have to try a few experiments,' Thornhill said. 'Try dropping in floats at various points along the Minnow and the Lyd.'

He looked across the water. There was a path on the other side of the Lyd leading to a narrow footbridge spanning the mouth of the Minnow. Beyond that were the allotments and the town's playing fields, with the slate roof of the Ferryman's Inn standing on the bank of the Lyd itself. There were people on the path and the footbridge, staring across the river.

'They're not going to see much,' Kirby said sourly. 'We're making a collection of the debris washed up on this bank. Do you want to have a look, sir?'

Thornhill nodded, and WPC Ailsmore led them beyond the shelter of the screens to a small pile of rubbish presided over by a small, wizened constable on the verge of retirement. Kirby crouched beside the pile and poked through it with a stick. There was a sodden shirt, part of a newspaper, fragments of wood in various stages of dissolution. And a beer bottle.

'We found that a few yards downstream from the screens,' Ailsmore said.

Kirby lifted it up carefully. It had lost its top, but it was still half full of liquid, probably river water, which had acted as ballast and prevented it from sinking.

'Not been long in the water.'

'No, Sarge.' Ailsmore's eyes flickered from Kirby to Thornhill, standing silently a few paces behind. 'Not a label I've seen before. Not around here, I mean.'

Kirby lifted the bottle a little closer and studied the label. 'India Pale Ale,' he read out slowly. 'Thorogood and Nephew, Elmbury.'

'What did you say?' Thornhill said.

'Elmbury, sir. Why?'

'Nothing. Or rather nothing to do with this.' He felt a spasm of guilt, like a twinge of moral rheumatism. 'It's just something my wife said the other day. Mentioned Elmbury. Nothing to do with this.'

Chapter Six

———◆◆◆———

The Drowner?

Trickles of cold water ran down Jill's bare legs and gathered in small, gleaming puddles on the linoleum. It was a warm day but the water was cold enough to bring out goose pimples on her skin. She was washing herself at the kitchen sink, using cold water because there wasn't any hot, and the novelty had soon worn off, scrubbed into oblivion by the sheer bloody inconvenience of it. Perhaps there was something to be said for being dirty, after all.

The Drowner? She must have seen the words in print, because she knew that Drowner had an initial capital. The sharp-edged bar of carbolic soap slipped from her wet hand and dropped on her unprotected foot. She swore. As she hopped up and down, still swearing, she was glad there was no one to see her, glad she was alone again. Then she concentrated entirely on finishing the masochistic business of washing as quickly as possible.

After she had cleared away the breakfast things and made the bed, she sat in the overgrown garden reading *The Vicar of Bullhampton*. She told herself that she was enjoying the book, that she deserved the holiday, and that she needed a rest. But Trollope still failed to hold her attention. Time and again she found her eyes drifting down to the broad sweep of the estuary.

Meanwhile, the problems re-emerged in her conscious mind like bubbles of air oozing out of the tidal mud along the banks of the river below.

She dared not think about the greatest problem. Not now. It would come back at night, in the early hours when she was defenceless. She concentrated on lesser ones, a form of protection. For example, how much did Charlotte know, or guess?

Her stated reason for visiting Walnut Tree Cottage was obviously a pretext. Jill had plenty of bread, and she was quite capable of buying more if she needed to. And there was no reason why the news of a drowned waitress in Lydmouth might have made her cut short her holiday. The *Gazette* was perfectly capable of carrying on without her, and in any case the death was probably no more than an unfortunate accident. Which meant there had been another reason for Charlotte's visit.

Richard Thornhill?

Who did have an interest in the dead waitress, whether or not the death was accidental. She had argued with him, upstairs in the bedroom, after Charlotte had driven away.

'Charlotte would have said if there was anything suspicious about the death,' she had told him. 'It's just a common-or-garden accident.'

'I need to be sure.'

'Then why don't you phone Brian Kirby and find out?'

Richard had stared out of the bedroom window, following the river with his eyes. He was wearing only his trousers, with the braces trailing; he was unshaven, hair unbrushed, the pale skin and curls of dark hair on his chest somehow mysterious, simultaneously dangerous and exciting like an undiscovered continent. 'I need to see for myself. Besides, Brian would think it odd if I just phoned in.'

'But you're off duty,' she had wailed, taken off guard by the strength of her sense of loss.

'I'm never off duty.' He had turned to face her, stroking her arm as if it was an animal in need of reassurance. 'I'm sorry. But with a bit of luck I should be back in a few hours. Certainly this afternoon. What will you do? Stay here?'

'I'll probably go out.' She had taken a step back and picked up her hairbrush, moving out of range of his hand. 'I'll see.'

She had said that more to establish her right to independent action than because she wanted to go out. But now, as Trollope fought a losing battle against nagging thoughts, going out seemed the only sensible thing to do. She threw down the book and went inside to get changed.

Twenty minutes later, she drove through the network of lanes separating Walnut Tree Cottage from Eastbury and turned left onto the main road to Lydmouth. Driving was too familiar an activity to make an effective distraction. If Charlotte knew, or guessed, about Richard – had she told Philip? Philip Wemyss-Brown was Charlotte's husband, and the editor of the *Lydmouth Gazette*, the paper which was largely owned by Charlotte. And there was a further complication: Charlotte knew that Philip had once asked Jill to marry him. It had been long before he met Charlotte, true, but the knowledge was quite enough to add a hint of mud to sully the clear waters of friendship. Jill was fond of Charlotte, and thought Charlotte was of her, but Charlotte also saw Jill as an employee and even as a rival. How would that affect what she did with what she knew or suspected?

Shopping mitigated so many of life's ills. There must be something she needed to buy. For a moment Jill toyed with the idea of buying something for Richard. But she knew that that was one luxury a woman in her situation could not afford.

He was still alien despite everything, still waiting to be explored like a strange country. Detective Inspector Richard Thornhill, head of CID, Lydmouth division, husband of Edith, father of David and Elizabeth. For an instant, Jill felt a stab of sympathy with Edith, as opposed to her more usual feelings of guilt about Richard's wife. Edith must often have been in the position that she was in now: playing second fiddle to a corpse.

Jill parked in the High Street. She spent three-quarters of an hour buying things for the cottage — ranging from a bar of decent soap to a bottle of sherry. Charlotte and Philip had taken her for a picnic to Walnut Tree Cottage the previous summer, but this was the first time she had stayed there. She had not realised it would be quite as primitive. Or that the primitive would stop being picturesque and become inconvenient instead.

As she was paying for her purchases in the chemist's, she heard someone say her name in a deep, husky voice. She turned round. A burly man in late middle age was smiling down at her. He had heavy shoulders, a long jaw and a narrow skull.

'Hello, Mr Broadbent.'

'Call me Bernie, my dear. Most people do.'

She smiled at him. He took her shopping bag while she was searching for her purse and later came outside with her. 'I was thinking of getting a cup of coffee in the Gardenia,' he said, nodding to the café a few doors up the street. 'But the place is stuffed with folk waiting to be served.'

'Have you heard that one of their waitresses has died?'

'Really? Which one?'

'Mattie Harris.'

Broadbent had lost his smile. He bent towards her, his close-set eyes both moist and hard, like wet grey pebbles. 'Who told you? When did this happen?'

Jill held her ground. 'Charlotte Wemyss-Brown mentioned it. The girl was found in the Lyd last night, I gather. Somewhere near New Bridge.'

The smile was back on his face now. He scratched his head. 'Mattie Harris. Now which was she? The little redhead or the beanpole?'

'I think she must have been the redhead.'

'Poor kid. I suppose it was an accident?'

'Charlotte didn't know.'

'I daresay the police have got a pretty good idea already.' Bernie Broadbent had recently become a county councillor, and was now the newest member of the Standing Joint Committee which superintended the activities of the police force. What complicated matters still further was the fact that he was related to Edith Thornhill. He glanced at his watch. 'Well, I must be getting along for lunch. Can you manage all that shopping?'

'Yes, thank you. By the way, Charlotte said something about perhaps the Drowner was responsible. Does that mean anything to you?'

Bernie laughed. 'Just an old story. Superstition. The Drowner's a sort of local bogey man. My nan used to tell my sister if she didn't read her Bible, the Drowner would get her the next time she was near the river.'

Bernie laughed again, though there was nothing particularly funny in what he'd said. Then he said goodbye and walked quickly away.

By now it was lunchtime. Jill went home to Church Cottage. Even after twenty-four hours absence, the cottage no longer felt quite like home. She spent a few minutes with her cat Alice, who was in the cupboard under the stairs nursing four young kittens. Alice was pleased to see her, but not immoderately so. Mary Sutton next door was coming in every day to provide food, and at present Alice had enough on her mind without bothering too much about humans. Two of the kittens were half-promised to Edith Thornhill.

There were tins of soup in the cupboards, and Jill had bought cheese to take back to Eastbury. She made lunch and ate it in the sitting room with a glass of sherry. Alice stayed in her cupboard. Jill realised she was gobbling the food as though desperate to get away. She should have gone out for lunch. There was nothing to distract her here.

Most of the time she thought about Charlotte's visit, rehearsing it in her memory, trying to extract every possible drop of significance from it. The need to know swelled like a balloon. After lunch. she rang Troy House on the off chance that Charlotte had returned from Chepstow. The familiar voice recited the telephone number slowly and clearly, as if making a public announcement to a crowd of idiots. Instantly the balloon burst.

'Charlotte? Is that you?'

'Yes, Jill. Of course it is. And what can I do for you?'

Jill knew it was impossible for her to say *What do you know about me and Richard?* It was impossible for her to enquire delicately what Charlotte knew and suspected, let alone to ask directly. They might be friends but there were some subjects they couldn't talk about. They lacked a shared language for the necessary concepts. Mutual forgiveness was not assured.

Instead she blurted out, choosing the question at random, 'Charlotte, who *is* the Drowner?'

Chapter Seven

─────◆◇◆─────

Just before lunch on Saturday morning, less than twenty-four hours after the discovery of Mattie Harris's body in the River Lyd, Robert Sedbury parked his car in Castle Street outside the Georgian house where he had spent so much of his adult life. He was a swarthy man who wore a permanently intent expression, like a man obsessed with an endless puzzle. When they were courting, his wife had once told him that he looked Byronic, an epithet he secretly cherished and she had long since forgotten.

A brass plate twinkled beside the dark-green front door. It had been there for nearly fifty years, and the brass had softened to a dull golden sheen, and the lettering was so worn that in places it was hardly legible. Not that it mattered, because everyone knew that it read Sedbury & Son, Auctioneers and Estate Agents. Technically, perhaps, it should have been Sedbury & Brown, since Henry Brown had been a partner for the past thirty years. But the firm had been called Sedbury & Son since the 1840s, and Robert felt that their clients might find a change of name unsettling, if not subversive.

The office would usually have been closed on Saturday, but as he had expected the door was unlocked. Robert went inside and glanced through the open door of the big front office where the articled clerks and the typist sat. The stools were empty and the typewriter was silent. Malcolm's cubby-hole by the fireplace was empty. The walls were lined with shelves bearing red ledgers containing a record of every transaction the firm had handled since the days of its founder Josiah Sedbury. There were more of them in the storerooms on the first and second floors of the house.

The sensible thing, Robert knew, would be to discard the older records or store them elsewhere – or even move to new and more spacious premises. But any of these would have involved a break in continuity that he was not willing to make. Both his son and his partner had suggested making changes, but Robert refused. He argued that the firm continued to grow and prosper precisely because it didn't change. People trusted it, just as their fathers had. Whatever the strength of his argument, Robert Sedbury retained control of the firm so his will prevailed.

He frowned, noticing that the temporary typist had once again failed to tidy her desk before leaving on Friday afternoon. She was messy, a slow and inaccurate typist, and surly with callers. She would have to go. No doubt about it, he thought, they would have to bite the bullet and appoint a new permanent typist. And they'd be damned lucky if they found one half as efficient as Violet Evans had been. The stupid girl.

Suppressing his irritation, he followed the hall to the two offices occupying what had once been the back parlour of the house. Robert's father had partitioned the room. Robert now occupied the larger section and Brown, his junior partner, had the smaller. Except Brown wasn't here: he was taking a month off to go jaunting round the Highlands. Robert felt a lightening of his heart. He opened the door and smiled at his son sitting behind Brown's desk.

'Hello, Dad.'

'How you getting on?'

'I've nearly finished the Victoria Road particulars. But you'd better check through them.'

'I will, but I'm sure they'll be fine.'

'I didn't realise you'd be coming in as well. I put the post on your desk.'

'Good lad. I've got some paperwork to catch up on. You'll not believe it, but that damned typist has misplaced half the Ruispidge correspondence. We're going to have to get someone new.'

'Permanently?'

'Yes. I've decided enough's enough. I can't keep that job open for Miss Evans any longer. She's a damned good secretary but you can't just have people waltzing off like that and not saying when they'll come back. And her reason for going, too. There's been a lot of talk. It's not the sort of thing that looks good. I don't want to give Sedbury's the wrong reputation.'

While Robert was speaking, he watched his son. Malcolm had picked up a paper knife and was fiddling with it, his eyes not meeting his father's. Their faces were very alike, Robert knew, peas from the same pod.

'You don't approve?' he said gruffly.

'You're the boss, Dad, it's up to you, of course. But she's a good worker, and the poor kid's had a tough time.'

'You're too soft-hearted.' But Robert liked the fact that his son was showing concern for the firm's doings, and if the truth were told he was proud of his kindness too. 'I'll think about it,' he said, and watched his son's face light up into a smile. 'But we'll have to make a decision soon.'

Robert went into his own office and sat down behind the big mahogany desk. The silver-framed faces of his family were drawn up in two encampments, one on either side of his blotter. His wife, his parents, his son, his daughters and his grandchildren. They were all there, bless them, all watching him. He sighed and began to open the post.

It was as well he had come in. There was an inquiry about

Wynstones from a Mr George Christie of Hampstead, London. Christie had written a month ago asking for details of houses for sale in the Lydmouth area. Robert had sent him the particulars of several which met Christie's criteria, and several more which didn't. It seemed that Mr Christie and his wife would be passing through Lydmouth on Sunday on their way to a family celebration in Swansea on the Bank Holiday Monday. Mr Christie realised that this was very short notice, and at an inconvenient time, but he wondered if it might be possible for them to view Wynstones as they passed through the area, perhaps around lunchtime. If it were, he would be obliged if Mr Sedbury would let him know, if necessary by telephone.

Robert glanced at the postmark on the envelope – Thursday. The letter had been delayed. He was tempted to ignore it, and write a civil note citing the delay as his reason for not getting in touch in time. He was due to play golf with Philip Wemyss-Brown early on Sunday afternoon and had no desire to break the engagement. On the other hand he would be extremely pleased if he could find someone willing to take Wynstones off the books.

It was a five-bedroomed house with all mains services and a one-acre garden on Narth Road, nearly a mile from the town centre. It was only twenty years old, and the Minnow ran along the bottom of the garden. But it had proved difficult to sell. Two years earlier, its previous owner, a retired bank manager, had committed suicide after he'd been diagnosed as having lung cancer. He had hanged himself from the banisters. His widow had stayed in the house but had died unexpectedly of pneumonia last November, reinforcing local opinion that there was a malign influence about the place. There was even a view that Wynstones was haunted. All this wouldn't necessarily have mattered if their heirs, the old man's nephew and niece, had been willing to accept reasonable offers for the place. But they had an inflated idea of its value, and had refused to let the price be dropped.

In the circumstances, someone like Mr Christie, a retired rubber planter recently returned from Malaya, might be an ideal choice. Mr Christie was a fisherman, it seemed, and in his letter he mentioned the river at the bottom of the garden. He sounded almost too good to be true. There was also a consideration that an inflated price meant an inflated commission.

Deferring the decision for a moment, Robert went into the front office to check the particulars on file and find the keys for Wynstones. House keys were kept on four rows of hooks in a cupboard in the left-hand alcove by the fireplace. They were labelled, and hung in alphabetical order by the name of the house or the street. Wynstones' keys should have been near the end – perhaps the last bunch. There was no sign of them.

He heard Malcolm coming slowly down the hall and turned as he reached the doorway.

'Have you seen the keys for Wynstones?'

Malcolm looked past him into the cupboard. 'Isn't that them on the second row down? Third from the left?'

Robert turned to look. 'No, that's nineteen Lyd Street.'

Malcolm opened the filing cabinet beside the typist's desk and was rummaged in the bottom drawer. 'Here they are.'

'What the devil are they doing there?'

'I think the girl must have got confused. Miss Evans used to put keys there which needed labels typed. Perhaps she thinks all keys go there.'

'More likely she doesn't think at all.'

Malcolm tossed the keys across the room to his father. 'Why do you need them anyway? Someone interested at last?'

'Chap called Christie. The only trouble is, he and his wife want to have a look at the place tomorrow lunchtime, and I'm down to play golf. Well, I suppose it will have to be work before pleasure.'

Malcolm bent down to push the drawer shut. 'Why don't I take them round?'

'You don't want to do that.'

'I've got nothing in particular on tomorrow, and I came with you when you took the last lot round. If they've got any questions I can't answer, you could always phone them in the evening.'

'Are you sure you wouldn't mind?'

Malcolm smiled and shook his head.

'Thanks, then. I think I'll take you up on that.'

Robert telephoned George Christie, who raised no objection. While he was on the phone, Robert heard a knock on the street door, followed by the sound of Malcolm and a man talking. A moment later, he went out of his room to find Malcolm and Bernie Broadbent in the front office.

'Robert,' said Bernie, lumbering towards him. 'I was just telling young Malcolm here, I happened to be passing, saw him through the window and I thought why not strike while the iron's hot. The early bird catches the worm, as my mam used to say. It's about that house—'

The telephone started to jangle.

'I'll answer it,' Malcolm offered.

Robert took Bernie along to his office. 'Which house?'

'Victoria Road.' Bernie settled himself into the visitor's chair, and patted his pockets, looking for pipe and matches. 'Number sixty-eight.'

Robert raised his eyebrows. 'It's not even on the market yet.'

'Yes, but it soon will be, won't it?'

'It's certainly a strong possibility,' Robert admitted. 'More than that, actually. We've been asked to handle the sale.' While he was speaking, his mind rapidly explored a series of possible connections. Bernie was the part-owner of a large engineering works on the outskirts of Lydmouth. One of the senior managers there was Stephen Shipston, whose half brother Wilfred Shipston was the owner of sixty-eight Victoria Road. 'You are aware that there's a sitting tenant? And their lease has at least another year to run.'

Bernie nodded as he lit his pipe.

'Perfectly respectable family,' Robert went on. 'I believe the man's a senior police officer. I'm sure Mr Shipston wouldn't mind me telling you that the house will definitely be going on the market next week. But I'm afraid we haven't yet completed—'

'Oh that's all right.' Bernie waved pipe smoke away from his face. 'I already know the house. And I know the sitting tenant, too – he's married to a cousin of mine. Naturally in the circumstances, if I buy the house, I'd be happy for them to continue there indefinitely. I'm thinking of it as a long-term investment, you see. So do you think you could have a word with Wilfred? Say I'm putting in an offer?'

'But you don't even know the asking price.'

'But I know Wilfred. And for that matter he knows me. I don't doubt you and him have already discussed the question of price. And between you you've decided on one that's on the steep side. Not unreasonable, just steep. Wilfred has got a hard head when it comes to business, but he's not stupid. Nor am I. And I know if he's made up his mind on a price, I know I've got about as much chance of persuading him to accept a lower offer as I have of getting the Rock of Gibraltar to turn a somersault. So why bother?'

'I'll let Mr Shipston know, of course—'

'One more thing, Robert, and I don't doubt it's close to your heart. The little matter of your commission. The way I look at it, the sale is going through you. You knew I was interested in acquiring residential property in Victoria Road, and you happened to tip me the wink.'

'I see.' Robert did – it was an open secret that Wilfred Shipston and his half brother were not on the best of terms. Bernie didn't want it to be known that he had advance warning of the sale via a leak in the family. Nice of him – suggested he valued Stephen Shipston as a manager. Either that or Bernie thought that someone else might be interested in the house and wanted to get in first. 'In fact, I think you did mention you were interested in the right sort of residential property a couple of months ago. At the Chamber of Commerce, was it?'

Bernie nodded. 'Very likely. So there's no question about it. You're due your commission.'

'The only thing is, what if Mr Shipston decides to see if he can get a slightly higher price on the open market?'

'I don't think he'll do that. He's hoping to buy some land in South Africa for that daughter of his. If the price is right, he'd prefer to have this sorted out sooner rather than later.' Bernie got to his feet. 'Well, mustn't keep you. Coming in on Saturday must mean you're busy. Many thanks, and give Wilfred my regards when you talk to him.'

Robert showed Bernie out. He chuckled quietly once the door was safely closed – what with the Victoria Road offer, and Mr Christie's letter about Wynstones, this was proving a potentially profitable morning. Still smiling, he opened the door of Malcolm's room, wanting to share the news. His son was talking on the phone.

'. . . It's a big blue thing,' Malcolm was saying. 'Plastic.' He looked up, saw his father in the doorway, beckoned him in just as Robert was on the brink of withdrawing. 'Must go – see you soon.' He put down the telephone. 'You look pleased.'

'That's because I am. Keep it to yourself, but I think I've just sold the Victoria Road house to Bernie Broadbent. Would you like a bite of lunch? My treat, I feel like celebrating.'

'Sorry – I can't manage today.' Malcolm pushed back his chair and stood up. 'I promised Bill I'd go out with him. He's got something he needs to talk about.'

'Not to worry. Some other time, perhaps.'

'Some other time.' He smiled at his father. 'Yes, I'd like that.'

Robert Sedbury watched his son pick up his crutch, manoeuvre his body round the desk and move slowly down the hall to the door as fast as the calliper and his withered legs would allow.

Chapter Eight

Miss Minnie Calder loved three things above everything else — God, Jimmy Leigh and her house in River Gardens, though not necessarily in that order. When one of them failed to live up to her expectations, she could usually find consolation in one of the others.

At present, as she drained potatoes into her gleaming sink, the cleanliness and convenience of the kitchen was some compensation for the shortcomings of Jimmy. Through the smart metal-framed window, she could see him digging what would eventually be the vegetable patch at the bottom of the little garden. This was part of his punishment for his terrible behaviour yesterday.

First, she had found him doing something very dirty and disgusting in his bedroom. Second, he'd run away while she was telling him off. Third, he had stolen a toy from the toyshop near the library, and run away with Mr Prout, the manager, at his heels. To make matters worse, Mr Prout was the organist at Lydmouth Baptist Chapel and a man whose opinion Minnie Calder valued highly. Fourth, Jimmy had stayed away from home for the rest of the afternoon and most of the evening, making her very worried indeed. Fifth, he had been brought back, wrapped in a blanket and wearing borrowed clothes, like a common criminal in a police car, which had parked outside her house in full view of all the neighbours. His own clothes were soaked, he had lost one of his shoes and he claimed he had lost the engine (which meant that she, Minnie Calder, would have to pay Mr Prout for it).

And to crown everything, he had found a dead body.

Six of the best on the hand with a ruler. No pocket money for a month. And he was going to turn that wasteland outside the kitchen window into the best garden in the street.

Jimmy wheeled a barrow-load of rubble and weeds down to the heap by the back fence. There was a gate in the fence, which gave onto the towpath along the Minnow. Minnie Calder's one reservation about her house was that it might prove to be damp because it was so near the river. They and their neighbours were the first tenants to live in the newly built River Gardens, and they'd only moved in three months ago, so the council officials' claim that the house would be as dry as a bone still had to stand the test of time.

Minnie Calder opened the window. 'Jimmy,' she called. 'Your dinner's almost ready. Come and get cleaned up. And make sure you take your boots off before you come in the house this time.'

She shut the window and mixed butter with the potatoes. While she was laying the table, she wondered if she should tell him what Mrs Sisal, their next-door neighbour, had said. She thought on the whole it would be wiser to do so. She bided her time. She waited until he was halfway through his meal – cold ham, boiled potatoes and a nice salad.

'You know that lady last night? The one you found?'

He looked at her, still chewing, and nodded.

'Shut your mouth while you're eating. What your mum and dad would have thought of your table manners I just don't know. Well, anyway, Mrs Sisal told me she heard it was Mattie Harris.'

Very slowly Jimmy laid down his knife and fork – not on his plate but on the tablecloth. His mouth was open but he was no longer chewing.

'Do shut your mouth,' Minnie told him angrily. 'How many times have I got to tell you?'

'Mattie? *Mattie?*'

'That's what she said. Mattie Harris. And I can't say I'm altogether surprised. By all accounts, she was a rackety girl. No better than she should be, I shouldn't wonder.'

'Mattie? Mattie?'

'That's what I said. Now pick up that knife and fork. Look at the mess you've made on the cloth.'

'But it can't be *Mattie*. It can't be.'

'Don't be silly. And finish your lunch.' Then the implication of what he had said sunk in. 'You didn't know her, did you?'

His eyes, large and round, met hers. At that moment there was a ring on the doorbell.

'Some people!' Minnie glanced up at the clock on the wall. 'You'd think they'd realise that people are having their dinners, wouldn't you?' She stood up, untying her apron and catching her reflection in the mirror below the clock. Thank heavens she'd powdered her nose, literally as well as metaphorically, before serving dinner. 'Get along with you, then. You might as well make yourself useful and see who's at the door.'

She followed Jimmy into the little hall. He opened the front door. On the doorstep was a fair-haired man wearing a suit and a bright blue and red tie. Beside him was a dark young woman, heavy about the hips, with short brown hair and very large brown eyes.

'Good afternoon, Mr Leigh,' the man said, bouncing up and down on the balls of his feet like an athlete before a race. 'I'm Detective Sergeant Kirby. This is my colleague WPC Ailsmore. You met her last night, remember.'

Jimmy Leigh spun round, face puckering. 'Auntie,' he whined, 'I don't want to—'

'We'd just like a few words,' the sergeant said. 'Nothing to worry about.'

Minnie Calder had been used to taking control of situations

all her adult life. She took control of this one. She put her hand on Jimmy's arm and drew him gently towards the stairs. 'Go up to your room, dear, for a moment. I'll have a word with the police officers first, and then we can all have a nice chat together. Nothing to worry about, is there?'

He galloped up the stairs to the security of his room, slamming the door behind him.

'We'll go in here, shall we?'

Minnie Calder led the police officers into the lounge, which was the only room in the house of which she was unreservedly proud. The furnishings were entirely new, in honour of River Gardens itself. None of your old hand-me-downs in here: from the pictures on the walls to the carpet on the floor, from the television in the corner to the coffee table in front of the electric fire, it was all shop-bought stuff, none of it more than six months old.

She settled them down and offered them tea, which rather to her relief they declined.

The sergeant put his hands on his knees and leant forward. 'Miss Calder, naturally we need to ask your nephew about what happened last night.' He had a London accent, and was altogether a bit too pleased with himself. 'Perhaps it would be easier if we got a few facts straight with you first, though. In the circumstances.'

The woman Ailsmore had snapped open a notebook and was ready to take notes.

'His full name, to begin with?' the sergeant said.

'James Henry Leigh.' She waved at the photograph on the mantelpiece, her sister in the wedding dress and the laughing man in the tight suit beside her, framed in chromium plate. 'They're his parents. He's an orphan. His dad went down at sea on one of the North Atlantic convoys, and his mother, my sister, she went just before the end of the war.' She noticed that the woman was no longer writing, and she thought the man was looking bored. She added with a note of defiance in her voice,

'Came to live with me in nineteen forty-five. Someone had to have him.'

'Tell me,' said the sergeant, 'how old is he?'

'Twenty-one,' said Minnie Calder. 'He'll be twenty-two come August.'

Chapter Nine

'Couldn't you come back later, Inspector?' said Mrs Browning. 'We're rushed off our feet. I mean, it's Saturday lunchtime, and I'm one girl down—'

'That's precisely why I'm here,' Thornhill pointed out. 'This probably won't take long.'

Reluctantly she allowed herself to be herded into her office at the back of the café. A dour steel filing cabinet was decorated with pictures of fluffy cats cut out from calendars. A teddy bear sat on the visitor's chair, his bottom resting on a copy of the *Financial Times*. Mrs Browning herself was plump and floated on a cloud of perfume, trailing scarves of chiffon, through the later stages of middle age. She had a small moustache on her upper lip and was reputed to have evicted a gang of drunken youths on Derby Day by force of personality alone.

'I knew it would end in trouble,' she said, sinking down behind her desk and taking a cigarette from the box in front of her. 'Oh, she was very plausible, I'll give her that, but in my experience a divorced woman means trouble of one sort or another.'

'Divorced?'

'That's what she said, anyway. I'm not entirely convinced that she was married in the first place. His name is Gary. Or was. Sergeant in the USAF. Showed me a photo of him once. Black as the ace of spades.' Cigarette smoke wreathed round her fingers and she smiled. 'Well-set-up man, though, there's no denying that.'

'How long has she worked here?' Thornhill asked.

'I took her on just before Christmas. She used to work at Pingry's.'

'The slaughterhouse in Mincing Lane?'

Mrs Browning nodded. 'She hated it. She was only a clerk-typist, but she couldn't avoid seeing things and hearing things. Couldn't stand the blood, she told me.'

'When did you last see her?'

'When she went off shift at six o'clock on Thursday evening.'

'Do you know what she planned to do?'

'She was going back home to her parents. They live in Eastbury. I've got the address if you want it.' Mrs Browning opened a drawer, pulled out a file and passed a sheet of paper to Thornhill. He made a note of the address.

'It was Thursday, so she was probably coming back into Lydmouth to go to the dance.'

'What dance?'

'The dance at the Ruispidge Hall. They usually have one there on Thursdays and Saturdays, and she always tried to go if she could. I never saw her dance myself, but Myra says she was a natural.'

Thornhill made a mental note to have a word with Myra, the stork-like waitress who was now doing the work of three as she tried to cope with the Saturday lunchtime rush.

Mrs Browning pursed her lips and breathed out a plume of smoke. 'I daresay it wasn't just the dancing. It was a good place to meet young men.'

Thornhill said, 'She liked young men? Was there a boyfriend?'

'None that I know of. But she was the sort of girl who attracts men like wasps round a honey pot. Encouraged it, too, the way she dressed. One day she turned up to work in a skirt so tight I had to make her go home and change it. Left nothing to the imagination, I can tell you. The other person who might be able to tell you about that kind of thing is Violet Evans. She works at Sedbury's in Castle Street. Nice girl, rather plump but such a sweet face and very pretty.'

Her voice trailed away and Thornhill sensed her attention was drifting into the café, monitoring the murmur of conversation, the chink of cutlery and the clatter of plates. She stubbed out her cigarette with an air of finality, as if implying that as far as she was concerned the conversation was over.

Thornhill sat back in his chair and stretched out his legs. 'You must have been concerned when she didn't turn up for work yesterday.'

Mrs Browning shook her head. 'She asked to have the day off. Needed to take her mother into hospital. It was an out-patients visit, and she wasn't sure how long it would last. Her mother's very frail, and Mattie didn't want her to go on the bus alone It was very inconvenient but like a fool I said yes.' She snapped open her handbag, took out a lace-trimmed handker-chief and dabbed her eyes. 'Such a silly girl. Used to make me so cross.'

She had a little more to add. She showed him a cupboard where the staff kept their things. Mattie's uniform was there, with the shoes that went with it, and a brown raincoat. There was nothing in the pockets of the coat. Thornhill talked to Myra, who had nothing to tell him apart from the fact that Mattie had been popular with the male customers but very good about sharing tips.

A few minutes later he went back to police headquarters. The smell of cooking in the café had made his mouth water, remind-ing him he hadn't had a proper meal since Edith had left. He sent a probationer to the canteen for a late breakfast with all the trimmings. He and Jill had picnicked in bed last night, licking the crumbs off each other, and then forgetting food altogether and allowing two plates to fall on the floor and break. Another appetite stirred.

The probationer returned with coffee the colour of battle-ships and a sandwich the colour of parchment. 'It's the Bank Holiday weekend, sir,' he said nervously. 'No hot meals.'

Thornhill waved him out of the office and picked up the sandwich. The phone started ringing as he was chewing the first mouthful.

'Thornhill,' said the voice of Superintendent Williamson in his ear. 'I'm surprised you haven't phoned me. What's all this about a body?'

He swallowed painfully. 'I was planning to phone you this afternoon, sir, when we've got a few more facts.' He wondered who had told Williamson about Mattie Harris. 'We've not got a great deal to go on yet.'

'I'll be the best judge of that.'

Thornhill said slowly, 'Mr Hendry asked me to take opera-tional charge of this, sir, since you're on sick leave.'

There was a silence at the other end of the line, the sort of silence you get in the interval between pulling a pin from a grenade and the resulting explosion. But when Williamson spoke, his voice was unsettlingly mild and silky. 'I know that, but I've still got my wits about me and I'm still head of CID in this force. Which means I like to keep an eye on what's happening in my patch. Understand?'

'Yes, sir. Last night a young man called Jimmy Leigh found the body of a young woman called Mattie Harris floating in the river just above New Bridge, on the Farnock bank. She was a waitress at the Gardenia Café. They've taken her down to the mortuary. The pathologist hasn't had a look at her yet, but there's no obvious sign of assault. But Doctor Bayswater pointed out that she seems to have dressed herself in a hurry. Or perhaps someone else dressed her.'

'No need to make things more complicated before you have to.'

'No, sir. There's a slight complication in that the young man who found the body has a mental age of twelve. He lives with his aunt in one of the new council houses in Temple-fields. Sergeant Kirby and WPC Ailsmore are interviewing them now. He was up before a juvenile court seven or eight years ago for petty theft. He's highly strung, apparently, and seems to be nervous around police officers. Nothing else known about him.'

'What have you got on Harris herself?'

'Not a great deal yet. Mrs Browning, the manageress of the Gardenia Café, says she claimed she was divorced. Lived with her parents in Eastbury. I'll go out and see them this afternoon. We've not yet traced anyone who admits to seeing her alive after six o'clock on the Thursday evening, which is when she went off duty at the Gardenia.'

'Is that all you've got?'

'Yes, sir.' Thornhill thought it was quite a lot for a man to achieve who was on leave and who, but for a landlady's double-booking, would have been building sandcastles with his children on a beach in Bournemouth.

'Keep me informed,' Williamson demanded. 'Ring me at home this evening, all right?'

'Yes, sir.'

'And if there's a major development, I want to know about it when it happens.'

Williamson slammed down the phone. Thornhill sighed. He pushed away the sandwich and took a sip of lukewarm coffee. The Superintendent was due to retire at the end of June. It was widely understood at police headquarters that after a recent case which had ended in a blaze of glory for Williamson, he would quietly cruise towards his retirement date in the privacy of his own home. He wasn't well, and he and Mr Hendry, the Chief Constable, seemed to have come to an arrangement. It must be hard to let go, Thornhill thought, and perhaps the possibility of another murder case, of one last triumph, was too much for the old man to resist. Williamson had aged terribly in the past year.

Losing his grip, they said in the canteen, and for once perhaps canteen rumour was right.

The phone rang again.

'*Lydmouth Gazette* would like a word with you, sir,' the switchboard clerk said. 'Would you like me to find someone else?'

'No, that's OK.' Thornhill felt his stomach lurch, as though someone had pressed an invisible button in an invisible lift, and he was suddenly descending very fast. 'Put them through.'

There was a click, then Jill's voice said, 'Inspector Thornhill?'

'Speaking.'

'This is Jill Francis at the *Lydmouth Gazette*.'

Otherwise known as Jill Darling. 'What can I do for you?' Memory had the answer. *Cover you in kisses, working downwards from your eyelids, seeing how candlelight turns your skin to a sea of golden shadows.*

'We understand that a young woman has been found dead in the river near New Bridge.'

'That is correct.' *Yes, and I understand that I love you, though I'm not sure you heard me tell you.* 'We are making inquiries. I believe Sergeant Kirby talked to Mr Wemyss-Brown earlier in the day.'

'Yes,' said Jill, and he imagined he heard laughter bubbling under the calmness of her voice. 'I just wondered if there'd been any further developments since then.'

'Nothing to speak of.' *Nothing to speak of on a telephone line. Just the sort of things you said when our heads were side-by-side on the same pillow. When our bodies were tangled together.*

'So you've not set a time for the inquest yet?'

'Not yet. But I imagine it will be as early as possible next week. Not Monday of course, because of the Bank Holiday, so most likely it will be Tuesday.'

'Perhaps I should contact you a little later?'

'Yes, that would be sensible.' *No, not sensible at all. It would be wonderful and terrifying, and it would probably end in sorrow. It would be full of glory and misery. He wanted her to contact him as soon as possible and as intimately as possible and for as long as possible.* 'You or Mr Wemyss-Brown could try again tomorrow, perhaps,' he suggested. 'I don't think I shall be available this evening. I shall be off duty then.'

'I see,' Jill said.

Thornhill hoped she did.

Chapter Ten

'It's so damned unfair,' Bill said, slopping beer on the grass. 'In fact the whole business has been a bloody disaster from start to finish.'

'Don't worry.' Malcolm Sedbury was trailing after him, dragging his useless legs. 'Ten to one it's in the bag. Or maybe she destroyed it. But either way, it's not a problem.'

Bill put down the tray with their drinks on the table nearest the car park. Malcolm settled down on the bench, propping his sticks against an empty chair. Still standing, Bill took a long pull of the beer, swallowing nearly half a pint. A woman at a nearby table was looking at him, which wasn't unusual. He was tall and fair-haired, with regular features and a fresh complexion. While he was doing his National Service, he had actually looked like a soldier, rather than a civilian in uncomfortable fancy dress.

Malcolm took a sip from his own glass, then lit a cigarette and pushed the packet across the table.

Bill took one. 'But what if—'

'Stop it. Just relax. There's no point in getting worked up.'

For a moment the two young men smoked in silence. They were sitting in the beer garden at the Golden Fox, a roadhouse some miles outside Lydmouth. They had come here for two reasons, because it was far enough out of town for there to be a good chance that they would meet no one they knew; and because Bill wanted to give the car a run. He had had his twenty-first birthday last month, and his parents had given him a second-hand MG TF, a rakish pre-war sports car. They could see the car now, its claret-coloured paint work gleaming in the sun. It was low-slung, and Malcolm found it difficult to get in and out of.

'It's as well I went into the office this morning,' he said slowly. 'We've had an enquiry for Wynstones.'

Bill sucked his little moustache. 'But that's—'

'Yes, I know. There's another complication. Dad couldn't find keys. That's all sorted out now, but he's still got them.'

'There must be something we can do. There has to be.'

'Of course there is. Simple enough. They want to look over the place tomorrow afternoon. And I'll be the one who shows them around.' Malcolm smiled. 'I wondered if you might be free to drive me?'

'Of course I will.' Bill leant forward, one hand fiddling with a button on his blazer. 'Are you sure it's going to be all right?'

'Yes. Don't worry.'

'Violet phoned this morning.'

Malcolm's dark eyebrows shot up. 'She phoned you at *home*?'

Bill nodded.

'Had she heard anything?'

'No, no.'

'How is she?'

'In a bit of a state. You just wouldn't believe how she's changed since that baby's come along. She's either nagging or crying.'

'I think Dad's going to sack her. And it's not entirely her fault that she's got that baby, is it?'

Bill turned his lean, handsome face aside and studied the toecaps of his shoes. 'It's her fault. She said it would be all right. It was the safe time of the month, so we didn't have to use anything. Much nicer like that.' He looked at Malcolm, his face a mixture of pride and fear. 'I'll make it all right, of course. But

I've got to bring Dad round to the idea, first. You know what he's like – it's a matter of choosing your time. Anything like this tends to make him hit the roof. I just can't rush it. You do see that, don't you?'

'I see.'

'Violet doesn't,' Bill continued. 'She wanted to know if I'd seen Mattie. She was expecting to see her yesterday, apparently.'

Malcolm sipped his beer, staring at the traffic moving up and down the main road fifty yards away.

'I just don't know what she's playing at,' Bill said, his voice rising.

'Perhaps you should go and see her – find out what's really going on.'

'I can't do that. She's living with her parents, for God's sake. If I turn up on their doorstep, I'd be asking for trouble. They'll know right away that it was me who put the bun in the oven. And I really wouldn't like to get on the wrong side of her dad.'

'Ted Evans? He always seemed pretty mild to me.'

'You don't last long as foreman on a building site if you're meek and mild.' Bill finished his beer. 'He's an ex-sergeant major in the Royal Marines. He's got a temper too. My father says he nearly killed this big Irish labourer who started giving him lip.' He pointed at Malcolm's glass, which was still half full. 'Do you want another one yet?'

Malcolm shook his head. 'Should you have much more on an empty stomach? I thought you were playing cricket this afternoon.'

'I cried off.' Bill stood up and hesitated, glass in hand. 'To be honest, I couldn't face it. Ted's the wicket keeper.'

'Wait a moment,' Malcolm said. 'If he's playing cricket, then he won't be at home this afternoon.'

Bill nodded, his eyes straying towards the door to the bar.

'Then we could drop in. Have a word with Violet.'

'But I told you – that would mean they'd guess I–'

'I said we, not you. You can drive me. She's one of our employees, remember, and that's why I need to see her.'

'But what if she's heard something?'

'We'll deal with that when and if we have to. So we just act normally. It's common sense.'

For a moment Bill stared at Malcolm, his lips moving but no sound emerging from them. Then he said gruffly, 'I'll just get another drink.'

Three-quarters of an hour later, they drove back to Lydmouth. Bill had three pints inside him, plus a sandwich to soak up some of the third, and he threw the car into the bends of the road with enthusiasm. Malcolm clutched the side of his seat. They roared down Chepstow Road and turned into Broadwell Drive. Bill stamped on the foot brake at the entrance to Broadwell Crescent.

'Christ.' He looked at the rutted surface of the roadway. 'I'm not taking her down there. You'd need a tractor for that. Do you mind walking?'

Malcolm shrugged. He did mind — he would always mind. But he had learned long ago that there was no point in complaining about it to other people. One just had to get on and do it.

They left the car by the kerb. There was no doubt where the Evanses lived. None of the other nine houses had roofs. The Crescent looked more like a bomb site than a building development. Still, Malcolm thought, his professional attention briefly engaged, not a bad investment in the long term: nice new little houses on the edge of town, all mod cons, near a bus route and the hospital, easy to sell in a few years' time.

The Evans' home was on the corner, as bright and neat as a doll's house marooned in a garden full of mud, builders' rubble and a pile of scaffolding. Bill pushed open the gate, and they walked slowly up the concrete path to the front door.

'Let me do the talking,' Malcolm murmured.

Bill nodded.

They rang the doorbell and waited. Malcolm had hoped Violet herself would answer it but a moment later the door was opened by a sturdy, middle-aged woman with a trace of Violet's prettiness lingering on her plump, freshly powdered face. Her welcoming smile faded. Malcolm had never met her before, but she would know who he was. He had the polio to thank for that.

'Mrs Evans? My name's Malcolm Sedbury. My father asked me to drop in and see how Violet is.'

'She's asleep, I'm afraid. She's — she's not been very well. I hope it's not inconvenienced your father.'

'Well, we do need to discuss what—' Malcolm began.

'I'm not asleep, Mother.'

Mrs Evans turned. Malcolm and Bill looked past her. Violet was coming down the stairs, carrying the baby in the crook of her arm. Her face was pale but still pretty. She was wearing a loose, flowery dress with buttons up the front, and Malcolm wondered if she'd been feeding the baby when they called. The thought of all that rich, voluptuous flesh made him feel almost ill with lust.

'Violet,' he said. 'How are you?'

'All right, thank you, Mr Malcolm.' Her eyes moved from him to Bill. 'It's kind of you to bother to come all this way.'

Her voice had changed, Malcolm thought — it was thinner, more tired than before. She needed a perm, too. The fine blonde hair straggled down her cheeks, most unlike the usual golden helmet.

'You'd best come in,' Mrs Evans said. She opened the door on the right of the hall. 'We'll go in the lounge, shall we?'

Not counting the baby, there were only four of them in the lounge, but that was enough to make the room seem cramped. The window looked out over the builders' wasteland at the front of the house. There were two threadbare armchairs, a little Utility table, and a sofa covered with what looked like blackout material, huddled together on a square of fraying carpet. The plaster had not yet been painted. But the curtains were new and bright, and a large cyclamen stood on the windowsill.

'Please sit down,' Mrs Evans said. 'We've only just moved in, as you can see, so we haven't got things quite straight yet.'

'It's a charming house,' Malcolm said, the patter flowing easily because he felt relieved, Violet couldn't have had the news. 'And a very nice location on the edge of town like this. You must be able to see fields from the back?'

Mrs Evans nodded, her face suddenly flushing with enthusiasm. 'It'll be lovely when the garden's done. Almost like being in the country.' As she spoke, her vowels broadened imperceptibly, and her face briefly relaxed.

'By the way,' Malcolm went on, 'this is my friend Bill Pembridge.'

'How do you do?' She said.

Suspicion returned to Mrs Evans' face and she seemed not to see his outstretched hand. 'Pleased to meet you, I'm sure.'

'And this is the baby,' Malcolm said, feeling like a curate in an Aldwych farce. 'Wearing pink, so I presume it's a girl. What's her name?'

'Grace,' Violet said looking at Bill, who was looking at the baby as if looking at a Martian.

'I won't beat about the bush,' Malcolm said. 'My father feels that he may soon have to advertise your job, Violet. We've had one or two temporaries, but it's not worked out very well.' He watched her face begin to disintegrate. The baby whimpered in her arms. 'Of course, if it were just up to me, I'd much rather have you back. But now you've got family responsibilities, we have to be realistic.'

Poor kid, poor bloody kid.

'There's always a chance Violet could make other arrangements about Baby,' Mrs Evans said. 'Do you think your father might be able to see his way to – well – keeping the job open until then?'

'It's hard to tell. I'll have a word with him.'

'He always seemed pleased with Violet's work.'

'We all were. But he is rather upset, I have to say.'

'That's understandable,' Mrs Evans said. 'Not the only one, either.'

'I'm trying to persuade him not to do anything in a hurry.' Malcolm smiled at Violet. 'We miss you at the office. But I thought it would be best to let you know the situation.'

'Very kind, I'm sure,' said Mrs Evans. 'Isn't it, Violet?'

The baby stopped whimpering and started howling. Violet shuffled her bottom to the edge of her chair and stood up. Malcolm darted a guilty glance at her, half hoping, half fearing, that the movement would reveal a glimpse of that wonderful body.

'Grace is hungry,' Violet announced. 'I'm going upstairs to feed her.'

Mrs Evans started to say something and then stopped. Ignoring her mother completely, Violet moved towards the door. Malcolm thought that Mrs Evans would have a better chance of winning an argument with an earthquake. The three of them watched in silence as Violet left the room, and then listened to Grace's high wails and Violet's slow, heavy footsteps mounting the stairs.

If she were like this now, Malcolm thought, how would she be when she heard the news?

Chapter Eleven

At present, Bernie Broadbent enjoyed driving. He ran over to Elmbury for a late lunch, partly to distract himself from this business about the Drowner, partly because he wanted to pay an unexpected visit to Crossways Garage, and mainly because he wanted to try out the car.

He had taken delivery of one of the new Riley RM series last week, the RMF with the 2.5 litre engine. You could do 0–60, they claimed, in just under 17 seconds. Bernie liked machines that worked well, he liked possessions that looked new and expensive, and he had a sentimental attachment to the Riley's slightly old-fashioned design. The long, lean bonnet and the elegant sweep of the running boards from the front mudguards reminded him of the sort of cars that twenty years ago he'd dreamt of owning.

Crossways Garage was a little outside the town. The owner was hoping to retire on the proceeds of the sale. Bernie was considering setting up a chain of garages in the area. He believed road use was bound to increase considerably in the next few years, and since servicing vehicles was such a major outlay for many of his other business interests, there would be a number of immediate practical advantages.

What he saw at Crossways Garage was on the whole favourable – a good team of mechanics, working six days a week, no obvious signs of slacking. The location was good and if he could buy that field at the back as well, there would be plenty of room for expansion. The owner himself was there, another good sign. Among other things, the man was a partner at Thorogood and Nephew, and when Bernie said something complimentary about the beer he had given him last month, he insisted on putting another crate of IPA in the boot of the Riley. All very satisfactory, Bernie thought, the sort of man you could do business with.

Relishing the Riley's power, he drove back to Lydmouth. He stopped for a sandwich on the way at the Golden Fox. As he pulled into the roadhouse's car park, he noticed young Pembridge and his friend Malcolm Sedbury driving off in an elderly MG.

Instead of going home when he reached Lydmouth, he drove down to the George V Sports Field near the allotments, the home ground for Lydmouth Cricket Club. He parked the Riley alongside a handful of other cars between the field and the river. White-clad figures moved with somnambulistic solemnity across the grass. Willow cracked on leather and a streak of red shot between two fielders and rolled over the boundary. There was a spatter of applause from the pavilion.

Ted Evans, who was armoured in wicket keeper's pads and gloves, shook his head sadly behind the batsman. Lydmouth were playing Ashbridge, and the visitors had chosen to bat first. Bernie glanced at the scoreboard. A new digit clacked into place, marking up the new four. No wickets had fallen yet. The visitors' opening partnership had already notched up a healthy forty-seven.

'Bernie, old chap!'

He turned. Stick in hand, Ray Williamson was walking rather uncertainly down the lane past the allotments towards him. Judging by his gait and the redness of his face, he had been refreshing himself at the Ferryman's Inn. Bernie held open the gate, and the two men walked slowly round the boundary of the field towards the pavilion.

'Not doing too well, are we?' Williamson said. 'Shame we didn't win the toss. Ten to one the Ashbridge captain realised our bowling was going to be weak today.'

'Why's that?'

'Young Pembridge had to cry off. It would be a different story if they had to face his yorkers.'

They had reached the pavilion now. The scorers perched on the veranda. A ragged arc of deckchairs and shooting sticks and picnic blankets spread along the front of the pavilion and extended on either side. Gerald Pembridge and Cyril George were sitting a little further back under the shade of an elm. Gerald waved Bernie and Williamson over.

'Not doing too well, I'm afraid,' Gerald said.

George smiled and nodded. 'Gerald's right.' Cyril George owned the largest building firm in the area, and he usually made a point of agreeing with Gerald Pembridge, because Gerald was the Council's Director of Planning.

'Missing Bill, I daresay,' Bernie said.

'Said he had a headache.' Gerald smiled. 'Wouldn't have stopped me playing when I was his age. But it's not just that. We're not fielding as well as we should be. Ted Evans is off form. Missed an easy catch at the end of the third over.'

'So we'll be drowning our sorrows rather than celebrating this evening,' Williamson said.

'You'll have to count me out, I'm afraid,' Gerald said quickly. 'It's one of my Saturdays.'

'Saturdays?' Williamson's large blue eyes slid towards Gerald. 'What do you do on your Saturdays?'

'Dance night,' Gerald reminded him. 'Mustn't disappoint my boys and girls.'

'Very public-spirited of you,' Bernie said.

Gerald smiled and with a graceful flick of his fingers smoothed back his hair. 'We all do our bit, eh?'

'Bring Edna round for a drink afterwards,' Cyril George suggested. 'The Sedburys are coming to dinner so they'll be there.'

Bernie glanced at a man passing with a cup and saucer in his hand. 'Looks like they've got an urn going inside. I could do with a cup of tea.'

'Me, too,' Williamson said.

He and Bernie said goodbye to the others and walked towards the door at the side of the pavilion. The score had risen to fifty-six and still no wickets had fallen.

'I don't suppose there's any news your end?' Bernie said softly.

'Nothing concrete.' Williamson took a pipe from the top pocket of his jacket and peered into the bowl. 'But I've had a word in the right ears. I'll keep my finger on what's happening, don't you worry.'

'Good man.'

'Gerald seems cool enough.'

'No reason why he shouldn't be,' Bernie said. 'Is there?'

They went into the pavilion. Williamson went to the lavatory. Bernie bought himself a cup of tea and strolled onto the veranda. The scorers were sitting in a world of their own at the end. Apart from them, only Lydmouth Cricket Club committee members were allowed on the veranda when a match was in progress. Bernie felt he'd had enough of Williamson's company for the time being, and Williamson was not on the committee.

Suddenly there was a burst of clapping. The Lydmouth umpire raised his finger. One of the batsmen tucked his bat under his arm and began the slow trudge back to the pavilion.

'Well, that's a start,' Bernie murmured to Robert Sedbury, who was leaning over the rail with a pipe in his mouth. 'I was beginning to think him and his partner would be out there till they pulled stumps.'

Sedbury smiled. 'So far it's just not been our afternoon, has it? It's not so much that they're playing well, but we're playing badly.'

'If only we had Bill Pembridge.'

'Just so.' Sedbury turned to look at Bernie. 'By the way, I had a word with Wilfred Shipston. I relayed your offer to him, subject to survey, and so on, of course. He's accepted.'

'I'm glad to hear it. I'd like to get it sorted out as quickly as possible.'

'You'll want to tell the Thornhills the good news, I expect?'

Bernie smiled, showing strong yellow teeth. 'That's something I shall enjoy.'

Chapter Twelve

———⊙◦◦⊙———

'There, dear. See? There's the Drowner.'

Charlotte Wemyss-Brown flung out a bejewelled hand and pointed at one of the pillars supporting the arch. Jill followed the direction of her finger with her eyes. They were in the south porch of the Parish Church of St John the Baptist. At the top of the pillar, forming the base of the arch, was a capital carved with vine leaves.

'The porch is early Perpendicular, but the archway is much earlier. First half of the thirteenth century at the latest. You have to stand a little to one side, and look upwards. Whoever carved the capital didn't want to make the Drowner too obvious.'

Jill craned her head and peered up into the carving. First she saw nothing but the leaves and the stems. Then she shifted her position a little and suddenly she saw the face of the Drowner. He looked like a fish seen from the front. His head was about the size of an egg, and about the same shape seen in cross-section. Some sort of carp, perhaps. He had a small mouth and staring eyes and something which might have been gill covers on either side. But he wasn't just a fish. The anonymous sculptor had contrived to add something human to the face, hints of consciousness, of malevolence.

'Isn't it rather odd – something like that in a church porch?'

'Surprisingly common, dear. You find these pagan survivals

tucked away in medieval churches all over the country. The most common is the Green Man. I suppose the Drowner is a sort of fishy variant. He was probably a Romano-Celtic deity originally, some sort of water god, but he seems to have got mixed up with a Welsh saint called Druoc in the Dark Ages.'

Jill reached up and touched the little stone face. She shivered.

'You're not the first to have done that, I expect,' Charlotte said.

'To touch it or to shiver?'

'Both. The story is, he's half man and half fish – sort of a local version of a merman, I suppose. He lives in the Lyd, and when the spirit moves him he drags women and children down into the deep and has his wicked way with them.'

'And then when he's had enough,' Jill went on slowly, 'he lets them float back to the surface. But of course by that time they're drowned. I remember now. The story's mentioned in the church guide.' She smiled at Charlotte. 'It's very comprehensive.'

If Charlotte had been the simpering kind, she would have simpered. 'A small thing, but my own,' she murmured.

'So now people are saying that Mattie Harris was taken by the Drowner?'

'People are still superstitious around here. When the spirit moves them. Especially the older ones. Most of the time, things like the Drowner are treated as a joke. But then, when someone's drowned, suddenly the joke doesn't seem quite so funny. And they start to wonder if perhaps there's something in it after all.'

'Why Mattie, I wonder?'

'The poor child probably just fell in. I wonder if anyone's told Violet Evans yet.'

'Who?'

'Violet Evans. She worked at Sedbury's until very recently. Rather large girl, but terribly sweet-natured. Lovely face. She was in my guide troop for a while. Comes from a nice, hard-working family. She and Mattie Harris were as thick as thieves, though and I can't help thinking that Mattie was a bad influence.' Charlotte lowered her voice. 'Violet had to leave Sedbury's very suddenly, It turned out she was more than eight months pregnant.'

'Surely someone noticed before that?'

'Apparently not. If anyone noticed, they just thought Violet was putting on a little bit more weight. Came as a complete surprise to everyone, even her own family.' Charlotte added with a touch of condescension, as a mother speaking to a childless woman: 'It can happen, you know — especially if it's a smallish baby.'

'What will they do?'

'Oh, they'll find a way of managing. People usually do. We see her mother, Mrs Evans, at church occasionally. I've heard they're planning to have the baby adopted. Probably the best thing for all concerned. Wouldn't you agree?'

'I don't know.'

'Such a pity, because the family are really making a big effort, and they're very respectable. Violet's father was the sexton at St John's when I was a girl. They've just bought a new house in Broadwell Crescent. Funny how things have changed.' Charlotte laughed, but without amusement. 'Anyway, dear, why are you so interested in all this?'

'Just curious.'

'You're on holiday. We can't have you rushing back to work at the first hint of a story.'

'Don't worry.'

The two women left the porch and strolled around the west end of the church and down to the gate. Charlotte's Rover was parked outside Church Cottage. She had been on her way to Clearland Court for a committee meeting and had stopped off to show Jill the Drowner. She climbed into the car and rolled down the window.

'You'll be all right, won't you?'

'Why shouldn't I be?'

'No reason — it's just that things can sometimes be very difficult. For a single woman, I mean.' Charlotte started the engine and rammed the car into first gear. 'Especially somewhere like Lydmouth. In some respects, of course, it's much easier when one's in town. The great advantage with London is that so few people know who one is.'

She smiled and revved the engine. The Rover surged away from the kerb. At the junction with the High Street, the car barely slackened speed before turning right, the manoeuvre heralded by a blast of car horns. Charlotte was an excellent driver but not a considerate one.

Jill shrugged, suddenly anxious to escape from Lydmouth, from the prying eyes and listening ears of all the people who knew who one was. She would go back to Eastbury, to the empty cottage, the wonderful view and *The Vicar of Bullhampton*.

She added a bag with a few more clothes to the shopping that was already in the car. As an afterthought, she fetched a blue silk dress, far too frivolous for the grimly rustic realities of Walnut Tree Cottage, especially if there were no one but herself to see it. She said goodbye to Alice and the kittens, who ignored her completely.

Once in the car, though, she changed her mind. An impulse made her drive along Chepstow Road. She turned right into Broadwell Drive. She had not been here for some time, and in her memory the cluster of raw new houses at the end had been a green field with a few cows in it. The only completed house was the one on the corner.

She would have driven away at that point, idle curiosity satisfied, but for the fact there was a pram parked in a patch of sunshine on the path by the front gate. It was a large vehicle, perhaps thirty years old, with purple and gold paint work and the sort of suspension Jill associated with state carriages at the Opening of Parliament. Jill felt a twinge inside her, half anxiety, half straightforward envy.

What is it like, having a baby?

Then the pram began to cry.

Two things happened simultaneously. Jill got out of the

car and stepped towards the gate, drawn by an urge to comfort that was as old as the human race. The front door opened. A fat young woman darted down the path, her ragged golden curls bouncing on either side of her face. She picked up the baby, who immediately fell silent. Only then did she look at Jill.

'Isn't she lovely?' Jill said, looking at the tiny face, framed in a sun bonnet, nuzzling against her mother's breast. 'They're so small at this age, so perfect.'

'Yes.' The woman nodded, acknowledging that an absolute like 'perfect' was really the only appropriate term for her daughter. She moved slightly, so Jill could have a better view.

'How old is she? She *is* a girl, isn't she?'

The woman nodded. 'Nearly three weeks.'

'What's her name?'

'Grace.'

'That's a beautiful name,' Jill said. 'And I'm sure she'll live up to it.'

The woman could only be Violet Evans. She was attractive, though her face was worried and the eyelids were puffy from tiredness or crying. She must have heard about Mattie.

'She's named after a friend of mine. Well in fact it's her second name.'

'Mattie Harris, by any chance?'

Jill wished she could bite the words back as soon as she said them. The baby had flustered her, addled her wits.

Violet's face went blank with surprise. 'How do you know?'

'Just a guess really.'

'Do you know Mattie?'

'No.' Jill looked at her watch. 'I must be going.'

'Have you heard something about her, then?' Violet said sharply. 'Why are you here?'

To make matters worse, the girl wasn't a fool. And she obviously hadn't heard what had happened. Jill came to a quick decision.

'Look, I'm afraid I've got some bad news for you. My name's Jill Francis, by the way, I work for the *Lydmouth Gazette*.' Jill watched Violet's mouth tremble. 'I'm afraid it's bad news about Mattie. I thought you must already know. I'm so sorry, but she's drowned.'

Violet's arms tightened around Grace. The baby's head jerked and she began to cry. Violet immediately relaxed her hold, cooed softly into the black feathery hair at the top of Grace's head. The cries subsided. When all was quiet, Violet laid the baby very carefully in the pram and covered her up. Then, at last, she turned to Jill, who was standing by the gate and feeling like the worst kind of fool.

'I'm so sorry,' Jill repeated. 'I didn't come to see you because of that. In fact, I didn't mean to come and see you at all. But the baby began to cry and — well, I came over.'

Violet put one hand on the gate post and studied Jill's face as though it concealed a puzzle she wanted to unravel. 'What happened — when?'

'I gather her body was found in the river near New Bridge late last night.'

'She couldn't swim. Used to laugh about it, said if you put her in the water, she'd sink like a stone. I think she was a bit scared, actually. Funny to think of Mattie being scared. Did she fall in?'

'No one's quite sure yet. They'll find out.'

'That explains it.'

'Explains what?'

'Why — why she didn't come and see me yesterday. We were going to meet yesterday evening. She wanted to see Grace. I was going to ask her to be Grace's godmother. I went to the Gardenia this morning. Myra, that's the other waitress, said she just hadn't turned up. Do you think she knew all along, do you think she knew Mattie was dead?'

'I'm sure she would have told you if she'd known. Probably the news hadn't reached them.'

Violet rubbed her eyes. 'It's awful, everything's so awful.'

'Were you very close?'

'She was my best friend. We met when we were four, first day at school. She came up to me and said, would I be her friend. And I said yes, so I was. And we stayed friends ever after, we stayed friends even when she went away with Gary. And then she came back to Lydmouth and everything was the same again. We were friends.'

As she spoke, Violet's voice rose steadily in volume. The words tumbled out, and so did the tears.

'I'm sorry,' Jill said, and felt the uselessness of her sorrow.

'I can't – I can't believe I'll never hear her laugh again. She used to say I was the large person with a little laugh, and she was the other way round. If you heard her laugh you would think she was six foot six. Used to laugh at everything.'

'Perhaps you should go and sit down, have a cup of tea,' Jill suggested.

'If she's not here, it changes everything.'

'Is there anything I can do?'

'No.' Violet looked up. 'Except tell me what am I going to do now.'

She shook her head, as if acknowledging the futility of what she had said. Then she nodded to Jill, sniffed, turned the pram and pushed it up the path to the house. Jill waited by the gate, watching Violet take Grace out of the pram and carry her into the house. As Violet closed the door, she raised a hand, half-heartedly waving goodbye.

Jill went back to the car and sat behind the steering wheel. She wondered why and how Mattie's death changed everything. She thought of Mattie, a small woman with a large laugh. She thought most about Grace, about the soft, perfect skin, the curve of the cheek, the straight little nose, the unbearably delicate hand with the nails like tiny pearls.

Jill's hands were on her lap. They rose of their own volition and settled, palms downward, on her stomach. Two words formed in her mind, and she heard herself say them aloud in a cold, clear voice, as unfamiliar as a stranger's.

'What if? What if?'

Chapter Thirteen

The heat and the humidity steadily increased in the afternoon. Thornhill took WPC Joan Ailsmore with him to Eastbury. He felt, in the usual cowardly masculine way, that women were better at coping with emotion than men. Taking her along would absolve him of any responsibility in that area. There was also the point that Joan had shown herself a sharp-eyed, competent officer in the few months she had been in Lydmouth, and Thornhill was beginning to wonder whether he should get her permanently out of uniform and into the CID.

Driving into Eastbury unsettled him. It seemed a baleful coincidence that Mattie Harris's parents and Walnut Tree Cottage should be in the same village. He must have driven past the Harrises' cottage on his way to Lydmouth this morning, leaving the warmly desirable sight of Jill Francis in her dressing gown for the chilly spectacle of Mattie Harris on a mortuary slab.

'There it is, sir,' WPC Ailsmore said, pointing out of the nearside window. 'Lower Slade.'

Thornhill pulled over and reversed the little Austin back to the gate. The cottage's name staggered in clumsy white letters across the peeling blue-green paint on the gate. The two police officers got out of the car. The house was at the foot of Eastbury Hill, its long front garden running down to the main road.

Thornhill glanced up and beyond it. He was almost sure that Walnut Tree Cottage was one of the roofs near the top. He wondered if Jill were there, waiting for him. The thought of her was distracting him from the job.

He pushed open the gate with unnecessary violence. They walked slowly up the cinder path to the half-glazed front door. Apart from a small area near the house, most of the garden had been devoted to fruit and vegetables. Caked earth, sprouting weeds and dead leaves told their own story: a neat and productive garden was gradually running to seed.

The house itself was attractive, at first sight. It was long and low with small windows. At some point in its life it had been colour-washed blue, and the paint had now faded to a soft blue-grey. Lichen blotched the stone tiles of the roof. The roof sagged and rippled under their weight. The tall chimney stack badly needed repointing.

Joan knocked on the door. They waited and then she knocked again. Then, through the glass, they saw a small man hunched over a stick making his way towards them through the gloom. He opened the door with some difficulty and peered up at them with soft, milky brown eyes.

'Good afternoon, sir. I'm Detective Inspector Thornhill from Lydmouth. This is my colleague, WPC Ailsmore. Are you Mr Harris?'

'Yes. Yes, that's right.'

'May we come in, sir? We need to talk to you.'

The old man wrinkled his forehead in confusion but stood back, holding the door wide. 'Mother's in the kitchen. We'd better go in there, if you don't mind.'

He shuffled away across the stone-flagged floor. Thornhill exchanged glances with Joan and followed. The house smelled of damp and cabbage, with other less pleasant smells beneath those. There were rooms on either side of the hall, made gloomy by half-drawn curtains and small windows. Mr Harris led them through a door at the back of the house. The kitchen was a hot, airless room with a range at one end. An old lady was sitting beside it in a rocking chair.

'Two police officers to see us, Mother,' Mr Harris said in a loud voice. 'Isn't that nice?'

The old woman looked up. She was small and monkey-like, sitting hunched forward, with a newspaper in her lap. She was the size of a ten-year-old child, Thornhill thought, but when she was younger perhaps she had a similar build to her daughter.

'I'm afraid we've got some bad news,' Thornhill said, wishing he was anywhere but here, wishing he could leave this part of the job to Joan Ailsmore. 'It's about your daughter.'

'Mattie?' The old man went to stand behind his wife's chair. He put one hand on her shoulder, and she lifted a hand like a paw and placed it on top of his. 'Is she dead?'

'I'm afraid she is, sir. We are very sorry.'

There was a silence. The old man scratched his chin with his free hand. Coke settled in the range. Thornhill listened to Joan's breathing, which was loud enough to make him wonder if she had a cold. Not wanting to stare at the Harrises' grief he looked at the room instead. There was a calendar with a picture of Salisbury Cathedral. Half a dozen sweet williams peeped out of a jam jar on a windowsill. A pile of library books was on one end of the dresser. The scullery was visible through an open door, with a tin bath hanging on the wall. No electricity, judging by the candles on the mantelpiece and the oil lamps on the table beside the fire and on the dresser.

It was the old woman who spoke first: 'How did it happen?'

'She was found in the river, I'm afraid. It's possible she may have drowned. Do you know if she could swim?'

'No. Never liked water, even when she was a baby.' The voice was so soft they had to lean forward and strain to hear what she was saying. 'Mattie hates water, doesn't she, Joe? Just like a cat.'

'Yes, dear.' The old man raised his head and looked at Thornhill. 'How did it happen? Did she fall in?'

'I'm afraid we don't yet know, sir. But we'll find out.'

'How are we going to manage?' Mrs Harris suddenly demanded, in a much stronger voice. 'I need Mattie. Who's going to do my feet?'

'Don't worry about that now,' Mr Harris said. 'The police don't want to hear about your feet, Mother.'

'She was found on Friday night,' Thornhill said. 'But we didn't find out who she was till this morning. Would you like me to ask someone else to make the formal identification? A relative, perhaps.'

The old man looked up. 'I'll do it. She's my daughter.' He hesitated, his features working. 'When – when did she die?'

'We're not yet sure. It may have been Thursday night. Were you surprised when she didn't come home?'

'No. She said she was going dancing, and if she missed the last bus she'd stay with Violet.'

'Our Mattie loves dancing,' Mrs Harris said. 'She always did. I remember Mrs Carnegie saying, that was her first teacher, that Mattie danced like a little fairy. No one else in the class could—'

'Violet?' Thornhill said.

'Violet Evans. Works at Sedbury's, the estate agents.'

Thornhill nodded, and Joan made a note.

'Such a sweet girl, Violet is,' Mrs Harris said. 'I've known her since she was a kiddy, she and Mattie used to go to school together when we had that place on Mincing Lane, and I never heard a cross word or saw a frown. Your Violet must have been born on a Sunday, that's what I told her mother. Mattie was born on a Wednesday.'

The monkey's face wrinkled still further. The paw tightened its grip on Mr Harris's hand.

'So you thought she was staying with Violet?' said Joan in response to a glance from Thornhill. 'Was that something she often did?'

'Once or twice a month.' Mr Harris was looking puzzled.

'Maybe there was a dance that was going on late. Or she was on earlies at the Gardenia.'

'They think the world of her at that café,' Mrs Harris announced. 'It's where a lot of smart people go, the Gardenia.'

'And you weren't worried when she didn't come back last night, either?' Joan continued.

'Not really. She said she might have to work late, a private party at the café, and if she did she'd stay with Violet.'

Mrs Harris leant forward. 'We're going to have a bathroom,' she confided. 'Our Mattie's going to arrange it. We're going to have the electric light, too.'

'They don't want to know about all that,' Mr Harris said. 'The police are busy people. You mustn't waste their time.'

'It's all right, Mr Harris,' Thornhill said. 'Tell me, when did you last see Mattie?'

'Thursday morning, when she went to work. We had break-fast together, and then she took Mother in a cup of tea just before she went to catch the bus. Seven twenty-five. That's when the bus comes.' The old man turned aside and stared at the win-dowsill with the sweet williams in the jam jar.

'What was she wearing, Mr Harris?' Joan asked brightly.

'She had her brown mac in case it rained. And a little beret.' He turned to face them, and Thornhill saw the tears glistening on his cheeks. 'Mrs Browning let her keep some clothes at the café for when she was going out. So she was wearing her wait-ress's uniform underneath.'

'What colour was the beret, sir?'

'Blue or black. I don't know. Navy-blue?'

'A lovely new handbag,' Mrs Harris murmured, turning her head to look up at her husband's face. 'Very smart, too. Mattie said she'd seen Lady Ruispidge's niece with a bag like that.'

'And what was the handbag like?' Joan waited, pencil poised. 'Large, small?'

She was hurrying the old man too much, thought Thornhill,

and he stepped forward to put his body between Joan and the couple by the range.

'Big, bright blue thing,' the old man said. 'Shiny.'

'You must ask her to show you her powder compact,' Mrs Harris suggested. 'It's in the handbag. Real gold and it's very beautiful. Very ladylike. Gary sent it to her. Gary's her husband.'

Mr Harris pulled away his hand in his agitation. 'The police don't want to know about Gary, Mother. He's an American airman who was married to Mattie, but they're divorced now. He's in Korea, I think she said.'

'Would you mind if we had a look at Mattie's bedroom, sir? Sometimes it can be helpful in cases like this.' Thornhill didn't specify how. 'If it's not too much trouble?'

'When's Mattie coming home?' Mrs Harris asked.

Mr Harris glanced at his wife, his expression a mixture of irritation and sadness. He hobbled towards the door to the scullery. 'This way, sir,' he said to Thornhill.

The scullery had a brick floor, a copper, a stone sink. One wall was made of a painted tongue-and-groove partition, with a small door at one end. Mr Harris opened the door, revealing a flight of steep uncarpeted stairs going up into the darkness.

'Do you mind going up there by yourselves? I can't manage the stairs because of my knees.'

'Is this the only way up, sir?'

The old man nodded. He stood back and Thornhill climbed slowly into the darkness, feeling his way with his hands tread by tread, with Joan at his heels. A rectangle of light told him he had reached a door. He stopped suddenly, feeling for the handle, and the WPC's solid body cannoned into him.

'Sorry, sir,' she said, sounding flustered.

He found a Suffolk latch high on the right-hand side, lifted it and pushed. Sunlight flooded onto the stairs. Thornhill stepped into the room, with Joan at his heels.

He had always found this an unsettling moment – because when people were in their most private places, they left traces of their personalities like fossils in rocks. He was closer to the living, breathing Mattie Harris in her bedroom than when he had stood beside her body in the mortuary. He heard the clatter of a poker from the kitchen below, followed by a dry, retching sound which might have been a sob.

The room was long and thin, following the dimensions of the kitchen below. It was lit by a single dormer window, which looked out on the roof of an outhouse leaning against the back wall of the kitchen, a small, terraced back garden now reverting to brambles and nettles, and the steep slope of Eastbury Hill. Thornhill guessed that the kitchen and scullery were more recent than the rest of the house, which was why the room was served by a separate staircase. A deep alcove extended over the scullery. But the bedroom seemed smaller and narrower than the kitchen because of the sloping roof.

'Nice and private, isn't it?' Joan said. She stared at the dressing table beside the window — two banks of drawers separated by a three-quarter length mirror with a gleaming walnut veneer — with an expression that was frankly envious. 'That must have cost a few bob.'

'Can't have been easy getting it up those stairs, either.' Thornhill glanced in the alcove, where there was a small wardrobe, rather humbler than the dressing table and recently covered with cream paint. 'See what you can find in there. That powder compact. Documents. Anything that strikes you as unusual.'

He walked down the room to the brass bedstead at the far end. It was large enough for two, though the horsehair mattress sagged in the middle like a valley so they would have to be two people who enjoyed being together. It was made — a strawberry-pink coverlet of what looked like satin with an eiderdown the same colour on top. He wondered if she had brought men here. Probably not, because of the parents just below.

On the bedside cupboard was a lamp and an empty ashtray on top of a copy of *Titbits*. He opened the cupboard. There was a jumble of things inside. He put the contents one by one on the bed. A packet of contraceptives, a leather writing case, matches, a torch, a packet of ten Weights with one cigarette inside, a jar of hand cream, another jar of cold cream for the face, nail varnish, a handkerchief trimmed with lace, a hairbrush with dark red hairs tangled in the bristles, and three hairpins. Last of all was a framed studio photograph of Mattie Harris smiling up at the camera, revealing a mouth full of irregular teeth. Not exactly pretty but she'd had something. It was hard to equate the living black-and-white woman with the technicoloured corpse in the mortuary.

'Just clothes in the wardrobe, sir,' Joan said. 'Nothing unusual, though I'd say she wasn't a shrinking violet.'

'Try the dressing table.'

'She was a lucky girl.' Joan picked up a powder puff and sniffed. 'That's Fleur de Rose. She's got a great big jar of the stuff.'

'Expensive?'

'I'll say. I just wish someone would buy me some.'

He turned abruptly, cutting off the conversation before it could develop further, and unzipped the writing case. Inside were several letters – some signed Gary and some signed Violet – whose contents seemed entirely innocuous, a dog-eared ration book, and a photograph of a black man in USAF uniform. There was a birth certificate, too, showing that at the time of Mattie's birth the Harrises had been living in Mincing Lane.

'Sir, something you should see.'

He glanced at Joan. She was leaning behind the dressing table, looking at the window.

'I think the catch has been forced.'

He joined her. It was a simple casement window. When they had come in, it had been open. Joan pointed at the window frame. The metal of the catch had been bent out of shape. The wood round it was dented. There were complementary marks on the mullion separating the two halves of the window. The catch had lost some of its paint and the metal beneath gleamed.

'Someone's jemmied it open.' Joan's face glowed, as if someone had given her a present. 'It looks like they used something that was round in cross-section – see the curve there in the wood – like a screwdriver, perhaps. And judging by the marks on the catch, it's been done recently.'

'Yes,' said Thornhill. 'I had noticed.'

She shot him a startled glance, and stepped backwards. It was a fine line, Thornhill knew, between keeping his officers keen while preventing them from becoming overconfident. Using his elbow in case there were prints, he lifted the latch, pushed the window open and leant over the sill.

The roof of an outhouse stretched away beneath him – slate here, rather than stone tiles, supporting the theory that the extension was younger than the main cottage. The outhouse was probably some sort of shed or workshop. Because the ground rose so steeply behind, the level of the first terrace in the back garden was no more than a foot below the lowest point of the outhouse's roof. And the gap between terrace and outhouse could not have been more than eighteen inches.

One of the slates had come adrift and there were one or two lighter scratches on the mottled dark grey.

He looked back at Joan. 'Looks like a break-in, doesn't it? We'll have a look outside before we go, and we'd better send the Scene of Crime boys along. It's possible the bedside cupboard was turned over as well. Any other signs – things out of place, things missing?'

'She seems to have kept things pretty tidy,' Joan said. 'But one of the drawers in the dressing table's in a mess.'

At Thornhill's nod, she pulled the drawers open one by one. Two held underwear, and a third scarves and handkerchiefs. These seemed undisturbed. But the fourth was a jumble of papers, cosmetics, and jewellery.

'What are the papers?' Thornhill asked.

'There's an estimate from a plumber's firm for putting in a

bathroom. Pay envelopes from the café. And there's a Post Office Savings Book.'

She passed it to him and he opened it. Nearly £190 – rather a lot of money for a waitress.

Joan was watching him, her eyes bright with intelligence. 'According to the pay envelopes, she earned between three and four pounds a week, depending on overtime.'

'So she was rather richer than you'd expect.'

'But the burglar wasn't interested in that. Look, sir.' Her enthusiasm outweighed her wariness of Thornhill. She pointed into the drawer at a thick gold chain with a pendant in the shape of an enamelled heart, set in gold. 'That must be worth at least thirty quid. Whoever broke in obviously wasn't trying to steal valuables. So what *was* he looking for?'

Chapter Fourteen

No way out of it – he'd have to see her.

The day had grown warmer. Trapped in the river valley of the Lyd, the air hung hot, damp and still over the town, wrapping it in an early evening haze. Bill Pembridge parked the MG on Chepstow Road, a hundred yards beyond Broadwell Drive, and followed the familiar path across the fields until he reached the meadow at the back of the half-built crescent. June Evans ran her home like military operation. Tea was at six. Then there was the clearing away. Then, if the weather was fine, Violet was expected to take Rab for a walk.

His timing was good. She was walking slowly along the line of the hedge on the far side of the meadow. The dog was chasing a rabbit. She saw Bill coming towards her and stood there, waiting for him. He felt a surge of sexual desire. My God, he thought, I'd like to drown in you. He pushed the thought away. It was too dangerous now. Besides, since the bloody baby Violet had changed.

As he drew near, he forced a smile. 'Darling,' he said. 'I just had to see you.'

He took her in his arms and kissed her. At the last moment she turned her head away, so his lips landed on her cheek.

'Don't,' she said. 'Someone might see.'

Her breasts nuzzled against him. They were huge and firm – must be the baby, he supposed – and they drew him like a pair of cushioned magnets. He looked away from her.

'Have you heard about Mattie?' she said.

He noticed her eyes were red-rimmed. 'Yes. Tragic, isn't it? I just don't know how it could have happened.'

'But didn't you –?'

'Oh no. She was fine when I last saw her.'

'I just can't believe it. I – I – keep thinking I see her. Out of the corner of my eye.'

'I know.' He pulled her closer and felt his body responding to her softness. 'Must have fallen in the water on her way home, I suppose. Poor kid.'

'You should have—'

'Darling, we haven't time for this.'

'But Mattie,' she wailed. 'On top of everything, Mattie having to die.'

His arms tightened round her. 'We've got to talk.'

'I can't stay long. I've got to get back to Grace.'

'She's lovely, isn't she? It was so good to see her.' Bill nuzzled Violet's hair with his lips. 'How is she?'

'She's fine. But they're trying to make me have her adopted.' A tremor ran through her body. 'Our baby.'

'Really?'

Clasped together, they stood there for a moment, neither speaking. Bill stroked her cheek. He felt the warmth of a tear running down his hand. It was odd, he thought, that grief could be sexually exciting. He wondered whether she might agree if he suggested they went into the trees over there and—

'Couldn't we get married now?' Violet said in a voice that sounded sodden with cold. 'Then they couldn't do anything. And Grace could be with us.'

'Darling, we've been through this. I've got to get through college first. Start earning my own living. That's the sensible time to get married. We discussed it – remember?' He stroked the blonde fluff on her forearms. 'Then we can settle down and be happy together.' He tried the effect of a smile. 'Nothing's changed.'

'But it *has* changed. We've got Grace to think about now.'

She'd changed too, Bill thought, and he wasn't sure he liked it. She was getting almost bossy. He said, 'Look, I know it must seem awful, but perhaps your parents are right.'

'What do you mean?'

'We should think about what's best for Grace. Perhaps she'd be happier if she was adopted. She's so young, she wouldn't miss you. Then we could start again.'

Violet pulled away from him. 'No,' she said. 'No, no, no.'

'Well, think about it, anyway. It's the sort of thing that perhaps a man sees more clearly.'

But she wasn't listening. She was staring over his shoulder. 'Oh my God,' she whispered, her hand flying to her throat.

Bill turned. Ted Evans was no more than 50 yards away, running towards them, the distance rapidly closing. He was still wearing his cricket whites. His face was red and his mouth was open, but he wasn't saying anything.

Rab had seen Ted too. Yapping happily, the dog ran towards him, his little legs twinkling in the evening sunlight. Scarcely breaking stride, Ted Evans kicked him out of his way, his boot catching the dog just behind his front legs. Bill thought he heard the crack of a snapping rib.

He pushed past Violet and started running. Running for the road, running for his car, and hoping to God that he was fitter and faster than Ted Evans with the blood lust upon him.

Chapter Fifteen

Edna Pembridge raised her eyes from Sergeant Kirby's warrant card. 'I suppose it's about the unfortunate incident on Saturday,' she said, wrinkling her little nose. 'That sort of thing is always a risk with young people, but I can assure you that I soon put a stop to it. One boy was definitely smelling of alcohol so the committee has banned him. Of course, the whole purpose of these evenings is to allow young people to mix, have some healthy exercise, but to do so in a thoroughly wholesome way.'

Kirby glanced at Joan Ailsmore and then said, 'So some of the kids got carried away and there was a bit of hanky panky at the back?'

'Nothing we couldn't cope with, Sergeant. Just a little horse-play during the Cuban Rumba. And I can't imagine who complained.'

'We haven't come about that, in fact, Mrs Pembridge. Is there somewhere quieter we can have a word?'

Twenty or thirty young people were bouncing round the Ruispidge Hall. The five-piece band on the little stage was pounding out a samba. There was a drummer, a pianist, a guitarist, a trumpeter and a bass player. Kirby noticed that the trumpet-player's eyes kept straying to the two police officers and his wife beside the tea urn.

'We'll go outside,' Mrs Pembridge decided. 'This way.'

She led them through a door at the back of the hall which gave on to a little yard, a patch of rutted gravel and mud. The Pembridges' Vauxhall was the only car parked there. At the back was a stile leading to a footpath, and over to the right were the playing fields, gardens and buildings of the Lydmouth High School for Girls.

'So you have a dance twice a week?' Joan asked. Kirby had brought her along at Thornhill's suggestion; not that he'd been reluctant.

'Thursdays and Saturdays. My husband and I are both on the Ruispidge Hall Committee. We try to help young people especially, because nowadays they face so many temptations. My husband plays in a little dance band so he can help with the music.'

'He plays here twice a week?'

'No – we have a rota, and my husband's band plays for perhaps one evening in three. Though in fact he's doing two in a row this week. But in any case one of us tries to put in an appearance on most dance evenings. Just to keep an eye on things.'

Joan made her eyes widen. 'Must mean a lot of work.'

'We like to help. Superintendent Williamson – you'll know him, of course, he's a very good friend of ours – was telling me only the other day that he thought most young people who turn to crime did so because they were bored. I don't think you could say our dancers were bored. I remember hearing Lady Ruispidge saying—'

'We'd like to show you a photograph, Mrs Pembridge,' Kirby interrupted. 'Don't want to take up too much of your time.'

He nodded to Joan, who brought out a photograph of Mattie Harris from a manila envelope. It was the studio shot Thornhill had found among her possessions at Lower Slade.

Mrs Pembridge's thin lips made a moue. 'That's the girl who had the accident.'

Kirby nodded. 'When did you last see her?'

'Thursday evening.'

'One of your regulars?'

'I suppose she was. Usually comes — came — once a week. She tended to be rather unsuitably dressed. Once or twice I had to have a word with her.'

'How do you mean?' Joan asked.

Mrs Pembridge shot her a suspicious look. 'Sometimes she revealed a little more than necessary. Some of our lads are very impressionable.'

'Was she a good dancer?'

'Yes, actually she was.' Mrs Pembridge smiled at Joan. 'Natural sense of rhythm, and very graceful, too. Of course one had to watch her with waltzes.'

Sounds like my kind of girl, Kirby thought, even though she had been the wrong shape. He turned towards Mrs Pembridge. 'Was she involved in the — the horseplay on Saturday?'

'No. She wasn't here. But I—'

'But she was here on Thursday. What time did she leave?'

'I'm sure I couldn't say.' Mrs Pembridge wrinkled her nose again. 'It must have been before the end, because usually the girls help me with the washing-up and so on, and I noticed she wasn't there then.'

'When did the dance finish?'

'Nine o'clock. We could ask Gerald — my husband. He was playing that evening. Mattie certainly came back in after the interval. He might remember when she left. Leaving early was unusual, come to think of it. She generally stayed until the end.'

'Was there anything else that was unusual?' Joan asked.

'She forgot to take her beret. It's still on the pegs. One of the girls mentioned it to me this evening.'

'What sort of mood was she in?'

'She seemed very lively. Even more so than usual. I remember her shrieking with laughter at something someone said. One could hear her over the music.' Mrs Pembridge looked at the hall, where the music was building to a climax. 'I really must go in. They'll need their teas in a moment. Would you excuse me?'

'What about a handbag?' Kirby asked.

Mrs Pembridge gave a high, nervous laugh. 'Mattie had her usual bag with her – one could hardly miss it. A big blue one, imitation patent leather. Quite remarkably flashy.' She edged a few paces nearer the door to the hall. 'She was wearing rather high heels, too. She always did, trying to make herself look taller, I suppose. She looked quite a sight, I can tell you, tottering along on them when she was in a hurry. I saw her practically running on them last Saturday actually—'

'Yes, but on—' Joan began.

Kirby nudged her into silence with his elbow. 'Saturday? But I thought you said she wasn't here on Saturday?'

'She wasn't. Other fish to fry, no doubt. Gerald wasn't playing that evening but I'd popped into the hall to make sure everything was all right. Just as well, as it turned out. But as I was going in I saw her walking by on the other side of the road. She didn't see me.'

'Which way was she walking, then?'

'That way.' Mrs Pembridge waved northwards. 'Towards Narth Road. Dressed up to the nines, leaving very little to the imagination, and as I said, those heels! She was rattling along at a fine pace for all that.'

But where had she been going to? As far as Kirby could see, she'd been walking away from everything in Lydmouth that might have interested her – from the bus station, from the pubs, from the Saturday dance at the Ruispidge Hall, from the Gardenia Café, from her friend Violet Evans.

The music stopped. Edna Pembridge slipped into the hall. Kirby jerked his head at Joan and followed. Mrs Pembridge was already behind the tea urn, turning a mob of thirsty and hungry young dancers into an orderly queue.

'Sandwiches this side, please, and tea the other. And don't try to push in, Kenneth Owen, your turn *will* come.'

The man who had been playing the trumpet was murmuring something in her ear. She looked at Kirby and beckoned him over.

'This is my husband, Sergeant—?'

'Kirby, ma'am.'

'He's just reminded me of something. You tell them, dear. I'm busy.'

Gerald Pembridge smiled at them. 'Shall we go outside? I could do with a cigarette.'

They went out of the main door and stood on the forecourt of Chepstow Road. Several of the lads were already out there, smoking, but they kept at a respectful distance. Pembridge lit a cigarette. He was a sleek, slim man, probably about fifty, wearing a dinner jacket. He would have looked younger if it hadn't been for the lines on his face and the suspicious darkness of his hair. He resembled a professional dancer, the sort that charms rich widows at afternoon tea dances. Kirby introduced himself and Joan and produced the photograph.

'Yes, that's Mattie Harris, all right. Poor little thing.'

'Can you remember when she left, sir?'

'About nine, I suppose. When the dance finished.'

'But she didn't help with the washing-up.'

'Probably slipped out, trying to avoid it. Not the sort of girl who liked wielding a tea towel.'

Kirby glanced over his shoulder. No one was in earshot. 'So what sort of girl was she, sir? Did you know her well?'

'She came quite often.' Pembridge straightened his bow tie. 'Rather older than most of the kids we get. Loved dancing. But she could be a rather – how can I put it? – a rather unsettling influence.' He tapped the side of his nose and lowered his voice. 'If you know what I mean.'

'Were any of the boys especially close to her?' Kirby murmured.

'No, not really. Half of them would have liked to have been, but that's a different story. She never actually did anything – ah – blatant. Not that we noticed anyway. Not until that last evening, that is. Which is what my wife wanted me to tell you.'

'This was in the hall, I take it?'

'No, it wasn't. As a matter of fact it was out here. Mattie used to come out for a cigarette in the break. Can't say one likes a woman who smokes in public, but that's neither here nor there. Anyway, my wife came out to call them in at the end of the interval. Mattie was talking to a young chap. Not one of ours. Must have been hanging around outside. And they weren't just talking. Not to mince words, she reached up and kissed him. I wasn't the only one to see it. Kenny Owen saw it too.'

'*Who* did she kiss?' Kirby said, wondering why some people never seemed to get to the point.

'The boy they say found her body. The one who's not quite right in the head. Not one of ours, as I said, but one sees him around. Jimmy something. I know – Jimmy Leigh.'

Chapter Sixteen

———◆◆◆———

At nearly nine o'clock, it was still light, still hot. Must be the heat making him restless, Bernie Broadbent decided, the heat and the worry.

He had spent the early part of evening with several other committee members of Lydmouth Cricket Club as well as most of the team, drowning the memory of their defeat at the hands of Ashbridge in the lounge bar and the garden of the Ferryman's Inn. Since most of the Ashbridge team were also there, celebrating their victory, this had not been an easy aim to achieve.

Ted Evans had joined them, saying even less than usual, but he hadn't stayed more than a few minutes. He'd been drinking spirits, several doubles in quick succession, as if he had other memories that needed drowning. A man to watch, Bernie Broadbent thought, a man to be wary of.

He drove slowly through the town in the Riley. Windows were down, and the radio filled the car with dance music that drifted into the streets to mark his passing. He had had rather more beer than was wise but there wasn't a policeman in Lydmouth who was likely to stop him. Not that he wasn't perfectly capable of driving. Life was all a matter of taking calculated risks, Bernie Broadbent thought, and he was expert at that.

He turned into Victoria Road and drew up outside number

sixty-eight, the house which now, to all intents and purposes, was his. Subject to survey and contract, of course, but he didn't anticipate any problems there. The Thornhills' little Austin was immediately in front of him. Now was as good a time as any.

Bernie got out of the car, pushed open the gate and walked slowly up to the porch. He rang the doorbell long and hard. While he waited he turned back to look at the Riley. The door opened, and he turned slowly to face Richard Thornhill.

'Evening, Richard. Hope I'm not disturbing you, but I'd like a word. Won't take long if you've got a moment now.'

Thornhill stood back, holding open the door. Bernie went into the house and lumbered straight down the hall towards the kitchen. His niece Edith usually tried to put him in the sitting room at the front but he preferred the kitchen.

'I was about to have a glass of beer,' Thornhill said. 'Would you like some?'

'Don't mind if I do.'

Bernie sat down in the Windsor chair, which had been pulled towards the open window, and felt for his pipe. Thornhill pushed a postcard across the table towards him. Picture upwards, showing a view of a beach.

'This came from Edith this morning. They seem to be having a good time.'

Thornhill went to fetch the beer. Bernie picked up the post-card, turned it over and read the message: *Weather lovely but sea a bit cool. D and E don't mind. Much discussion about names for kittens. The digs are very nice, though a bit crowded. We all wish you were here. Much love, Edith.* Thornhill came back into the room with a bottle and two glasses.

'When are they coming back?' Bernie asked, watching the beer gliding into the glass.

'Monday evening.'

'So you're roughing it by yourself in the meantime?'

'I'm meant to be doing a spot of decorating.'

Bernie began to fill his pipe. 'I imagine the Harris girl

turning up like that has thrown a spanner in the works.'

Thornhill smiled. 'You could say that.'

'Ray Williamson said he thought it should be quite straight-forward. That's some consolation.'

'Early days yet.'

Bernie leant forward to take the glass Thornhill was holding out to him. 'No reason for concern, is there?'

'Just a few questions that need answering.'

Damn the man, Bernie thought — any other officer in Richard Thornhill's position would have talked quite freely about the case. The two of them were practically family, and of course Bernie was on the Standing Joint Committee, so in a sense he was one of Richard's bosses. What made the man tick? Bernie knew how most people worked, what you had to do to bring them round to your point of view. But there were a few like his cousin's husband whose inner machinery was tucked away out of sight.

He sipped his beer and stared out at the little back garden with its row of fruit trees espaliered against one wall. 'You've got access at the back, haven't you?'

'Yes.' Thornhill looked sharply at him. 'As a matter of fact we have.'

'You ought to get a garage down there. You could fit one in beyond the pear trees.'

'Yes, it's an idea.' Thornhill hesitated. 'I suppose if we ever buy the house, we'll consider it seriously.'

Bernie knew this had been a sore point between Edith and Richard. She had inherited a little money from her mother, which she had decided to put towards David's education. Richard would have preferred it used as a deposit on the house. It was typical of the man that neither he nor Edith had ever hinted that a loan from Bernie would solve the problem.

'Something I should tell you,' Bernie said, and then drew out the suspense by taking his time over lighting the pipe. 'I've a feeling you'll be getting that garage after all.'

'That's a decision for Mr Shipston.'

'I've put in an offer for the house, Richard. Shipston accepted it this afternoon.'

There was a moment's silence. That's floored him, Bernie thought with some satisfaction.

'What about our lease?'

'I'm buying the house with a sitting tenant. That's not a problem. Shipston's side of your contract with him will simply be transferred to me.'

'People might feel there's something rather odd about the situation.'

Bernie pantomimed surprise. 'Why?'

'Because Edith's your cousin, you're on the Standing Joint Committee, and I'm a police officer.'

Bernie shook his head. 'Nothing underhand about it, lad. I'm not making a secret of it. Naturally, I'll mention it to James Hendry, just make sure it's all above board. But he's not going to object. And if your chief constable's happy with it, then don't you think you should be too?'

Richard swallowed a mouthful of beer. 'Why?'

'Why did I want to buy it? It's more a question of why wouldn't I want to buy it. Because a house like this is an investment — nice, solid Victorian semi, a stone's throw from the park. And it will be a nice little earner while it appreciates in value.'

To his surprise, Richard threw his head back and laughed.

'What's so funny?'

'So you're planning to increase the value of your desirable freehold property by adding a garage?'

'Why not?' Bernie smiled, uncertain whether Richard was genuinely amused or not. 'We'd better have a toast, eh? To our new relationship.'

The two men chinked their glasses together and drained the rest of their beer.

'Another?' Richard said.

'No. You'll need to get on with your decorating, I daresay.'

He took Richard outside to admire the Riley and drove home. He had the windows open but he didn't bother with the radio. The air was stuffy and he had a headache. What must it be like to have a wife and children? A home you could decorate for them? The beer was making him maudlin.

On Chepstow Road, he noticed a crowd of young people milling around the Ruispidge Hall. Probably most of them were talking about Mattie Harris. He guessed that the Saturday dance had just finished. It looked as if that dried-up stick Edna Pembridge was berating an unfortunate lad.

The sight of those young people made his heart beat a little faster. So fresh, so innocent. He turned left into Narth Road. The grounds of the Lydmouth High School for Girls swept past him on the left-hand side. A moment later he turned right through the open gates of Netherfield, set between tall privet hedges.

The drive wound through the shrubbery between the house and the road, designed to bring visitors unexpectedly upon the house in all its white splendour. He left the car on the tarmac sweep outside the front door. Halfway between the Riley and the house, he looked first at one and then at the other. Yes, it was a smart car. Desirable, even. So in its way was the house, stark and bright like an ocean liner, faintly luminous in the gathering twilight. An architect had built it for himself during the 1930s, and there had been articles about it in several magazines. For once the thrill of ownership failed to reassure him.

Suddenly he changed his mind. Instead of going into the house, he walked round the side, past the garage block and the little vegetable garden tucked behind it, and down the long, sloping lawn. The land swept down to the Minnow. He had just under an acre. Lines of trees marked the tall fences on either side. Most of it was laid to lawn, though there was a hard tennis court on one side, which Bernie had never used. During the 1930s, there had been garden parties here.

He followed the path down to the river, not because he particularly wanted to go, but because following the lie of the land was slightly easier than standing still. He sat down on a wrought-iron bench, pulled out his pipe and tried to relax.

Two minutes later, restlessness drove him back to the house. His footfalls echoed on the parquet floors. The mirror in the hall showed him his pale, obstinate face. He turned on the radiogram in the drawing room and tried to fill the house with dance music. He walked from room to room, while the syncopated rhythms ebbed and flowed around him. There was so much empty space.

While he walked, his mind lurched drunkenly to and fro like a daddy long legs. Usually his mind was as disciplined as his body. Not always, though. Were there more moments of anarchy than there used to be?

Those young people — never learned how to dance — she was a beautiful dancer — poor kid — well if Ray can't, no one can. But Gerald? You've got to hand it to Richard — wonder what he and Edith are like when they — nice children, never know what to say to them. Well, anyone can see it's a beautiful car — yes, that house needs a garage, maybe leave room in it for a work bench — God, I wish I was young — more beer? —This could be tricky, look, very tricky, but there's a funny side to it — My God, they're so beautiful, and they don't realise it —

He reached the kitchen, which always reminded him of an operating theatre. Not a room to sit in, like the Thornhills', but a room designed for work. He went through to the pantry and took a bottle of beer from the crate on the floor. Back in the kitchen, he opened drawer after drawer, searching for a bottle opener. He knew there was one in the cocktail cabinet in the drawing room, and probably another in the dining room sideboard. But there must be one in the kitchen, too.

His inability to find a bottle opener in his own kitchen suddenly assumed monstrous proportions. It was the final confession of failure, of his inability to cope. He slammed the bottle down on the table, jarring his wrist. He stormed out of the kitchen, through the hall and out of the front door.

There was the Riley, here were the keys. He knew that only

one thing would calm him now. He got into the car. Just before he started the engine, the telephone began to ring in the house.

Ray Williamson, he guessed. Or Gerald Pembridge. *Let them wait.*

The engine fired. He drove down the drive, turned into Narth Road and had soon left the town behind him.

The phone rang for thirty-two rings and then stopped.

Chapter Seventeen

———◆◇◆———

The roll of thunder boomed like distant artillery fire further down the estuary. Jill twitched, and her hand knocked *The Vicar of Bullhampton* from the arm of her chair.

She picked up the book and tried to concentrate. It was still very warm, though in the last half hour it had grown much darker. She was sitting by the open window of the bedroom with a hurricane lamp on the sill beside her. Four hours ago she had put on the blue silk dress. One hour ago she'd taken it off and hung it up in the wardrobe. She had scrubbed off her make-up and put on her old dressing gown.

She gave up the struggle to get to grips with the inhabitants of Bullhampton. She lit a cigarette and stared down at the twinkling yellow lights of the village, at the darkness of the estuary and the outline of the hills on the other side. There was no doubt that Charlotte suspected something. She'd as good as warned Jill off. Besides, Jill knew — none better — that having affairs with married men was not a recipe for happiness. Then there was the other worry, the one that underlay them all, the deepest, darkest irony of all.

The first time they'd done it, in Church Cottage?

Shabby subterfuges, she thought, routine deceptions — is this really what I want? She knew, too, that Richard would always put his job first. Sometimes she thought it was one of the things she loved about him, the fact that he wasn't morally flexible in the way most other men were. Though if committing adultery wasn't a sign of moral flexibility, then what was? Perhaps that part of his life was in another compartment. Men were good at doing that – putting up barriers, dividing up their lives with watertight bulkheads.

She heard a car in the lane. Dear God, it was slowing. The car stopped. The shed doors screeched, which meant the car must be Richard's. They had arranged that she would leave her car outside so he could tuck his out of sight. She flicked the end of her cigarette through the twilight to the long grass below the terrace. What a fool she'd been to remove her make-up as well as the dress. She lifted the hurricane lamp on to the chest of drawers and quickly brushed her hair.

Richard's footsteps on the path below. She knew they were his – fast and light – just as she knew the way his skin smelled in the crook between neck and shoulder. She heard him softly call her name.

She went back to the window and looked down at him. He was wearing an open-necked shirt and carrying a jacket slung over his shoulder.

'May I come in?'

'Of course. Wait.'

She went downstairs and slid back the bolts of the door. He slipped inside and tossed the jacket on to a chair.

'You must have thought I wasn't coming. I tried to phone Church Cottage but you weren't there.' He stretched out his hand and gently touched her cheek. 'I am sorry.'

'It's all right. I understand.'

'I would have been earlier. Bernie dropped in.' His Adam's apple rose and fell. 'He's buying our house.'

'He's *what*?'

'Shipston wanted to sell. He gave us first refusal.' Richard hesitated, leaving an absence, a sense of things unsaid. 'We couldn't afford it.'

'What does he want to do with it?'

'Nothing. We can stay there, as before. Except he's going to put in a garage and do God knows what else.'

'He's not buying a house,' Jill said. 'He's buying a family.'

'Yes. I don't like it. But there's not a lot I can do. He's going to talk to Hendry.'

She drew the dressing gown more tightly around her. 'Would you like something? A sandwich? A drink?'

'Tea. I'll make it.'

She stood in the kitchen doorway, watching him struggle to get the Primus stove alight.

'I'm afraid I can't stay long. I really should look in at head-quarters, have a word with Brian Kirby.'

'I think Charlotte suspects something.'

Richard dropped the spoon on the table. She watched it spin and fall to the quarry-tiled floor. Neither of them made a move to pick it up.

'How?' he said.

Jill shrugged. 'She can put two and two together and make five as well as anyone. And she was warning me this afternoon, terribly, terribly tactfully, that Lydmouth wasn't the sort of place where you could hope to keep something like this quiet.'

Something like this, she thought, something like what? A friendship? A quick fling? An affair?

'We'll have to be careful.'

Jill said slowly, 'Are you sure you want this to go on? With all it entails?'

He came round the kitchen table and took both her hands in his. 'Of course I do. You know I love you.'

She bowed her head against his chest, and they were silent for a moment. He had told her that he loved her once before but that had been when they were making love, so it hardly counted. Then, she had not replied in case the words belonged only to the moment. Now, in the flickering light of a hurricane lamp in a damp little kitchen, the words meant something different.

'I wish this hadn't happened now.'

'Us?' she said shocked, pulling away from him.

'No, no. Mattie Harris dying. God knows we've little enough time as it is. And the trouble is, I'm afraid her death wasn't straightforward.'

'What do you mean?'

Jill wished she could take back the question as soon as the words left her lips. She had promised herself that she wouldn't show any curiosity about his work. It would put undue pressure on him, take too much for granted. She was a journalist, after all.

But he was replying, without any hesitation. 'There are signs that either she got dressed in rather a hurry or someone else dressed her. Perhaps after she'd died.'

'But she was drowned, wasn't she?'

'So it seems. But of course we can't even be sure until we have the results of the post-mortem.'

Somehow his arms had come around her again and her head was back on his chest. She felt the beating of his heart through the shirt. She touched the spot with her finger.

'There's another thing,' Richard went on. 'She told Mrs Browning at the Gardenia that she needed to have the day off so she could take her mother to hospital. Then I went to see her parents. She'd told them that she was going to a dance on Thursday night, and that she might not be back at all – that she'd stay with a friend. They thought she was working at the café as usual yesterday. She said that she might have to work late, in which case she'd stay with the friend again on Friday night. So she must have had something planned for Friday. The question is, what?'

'And whatever it was can't have happened – that's assuming she died on Thursday night.'

'We can't even be sure about that yet.'

'Was the friend Violet Evans?'

He looked down at her face. 'How did you know?'

'Charlotte mentioned that Mattie and Violet were friends. So I went to see her.'

'Why?'

'I don't know. I just wondered where she lived, and I was at a loose end. Charlotte had upset me a little, I think... I wasn't going to talk to Violet, but she was in the garden, with her baby, and we just started chatting. In fact, I rather wish I hadn't gone. She hadn't heard about Mattie. She was awfully upset.'

'Did she mention if she was going dancing on Thursday?'

Jill shook her head. 'I wouldn't think she had much time for that sort of thing. I got the impression that life's rather difficult for her at present. She's living at home with her parents, and she's got the baby to look after. I don't think there's a father on the scene. But she was expecting to see Mattie on Friday evening.'

'Are you sure?'

'That's what she said.'

'Did Violet say why?'

'No particular reason.' Jill felt a surge of irritation. 'They didn't need a *reason*. They were friends. Violet said she was going to ask Mattie to be the baby's godmother.'

The kettle had come to the boil. She watched him making the tea, his movements precise and carefully thought out as though he were a scientist conducting an experiment. He took the tray into the living room, where they sat primly side by side on the little sofa.

'What about clothes?' Jill said suddenly. 'If she was staying somewhere overnight, wouldn't she want to change?'

'She kept some at the Gardenia. She left her uniform there on Thursday evening and changed into a skirt and blouse. She was carrying a large handbag as well, which we haven't traced. Williamson's showing an interest in the case too.'

'But isn't he retiring in a week or two? And I thought he was on sick leave.'

'He is. There's no reason for him to want to stick his oar in. But that's what he's doing. I had to phone him earlier this evening. He wants me to phone him at least once a day.'

It was much easier talking about a dead girl than it was talking about whatever was happening between them, and what would happen. Richard bent forward to pour the tea. His nearness was somehow threatening. Jill wanted to put her hand under his shirt and stroke his chest. Part of her didn't want to feel that way, because it made her realise that her body was no longer solely under her control. He passed her a cup and saucer. This was only the second time that he had brought her a cup of tea, but it was precisely the colour and strength that she liked. He was a man who attended to detail. She wasn't sure if she liked this characteristic or not.

'Joan Ailsmore and I took a look at Mattie's bedroom in her parents' cottage.'

'Oh – you took Joan Ailsmore, did you?'

'Useful to have a woman, sometimes. She's very keen.'

And quite attractive, Jill thought, if a little broad in the beam.

'I might suggest she applies for a transfer to CID. We've never had a woman officer, but there's no reason why we shouldn't. Anyway, we found a couple of odd things. Mattie seemed surprisingly well off for someone who was a waitress. She'd spent a bit of money on furniture. No sign of a hire purchase agreement, either. She spent money on clothes. She was planning to put a bathroom in. She'd even got an estimate from the plumber. There was nearly a couple of hundred pounds in her Post Office Savings Book.'

'Wasn't she married or something? Perhaps that's where the money came from.'

'I think it was probably "or something". No sign of a marriage certificate. He was an American airman called Gary, a Negro, and apparently he's in Korea at present. We'll check, as far as we can, but I don't think it seems likely.'

They sipped tea in silence for a moment while Jill thought about WPC Ailsmore.

Then Richard cleared his throat and said, 'Do you mind me talking like this? It's something I've never done before, not about work. Perhaps you'd rather –'

'Of course I don't mind.' She put her hand on his and squeezed it gently. 'And you haven't said anything about keeping it to myself, which can't have been easy.'

They smiled at each other. The tension between them evaporated. Richard put down his cup and sat back. It was natural for Jill to nestle against him, natural to feel the weight of his arm on her shoulders.

'There's one more thing,' he went on. 'And then I'll stop talking about it, I promise. Mattie's bedroom was separate from the rest of the house. The stairs are too awkward for the parents. But someone had broken in recently. They'd climbed up and forced a window. No sign of anything missing – she had a few odds and ends of jewellery, and they were still there.'

Jill's hand crept inside his shirt and stroked the hair on his chest. 'When do you have to go back?'

'I should have gone.' His hand came round and stroked her leg, slipping into the gap between the edges of the dressing gown. 'I shouldn't be here in the first place. Say half an hour?'

Jill said breathlessly, 'Do you know what Alec Sutton is always saying?' Sutton was the vicar, and Jill's landlord. 'Part of his stock in trade – the sort of thing he regales the faithful with on Sundays. *God said, take what you want, and pay for it.*'

She shivered. Mattie Harris was dead. She couldn't pay for anything any more. Richard stroked her legs, his hand slipping between her knees and sliding gently between her thighs.

'How could I pay for you? You're beyond price,' he said, which was a very satisfactory thing to say. Then he kissed her.

Chapter Eighteen

At nine forty-five, Sergeant Brian Kirby tried Thornhill's home number once again. Once again, there was no answer. He dropped the phone into its cradle. Not like the guv'nor – Thornhill had said he'd try and call in for a word earlier in the evening; he should have been in touch by now.

Cigarette drooping from the corner of his mouth, Kirby looked at Joan Ailsmore. She was sitting on the edge of the neighbouring desk, swinging what looked to Kirby like a rather nice pair of legs. They were the only people in the long CID Office. The typewriters were silent; the ashtrays and waste-paper baskets were overflowing, waiting for the morning visit of the cleaners. He raised his eyebrows at her.

'What are you going to do, Sarge?' she said.

Kirby had already considered the alternatives. In Thornhill's absence, he could in theory refer the matter to Williamson, even though Williamson was technically on leave. Or he could use his initiative.

'Come on,' he said, pushing back his chair and stubbing out the cigarette. 'Let's go visiting.'

Behind the main building of police headquarters was a large yard littered with temporary offices, sheds and vehicles. St John's clock was striking the quarters. Kirby slipped into the driving seat of a two-tone blue Hillman Minx, which CID had recently acquired for its exclusive use on a trial basis following months of negotiation with the Assistant Chief Constable, the Chief Constable and the Standing Joint Committee. Joan climbed into the passenger seat, not lingering outside the door waiting for him to open it like most of his girlfriends tended to do. She had grown used to being a police officer first and a lady second. She had spent two years pounding the streets of Birmingham before transferring to Lydmouth, which was another point in her favour. Lydmouth was all very well but there were far too many country bumpkins for comfort.

The clock began to strike ten as Kirby started the engine. He said nothing until they were driving down the High Street towards Templefields.

'Let me do most of the talking,' he said. 'Chip in if there's a long pause and you see me glancing at you. Don't come down too hard on them, though.'

'So you don't think it's him, then?'

For an instant he looked towards her, his face splitting into a grin. 'No – because I'll be the one who's being hard on them.'

'So what *do* you think?'

'It's him. Course it bloody is.'

'But he found her.'

'Someone had to.' Kirby slowed, signalling right. 'Or, just as likely, he set it up.'

'Jimmy? But I thought that at best he was about nine pence in the shilling.'

'He's cunning enough in his way. That type often is.' Down the hill he saw the lights of the station, New Bridge beyond. He turned left. 'I'm not saying he planned anything. If it was him, he probably didn't plan to kill her, any more than he planned to find her. That sort of mind always thinks in the short term. But once he'd jumped off the bridge and was in the water, it's just the sort of crackpot logic you'd expect. He found the body, so no one would think he'd done it.'

By now they were running down Mincing Lane. The sound of a piano drifted through the open window of the King's Head. Near the far end, just before the entrance to the slaughterhouse, he took another left turn. A moment later they were in River Gardens. There were lights on in most of the neat, little semi-detached houses, including Minnie Calder's.

Silent now, they left the car and walked up her path. Joan rang the bell. They waited a moment, noticing the twitch of a curtain in the front window. Miss Calder herself opened the door.

'What sort of a time is this?' She was wearing a dressing gown, and her hair was armoured with curlers covered with a scarf. 'I thought we'd seen the last of you today.'

As she was speaking, Kirby heard running feet on the landing and the door slamming above their heads.

'Who's that?'

'Jimmy, of course.' She folded her arms across her chest and stared up at him. 'Going to tidy his room before he gets ready for bed.'

'We've just got a few more questions, Miss Calder.' Kirby edged towards her, and she stepped back a pace. 'We'd like to ask Jimmy one or two things.'

She jerked her head at the lounge door. 'All right. We'll go in there. You can talk to me first.'

The little room smelt of peppermint and plastic. The air was stale and still. Miss Calder closed the door. She didn't ask them to sit down.

'Well?'

'Could you tell us where you were on Thursday night?'

'Me? Why?'

Kirby let the silence lengthen.

'It's housey-housey night,' she went on. 'Upstairs at the King's Head.'

'When did you get back?'

Her eyes slid away from his face to the clock over the electric fire. 'Tennish? I don't know. Quarter past? Mrs Halleran would know.'

Kirby was sure she would. The trouble was, the King's Head had a well-deserved reputation for unorthodox opening hours, and it was more than likely that Mrs Halleran had granted herself an extension on the night in question. Especially when she had people gambling and drinking upstairs and the old black-out blinds pulled down.

'Was Jimmy here at home?'

'How do I know?'

'You didn't check on him, then?'

She shook her head. 'He's not a baby. Anyway, I thought he'd be asleep.'

'He's not asleep now, is he? And it's the same time.'

'He's had an upsetting day, Sergeant. So it's not surprising he's finding it hard to settle, is it?'

They were still standing in a huddle between the sofa and the door. Kirby asked if they could sit, and Miss Calder grudgingly agreed. He met Joan's eyes, and waited.

'It can't always be easy looking after Jimmy,' she said. 'Must be a big responsibility.'

Miss Calder sniffed, but in a way that signified a grudging assent. 'When all's said and done, a boy needs someone to look after him, and Jimmy's always going to be a boy. So when my sister died I didn't really have any choice. They were very good at the hospital, I'll say that for them.'

'You were a nurse?'

There was another assenting sniff. 'Lived for my work, that's what my sister used to say. And she wasn't so far wrong. Still – that's all water under the bridge.'

'Jimmy's always been a little slower than other boys?'

'Yes. My sister used to say it was the polio that did it, but anyone with a little medical knowledge could have told her that was nonsense.'

'He must have made a very good recovery.'

This time Joan was rewarded with an actual smile. 'To look at him now, you wouldn't think they thought he'd never pull through, would you? Then they were sure he'd be crippled for life. But now he's as good as new.'

The smile mutated into something alarmingly like a simper, as out of place on that gaunt face as a pink ribbon on a man-eating tiger. 'Mind you, Doctor Fairclough said it was all down to the nursing, and I did a lot of that myself. He was in the old Cottage Hospital, you see, which was where I was working during the war.'

Kirby leant forward. 'He's a big lad, Miss Calder, a grown man, even if he's a bit slow. What's he like about girls?'

She looked at him as if he'd mouthed an obscenity. 'Our Jimmy's not interested in that sort of thing.'

'How do you know?'

'You only have to look at him.' Her hands plucked the wool of her dressing gown. 'He's still playing with toys.'

Kirby smiled. 'I'm very glad you reminded me of that, Miss Calder. It was an engine, wasn't it? A little clockwork engine.'

She glared at him. 'You can't be bothering about a thing like that now.'

'Stealing's stealing whenever it happens,' Kirby said virtuously. 'I hope he's returned it by now?'

'Not yet. There hasn't been time.'

'So you've got it, have you? I thought Jimmy had hidden it.'

'No, he hasn't brought it back yet. He can be very obstinate sometimes. But there's nothing for you to worry about. I'll pay for it, whatever happens, don't you worry about that. I'll see Mr Prout at Chapel tomorrow and I'll have a word with him.'

'Looks bad – the fact he's not returned it.'

'But if I pay for it –'

'Even so, Miss Calder.' Kirby shook his head slowly, looking shocked. 'We may still have to press charges.'

Silenced for a moment, she stared blankly at him. He looked at her ringless hands twisting on her lap, noticing the trimmed nails, the rough skin and the thickening of the finger joints. Joan kept quiet.

'It all depends,' Kirby said at last, as if making a concession out of the generosity of his heart. 'If Jimmy helped us in other ways, it would make it easier to put in a good word for him.'

'Helped you? How?'

'We need to talk to him, Miss Calder.'

'Can't it wait till the morning?'

'No.'

The hands fell apart, palms upwards, submitting. She stood up, looking from Kirby to Joan. 'All right. I'll fetch him. But about that engine, can you —?'

'I can't make any promises.' Kirby stood up too. 'But you won't regret this. I think it would be better if we talk to him alone. We'll go upstairs, shall we? I'd like to see his room.'

'I want to be there as well, all right? He might say something he didn't mean or let you—'

'Let us what?'

'You know. Twist things.'

Kirby adopted an expression blending outrage, sorrow and incredulity. 'You've been watching too many American films, Miss Calder. We're not like that.' He glanced at Joan, and saw a reciprocal glimmer of understanding in her eyes.

'The sergeant's right,' she said, smiling. 'The point is, if we talk to Jimmy while you're in the room, he may feel a bit awkward. Might be a distraction.'

'If you'd prefer it, we'll take him down to the station,' Kirby said. 'To an interview room, which would be far more inconvenient for us. And I daresay it won't do him much good, either. But if that's what you want, Miss Calder, that's what you want. Will you call him down?'

'Wouldn't it be more comfortable for him at home?' Joan asked, the voice of sweet reason as opposed to Kirby's voice of unbending authority.

Minnie Calder said, 'All right — have it your own way. But I don't want you frightening him. He's only a boy, when all's said and done.'

She took them upstairs to a little landing with three closed doors. She opened one of the doors a few inches without knocking.

'There's a policeman to see you, Jimmy, and a lady policeman.'

The boy's white face appeared in the crack between door and jamb. 'Why?'

'They want to ask you some questions. Just tell the truth. There's nothing to worry about.'

Kirby smiled at Miss Calder. 'So we'll see you downstairs, shall we? Shouldn't be more than a few minutes.'

She left them at last, her footsteps slow and reluctant on the stairs. Jimmy retreated into his room and sat down on the narrow bed. Kirby followed Joan inside and shut the door behind them. It was a boy's room. Miniature Grenadier Guards marched across the bedside table, playing soundless instruments. Pictures of cricketers had been laboriously snipped from newspapers and fixed with drawing pins to the door of a free-standing cupboard. The little bookshelf was laden with annuals and comics. Joan stepped on a toy lorry, and muttered an apology.

Jimmy looked up at once. 'Is it bent?'

Kirby picked up the lorry and squinted at it. 'Looks fine to me.'

Still holding the toy, he crossed to the window and pulled aside one of the striped curtains. The room faced the back of the house and at this time of evening there wasn't much to be seen. Light from the kitchen window spilled into the little back garden. A wheelbarrow stood with its handles in the air like the hands of a highway man's victim, propped against the back fence near the gate to the footpath. The Minnow was invisible beyond the fence. He turned and looked at the man-boy on the bed. If something inside his mind hadn't stopped growing, he would have been handsome, tall and slim. He noticed that Jimmy was darting sly little glances at Joan.

'Why didn't you tell us that you knew Mattie?' Kirby said sharply.

Jimmy's head jerked towards him. 'Me? Who told you that? It's a lie.'

'No, it isn't, Jimmy,' Kirby said. 'In fact, you knew her pretty well. No girl would kiss a boy unless she knew him pretty well, would she?'

He watched the white face redden.

'It's a lie. Someone's making up stories.'

'You're the one making up stories, if you say you didn't know her. Come off it, Jimmy, this isn't getting us anywhere. Someone saw her kissing you in broad daylight. Not the sort of person who tells lies, either.'

Jimmy hung his head. 'I knew her a bit,' he mumbled.

'How much is a bit?'

Jimmy shrugged. Kirby stretched out his arm and put his fingers beneath Jimmy's chin. He forced Jimmy's head up, until the two of them were face-to-face. 'You've got to do better than this, Jimmy. Because otherwise I'm taking you down to the station, and I'm locking you in a cell. You're not going to like it in our cells.'

He increased the pressure, squeezing Jimmy's chin between his fingers. The man-boy yelped.

'And you know when she was seen kissing you?' Kirby went on, as relentless as fate. 'Thursday evening. And you know something else? No one saw her alive after that.'

Jimmy's trembling became more violent. 'I didn't kill her,' he said, 'I didn't kill her, I swear it on the Bible. She was my *friend*.'

Kirby released his hold and Jimmy's head fell forward as if his neck had snapped. He glanced at Joan.

'She was a nice girl,' Joan said softly. 'That's what everyone says.'

Jimmy nodded.

'She used to talk to you, I expect?'

Jimmy looked up. 'I used to help her.'

'How?'

He scratched his head, dislodging a little shower of dandruff and dried grease. 'Used to carry her bags. Used to make sure she was all right.'

Kirby's attention sharpened.

'That was kind of you,' Joan went on. 'She must have been very grateful. So you sort of kept an eye on her?'

'Because she was my friend.'

'And how did you look after her?'

'I walked with her. No one would say nasty things to her if I was there. They knew I'd hit them if they did.'

Kirby was pretending to examine the contents of the book-case. The lad might be a half wit, but he was a well-muscled one.

'It's not nice when people say nasty things to ladies,' said Joan. 'Did people do that to Mattie?'

Jimmy shook his head. 'They wouldn't, would they? Not while I was there.'

You couldn't argue with that sort of logic, Kirby thought.

'So what happened on Thursday?' Joan went on. 'Did you look after her in the evening, after you saw her at the Ruispidge Hall?'

'No.' His face trembled. 'No. She told me not to. She told me to go away.' The man-boy stared at his hands, his shoulders twitching. 'I wanted to go with her. But she said no, said she'd be all right.'

Poor kid, Kirby thought, jolted unexpectedly into pity. That girl must have really meant something.

'Did you see where she went to on Thursday evening? After she left the Ruispidge Hall?'

'No. She just walked off.'

'Which way?'

'Towards – towards Narth Road. Like she did last weekend.'

'What do you mean?' Kirby interrupted. 'What was she doing last weekend?'

Jimmy flinched. 'Nothing. I done nothing.'

Joan leant forward and patted his hand. 'We know that, Jimmy. Sergeant Kirby just wants to know where you saw her go, that's all.'

'That's all,' echoed Kirby, feeling that Joan Ailsmore had somehow arrested control of the interview from him without his noticing.

'It was Saturday night,' Jimmy said.

'Can you remember what sort of time?' she pressed.

Jimmy frowned, then his face broke into a broad smile. 'Must have been about eight o'clock. People were coming out of the cinema.'

'Good boy. That's how a detective thinks. So the first house had just ended.'

'Mattie was walking up from the bus station, so I said I'd go with her, keep her safe. So we walked all the way to Narth Road.' He pointed at a maroon short-sleeved jersey draped over the back of a chair. 'I was wearing my new jumper. She said I looked very smart.'

'So you walked her all the way to Narth Road. That was kind of you. Did she talk to anyone on the way?'

'No. Just to me. She always talked to me. Except near Ruispidge Hall because someone was watching. So she made me walk behind.'

'And where did you say goodbye to her?'

'When she got to the house where she was going.'

'Whose house was that? Do you know?'

Jimmy shook his head again.

'Who was she going to see?'

'Just a friend.'

'So where was the house, son?' Kirby said, unable to restrain himself. 'Which side of the road was it?'

Jimmy thought for a moment and then looked at Joan and held up his right hand.

'Was it a long way from Chepstow Road?' she asked.

'Not far.' He screwed up his forehead again. 'There were big metal gates. White ones – with Ns in them.'

Kirby's head jerked up as if he'd been stung by a wasp. 'Ns?'

Jimmy shied away from him.

'The letter N?' Joan said. 'That's what you mean, isn't it?' She waited for Jimmy's nod. 'Good boy. And you didn't see her again that evening?'

'No.'

'Did you ever go with her when she went to visit friends' houses at other times?'

'No. Just when she went to see Violet. Do you know Violet? Violet's nice. She gave me some chocolate.'

'What about other friends?'

'She's got lots of friends.'

'Any special friends like you? Ones she might have kissed?'

He blew through his lips, reminding Kirby of a cow. 'Maybe.'

'Did you see her kissing anyone else?'

'Once. But she said I wasn't to tell.'

'It's all right now,' Joan said, bending closer and touching his leg, just for an instant. 'She wouldn't mind you telling us. Who was it?'

'I don't know.' He stared at Joan's hand. 'It was in the park.'

'Jubilee Park?'

He nodded. 'I was sort of keeping an eye on her and she didn't know. And this man came up and they started kissing and cuddling. Afterwards I asked her who he was and she told me not to tell.'

'What was he like?'

Jimmy shrugged.

'Young?' Kirby suggested. 'Old?'

'Very old.'

'Was he wearing a hat?'

'I don't remember.'

They questioned him for another five minutes but drew no more out of him, or nothing worth having. Jimmy remembered nothing about the man apart from the fact he was old. He couldn't even remember when he had seen the man with Mattie in the park — it could have been weeks or even months ago. He was almost equally vague about Thursday evening. He said he'd wandered around the town after leaving Mattie, and then gone home to sleep. He couldn't remember meeting anyone who knew him. His aunt had been out at the King's Head when he returned, and he hadn't seen her until Friday morning.

Kirby had had enough. Leaving Joan to make soothing conversation with Jimmy, he went into the spotless bathroom for a leak. Christ, the place was so clean you could eat your dinner off the floor. Afterwards, he and Joan went downstairs. Minnie Calder was waiting for them in the hall.

'Well?' she demanded. 'What are you going to do about that engine?'

'I'll have a word with my colleagues, Miss,' Kirby said.

'Did he say anything?'

Kirby gave a non-committal grunt and edged past her to the door.

'So you're not going to arrest him?' she persisted.

Kirby opened the door and the relatively fresh evening air flowed into the still atmosphere of the house. 'We may have to come back to ask you or him some more questions, Miss Calder. But that's all for tonight.'

He and Joan left the house. Neither of them said anything until they were back in the car, driving down Mincing Lane.

'Wouldn't like to have her as my auntie.' Joan glanced at him and he smelt her perfume. 'Was it all right in there? What I was doing, I mean?'

'You were fine,' Kirby said curtly.

'So what you think? Are we on to something?'

'I doubt it. Not with him.'

'But why?' Almost at once, she answered her own question. 'It's that house in Narth Road, the one with the white gates. Do you know whose it is?'

For a while, Kirby said nothing. Not until he'd turned out of Mincing Lane and driven up to the High Street. Not until he'd turned into police headquarters and switched off the engine. He knew Joan would find out sooner or later – it was only human nature to be curious and there was only one house in Narth Road with white gates with Ns woven into the curls and twists of the wrought iron.

He offered her a cigarette, lit hers and his and stared at her through the smoke that filled the little car. 'Keep it under your hat for now,' he said. 'We'll tell the Guv'nor but no one else.'

'So are you going to tell *me*?' Joan said. 'Or do I just use my vivid imagination?'

Kirby grinned at her. 'You can use your vivid imagination to work out why Mattie Harris was dressed up to the nines on Saturday night and paying what was apparently a social call on a County Councillor and a member of the Standing Joint Committee.'

'Sarge?' Joan picked a shred of tobacco from her lips. 'Are you having me on?'

'I wish I bloody was. And I hope to Christ that Jimmy's lying through his teeth. Because otherwise we're in trouble. That house is called Netherfield, and it belongs to Bernie Broadbent.'

Chapter Nineteen

Malcolm Sedbury thought his father was one of the worst and one of the best things in his life. He could remember when the old man had seemed roughly on a par with God Almighty. In those days he'd been much easier to cope with than he was now. The polio was partly to blame, of course, but you couldn't blame that for everything.

On Saturday evening, his parents dressed for dinner because they were dining at the Georges' house, and Mr and Mrs Pembridge were going to join them for a drink after the dance at the Ruispidge Hall was over. His father came down to the drawing room, a stiff and unfamiliar figure in his dark clothes, and poured himself a whisky and soda. He joined Malcolm, who was reading in a chair beside the open French windows.

'Found these in my dressing room this evening,' Robert said awkwardly, taking a slim leather case from the pocket of his dinner jacket. 'Used to be your grandfather's. I wondered if you might like them.'

With the slightest of sighs, Malcolm laid down his detective novel on the arm of the chair and took the case. His father twiddled with his black bow tie. Malcolm opened the catch and lifted the lid. Inside on a bed of blue watered silk was a pair of cut-throat razors with ivory handles tipped with silver. He took one of them out and opened it.

'I'd be careful, if I were you,' his father said. 'Damned sharp. Last time I used a cut-throat was on the day I married your mother.' He smiled, a little sheepishly. 'Seemed the right thing to do, somehow. Of course they're not very practical these days, but I thought you'd like to have them. There's a strop upstairs. You can have that as well. I – I'll show you how to use it.'

'Thanks, Dad.' *For my wedding?* Malcolm closed the razor and slipped it back into its case.

'I'd better go and ginger your mother up. We're going to be late.'

Malcolm picked up his book again.

'Have you got any plans for this evening?'

Malcolm looked up. 'I might drop in on Bill. I'll see.'

When at last his parents left, Malcolm limped into his father's study. He tried the drawers of the desk and, finding them locked, swore under his breath. It would have simplified things so much if for once his father had forgotten. Nothing else was locked, only the desk. 'Some of the work we do is confidential,' his father had told Malcolm more than once. 'We owe it to our clients to make sure that no one can pry.'

He went into the kitchen. His mother had left a plate of ham and salad in the larder. He ate a few mouthfuls, but couldn't stomach the rest. He scraped it into the dustbin and covered it with an old newspaper so she wouldn't fuss. He returned to the study and phoned the Pembridges'. Bill answered.

'Had any luck?' Bill's voice was already slightly slurred.

'No. Nothing we can do about it. But it doesn't matter. We'll just have to wait.'

'Come over and have a drink.'

'OK.'

'I'll come and fetch you,' Bill said.

'Don't bother. I'll walk.'

Malcolm collected his sticks and left the house. In one sense he was proud of those sticks. It had been a long slow business, first the wheelchair, then the crutches and now just the sticks. It had taken literally years of practice but now he could move along a level, firm surface with surprising speed. Sometimes he caught sight of himself in a shop window and wanted to retch with distaste. He thought he looked like an ungainly spider scuttling along from one dark hiding place to another. He hated the thought that people were looking at him, were laughing at him behind his back. He hated the knowledge that he would always be different.

The Pembridges' house was in Albert Road on the other side of the park, only a few hundred yards away from where the Sedburys lived. Two old beech trees stood like sentries between the house and the road and gave the house its name. Malcolm limped up the drive and found Bill in the garden. There was a circular goldfish pond on the lawn and Bill had set up a couple of deckchairs beside it. On the grass between the chairs was a table holding a decanter of whisky, a siphon of soda and two glasses. Bill had his feet up on the broad parapet of the pond. It was still light, but the glow of his cigarette danced like a firefly. He looked up, glass halfway to his lips, and Malcolm saw the relief in his face.

'Take a pew,' Bill said. 'Scotch? Thought we'd sit outside. So bloody hot.'

Malcolm lowered himself awkwardly into the deckchair. Deckchairs were a trial because they were so hard to get out of. Bill had already poured a couple of inches into a glass. He gave it a token squirt of soda and passed the drink to Malcolm.

'It is hot,' he repeated. 'It's not just me, is it?'

'No.' Malcolm sipped his drink.

Bill waved his forefinger at the pond. 'What I want to know is how we could be so bloody stupid.'

'We had a lot to think about. And anyway, there's nothing to worry about.'

'Nothing to worry about? Christ, Malcolm—'

'I've got a plan.'

There was a silence. Bill craned his head. Malcolm sometimes wondered what would happen if they found themselves in a situation where he didn't have a plan. It had always been like this, even before the polio. It was one of the few things that had survived from that other life, when his legs had been as strong as anybody's, when he had been just like everybody else. In that other life, Mr Herrick, who used to coach the Under-13 cricket XI at Ashbridge, had said he might make a useful county player one day.

'I had an idea,' Malcolm said. 'It'll simplify everything. We could kill two birds with one stone. What we'll do is make it easy for everyone.'

'I knew you'd think of something. So what are we going to do?'

Malcolm told him. Bill's face was shiny, though it was hard to tell whether it was the alcohol making him sweat, or the heat, or simply relief. They had another whisky.

'I'd better be careful,' Malcolm said. 'I'm not sure I'm going to be able to walk back if I have another.'

'Not a problem,' Bill announced, waving his glass expansively. 'My pa will run you back. That's what the old man's there for.'

They sat smoking and drinking as the light leeched out of the sky. Albert Road was on high ground. Beyond the roofs of the town was a grey-green patchwork of open countryside with the darker hills of the forest beyond.

'Thanks, old chap,' Bill said at one point.

'That's OK.'

'Funny old thing. Life, I mean. You know Violet?'

'Of course I know Violet.'

'I saw her this evening. I think I'm getting cold feet.'

'Because of all this?'

'Partly, I suppose.' Bill's perfect profile was outlined against the darkening sky. 'Then there's the baby. I could hardly go to university with a baby, could I? Anyway, Pa would probably throw me out of the house. I mean, it wouldn't be fair to any of us – me, Violet or the baby.'

'Did you say anything to her?'

'Not exactly. We – we were interrupted. God, I feel a heel. She's not having a very good time at home at present. And then there's this business with Mattie.'

'Yes.' Malcolm sipped his drink. 'But sometimes you have to be cruel to be kind.'

'That's it. That's just it.' Bill's enthusiasm for this line of argument was almost indecent. 'Men are better at that sort of decision than girls, I think. We don't let our hearts rule our heads in the same way. Someone has to do the thinking, don't they?'

'True enough.' Malcolm felt the familiar blend of exasperation, envy and affection. 'If I were you, though, I'd go away once you've told her. Get right away from Lydmouth for a few weeks.'

Bill nodded. 'Her father saw me this evening.'

'Then I wouldn't leave telling her too long. Get it done quickly and get out of the way.'

'I can't wait for autumn,' Bill said softly. 'Get away from the whole bloody mess.'

Malcolm grunted. Now his National Service was out of the way, Bill could take up his place to read law at University College London. Whereas he would be stuck in Lydmouth without anyone to talk to.

'Think of it,' Bill went on. 'London, all those girls. Shame you can't come with me.'

'One day,' Malcolm murmured. One day, he promised himself, he would escape from Lydmouth. There must be more to life than being the son in Sedbury & Son, even if you couldn't walk properly.

'When you're qualified,' Bill said, mirroring Malcolm's thoughts, 'that'll be the time for you to come up. They must need bags of estate agents and surveyors in London. We'll have a flat together, a flat in Chelsea.'

This was a familiar version of the future. Malcolm cheered up a little as they tossed their plans for life in London backwards and forwards between them, just as they'd done so many times before. The sky grew darker and darker. Bill found it increasingly difficult to remember what he was saying, but it didn't matter because Malcolm knew.

'A lot of pebbles on the beach in London,' Bill said, enunciating each word with great care. 'We'll find a nice one for you, old lad, don't you worry.'

Bill slipped into a doze. His mouth fell open and he snored quietly. Malcolm drank another glass of whisky and watched a hedgehog picking its way across the lawn. He thought about pebbles on beaches and he thought about Mattie Harris. He knew he should be going. Mr and Mrs Pembridge would soon be back. He didn't want the indignity of being taken home as though he were a tired child at the end of a party.

He fumbled for a cigarette, found the packet was empty and instead took out a pipe his mother has given him for his last birthday. She told him it made him look grown up. He gripped the bowl and rotated it in his hand, wondering if he had the energy to look for his tobacco.

All those pebbles on the beach. But now one of them was no longer called Mattie Harris.

His hands convulsed. One gripped the bowl of the briar, the other the stem. With one easy twist he snapped the pipe in two. That was one thing about being a cripple. You had strong hands.

There was a roll of thunder somewhere down the river. For some reason it reminded him of laughter, Mattie's laughter.

Chapter Twenty

'I was out,' Richard Thornhill said. 'If you'd tried a little later, you would have caught me in. You'd better tell me what happened.'

He listened while Kirby explained the events of the previous evening. They were in Thornhill's office at police headquarters. On the other side of the big sash window, far too big for the cramped little office, rain fell incessantly from a grey sky. The weather had broken at last but it seemed not to have made any difference to the mugginess of the atmosphere.

Bells rang, faintly and far away, summoning the faithful to St John's, where Alec Sutton, the vicar, would tell them that God would let them take what they wanted as long as they paid for it. Thornhill put his hand to his face, ostensibly to rub his nose, but really to smell his fingers. There was still a hint of Jill there, he thought, something had lingered, some little part of her. Kirby droned on. Brian was far too shrewd for comfort – maybe he smelled a rat.

Thornhill slapped his hand on the blotter. 'So what you're saying is that Mattie knew Jimmy Leigh well enough to kiss him, and that they were seen together on Thursday evening. Gerald Pembridge saw that kiss and so did one of the lads at the dance. But when you talked to Jimmy, he threw a spanner in the works by saying he'd seen Mattie paying a call on Councillor Broadbent the previous weekend.'

'Yes, sir, but—'

'This man he saw her with in the park. Could it have been Broadbent?'

'No, sir. WPC Ailsmore went back to see Leigh this morning with a photo. It wasn't Broadbent. Or so he said.'

'Any news from the lab?'

Kirby shook his head.

'Have you phoned them this morning?'

'No, sir. What with the Bank Holiday weekend, they—'

'Try phoning them, Brian. And I'd like to see the report on the search of the riverbank.'

Kirby left the room. Even in a hierarchical organisation like the police force, you sometimes had to make it quite clear who was the boss. Perhaps especially in the police force. Thornhill knew that he should have kept in contact with headquarters yesterday evening, that his failure to do so had left him open to criticism. The best defence was attack. He shut his mind to the knowledge that if he continued to see Jill Francis like this, he would have to spend more and more time on the offensive.

He knew he should phone Williamson but decided to put it off a little longer. Instead he leafed through the contents of his in-tray. There was nothing of interest except the photographs – of the riverbank where Mattie had been found, and of Mattie herself in the mortuary. He skimmed through the prints. People had liked Mattie, even loved her. But the photographs of that plain face with its thin features gave you no indication of why. If Bernie had been one of her conquests, all hell would break loose. He lingered over a photograph of the objects found near Mattie's body in the river and on the bank. Among them was the beer bottle, with its label clearly readable:

India Pale Ale
Thorogood and Nephew
Elmbury.

There was a tap on the door and Kirby returned.

'They've not had time to do her yet,' he said stiffly. 'Doctor Murray's away for the weekend.' He put the report on Thornhill's desk. 'Nothing new, I'm afraid.'

Thornhill flicked through it. 'Good. So you tested the currents?'

'Yes, Guv. We put cork floats in the Minnow and the Lyd, three in each. Five of them ended up within fifty yards of where we found the body.'

'WPC Ailsmore – what's your impression of her?'

'She did well last night, sir. She got Jimmy Leigh to talk. Coaxed it out of him. In fact I was wondering . . .'

'What?'

'Whether there might even be a case for having a woman permanently on the strength.'

'We'll see.'

Thornhill's eyes met Kirby's, and for an instant the two men understood each other perfectly. Superintendent Williamson would never have countenanced the idea of a woman in the CID. But Williamson very nearly belonged to history. It was barely possible to imagine what the CID might be like after his passing.

'Councillor Broadbent,' Thornhill said slowly. 'We'll go and see if he's at home.'

Just for a moment Kirby looked surprised. 'Right, sir. Which car?'

'We'll go in mine.'

Thornhill knew the reason for the surprise. Kirby knew, just as the whole of the force probably knew by now, that Bernie Broadbent was Edith Thornhill's cousin. Soon they'd probably discover that Bernie owned the very house the Thornhills lived in. Kirby had half expected Thornhill to have a private word with Bernie first. It was the way things happened in Lydmouth, and almost everywhere else. Everyone was equal before the law but, in the eyes of the average police officer, wealthy relatives who were county councillors and members of the Standing Joint Committee were slightly more equal than most.

The streets were empty, drugged with the calm of Sunday morning. The rain had stopped. By the time they reached Narth Road, the sun was trying to break through the clouds. The tall white gates of Netherfield stood open. The little Austin purred up the drive. Kirby pursed his lips and whistled when he saw the Wolseley parked outside the front door.

'Nice motor. Is that his? Must be new.'

'It is.'

Thornhill's eyes swept the length of the big white house. Jill had once told him that she thought Netherfield a beautiful building, but he couldn't understand why. It was more like a large iced cake than a home where people might live.

Kirby rang the doorbell. A moment later, Bernie appeared, his bloodshot eyes peering past Kirby to Thornhill.

'Morning,' he grunted. 'And what can I do for you?'

'We'd like a word, sir,' Thornhill said. 'May we come in?'

'Of course you can.'

Bernie took them into a large drawing room at the back of the house. It was full of modern furniture and slightly less impersonal than a hotel lounge. French windows gave onto a paved area where cushioned chairs were arranged round a table. A pot of tea and a half-eaten slice of toast had been abandoned on top of a pile of newspapers. A cup, saucer and a plate stood on a tray beside it.

'Disturbed your breakfast, have we?' Thornhill said.

'Such as it was.' Bernie smiled, and charm flowed like sunlight through the wrinkles of his face. 'Had a late night. Do you want some coffee? A drink?'

'No, thank you. Look, sir, I might as well come straight to the point.'

'No need to be so formal, lad. I'm sure Sergeant Kirby knows we're by way of being related.'

'Yes, sir. We've called about Mattie Harris.'

The thick eyebrows shot up. 'The girl who got herself drowned?'

'We don't yet know how she died. Not for sure. Did you know her?'

Bernie shrugged his heavy shoulders. 'Not by name. But I must have seen her. They tell me she worked at the Gardenia, and I sometimes drop in for a cup of coffee. Was she the waitress with red hair?'

'That's right.'

'Poor kid. What does it look like? Could she swim?'

'Apparently not, sir.'

Bernie yawned. 'Very sad, in any case.'

'Would you mind telling me what you were doing on Saturday evening, sir? Not yesterday. Last weekend.'

'Saturday? What is this, Richard? What are you driving at?' Bernie waited a moment, but Thornhill didn't answer. 'I was here, I think. Catching up on paperwork, watching a bit of television. Why?'

'Did you see Mattie Harris?'

'Don't be stupid, man. Whatever gave you that idea?'

'We have a witness who saw her turning into the drive of Netherfield.'

'Then either your witness was mistaken or she didn't come up to the house. Maybe she ducked into the bushes near the gate. Wanted to touch up her make-up? Taken short? I could think of a dozen reasons. All I know is she didn't come here.'

Thornhill smiled, aware of Kirby standing silently at his elbow like the recording angel. 'Thank you, sir – that seems quite straightforward.'

Bernie's irritation subsided. 'While you're here, Richard, let me give you something for Edith.'

Thornhill stiffened. 'What?'

'I've got some early roses. I've got a standard in that corner of the vegetable garden by the greenhouse. She's coming back tomorrow, isn't she, so if I cut them now and you put them in water when you get home, they should be fine. It won't take a moment.'

He led them along the back of the house, round the garage block and into the vegetable garden. The roses were a soft delicate pink that made Thornhill think of a baby's skin. Bernie found a trug in the greenhouse and snipped off a dozen blooms.

'There you are,' Bernie said when he'd finished, handing the trug to Kirby. 'She loves roses, your Edith does. I remember her in my mother's garden when she was a girl, smelling them and smiling. Looked like she'd gone to heaven.' He gave Thornhill a lopsided grin. 'Look at the way the rain's caught on the petals. The drops are like diamonds, aren't they?'

Thornhill smiled back. 'Would you mind if we wander down and have a look at the river, sir?'

The geniality left Bernie's face. 'Of course. Be my guest.'

Thornhill and Kirby walked slowly down to the river, Kirby still carrying the trug, self-consciously like a bridesmaid with a bouquet.

'Why the river?' Kirby said when they were out of Bernie's hearing.

'Mattie must have gone into the water somewhere.'

'But you don't think —?'

'I'm not thinking, Brian. I'm just looking.'

They walked slowly along the thirty yards of river frontage that belonged to Bernie. Netherfield was on the outskirts of town so the water was free of rubbish, and much cleaner than it was lower down. The Minnow at this point was narrower than it became when it flowed through Templefields, and much narrower than the Lyd itself where Mattie had been found. But it looked deep, swollen with last night's rain.

'It's possible you know,' Thornhill said softly, almost to himself. 'Her body could have been swept right into town.'

Kirby said nothing, still angry at Thornhill's treatment of him earlier in the morning. That was one advantage of having children, Thornhill thought – you realised when experienced police officers were sulking. He guessed that the other reason why his sergeant was so uncharacteristically quiet was because of where he was. Kirby had a keen sense of what was due to those with influence. And in Lydmouth, you didn't get much more influential than Bernie Broadbent.

They walked back up the garden. Bernie was leafing through a magazine and smoking a pipe. The remains of breakfast had vanished. In their place was a glass and a bottle of beer.

Bernie looked up. 'Found any clues, Richard? No, you don't have to answer. I don't suppose I can tempt you to a glass of beer, can I?'

Thornhill looked automatically at the bottle on the table. He felt rather than saw Kirby stiffen beside him. He picked up the bottle and looked at the label.

'Yes,' he heard Bernie saying. 'Thorogood and Nephew. Do you know it? Nice little brewery in Elmbury.'

Chapter Twenty-one

The smell of roasting mutton and boiling cabbage hung heavily over the Bull Hotel. Raymond Williamson felt saliva gathering in his mouth and washed it down with another mouthful of beer.

He had been in the saloon bar of the Bull Hotel since it opened at midday. After a brief lull, the rain had returned. The room had grown so dark that the barman had switched on the lights. While he waited, Williamson doodled with his propelling pencil, covering the beer mats on the table with pictures of cats. He was hardly aware he was doing it. He always drew cats when his mind was occupied, when he was worried. Always the same cat.

Gerald Pembridge arrived halfway through the second pint. 'No sign of Bernie yet?'

Williamson shook his head. He raised his finger to the barman, who nodded and took down the tankard they kept for Pembridge.

'I would have been earlier,' Pembridge went on. 'But Edna took the car to church and Bill's off somewhere in the MG. Probably trying to impress some girl, the lucky devil. Anyway, Muggins had to walk, and of course the sky opened.' While he was speaking, he dabbed at his smooth, lean face with a handkerchief. 'We had some of your people at the Ruispidge Hall last night.'

Williamson opened his mouth to speak, caught sight of the approaching barman and shut it again. He waited until Pembridge had had his first swallow of beer.

'Who was it?'

'Chap called Kirby. Plain-clothes man. He had a woman with him.' Pembridge wiped away a moustache of foam with his handkerchief. 'Getting it on the job, these days, eh?'

'And what happened?'

'You haven't heard? I thought you'd—'

'I'll hear,' Williamson said grimly. 'But I'm technically on leave. And Hendry's given the case to Thornhill. So it isn't quite as straightforward as it would usually be.'

'We were playing when they got there, so they talked to Edna at first.' Pembridge spoke in a rapid monotone. 'She told them that Mattie was one of our regulars, that she was a bit flighty. Said she hadn't been there on Saturday, but Edna had seen her all dressed up, so thought she was going somewhere. And of course she mentioned that Mattie had come to the dance on Thursday night. Said she seemed excited.' Pembridge paused for more beer, his eyes panning round the room. He leant closer, lowering his voice still further. 'Then I talked to them. Told them I saw Mattie kissing Jimmy Leigh on Thursday evening, outside the Ruispidge Hall. One of the lads saw her do it too, so he confirmed it.'

'Just as well,' Williamson said. 'Just as well you did see them.'

'They talked to me later, and I confirmed everything Edna had told them. Not a problem.'

Williamson nodded slowly. 'I'll have a word with the Chief Constable. I'm going to have to leave you in a moment. I promised Bunty I'd to be back before one.'

'Time for another one? Here's Bernie.'

Broadbent strolled across the bar. He waved at them, but paused to exchange banter with two acquaintances propping up the counter. Finally he settled at their table. When they were alone, the smile left his face.

'I've just had a visit from Richard Thornhill and Brian Kirby. That's why I'm late.'

'They came to Netherfield?' Pembridge said quickly. 'Why?'

'Someone saw Mattie Harris turning into the drive last weekend.'

Williamson was engaged in turning a splash of beer on the polished top of the table into the head of a cat. 'Who?' he said.

'They wouldn't say.'

'I'll find out.'

'Good man,' Bernie said. 'Anyway, I said I hadn't seen her. Even if she did duck into the drive, it didn't mean she came up to the house. I told them I had a quiet evening at home.'

'Of all the bloody luck,' Pembridge said, flushing.

'Don't worry,' Williamson said. 'The point is what happened on Thursday night not Saturday. That's what the police are interested in.'

'They went down the garden and had a look at the river,' Bernie went on, smoke wreathing round his head. 'Why would they want to do that?'

Williamson lifted his head. 'Just checking. Mattie must have gone into the water at some point. Young Thornhill knows his job.' He looked up at the clock above the bar and the roasting mutton teased his nostrils. 'I've got to go.'

He swallowed the rest of his beer and said goodbye, promising to keep the others informed. The cobbled yard at the back of the hotel was wet and slippery. Swearing softly at the rain, he climbed into his car and started the engine. But for a moment he didn't drive off. He stared at the windscreen wipers sliding to and fro across the windscreen like dancing stick insects. The real problem was Richard Thornhill. He was reasonably sure he could deal with anyone else, even Brian Kirby, even the Chief Constable. But Thornhill was always an unknown quantity.

Marches to a different drummer from everyone else. I should have got a local man for the job, then life would have been much simpler.

He released the handbrake and let out the clutch. It was a 10-

to-15 minute drive home. He and Bunty shared a five-bedroomed house built by Cyril George on the outskirts of a village four miles from Lydmouth. By the time he got home Bunty would be on her third sherry, and staring sadly at the clock.

His route took him into Chepstow Road, and then out of Lydmouth by Narth Road. There was little traffic. The car in front of him, a little two-seater, turned into Narth Road too. It accelerated immediately, though they were still within the built-up area, and Williamson guessed it was doing at least 15 mph more than the speed limit. Not his problem, these days, thank God.

He followed more slowly, passing the Lydmouth High School for Girls on the left and then the gates of Netherfield on the right. Once out of town he accelerated, and soon caught up with the sports car in front. A moment later, it began to slow, signalling right.

As the sports car turned into the lane on the right, Williamson saw the two people inside. Bill Pembridge was driving, and beside him was not a girl, but poor old Malcolm Sedbury.

Williamson knew that lane. It led to a house where an old chap had topped himself a year or so back. Straightforward case of suicide. Brian Kirby had handled it. What was the name of the place? Bloody memory was going.

Not as young as I was.

He drove on. The rain stopped, and once again watery sunlight struggled to worm its way through the cloud cover. He worked at the question of the house's name, like a dog trying to get to the marrow inside a bone. It kept his mind busy. Kept him from thinking about other things.

The answer came to him as he reached his own house. He had put large stones along the grass verge of the road outside his front garden to prevent people from parking there. *Stones.*

That was the house's name – Wynstones.

Chapter Twenty-two

'Damn it,' Bill said. 'Looks like they're already here. What the hell are we going to do?'

In his irritation, he stamped on the brake. The MG rocked to a halt beside a Humber saloon parked in front of the garage doors.

Malcolm felt for the door handle. 'Don't worry. It's stopped raining so I can show them the garden first.'

Like so many returning colonials, Mr and Mrs Christie gave the impression that they were more English than the English. He was a tall, elegant man in a tweed jacket of antique cut, flannels and gleaming brogues. His wife was small, packed neatly and unobtrusively into a fawn cashmere twin set, with a string of pearls round her neck and a lined face the colour of uncooked dough.

Malcolm pushed open the door. 'Mr and Mrs Christie? I'm Malcolm Sedbury. I hope you haven't been waiting long.'

For a moment Mr and Mrs Christie behaved quite naturally, just as they would have done if Malcolm had been normal. Then they saw him struggling out of the car, saw the sticks. Their faces changed. Malcolm had grown expert in identifying that flicker of embarrassment, that twinge of pity, that twitch of distaste.

When at last he was upright, he shook hands with the

Christies and introduced Bill. 'I thought we'd take a look at the garden first, while the rain holds off,' he said. 'Bill can open up the house for us.' He smiled at Christie. 'And I expect you'd like to see the river. My father tells me you're an angler.'

The thin, dry face of Mr Christie blossomed into life, like a desert in the rain. Mrs Christie gave an audible sigh. Malcolm removed the boathouse key from the ring and tossed the rest of the keys to Bill. Mr Christie began to talk about the fish he had caught and nearly caught, mainly salmon and trout, ranging freely through the years of his life.

While Mr Christie talked, the three of them moved slowly down the path which led along the side of the house and into the back garden. The odd thing was, Malcolm noticed, that all of Mr Christie's fishing exploits had taken place in the British Isles. If he had fished while he was out in Malaya, presumably for most of his working life, he preferred not to mention it. Perhaps Malayan fish were in some way inferior to British ones.

Mrs Christie showed signs of wanting to linger to examine the sunken rose garden, to study the condition of the turf of the croquet lawn, to sniff the honeysuckle growing in sweet-smelling profusion along the south wall of a little summerhouse halfway down the lawn. But her husband swept them on, towards the river.

'Yes,' Malcolm said, answering one of the few questions that Mr Christie bothered to direct to him. 'We've checked with the solicitor, and we have it in writing. The fishing rights do go with the house.'

While he limped and talked, he also worried about what was happening in the house. He would have liked to have looked over his shoulder, pointless though it would have been, because Bill would hardly be standing waving, at one of the windows.

When they reached the river, Mr Christie gazed happily across the water and nodded. Meanwhile Mrs Christie asked Malcolm if there were any sign of damp in the house.

'Dry as a bone, Mrs Christie. That's the advantage of a

modern house. There's a very effective damp-proof course.'

'Ah – the boathouse,' cried Mr Christie and his strangled Edwardian vowels so mangled the words that for a moment Malcolm thought he had spoken in Malay, not English.

'I've got the key, sir,' Malcolm said. 'Would you like a look inside?'

It was a small wooden building leaning against the boundary wall of the garden, at the head of a short slipway down to the Minnow. The door at the back was padlocked. Malcolm unlocked it. The damp had swollen the wood and for a moment he wrestled with the door. He was aware of Mrs Christie nudging her husband.

'Let me,' Mr Christie said. 'I'll have it open in a jiffy.'

'No need, sir, thank you.'

Malcolm pulled the door open. Inside was a small clinker-built rowing boat, while on the wall hung an outboard motor.

'And this goes with the house, too?' Mr Christie said.

'In theory the boat and motor are for sale separately.' Malcolm noticed the floor was wet. 'But I think the vendors would listen to any reasonable offer. By the way, we've taken the boat out once or twice while the house has been empty, and turned over the engine. It's all in working order.'

'Splendid, splendid.'

It was at this point that things began to go wrong. It was Mrs Christie's fault. Instead of allowing Malcolm to guide them through the rhododendrons which clustered near the one side of the house the Christies had not so far seen, she made a beeline for the sunken rose garden. She gazed at the bushes in need of pruning and said cheerfully that she thought there was a great deal of work to be done here. While she was in the rose garden, her husband lost patience with her and walked to the front of the house, retracing his steps along the path by the garage.

The timing was unfortunate. Bill was part way between the front door and the MG, his head turned towards the other side of the house, the side with the rhododendrons. Malcolm let one of his sticks clang against a drainpipe. Bill's head jerked towards the sound. He gave them a quick wave and veered away, turning through 180 degrees and slipping out of sight round the corner of the house.

At least the Christies appeared to have noticed nothing. They were absorbed in their own concerns. Besides they knew Bill had come with Malcolm, of course, but they had no idea of his status – whether he was a friend or an employee, for example – or of what he was doing.

Malcolm steered the Christies towards the front door, hoping Bill would be able to work his way back to the car unobserved. At this point there was a further problem. Mr Christie was here for the river. He had no interest in the house. Mrs Christie, on the other hand, wanted to see every room. She wanted to calculate how many towels you could get in the airing cupboard, how many guests you could comfortably seat in the dining room, and discuss the availability of domestic help.

'It's very clean for a house that hasn't been lived in for a while,' she said approvingly. 'And well aired, too.'

Meanwhile Mr Christie was fiddling with the bolts on the back door.

'There's a woman who comes in for one morning a week,' Malcolm said. 'She keeps the place tidy, and generally keeps an eye on things. If you decide to take the house, I daresay she could be persuaded to work longer hours.'

Mr Christie had got the door open now.

'I do miss the servants,' Mrs Christie confided. 'Staff was never a problem out there. We had such a lovely butler. But one could hardly bring him home with us.'

'I'll just pop down the garden again,' Mr Christie said, slipping through the door. 'Take another look at the river.'

'Ooh,' said Mrs Christie. 'It's quite a nice sized larder, I'll say that for it.'

'North-facing, of course. With just a hint of east, perhaps, but very little.'

'And is this the pantry?' asked Mrs Christie, moving on to another door.

Through the kitchen window Malcolm had a good view down the garden. Mr Christie was advancing slowly but steadily towards the river. Bill, who had been attempting to move discreetly round the house via the rose garden and the garage, had been forced to retreat down to the riverbank itself. Even at this distance Malcolm could see the bulge under his jacket.

Even poor obsessed Christie could hardly miss it. Not when he got closer.

The possibility — *the probability* — churned inside her like broken glass. As she walked back to the cottage the rain returned, fat drops of it, falling slowly out of the sky and hitting bare skin with the impact of a flicking finger. She scooped up the two chairs, pushed them into the shelter of the porch and went into the cottage.

'So much for my dirty weekend,' she said aloud.

She sat down beside the window, lit a cigarette and opened *The Vicar of Bullhampton*.

Chapter Twenty-four

Ted Evans was on his way home from the allotments when he saw Bill Pembridge. The boy was wandering down the towpath from the Ferryman, cigarette in hand, and whistling. Dapper in blazer and cravat, he hadn't a bloody care in the world. Not yet.

The fact young Pembridge was *here* was another injury. Ted's allotment was more than a source of fresh vegetables. It was a consolation. It was an extension of his personality. It was perhaps the only place in the world where he felt truly himself. It was private.

As spring gave way to summer, he spent more and more time down here. There were forty allotments, identical in size, each as idiosyncratic as their owners. Ted's was one of the neatest. His plants might have been on a parade ground; his shed had been recently creosoted; and a weed had only to show its head to be exterminated. He knew most of the other allotment holders, but by and large few of them talked to him, except on strictly practical matters such as how to keep out rabbits and precisely when vegetable marrows should be moved to open ground.

As usual on fine Sundays, he had spent most of the afternoon working down here. When he saw Bill Pembridge, he pulled back into the shelter of an ash tree. All the worry, all the fear, all the frustration coalesced into a single shaft of anger, hard as granite. He propped the bicycle carefully against the tree and walked out into the towpath.

Young Pembridge was not ten yards away. He stopped at once, his eyes widening.

Toffee-nosed bastard's scared shitless.

'Right,' Ted said slowly. 'Time you and I had a little chat.'

'Look, Mr Evans, I'm afraid I'm in a bit of a hurry. Couldn't I—'

'You're in a bit of a hurry to leave my girl in the lurch.'

'Violet? I don't know what you mean.'

'Have you forgotten yesterday already?'

'I – I happened to bump into her when I was walking. Just stopped to pass the time of day. Perfectly—'

'Shut up,' Ted said softly. 'You met her by arrangement. She told me. And as soon as you saw me coming, you ran off. I always had you down as a windy bugger, and I was right.'

Bill's eyes darted from side to side, looking for a way out. There wasn't one. There was the Lyd on one side, the fence of the allotments on the other. He could turn tail and run, or he could advance. And in either case Ted was going to get him.

'It was you,' Ted said. 'It was you got my girl in the family way.'

'I assure you—'

'Your assurances aren't worth a tinker's fart.' He took a step closer to Bill. 'So what you going to do?'

'What about, Mr Evans?'

'Violet. I expect you said you'd marry her, or some such nonsense. That's what boys like you usually say to girls like Violet. But you've got it wrong, haven't you? Because boys like you aren't usually so stupid. It's not a good idea to make a fool of a girl who has a father like me.'

With the last word – *me* – Ted's left fist shot out. Pain jarred down his arm as it connected with the corner of Pembridge's mouth. The boy threw up his arms, trying to protect his face, but he was too slow to prevent Ted's other fist from slamming against his cheekbone, just below the left eye. He howled, his hands clamped over his face, and blood beginning to seep through the fingers. Ted took careful aim and kicked him in the crotch. The lad doubled up.

Ted felt very calm. Now there was all the time in the world. He wondered what to do next. Break an arm, perhaps? Or something more painful, less likely to heal. Or put the bugger permanently out of his misery so he'd never hurt another girl again. All those choices, and all of them easy. That was the wonderful thing about violence, he thought, it made everything so simple.

'Please, Mr Evans, please,' blubbered the boy, blowing bubbles of blood from his broken mouth. 'I'll marry her, I'll do anything.'

The snivelling little bastard actually fell to his knees and tried to cling to Ted's legs. Suddenly his anger was replaced by an infinite contempt. He grabbed the boy by the armpits, lifted him up until they were looking into each other's eyes.

'I wouldn't let you marry my girl if you were the last man in the world.'

Lingeringly, like a lover, Ted stared at the broken face and smiled.

'Please, sir, please—'

He spat. He watched his spittle slide down Bill Pembridge's forehead and creep into his left eye socket. Then he hauled the boy like a sack of coal down the bank and threw him into the river. The boy's arms thrashed the water. He gasped and spluttered. Streaks of blood curled like tendrils of seaweed around him.

'If the bloody Drowner doesn't get you,' Ted said 'I will.'

Chapter Twenty-five

Parked outside police headquarters was a small black Austin with a bunch of roses on the back seat. Were they a bad omen?

Roses depressed Malcolm Sedbury. When he'd returned home on the day he jumped off New Bridge, all those years ago, his mother had been pruning the bushes at the front of the house. She'd seen his soaking clothes, plied him with questions like an interrogating counsel, told him off and sent him to bed without any supper. So, even afterwards, roses had remained in his mind, linked to a fearful, angry voice, linked to the heroic jump off New Bridge, linked to the last days before the polio struck.

There were steps up to the front door of the police station. Malcolm knew he would be able to manage them, though he hated steps because they made him look even more ungainly than usual. He had almost reached the top when a uniformed constable appeared on the other side of the door, opened it and solicitously asked him if he needed a hand.

Malcolm smiled, said he was fine, let himself be ushered down the hallway to the reception counter. There were people waiting, members of the public, and he felt he was running the gauntlet of their eyes. Behind the desk was a uniformed sergeant, who leant forward to hear what Malcolm was saying. It seemed to Malcolm that the man was paying him exaggerated attention, perhaps believing that because he could not walk properly he might not be able to speak properly either. Or think properly, for that matter.

'Good morning, my name's Malcolm Sedbury. Listen, I think I have some information about the accident near New Bridge last week. The one involving Mattie Harris.'

The sergeant nodded. 'What sort of information?'

'I must have seen her just before it happened. Or rather, not seen her — heard her.'

'Wait a moment, son.'

The sergeant went behind a glass partition, and Malcolm heard the rumble of voices. He reappeared a moment later and murmured to Malcolm, 'Someone will be down to see you in a moment. Perhaps you'd like to take a seat?'

He waited on a bench, carefully avoiding the eyes of other people and willing himself not only to look calm but to be calm. He sat very still, breathed slowly, made sure his hands rested naturally on his legs. He wondered why the others were here on a Bank Holiday Monday. It seemed strange that anyone else should have business with the police except himself.

He heard voices and looked up. Behind the counter, a slim man in a dark suit was glancing through some papers. The sergeant lifted the flap to allow the man into the hallway. He came over to Malcolm.

'Mr Sedbury? I'm Detective Inspector Thornhill.'

Malcolm struggled to his feet. He wondered if one shook hands with a plain-clothes police officer. Probably not.

'If you'd like to come with me,' Thornhill said, 'we can talk more comfortably in here.'

He opened a door and led the way into a large square room at the front of the building. There was a scratched mahogany table surrounded by a disorderly crowd of chairs.

'Do sit down,' Thornhill said.

Malcolm hooked the sticks over the back of a chair. One of

them slipped and fell to the floor. Thornhill scooped it up and returned it to him without comment.

'I understand you have some information about the girl who was found in the river last week.'

'Yes, that's correct. I think my friend and I may have heard her on the evening before she died.'

'Heard her?'

'It was pretty dark.'

'When exactly was this, sir?'

'Thursday evening, must have been about a quarter-past ten. I was with a friend – Bill Pembridge – and we'd stopped at the Ferryman's Inn for a drink and to buy some cigarettes. You know there's a beer garden beside the river?'

Thornhill nodded.

'We were sitting there, near the pub. We saw a couple in the field next door. You know – the one towards the allotments. Sometimes – sometimes couples go there.'

Thornhill's mouth twitched. 'When they want a little peace and quiet.'

Malcolm smiled. 'Yes. Well the girl was Mattie. And she was with a man.'

'Did you recognise him?'

'No. He was taller than her, quite burly, but that's all I know. He had his back to us, you see, and it was very nearly dark.'

'But you recognised her.'

'Not so much by the way she looked, though. It was because of her laugh. Mattie had a very distinctive laugh. Sort of throaty.'

'So you knew her? Personally, I mean?'

'Not really. But one saw her around. She was a striking girl, Inspector – all that red hair. And I noticed her in the Gardenia several times – you knew she was a waitress there?'

Thornhill nodded. 'What were she and the man doing?'

'They were – cuddling.'

'So there was no sign of a quarrel, for example?'

'Not that we noticed. But we were only there for a few

minutes, and we weren't paying much attention. As I've said, all I know is that she laughed.'

'And what happened then?'

'We went home,' Malcolm said. 'I would have come and seen you before, but I didn't realise that the girl in the river was Mattie Harris until yesterday.'

'How did you find out?'

'Mr and Mrs Pembridge mentioned it to my parents on Saturday evening. Mattie used to go dancing at the Ruispidge Hall, and they said that the police had been round to talk to them. Then my father mentioned it to me last night, and I thought I'd better come in and see you.'

Thornhill asked a few more questions but Malcolm realised that the interview had run out of steam. Thornhill asked him to make a statement, and brought down a young constable for the purpose.

Half an hour later, Malcolm struggled down the steps to the High Street. The rain had returned, and the pavement was speckled with dark drops like wet toffees. He heard the door opening and looked back. Inspector Thornhill loomed above him.

'Will you tell your friend Bill Pembridge to drop in some time, please? We'd like to take a statement from him as well.'

Malcolm nodded.

'You're going to get soaked.' Thornhill's voice was curt. 'Do you want a lift?'

'I thought I'd drop in on Bill Pembridge, actually.'

'Where does he live?'

'Albert Road.'

'I can drop you there if that would help.'

The rain was falling more heavily now, and the offer was suddenly attractive. Malcolm clambered into the passenger seat of the little Austin. The car smelt stiflingly of roses. Thornhill drove in silence, making no attempt at conversation. Were all detectives like this, Malcolm wondered? Thornhill turned into the drive of the Pembridges' house and dropped Malcolm at the front door.

'Remember – ask young Pembridge to look in. Tell him to ask for me or for Sergeant Kirby. Goodbye.'

As the sound of the engine diminished, Malcolm heard a distant trumpet playing a blues scale. He rang the bell. It was Bill who opened the door, first to Malcolm's relief and then to his surprise.

'What the hell have you been doing with yourself?'

Bill grimaced, wincing with the pain the movement caused him. 'Ran into Ted Evans yesterday. On my way back from the Ferryman.'

Malcolm said quickly, 'Did that –?'

'It was fine. I was feeling quite pleased with myself, actually. Then that bastard Evans jumped out at me as I was passing the allotments.'

Bill's voice had been rising in volume as he spoke, and Malcolm frowned a warning.

'Don't worry,' Bill said. 'Pa's upstairs pretending he's Louis Armstrong and my mother's out doing good somewhere.'

'What did Evans say?'

'It's finally penetrated his thick skull that I'm the baby's father. So he slung a few insults at me and tried to beat me up.'

Malcolm was tempted to say that it looked like Evans had succeeded.

'I gave as good as I got,' Bill continued. 'But he took me by surprise at the beginning.' He touched his face gingerly. 'I thought he'd broken my nose. He was completely out of control. The best thing to do was just get out of his way.'

Malcolm thought about the narrow towpath between the allotments and the river. 'And how did you do that?'

'I dived into the river and swam off.' Bill shrugged, miming nonchalance. 'Quite refreshing, really. First swim of the year.'

'The man's a menace,' Malcolm snapped. 'Have you been to the police?'

'Well, no. It would look bad, wouldn't it? And the whole business would have to come out.' His eyes flickered as though a light had briefly dazzled them. 'Wouldn't be fair on Violet.'

'Perhaps you're right. The police might start asking why you were down there in the first place. What about your parents?'

'I told them I walked into a door.'

'And they *believed* you?'

'They'd believe anything I'd say.' Bill's voice was bitter. 'You know what they're like.'

Malcolm did. He had sometimes wished he had parents like Bill's, the sort that left you alone, who didn't try and wrap you in cotton wool; who didn't really mind what you did as long as you didn't complicate their lives or make them lose face with their friends. Mr Pembridge was always working, apart from his evenings with his little band. Mrs Pembridge had her committees. All of which left Bill as free as a bird.

'Be gentle with Violet. At breakfast, Dad said he's decided to give her the sack. He's going to write to her this morning.'

'Poor kid,' Bill said automatically. 'Still, she'll manage – she's a good secretary. They get paid a mint these days.'

The trumpet playing stopped.

'He'll be coming down for his elevenses,' Bill said. 'Regular as his bloody bowels.'

'Let's go.'

'Where?'

'Anywhere.'

Five minutes later, they were in the MG, driving out of town in the direction of Eastbury with the rain thrumming on the hood and the water on the windscreen lending shiny distortions to the world on the other side, discreetly unsettling like an unexpected glimpse into the freak show tent at a circus.

'The police want a statement from you,' Malcolm said.

'You've been? I thought you were going to wait till this afternoon.'

'I was. But then it seemed better to get it over with.'

'What happened?'

'I saw an inspector called Thornhill. Plain clothes.'

'He didn't –?'

'It all went very well. Why shouldn't it? The police need all the help they can get from members of the public.' Malcolm darted a glance at Bill. 'Perhaps you should wait till tomorrow before going to see them. They might not believe that business about the door.'

Bill's knuckles whitened on the steering wheel. 'Actually, I made it sound rather better than it was. I thought – I thought he was going to kill me. He's the sort of man who might.'

'He's a menace.' Malcolm flexed his fingers. 'He should be locked up where he can't do any more damage.'

Chapter Twenty-six

It was WPC Ailsmore whose eyes caught the glint of gold near the water's edge.

'There, Sarge,' Joan said, pointing downwards, her face flushing and looking remarkably pretty in her excitement. 'Just there.'

She and Kirby were in the meadow beyond the beer garden of the Ferryman's Inn. The path along the bank was a faint, muddy ghost. Few people had reason to venture beyond the allotments, the cricket ground and the pub. The rain was back, drizzling steadily out of a dark sky. Joan was dressed for it in raincoat, headscarf and wellingtons. But Kirby had left his mackintosh at his lodgings, and was getting steadily wetter.

At this point the bank shelved. The soft ground was scarred with generations of hoof prints. When there were cattle in the field, they came here to drink. The place was a SOCO's nightmare. Their chances of finding traces of Mattie Harris in that pock-marked morass were so small as to be barely worth mentioning.

The slim gold powder compact was in an indentation made by a hoof. They couldn't have seen it from the path, which skirted the rim of the cows' drinking place. You had to be down by the water's edge. Joan bent forward, hand outstretched.

'Don't touch it,' Kirby snapped.

He edged forward, shook out his handkerchief and crouched. He picked up the compact, using the handkerchief to protect the surface, and dropped it in a brown envelope.

'What do you think?'

'There's a gold compact listed among the possessions we think she had in the handbag,' Kirby said. 'We're going to have to search this whole bloody meadow. The bag's blue plastic and on the large side.'

'So it shouldn't be that hard to find.'

'If it's here.'

They spent the next quarter of an hour picking their way up and down the meadow, heads bent, searching for anything that might relate to Mattie Harris. They found cigarette ends, a decaying condom, and an empty beer bottle in the angle at the corner of the field where two hedges met under the shelter of an English Maple. No surprises there. In the summertime, courting couples slipped out of the pub and into the meadow. Kirby had brought a girl here himself. The wind carried the sound of St. John's clock striking half-past eleven.

He shook himself like a wet spaniel, shaking away memories as well as rain. 'Let's see if Belper is back.'

They left the meadow and walked up through the beer garden to the Ferryman's Inn. They had parked the CID's Hillman in the yard at the side. In the interval, it had been joined by a pre-war Morris van, painted beige and streaked with rust. A door banged. A balding, middle-aged man came out of the pub. His stomach pushed down the waistband of his trousers and thrust against the buttons of his shirt.

'We're not open till twelve. And apart from patrons' cars, the yard's private property.'

'Mr Belper?' Kirby produced his warrant card. 'Detective Sergeant Kirby. This is my colleague WPC Ailsmore. We'd like to ask you a few questions.'

The man's face remained surly but now there was an element

of wariness too. He rubbed his close-cropped beard. 'What about?'

'Let's go inside, shall we?' Kirby suggested. 'I'm getting tired of standing in the rain.'

Belper shrugged. Without a word, he led the way back into the house. 'Wipe your feet. The wife washed the floor this morning.'

They sat in the public bar. The pumps were still covered, but otherwise it was ready for opening time. Mrs Belper, a shrivelled woman who looked a good ten years older than her husband, peeped into the bar, saw the visitors and scuttled away into the back of the building.

'I won't keep you long, sir,' Kirby said, thinking longingly of a nice glass of whisky to keep out the damp. 'We're just making some inquiries about a girl who may have been in here on Thursday night.'

'Thursday? We were packed. There was a coachload down from Birmingham, some angling club. We had half the cricket club in as well. Someone's birthday plus the regulars. And it was a fine evening so we had quite a few people who just thought it would be nice to wander along for a drink.'

It was a full answer, too full? Or was it just that Belper had decided he might as well co-operate because their visit had nothing to do with the Ferryman itself. He was said to be a surly bastard. Most publicans cultivated a friendly relationship with the police but he had never bothered. He was as surly with police officers as with anyone else. On the other hand he kept within the letter of the law and had his own ways of dealing with troublesome customers.

'Did you know Mattie Harris?'

Belper shook his head. 'That girl they found drowned down by New Bridge?'

'That's it.'

'That was on Friday.'

'There's a chance she'd been in the water since Thursday.'

'Never seen her, not to my knowledge. That doesn't mean she hasn't been here. Half my customers I don't know from Adam. Especially in the summer.'

'But you knew her name.'

'Course I do. Everyone in Lydmouth knows her name by now.'

Kirby nodded, conceding the point. 'She was a small girl, with a lot of red hair. People noticed her. She laughed a lot.'

'Well I didn't notice her. Most of my customers laugh too much.' Belper pulled out a tobacco pouch and began to roll a cigarette. 'Mind you, she could have been here but not in the pub. The garden was packed on Thursday. And if someone else came in to buy the drinks, there's no reason why we should have seen her.'

'Do you know if anyone went into the meadow on Thursday evening?'

'How should I know? I was stuck behind the bar.'

Kirby tried to establish whether Belper could identify anyone who had been in the beer garden on Thursday evening. But Belper claimed not to have been into the garden. They had been short staffed that evening, and he thought that neither his wife nor the barmaid had been out there either, except for a couple of forays to collect glasses. Kirby asked him to talk to his wife and the barmaid and between them make a list of any customers they knew by name who had been at the Ferryman on Thursday evening. He glanced at his watch. There was nothing else to learn here. It was time to get back to the station with the compact.

On the way out, though, he stopped in the passage beside the door to the yard. 'Do you happen to know Malcolm Sedbury, Mr Belper? Or Bill Pembridge?'

'Young Pembridge? Yes, he's in the club eleven. Couldn't play on Saturday, which is probably the reason we lost to Ashbridge. No sense of responsibility, that's the trouble with that generation.'

'Was he here on Thursday evening?'

Belper scratched his beard, raking his fingernails through the coarse, greasy hair. 'Yes, I think he was. Like I said, there were other people from the cricket club there as well. But I'm pretty sure he came in a bit later. After the rest of them. Must have been out in the garden, because I didn't see him after he bought a couple of drinks and a packet of cigarettes.'

All in all, Kirby thought as they drove back to police headquarters, not a bad morning's work, even if a wet one. If the compact turned out to be Mattie's, young Sedbury's sighting was corroborated. They had a time and place where she had last been seen.

Say the evening had ended in sex with A N Other in that meadow. Mattie would have got dressed in the darkness. Ten to one she'd been drunk. She could have fallen in the river and been too drunk to save herself. Not far down to New Bridge from the Ferryman, and the current coming in from the Minnow on the western bank would have swept her across to the eastern bank of the Lyd, under the willows where she'd been found.

Alternatively –

'Did she fall or was she pushed?' Joan said, her mind running in parallel with his, a coincidence he wasn't sure he liked. 'That's the question, Sarge, isn't it?'

They parked the car behind the headquarters building. Kirby fished the envelope out of his pocket.

'Can I have a look at it?' Joan said, 'If I was careful.'

'I don't see why not.' It was a small car, and Kirby liked being close to Joan. Looking at the powder compact together would bring them even closer. 'But don't touch it. Let me do that.'

He upturned the envelope over the palm of his hand and slid out the compact, still swathed in his handkerchief. He carefully unwrapped it.

'It is gold,' Joan said, a trace of envy in her voice. 'Can you open it?'

She was very close to him now. Kirby held himself rigidly, knowing that if he moved an inch towards her, their arms would come in contact. He liked the perfume she was wearing. Mainly to prolong the moment, he gently pushed the catch on the side of the compact.

The powder was dry but the glass inside the lid had cracked. Joan touched his arm and leant even closer. His skin tingled. Her nose six inches away from the compact, she sniffed.

'Fleur de Rose, I think,' she said. 'She had a jar of the stuff in her room.'

'Not cheap?'

'Costs a fortune. She must have been getting money from somewhere.'

Kirby closed the compact, folded the handkerchief around it and slid it back into the envelope. 'We'd better find the Guv'nor. That's assuming he's not sneaked off somewhere.'

They went upstairs. Thornhill was in his office, listening to someone speaking to him on the telephone. He waved Kirby and Joan inside and pointed to chairs.

'All right,' he said to whoever was on the other end of the line. 'Not much we can do about that now. It all depends on the Chief Constable, obviously . . . Thanks, bye.' He put down the phone and looked across the desk. 'Well?'

'We found a powder compact that might be Mattie Harris's in the field beside the Ferryman. It was on the riverbank, down by the water. No other traces of her in the field, not as far as we could see, but the landlord confirms young Pembridge was at the pub on Thursday evening.'

'Could she have fallen in by accident?'

'It's possible. She couldn't swim, and say she was drunk and alone in the dark—'

'It's not possible,' Thornhill said flatly. 'That was the lab on the phone.'

'So didn't she drown?'

'Oh yes. She drowned all right. And just before she died, she drank a hell of a lot of gin. Hard to be sure but it could have been as much as half a bottle or more. There's another thing –

she was three months pregnant when she died.'

'So that's another possible motive. Maybe for suicide?'

Thornhill shook his head. 'There was bruising on her shoulders, too. Almost certainly inflicted at the time of death by someone standing behind her.'

Joan opened her mouth but wisely held her peace. This wasn't the sort of situation where a humble WPC could make a useful contribution.

Kirby said hesitantly, 'So we're looking at the possibility of murder, sir? Someone held her in the river, kept her head submerged until she drowned?'

'Not in the river, Brian. That's the other complication. It's not river water in her airways. It's tap water. With a high concentration of bath salts.'

Chapter Twenty-seven

The Sunday passed by, with more or less of conversation respecting the murder; and so also the Monday morning.

Jill was on page three hundred ans sixty-three of *The Vicar of Bullhampton*. Only another one hundred and fifty to go. While she read, the old worry circled her mind like a bomber searching for the most effective place to drop its load.

The Trollope novel had less to do with clerical life than the title might suggest. Someone had murdered one of the farmers who lived in the village, and one of the chief suspects was the reckless son of the local miller. To make matters worse, the miller had a beautiful daughter, a fallen woman who had been cohabiting with another suspect. It seemed that almost everyone was willing to believe the worst of the brother and sister, for reasons which had little to do with the weight of evidence. In Trollope's world, women who had sex outside marriage were doubly victimised. Men took their pleasure from them, and then left scot-free, leaving the women to pay the price. Meanwhile society condoned what the men did while treating the women as pariahs.

Had things changed that much in eighty years? Had things been any different for Mattie Harris? Were they any different for Jill Francis? If your emotions and actions failed to fit into the current social framework, where did that leave you?

It left you out in the cold, that's where.

She heard the sound of Richard's car through the open window. She hadn't been expecting him. Edith and the children were coming home this evening. There was time to check her make-up and her hair in the mirror over the fireplace. But was there time to decide what she was going to say, or do?

He ran along the path in the rain, stood dripping in the porch and shrugged off his raincoat. He came through to the little living room and looked at her. She was standing with one arm resting on the back of the sofa, her fingers worrying the rough fabric. She didn't know what to say to him so she waited for him to speak first.

'I'm sorry,' he said, taking her by surprise. 'I shouldn't have dragged you into this.'

'Don't worry. I'm catching up on my reading.'

'I don't mean this weekend. Or not just that.'

She stared miserably at him and saw an answering misery in his face.

'So do you think we should stop?' Jill said.

'That would be the sensible thing.' He swallowed. 'Soon after we met – do you remember? – I thought I could drown in your eyes. Now I feel, the more I know you, the more I am drowning.' His mouth twisted. 'And all I want is to go on drowning.'

There were three feet between them, and it felt as though he were on the other side of the world. Jill thought of the miller's daughter.

'Richard, I've missed my period.'

Something flared in his eyes. 'You might be pregnant?'

'It's possible. That first time – at Church Cottage.' She looked at the carpet. 'Just after the kittens had been born.'

'Dear God.'

'I can't go through an abortion. Not again. I won't.'

He knew about that unhappy episode in her life, before she came to Lydmouth. He knew that in a sense it had been the reason why she'd come to Lydmouth in the first place.

'No. I understand that.' He sat down abruptly, as if his legs no longer wanted to bear his weight. 'I'll do whatever I can.'

'I have to leave Lydmouth.'

'Of course. And so will I.'

'Don't be silly. You can't leave Edith and the children. You can't leave your job.' Part of her was delighted that he should apparently be considering it, and part of her was horrified, for her sake as much as his. 'I just won't let you.'

'Darling,' Thornhill said slowly, as though trying out a word from a foreign language. 'I don't want to be apart from you. And if you're pregnant, it's my responsibility as much as yours.'

'Later. We'll talk about it later.' She crouched beside him, took his hands, which were cold. 'Anyway, why are you here? You should be working.'

'I have to see the Harrises again.' His fingers gripped hers. 'Mattie was pregnant when she died. There's bath water in her airways, not river water. And there's bruising on her shoulders.'

'Oh God. So it's looking like murder?'

'Just a possibility that the bruising was inflicted before death. So the drowning itself might have been accidental. She was very drunk. Drunk enough to have passed out.'

'In that case,' Jill said in a bright, hard voice, while her mind filled with unwanted memories, 'it's pretty obvious what she was doing.'

'How do you mean?'

'She was getting absolutely plastered and having a very hot bath. She was trying to induce an abortion, Richard. I tried it myself like that, once, and it didn't bloody work.'

Chapter Twenty-eight

By six o'clock, there was little more Thornhill could do. He knew he should phone Williamson but there was no hurry about that. Edith and the children were due to reach Lydmouth at six thirty-nine. Trains were often delayed on bank holidays so he wasn't going to meet them at the station. They were going to take a taxi. If he left headquarters now, that would give him about half an hour at home before they arrived. There was nothing to keep him here.

He had talked on the telephone with the Chief Constable, who was in a bad mood because the rain had ruined his afternoon of golf. On his way back from seeing Jill at Walnut Tree Cottage, he had been to see Mattie Harris's parents, which had served no purpose at all except to upset them still further. Mr Harris could not believe that anyone might have wanted to harm their daughter. Thornhill had not had the heart to tell him that she had been both drunk and pregnant at the time of her death.

Meanwhile, Brian Kirby had been co-ordinating a search of the Ferryman's beer garden and the field beside it. When the pub opened for the evening, a team of officers would question the customers. Thornhill needed to talk to Violet Evans, but had decided to leave that until the morning. He wanted to take Joan Ailsmore with him, and she was at present tied up at the

Ferryman's Inn. Jimmy Leigh could wait as well.

The fingerprint department had examined the compact. There were two of Mattie's smudged prints inside, but they found no prints whatsoever on the outside of the compact.

'Clean as a whistle, sir,' the sergeant in charge of the department had said. 'Makes you think, eh?'

'Could it have happened naturally?' Thornhill had asked. 'Washed off in the rain? Rubbing on something in a handbag?'

The old sergeant had shaken his head. 'You'd expect to find something. No, it's like someone polished the outside of the case.'

Thornhill drove back to Victoria Road. The car smelt like a hearse because of the roses, which were now beginning to wilt. It suddenly occurred to him that Jill might have noticed them on the back seat of the car either today or yesterday. At first she might have thought they were for her but then guessed they were for Edith. He banged the steering wheel as he turned into Chepstow Road. How could he have been so foolish? He could so easily have explained that they were a present to Edith from Bernie Broadbent.

My new landlord.

He banged the steering wheel again. No relief there – just a sense of his own foolishness to add to the frustration he felt, plus a painful hand.

The house smelt stale and looked grubby. He had a vague idea that Edith usually aired the place once a day so he went from room to room, downstairs and upstairs, and opened the windows. In some ways, this was not a good idea because it gave him an opportunity to see what a mess everything was in. Edith had been away for three nights, and already everything was falling apart. He made a sketchy attempt to pull the coverlet over the bed and straighten the eiderdown. In the bathroom, he put the cap on the toothpaste and stacked his shaving things neatly in the glass dish Edith had provided for the purpose.

Downstairs was more difficult. The sitting room was at least tidy because he hadn't been in there, though it seemed to have acquired a thick layer of dust since Edith left. He could safely ignore the room they called the dining room because that was only partly furnished and needed decorating. By tacit consent it did not require quite the same standard of cleanliness and tidiness as the rest of the house. But the stepladder, the new brushes, the rolls of wallpaper and the tins of paint told a silent tale of another failure.

The real problems, however, lurked in the kitchen and the scullery. There was a pile of dirty crockery in the sink and the top of the cooker needed cleaning. Making a cooked breakfast had been a mistake. The history of what he had eaten and drunk in the house was plain to see on the kitchen table. There was also a bottle of whisky, a shameful indulgence, which Thornhill immediately put away in the dresser. He found the postcard from Edith on the table under the newspaper, and put it in the place of honour on the mantelpiece. It was then that he discovered the boiler was out. So there would be no hot water for at least an hour and a half, possibly longer.

Still on his best domestic behaviour, he changed out of his suit into a collarless shirt and an elderly pair of corduroy trousers. Kneeling before the boiler, he started to riddle the grate. The doorbell rang. He swore, dropped the poker on the hearth and went to answer the door. A moment later, he found himself staring into the red face and chilly blue eyes of Detective Superintendent Ray Williamson.

'Didn't expect to find you relaxing at home,' Williamson said.

'There was nothing I could usefully do today, sir. And I am technically on leave.'

Williamson grunted. 'Aren't you going to ask me in?'

'Of course, sir. This way.'

Thornhill showed him into the dusty sitting room and settled him in an armchair beside the empty fireplace. As far as he could remember, Williamson had never been inside the house before. The Superintendent was not a man who believed in socialising with inferiors.

'I was expecting you to phone me today, Thornhill.'

'I was intending to this evening, sir. I was waiting to hear from Sergeant Kirby first.'

'What's he up to?'

'Conducting a search of the area around the Ferryman's Inn, and talking to the customers.'

'Are you sure you can justify the time you're spending on this? I've heard nothing that convinces me this isn't an accident. Silly little girl has a bit to drink, falls in the river, all very sad – but not really anything to do with CID.'

'But a number of features about the case aren't straightforward. In fact some of them are downright suspicious.'

Williamson waved a hand. 'Young Pembridge and his friend Sedbury seeing Mattie Harris fighting with a man on the banks of the river. It's all over town.'

Which meant that as usual someone at police headquarters had been talking out of turn.

'Malcolm Sedbury told me he saw no sign of a quarrel.'

'There you are,' Williamson went on. 'Just the sort of hysterical rumour you tend to get in these cases. People try and make things complicated. They don't want there to be a simple explanation. They want something more sensational.' He scratched his thigh. 'Anyway, Pembridge and Sedbury were probably half cut at the time.'

'There are other features, sir. I talked to Mr Hendry this afternoon, and he feels we've got no choice now but to treat this as a possible murder investigation.'

There was a long silence. Williamson's face seemed to lose some of its colour. He listened in silence while Thornhill listed the pieces of evidence. The unexpected affluence of Mattie Harris; the conflicting lies she'd told her parents and her employer; the discovery of her powder compact near the Ferryman's Inn, wiped clean of prints; the fact she had dressed, or possibly been dressed, so carelessly; the pathologist's findings, particularly the bruising, the pregnancy, and the bath water in the airways; and then there was the strange intimacy with Jimmy Leigh, and the man-boy's claim that he'd seen Mattie turning into Bernie Broadbent's drive the previous weekend.

'Poppycock,' said Williamson, at last. 'You can't rely on what someone like that says. A pound to a penny he made it up — trying to make himself interesting. I wouldn't go around repeating that if I were you.'

'But, sir—'

'But as to the other evidence, I see your point.' Williamson's tone had become almost conciliatory. 'At first sight, there do seem to be some unanswered questions. When's the inquest?'

'Tomorrow sir. We'll ask for an adjournment, of course.'

'Even so,' Williamson went on, his voice slow and dreamy, 'I shouldn't be surprised if it was an accident in the end in some form or another. Some girls ask for trouble, you know. We may never know the long and the short of it.' His eyes met Thornhill's for an instant. 'And perhaps it's better that way.'

You poor old man, in a few short weeks you'll finally be a back number. And already there's no reason why anyone should take much notice of you.

But even as he thought this, Thornhill was trying to interpret the expression on Williamson's face. It looked almost as if Williamson felt sorry for him, which made no sense at all.

The Superintendent stood up. 'A nod's as good as a wink, Thornhill, that's what I always say. Keep me posted. I expect a phone call tomorrow, all right?'

Williamson went into the hall and saw the bunch of roses, now looking even more in need of water than before on the hall table. 'They're early, aren't they? I'd get them in water if I were you.'

The front door banged, and Thornhill was alone again. He carried the roses into the kitchen, filled a vase with water and stuffed the stems into it, pricking his finger on a thorn. You probably had to do things to roses before you put them in water

– snip leaves off, or do something to the ends – but there wasn't time for refinements like that. He picked up the poker again and jabbed it into the grate, wishing he knew what Williamson had been getting at.

He had just lit the boiler when he heard Edith's key in the door. He went into the hall and the children flung their hard little bodies at him. He felt a surge of love. Three days had changed them, and him. They looked slightly larger than he remembered, and somehow more vivid.

'Daddy,' Elizabeth said, 'Daddy, I rode on a donkey called George. Couldn't we have a donkey?'

'I've got a new penknife, Dad.' David pulled away and tugged his father's arm. 'It's got five things in it. Do you want to see it?'

Edith herself came into the house, putting away her purse, followed by the taxi driver with their suitcases. The children rushed upstairs. Edith hugged Thornhill with an enthusiasm that took him by surprise. She seemed unsettlingly tall, her body oddly substantial, imbued with a strange familiarity like a smell associated with childhood and rarely encountered since then.

'I've missed you,' she murmured. She stood back and looked at him, taking in the shirtsleeves and corduroys. 'You're filthy. What have you been doing?'

'The boiler went out. I've been trying to get it alight.'

'You poor thing.' She linked her arm through his and drew him into the kitchen. Her eyes immediately fell on the vase of roses on the table. 'Oh they're lovely! You are kind.'

For an instant he wished it were possible to lie. 'Not from me, I'm afraid. From Uncle Bernie – first of the year, apparently.'

She lifted the vase and smelt them. He could never understand her taste for flowers, why they gave her such satisfaction. There was something sensual in her pleasure, a sensuality expressed in a language he couldn't understand. He felt aggrieved.

'And how's the decorating?'

For an instant he stared blankly at her. He had been so taken up with the events of the weekend, with Jill on the one hand and the Harris case on the other, that he'd forgotten that Edith knew nothing about the investigation. He explained what had happened, watching the happiness seep away from her face. Meanwhile the children thundered around over their heads, rediscovering their bedrooms and their possessions.

'And that's why the house is in such a mess, I'm afraid,' he concluded, knowing that he was only telling part of the truth, for it probably would have been in a mess in any case. Taken unawares by his own sincerity, he added, 'It's been very strange without you and the children here.'

'We're here now.' Edith was perceptibly rising to the challenge, and clearly enjoying doing so. 'We'll soon have things back to normal. Now I'd better see what's in the larder. I bet you haven't even managed to heat up the stew I left.'

'I forgot all about it.'

'It should be all right still. We can have that this evening. Come and put the kettle on while I see what else we've got.'

She was smiling, serene in her control of the house, in her control of him. For the moment, he was content to play along with it. Not just content – he wanted to.

'There's some news,' he said. 'Bernie came round and—'

The phone began to ring in the dining room. Edith's smile faltered.

'I'll answer it.' Thornhill went into the next room and picked up the phone, which was standing on the bookcase beside an unopened tin of paint.

'Sir?' Brian Kirby's voice. 'We've had a bit of a problem. Thought I'd better let you know.'

'What's happened?'

'Somehow the news got out that Jimmy Leigh knew Mattie Harris. And people have been saying he was seen quarrelling with her near the Ferryman on Thursday evening.'

The quirky logic of rumour led swiftly to the next step. 'So they're saying Jimmy killed her?'

'Yes, sir. But it's worse than that. A bunch of lads got tanked up in the King's Head at lunchtime. Two of them used to know Mattie when she worked at the slaughterhouse at the end of Mincing Lane. They got a bit heated. Then some bright spark decided they'd take the law into their own hands.'

Chapter Twenty-nine

When the postman called on Tuesday morning, Violet Evans was eating her second breakfast, unless you counted the slices of toast she had when she first woke up, in which case it would be her third. Her father, just back from his ritual trip to the outside lavatory, was putting on his bicycle clips in the hall while her mother packed his sandwiches into the khaki bag he took to work.

There was only one letter. Ted stooped, picked it up from the mat and brought it to Violet, who was watching him through the open door of the kitchen. Without a word, he laid it beside her plate. It was a good quality white envelope, with her name and address typed unevenly with one spelling mistake and two crossings out. Violet knew both the stationery and the typeface very well.

She put down her spoon and opened the envelope. Robert Sedbury regretted that he found it necessary to terminate her employment with Sedbury & Son. He would send what was owed to her by separate enclosure. Sedbury & Son would be willing to provide her with references, should she require them, but it was only fair to say that while her standard of work had on the whole been excellent her sudden, unexplained departure from the job was not something they could reasonably be expected to conceal from a possible future employer. Mr Sedbury was hers sincerely.

Violet handed the letter to her father, knowing that there was nothing to be gained from waiting. She watched him reading it slowly and deliberately. It was old Sedbury's decision, she guessed, no one else's. Malcolm would have helped her if he could. Mr Brown might have come round in time to the idea of an unmarried mother working at Sedbury's. But not Mr Sedbury himself. He could be as soft as butter sometimes – you had only to look at him with Malcolm – but he was a man who judged others as harshly as he judged himself. The silly old fusspot thought the good name of Sedbury & Son was roughly as sacred as the Royal Family's.

Her father dropped the letter. Before it hit the table it caught a current of air and zigzagged down to the floor.

'You stupid girl,' he said softly. 'We were depending on you. I'm going to have to see Mr George, Mother, there's no alternative.'

'What do you mean?' June said.

'I mean we can't afford this house. Can't afford the mortgage. Not without Violet's wage. Simple as that.'

'Surely Mr George will understand?'

'He's a businessman. He's not a bloody philanthropist. The best we can hope for is that he'll agree to buy the house back off us, and give us enough to pay off the mortgage. Otherwise we have to put it on the open market and let someone like Sedbury's take a commission. That's if the building society doesn't fore-close before it's sold.'

'But where are we going to live?'

'God knows.' Ted Evans snatched his bag from his wife's hands and stalked down the hall to the front door. 'And as for you my girl, you know what your gran used to say about girls who got themselves in the family way? Better dead than unwed. Maybe she wasn't so far wrong.'

He let himself out of the house, and Violet noticed that even in his anger he closed the door gently. He was a man who respected the inanimate materials he worked with.

Grace, in her pram outside the open back door, began to cry. Violet blundered towards the sound, the need to nurse her daughter temporarily outweighing her fear and her shock. But her mother had got there first. She picked up Grace, rocking her to and fro into silence.

'Just a bit of wind, I daresay,' June said.

'I'll take her, if you want.'

'You'd better let me do it, Vi. Been thinking.'

'What do you mean?'

'I've never seen your dad like that. You were always his favourite, but now . . . He's not a man to change his mind, my love, you know that.'

Violet sat down heavily on one of the kitchen chairs and rested her hands palms down on the table. 'I don't understand what you're saying. I don't understand anything.'

'I hate to say this, but you'd be better off out of here.' June sat down at the table, Grace cradled in her arm, and stroked one of Violet's hands as though it were a cat. 'He's not going to forgive and forget. I don't know what we're going to do if we have to sell this house. Go back into lodgings, I suppose, and there won't be much money around if we lose the deposit we put down. He seems to think we will. And it's not as if you'd be able to help with the money. It's not going to be easy for you to find a proper job round here.'

'You're sending me away?'

'It could be best for all concerned, my love. Just for a year or two. We'd stay in touch, of course, I'd come and see you. You could go to Cardiff, or somewhere. Not far for me to come on the train, eh? Get yourself a job as a secretary. You've got the skills, we all know that, and perhaps you'd find an employer who'd understand when you told him about why you had to leave Sedbury's.'

'But what about Grace? I can't take her to work with me. And I won't know anyone in Cardiff. There'd be no one to leave her with.'

'Best thing to do is to leave her with me.' June sat back and swayed to and fro, Grace clamped to her shoulder. 'Maybe we should let Baby think I'm her mother. My love, I do know how cruel this must sound, but this way would be better for everyone in the long run. Especially for Grace.'

Violet gave a little gasp. She stood up. If Mattie were here, she thought, it would all be different. Mattie would know what to do.

June didn't move. There were tears in her eyes. Grace was asleep, dribbling on her grandmother's pinafore. Violet held on to the edge of the table, swaying as though she were drunk. She opened her mouth but found no words to say. She blundered out of the kitchen and up to the room she shared with Grace.

Downstairs, everything was silent. Violet imagined her mother rocking Grace to and fro, to and fro. I'm useless, she told her reflection in the mirror, fat and useless, nobody wants me, nobody needs me. Even Grace will do better with Mum. Mum knows what to do with babies.

Routine broke in. Staring at the mirror was what she always did after breakfast. Automatically her hand reached for the cold cream. She followed the process stage by stage. Like a familiar prayer, one part led to another. Like a prayer, too, it gave her something to think about. She found herself applying the make-up with more than usual care — with the attention to detail she would have used if she were going out to work at Sedbury's in a few minutes' time. But not quite like that, either, because Mr Sedbury thought girls who wore make-up were common so you had to be careful what you used. But there was no longer any need to worry about Mr Sedbury's disapproval. She brushed a darker eye shadow above her eyes and coated her long lashes with mascara. She decided on a touch of rouge on the cheeks and a bright red lipstick which Mattie had given her for her birthday.

Her face changed in front of her. So did her mood. When she dressed, she chose a light, summery frock that Bill had liked, or said he did, and a pair of green suede shoes with peep toes, open sides and high heels. It took another five minutes to find the most suitable hat, handbag and pair of gloves.

She went downstairs. Grace was asleep in her pram again. Her mother was washing up.

'Where are you going to like that?' June asked, half curious, half worried.

'I'm going out.'

June opened her mouth to say something, changed her mind and said something else: 'You'll take a mac, won't you, or at least a brolly. It may be sunny now but there's more rain forecast.'

Violet shrugged. 'I'll see you later.'

Her mother might want to pretend everything was normal but there was no reason why she should, not now. 'Violet –' she heard her mother beginning as she closed the front door, as gently as her father had down. He wouldn't be able to hold that against her, at least. She walked out of the crescent and down Broadwell Drive to Chepstow Road. It must be her lucky day – there was a bus approaching the stop. A few minutes later she was at the bus station in the centre of town and found a number seven waiting for her.

It was still her lucky day. The bus followed the road that ran roughly parallel to the Lyd, the road that passed through Eastbury. She talked to no one on the way. No one sat down next to her, either, probably, she thought, because there wasn't enough room. Who cared? She stared out of the window looking at the swollen river tumbling down towards the sea. She didn't want to talk to anyone, anyway, and they wouldn't want to talk to her. They weren't interested in her problems, and why should they be? The only person Violet wanted to talk to was Mattie Harris, and she was dead.

Violet left the bus at the stop opposite the one shop in the village. She walked back up the road to Lower Slade Cottage, slowly because of the unfamiliar high heels. The shoes pinched. She had known Mattie's parents for most of her life. They were much older than hers, more like grandparents than parents.

'Funny, isn't it?' Mattie had said to Violet once. 'They spent all those years trying to have a family, and it wasn't until they gave up hoping that I came along. That's why they fuss so much.'

Mattie had told her that her parents were showing their age now, that her mother in particular was beginning to lose her marbles, but the reality that faced her in that low, hot kitchen came as a shock to Violet. It was a place of restless, useless movement: Mrs Harris sitting by the fire moaning softly as she rocked herself to and fro; Mr Harris, shuffling about the room, eternally busy, trying to make better what must always grow worse.

'Who is it?' Mrs Harris asked.

'It's Violet, Mother. Violet Evans. Mattie's friend. Sit down, Vi. Would you like some tea? Or a biscuit? Mother likes a biscuit, too, don't you?'

'Not for me, thank you.' Violet smiled and settled herself in the chair that Mr Harris had pulled out for her. 'I'm sorry about Mattie.'

'Yes. I don't think Mother has quite taken it in yet. But she knows something's wrong.' He shambled across the room to pat his wife's hand.

'Who's she?' Mrs Harris demanded, beginning to tremble.

'It's all right, dear, it's only Vi. You remember? Mattie's friend Violet? They used to live next door to us in Mincing Lane.'

'Should I go?' Violet whispered.

'No, no. It's all right. Nice for Mother to have a bit of company.' He let go of his wife's hand and bent nearer to Violet. 'That policeman came round, the inspector. He's been twice now. Full of questions.' The old man's voice rose, becoming petulant. 'I won't have them bothering Mother. It's not fair.'

No, Violet thought, it wasn't fair. Nothing was fair.

'But who would want to hurt Mattie?' Mr Harris had cut himself while shaving that morning, and the smear of caked blood was a dark purple sickle moon on his chalk-white face. 'She hadn't an enemy in the world. You know Mattie — everyone likes her.'

'Hurt her? But—'

'My little girl. Hurt? killed, maybe.'

'She was my best friend,' Violet said suddenly. 'I'll never have a friend like her.'

Mattie murdered?

She began to cry, without shame. She cried for all of them – for Mattie, Mattie's parents and herself. The running mascara stung her eyes and blurred her vision. The Harrises wavered like ghosts. How could you replace someone like Mattie? Mattie always knew what to do. Mattie would have known what to do about Grace. Mattie would have known what to do about Bill. When Mattie died, parts of other people died with her, and parts of their futures too.

'There, there,' Mr Harris said, patting her head with one hand and holding out a greasy tea towel with the other. 'Give your nose a good blow, that's what I always tell Mother when she's having a cry. It'll make you feel better.'

As she took the tea towel, Violet looked up at Mr Harris's face. There were tears in his eyes, too.

'Killed? Are you sure? Is that what the police said?'

'No.' Mr Harris stared at her face, as though looking for the answer there. 'Not quite. Just that their enquiries are going on and perhaps it wasn't an accident. But the way the inspector was talking, the things he was asking, what else could it be? Someone killed her, someone killed our Mattie.'

'If you knew who, would it help? Or if you knew why?'

The old man shrugged. 'How could it help? The only thing that could help would be if Mattie came back.'

'When's Mattie coming home?' Mrs Harris suddenly demanded behind them. 'Will we go when Mattie comes back? And who's that girl you've got there?'

Mr Harris turned away to soothe her. Violet put the tea towel on the table and found a handkerchief in her handbag. She blew her nose and wiped her eyes, half-listening to the soothing murmur of Mr Harris's voice.

Mattie murdered?

'When did you say Mattie was coming to take us away?' Mrs Harris asked.

'Soon,' Mr Harris replied. 'Quite soon, I expect.'

With half an ear tuned to the Harrises' questions and answers, Violet glanced at the litter of objects on the table beside her. It looked as if Mr Harris had been trying to do at least six things at once – writing a letter to a funeral director, making a shopping list, doing the accounts, peeling two potatoes, setting a mousetrap and sewing a button on a large, off-white garment which might have been one of Mrs Harris's nightdresses. For an instant, Violet's despair spilled over from herself and onto the Harrises. *Mattie murdered?* She picked up the knife and the partly peeled potato and removed the rest of the skin with the attention of detail she used to devote to a piece of embroidery. She had just finished the second potato when Mr Harris returned to the table.

'Tea,' he said, frowning. 'Wasn't I making you some tea?'

'Not for me, thank you. I'm not thirsty.'

He passed a hand over his forehead. 'There was something I was doing, wasn't there?' His eyes fell on the potatoes and he frowned. Then his face lightened. 'You shouldn't have, Violet. Really, Mother and me can manage.'

'I know you can. What are you doing about shopping?'

'Mrs Williams next door. No, we're fine. Doctor wanted to put Mother in a home, but I wouldn't let him. She's happier with me. They wouldn't know what she likes.'

'No, they wouldn't. Is there something I could do to help while I'm here?'

His eyes watered. 'You're a good girl. Mattie always said you were a good girl and she was right.' He shook his head. He looked round the room. 'But there's nothing. Nothing except the library books.'

'You'd like me to change them?'

'No – just take them back. They were our Mattie's, look, and they're due back tomorrow. The fines soon mount up if you're late.'

Violet bit her lip. 'Yes, they do.'

'And there are three of them, so in no time at all it'd come to a tidy sum. Mrs Williams would take them but she doesn't get into Lydmouth very often. Not unless her daughter takes her.'

'That's fine. I'd *like* to take them back.'

Mr Harris took three novels from the dresser and passed them to Violet, who squeezed them into her handbag.

'Mattie liked a good book. Proper little scholar, she was.'

The books were called *The Song Of the Heart*, *Love's Wild Dreamer* and *My Kingdom For a Kiss*.

Violet had to leave. If she stayed much longer in that hot, smelly room, she would faint. When she said goodbye to Mrs Harris, the old lady asked her who she was and when Mattie was coming to take them away.

Mattie murdered?

'Not so good today,' whispered Mr Harris as he showed Violet to the front door. 'She's all right of course, but not quite at her best. She'll be better tomorrow.'

'Yes,' Violet said. 'I'm sure she will.'

Chapter Thirty

Richard Thornhill saw her just a moment too late. There was no time to nip into the refuge of the Gents, no time to retreat to the car, no time even to fall to one knee and tie his shoelace, while pretending to be deaf and blind to everything happening around him.

When their eyes met, they were on either side of the glazed panels of the hospital's main doors. He wasn't surprised to see Charlotte Wemyss-Brown there. She juggled a legendary quantity of charitable commitments and probably at least half a dozen of them had something to do with the hospital and its patients.

He held open the door for her and she surged outside.

'Good morning, Mr Thornhill.' Charlotte now called Edith by her Christian name, but Thornhill was still several rungs below his wife on the hierarchy of acquaintance. 'Terrible business, isn't it?'

Thornhill wished he'd gone to interview Violet Evans himself, instead of sending Kirby to see her with Joan Ailsmore. 'What is?'

'That poor boy – Jimmy Leigh. Sheer persecution. Those drunken louts set themselves up as judge and jury. They could have killed him. No thanks to them that they didn't. You have arrested them, I hope?'

Thornhill admitted that some arrests had been made.

'Then I hope you make sure they're dealt with the full severity of the law. Will they go to prison?'

Thornhill pointed out that what happened next was up to the magistrates, not to him.

'Nonsense.' Charlotte moved a couple of steps to the left, forcing Thornhill to make a mirror manoeuvre, which led to his being neatly trapped in the angle between the main wall of the hospital and the porch. 'You can't expect me to believe that the magistrates won't take account of what the police say.'

Thornhill pointed out that in any case the CID had not been involved in the arrests. This was a matter for his colleagues in Uniformed Branch.

Charlotte waved her fingers and made a noise that sounded like *Pfuh!* 'I've known the poor boy for years. I'm quite sure he wouldn't hurt a fly. I used to know his aunt quite well when she was a nurse at the Cottage Hospital. Poor woman – so terribly upset when he went down with polio, and then she actually had to nurse him. Still, at least that story had a happy ending.' She glared up at Thornhill, her chest bulging like a pigeon's beneath her raincoat. 'And this story will have a happy ending, too, I'm sure. At least as far as Jimmy is concerned.'

She made the words sound like a threat. But despite her obvious sincerity, Thornhill had the odd sensation that her indignation wasn't quite real. No – that was wrong, he thought immediately, the indignation was real enough. But perhaps it was caused by something other than the plight of Jimmy Leigh. He glimpsed an element of calculation in Charlotte's face and wished he was elsewhere. He hadn't lived in Lydmouth for long before he realised that only a fool would want to quarrel with Charlotte Wemyss-Brown, and only a double fool would underestimate her.

'By the way, what happened at the inquest this morning?'

'It's been adjourned.'

'We all know what that means. But don't go looking for the

culprit in the wrong place, Mr Thornhill. Jimmy was nowhere near the Ferryman at half-past ten. And in any case he's always been a *gentle* giant. Personally I believe that we have a duty to protect vulnerable members of society.' She paused, gathering strength, like a swimmer waiting for the precise moment to dive into a wave. 'Men *and* women. Women *especially*, don't you agree?'

Thornhill nodded, feeling that he was literally and metaphorically with his back to the wall. He knew that Charlotte was at last coming to the point, and that it was the one point he did not want her to reach.

'Women have their reputation to consider. A woman's good name is prized above rubies, Mr Thornhill, I don't need to tell you that.'

'No,' Thornhill agreed. 'And now, if you'll excuse me—'

'It's not just a matter of reputation, either, is it?' Charlotte swung her handbag like a medieval bishop trying out the weight of his mace before a duel to the death on the battlefield. 'There's no doubt that we women are the weaker sex, partly because we're so sensitive. Take Miss Francis, for example.'

Thornhill wished he could.

'She's very sensitive, and she's been under a great deal of strain lately, and now her health is beginning to suffer. My husband and I have had to insist she takes some time off work. Men are much more robust in that sort of way.'

Rain began to fall from the sky once again. Charlotte ignored it.

'And how are dear Edith and the children? Back from Bournemouth yet?'

'Yesterday evening. They're very well, thank you.'

'Do give her my best wishes. So nice to talk to you, Mr Thornhill, but I must be getting on. Goodbye.'

Charlotte turned away without a smile, and strode towards the car park. Thornhill went into the hospital. His hands were sweating. Usually he could cope with Charlotte Wemyss-Brown. But usually he was not guilty of adultery. There was no doubt that she either knew or suspected something. She had warned him off Jill unmistakably, and taken the trouble to spell out some of the reasons why such a friendship was completely unsuitable. He shivered, going hot and cold like a man with a fever. The idea of Charlotte knowing was a nightmare. Who would she tell?

He went into the hospital. Jimmy Leigh was in one of the men's wards, at the end of the long room, near the window. He was sitting fully dressed on his bed with his back to everyone else, staring at the rain falling on the sodden lawn.

'Poor lad,' murmured the ward sister to Thornhill. 'It makes my blood boil.'

'You're not keeping him in?'

'There's no need, Inspector. He had a ducking and a bit of a shock but that's all, luckily. No thanks to that gang who did it. Throwing him off New Bridge like that – they could have killed him.'

'They didn't actually throw him off, Sister. They chased him down to the river, and he jumped in.'

'What does it matter?' Her thin shoulders twitched. 'The result's the same. Luckily Miss Calder will be able to keep an eye on him when he's back at home. You knew she was a nurse?'

'Yes.'

'I used to work with her at the Cottage Hospital. She's coming in to fetch him at midday.'

'I can run him home if that would help,' Thornhill said suddenly.

They had been walking more and more slowly, delaying their arrival at the end of the ward. At this point, the sister stopped altogether.

'That would be kind. I know Miss Calder will be in all morning. She had a man coming with a load of turf for the garden.' She moved on to Jimmy's bed. 'Jimmy, dear,' she said brightly, raising the volume of her voice considerably as though he were deaf. 'Here's Inspector Thornhill to have a chat with you.

And he's very kindly offered to take you home to Auntie Minnie in his car. Isn't that nice of him?'

Jimmy looked up and nodded. Thornhill wondered what, if anything, he was thinking. The man-boy was neatly dressed in flannels, a short-sleeved jersey, a white shirt and a tie. The sister helped him into his sports jacket and brushed the shoulders.

'Give my love to Auntie, Jimmy, and you can tell her from me you've been a very good boy.'

He smiled down at her, his face transformed, and she smiled back. It was as if the sun had slipped out from the clouds in Jimmy's mind, revealing a glimpse of what might have been. Just as suddenly it slipped back.

He picked up his little suitcase and walked with Thornhill down the ward. When they reached the doors, Thornhill looked over his shoulder. The sister was still watching them. Jimmy barged through the doors as if making his escape. Neither of them spoke until they were in the car.

'How are you feeling?' Thornhill asked.

'Fine.'

'You don't like hospitals very much.'

'Hate them.'

Thornhill put the key in the ignition but did not start the engine. 'I know you've already told PC Hemlett what happened.'

'They broke my fishing rod. That Fred Baker did it. Will they punish him?'

'We'll see.'

Jimmy had been fishing in the Minnow when the gang from the King's Head had found him yesterday afternoon. They'd chased him like a fox through Templefields, baying and shouting, down to the river. Jimmy jumped off New Bridge. They threw stones at him as he swam away, fortunately without doing much damage, perhaps because they were so drunk. Then the police had arrived, and the ambulance.

'Why did you jump in the river? You're a good runner, they

tell me. You could have run somewhere where you could have asked for help.'

Jimmy shook his head violently. 'Who'd help? Thought I'd jump in for the Drowner again.' His lips twisted. 'But he didn't want me, did he? My dad drowned – did you know that?'

'You were trying to kill yourself?'

Jimmy shrugged. 'Course not. But I can swim, look. Drowner knows that.' He looked quickly at Thornhill, then away. 'Are you going to send *me* to prison, sir?'

'Prison? Why should we do that?'

'That engine, sir. I thought—'

'There's no question of that, Jimmy, I promise you. You can put it out of your mind.'

'Can I keep the engine?'

Thornhill tried not to smile. 'That I don't know. When all's said and done, you stole it, so the toyshop will have to have either the engine or the money, won't they?'

Jimmy nodded slowly.

'I wanted to talk to you about something else,' Thornhill went on. 'Do you remember when Mr Kirby came to see you on Saturday night?'

'With the nice lady?'

'With the nice lady. Do you know who Mr Broadbent is?'

Jimmy nodded. Like Charlotte, Bernie Broadbent was one of the better known citizens of Lydmouth, especially since his election to the Council.

'I wondered if you'd ever seen him with Mattie?'

A shake of the head.

'Are you sure?'

Jimmy nodded.

'You told Mr Kirby she went to a house in Narth Road. You saw her kissing an old man in the park. And you've seen her going to the Evanses' house. Have you seen her with anyone else?'

Thornhill took Jimmy backwards and forwards over much of the same ground that Kirby and Joan Ailsmore had covered.

Nothing new emerged. Whenever Thornhill probed too hard, the man-boy either said he didn't know or retreated into silence. It was a textbook illustration of the fact that slow-witted people were harder to question than quick-witted ones.

At last Thornhill started the engine. They drove out of the grounds of the RAF hospital and turned left into Chepstow Road. They stopped at the zebra crossing in the High Street to allow a gaggle of mothers and toddlers to cross the road. Jimmy stared vacantly out of the passenger window. Thornhill drummed his fingers against the steering wheel, his mind running ahead to the rest of the morning.

'That's him,' Jimmy said suddenly.

Thornhill turned his head. 'Who?'

Jimmy pointed out of the window. They were outside a large Victorian house, set back from the road and now used as council offices. A tall man slammed the door of a car on the forecourt and strode towards the main entrance. It was Gerald Pembridge. Thornhill remembered belatedly that the building housed the Planning Department.

'How do you mean – that's him?'

Jimmy looked at Thornhill, his eyes wide and very clear. 'That's the one you was asking about, sir. That dirty old man. The one who was kissing Mattie in the park.'

Chapter Thirty-one

'See her?' the woman in the queue said. 'Do you know who that is? That's Violet Evans. That's who the police should talk to. Just look at the heels on those shoes.'

As one woman, the five people in the shop turned to look out of the window. Jill was among them, the last in the queue. She'd walked down from Walnut Tree Cottage to buy cigarettes she didn't yet need. She'd wanted an excuse to get out, even in the rain. But it wasn't raining now and she was uncomfortably hot under her mackintosh.

'Worked at Sedbury's,' the woman continued. She had a wart on her left cheek that rose and fell as she talked. 'Got herself in the family way – did you know that? – so she had to leave. Mattie and her were always together. She'd know about the boyfriends if anyone would.'

'You did say streaky, Mrs Fish?' said the woman behind the counter. 'Not middle?'

Jill slipped outside. Violet Evans was standing with her head bowed at the bus stop. When Jill said hello, Violet gasped and the colour rushed to her cheeks. Like a guilty thing surprised, Jill thought, knowing that guilt takes forms that perhaps even Wordsworth never dreamt of. Violet had been crying recently and her mascara had run. She had the sort of face that makes young men kill dragons and old men make fools of themselves. She had obviously made an effort with her clothes, and Jill wondered why.

'How's Grace?' she asked.

The girl's face lightened. 'She's lovely. She's put on another pound already.'

'She's very beautiful.' Jill heard the wistfulness in her own voice and rushed on, 'I'm staying in a cottage on the hill here. Just a little holiday.'

'I came to see Mattie's parents.' Violet's lips trembled. 'I just don't know what they're going to do now she's gone.'

'Do they have other children?'

'Mattie was an only child. No other family at all, or not close ones. And they're not very well, look, especially Mattie's mum. And of course all this about it not being an accident has made it even worse for them. Had you heard?'

Jill said carefully, 'The police have to make quite sure of everything when somebody dies unexpectedly.'

'She was murdered, I know she was. Some man killed her. I do miss her.'

'Of course you do.'

While they were talking, Violet and Jill drifted towards a bench near the bus stop, out of sight of the shop window. They both sat down. It was as if the movement released something in Violet.

'I don't think Grace's daddy wants to marry me any more.' She looked imploringly at Jill. 'You won't tell anyone, will you?'

'No.'

'Mum and Dad want me to leave Grace with them. They want me to go to Cardiff or somewhere, get another job, try and make a new start where no one knows what's happened.'

'And what do you think about that?'

'I'm not going to leave Grace. I won't let them take her away from me.' She opened a large, bulging handbag and fumbled for cigarettes. 'It's funny. I've never been as miserable as this but Grace is the best thing that ever happened to me. But it's because of Grace I feel miserable. Doesn't make sense, does it?'

'Sometimes things don't.'

'They do for other people. They don't get into messes. They always know what to do.'

'I'm not sure I do.'

Violet offered cigarettes, which Jill refused. She watched the girl lighting up, noticing the swollen rims under the eyes and the worry lines in the forehead.

'What I don't know,' Violet went on in a sudden rush of words, 'is whether I should go to the police.'

'What about?'

'Mattie.'

'Do you know something about how she died?'

Violet shook her head. She stared down at her handbag, still open on her lap. Jill followed the direction of her gaze and noticed there were two or three library books in the bag. Romantic novels. Was it any wonder that your expectations were dashed when you fed your hopes on stories with titles like *Love's Wild Dreamer*? On the other hand, perhaps reading Jane Austen and the Brontë sisters had had a similar effect on her so she had no grounds for feeling smug.

'It didn't mean anything to her.' Violet snapped the handbag shut. 'She was like a man. Just something you did.'

'What was?'

'You know. Doing it.'

'Do you think that had something to do with how she died?'

Violet looked at her with wide, wondering eyes. They were very blue, fringed with thick dark lashes like a doll's. But she must be a long way from being a fool.

'Do you?' Jill prompted.

'You won't tell anyone? Promise?'

'Yes.'

She tapped ash from her cigarette. 'She called them the old

men. Most of them were old. Well, quite old. Used to laugh at them, at the things they wanted.'

'Did she mention their names?'

'Oh, no,' Violet said quickly.

'Why did she do it?'

'For the money, of course. She wanted to get her mum and dad a bathroom, look, have the electric laid on. She couldn't do that on what they pay at the Gardenia.'

'I don't suppose she could.'

'She used to say, what did it matter? Probably their wives didn't want to do it any more. No one would ever find out, because the men would be too scared to say anything. Sometimes it was fun. And she said sometimes it was a bit of a laugh. There was one man who couldn't do it, but he paid her just the same, paid her to pretend he'd had her. Gave her *ten pounds*.' She laughed, a bubble of mirth rising up unexpected to the surface of her misery. 'But I expect you think it's awful, a girl doing something like that. Taking money and all.'

'No I don't. But I do think you should tell the police about this.'

Violet shook her head. 'I don't know. Mattie's dad – it'd break his heart.'

'Look, Violet,' Jill said. 'Even so, it would be a good idea to tell them. If you like, I'll drive you into Lydmouth. It won't take me long to walk back to the cottage and fetch the car.'

'No,' the girl said. 'I'd like to think it over first, if you don't mind.' She dropped the cigarette and squashed it under a green suede shoe. 'Anyway, here's the bus so I needn't trouble you. But thank you all the same.'

The single decker drew up at the stop. Violet almost ran to join the head-scarved women filing inside. As the bus pulled away, she looked out of the window and raised her hand just above the sill in a token wave.

Jill stayed on the bench for a moment, turning over in her mind what Violet had told her. Confidence or not, she knew she would have to tell Richard. She knew too that she'd frightened the girl off. She'd made a fool of herself again.

But had Mattie made a fool of herself as well, paid too high a price for a ten-pound note and a bit of a laugh?

Chapter Thirty-two

'He'll see me,' Thornhill said, slapping his warrant card on the counter and then sweeping it away. 'Just tell him I'm here, will you?'

The secretary gave him a startled look. She tapped on the door of the inner office and slipped inside, closing the door quickly behind her but not before a burst of laughter had escaped. A moment later, Gerald Pembridge came out, smoothing his dark hair with long white fingers, with the secretary trailing behind him. He cut an elegant figure in a dark pin-striped suit which made him look slimmer than he was.

'Yes, Inspector? What is it?'

'I'd like to ask you a few questions, sir.'

'Can't it wait? I'm in the middle of a most important meeting. Have you had a word with that sergeant of yours? I told him everything I knew.'

'There was one thing you didn't discuss with him, sir.'

Pembridge flicked his fingers in an oddly effeminate gesture. 'Oh, all right. Let's get it over with.' He turned to his secretary. 'Tell them I've been called away for a few minutes. See if any of them would like some more coffee.' He turned back to Thornhill. 'There's an empty office next door. We can use that.'

The room was cramped and smelled of mothballs.

Pembridge did not offer Thornhill a seat. He stood by the window, staring down at the High Street below.

'I wanted to ask you about Mattie Harris,' Thornhill said.

'Mattie?' Pembridge turned to face the room. He had small, streamlined features, surprisingly delicate for a man of his size. 'I don't think I can add anything to what my wife and I told your sergeant.'

'I think you can, sir. We have a witness who saw you kissing Mattie Harris in Jubilee Park a few weeks ago. I thought you might perhaps like to comment.'

Pembridge's head jerked towards Thornhill. 'Nonsense.' He tried a light laugh and failed miserably. 'They must have been mistaken.'

'No, sir. The light was good, and the witness recognised you both.'

Pembridge started to say something, stopped and sat down at the bare desk instead. 'Look, there's a perfectly innocent explanation. I realise it must look bad, Inspector, but – well – she was asking about accommodation, and I'd given her a bit of advice about council flats. Gave me a peck on the cheek because she was grateful. An affectionate girl, you know. And she knew me quite well because of coming to the dances. Nothing in it, really, nothing that need concern you.'

He ran out of words and stared miserably at the scarred and ink-blotched surface of the desk. Thornhill sat down opposite him without being asked. From this angle he noticed that Pembridge was going bald at the top of his head, and had artfully arranged his hair to conceal the circle of white skin beneath.

'Not just a peck on the cheek, sir,' Thornhill said slowly. 'Kissing and cuddling was how it was described to me.'

Pembridge put his head in his hands, revealing more of the bald patch. 'Look, I've been a bloody fool, but need this go any further? It would kill Edna if she found out.'

Thornhill let the silence lengthen. Then he took out his

notebook, flipped it open and said with a parade-ground snap in his voice, 'Tell me what happened. How did it start?'

'She came to the Ruispidge Hall – one of our regulars. One couldn't help but notice her. Not pretty, exactly but . . . I don't know, she had something. When she laughed, she made you want to laugh with her. Beautiful dancer, too.' He shrugged. 'There I was, blowing away on stage, and she always seemed to be looking in my direction.'

'But if you were up on the stage playing your trumpet, you can't have had much time for conversation.'

For an instant Pembridge leered. 'How much time do you need with a girl like that? We used to chat a bit in the interval. She rather liked my playing.' He shot out a cuff, exposing a heavy gold cuff link, unconsciously preening. 'One evening in March, Edna was ill so I was by myself. Mattie stayed behind to help me tidy up. That – that was the first time.'

Thornhill wondered where they'd done it. On the stage? Something about this interview made him feel ashamed of himself, as if this were a dream and he'd found himself thumbing through dirty postcards.

'How many times were there?'

'Not many – two – no, three other times.'

'Where?'

'Once in the Ruispidge Hall, and once here. And then the last time in the park. I was so stupid. So many risks.'

'When were you planning to see her again?'

Pembridge shook his head vigorously. 'We'd decided it was time to finish the affair – if you can call it that. At the end of April – that time in the park was the final fling. Edna was – well, not exactly suspicious, but . . . also, there was the question of the money.'

'Which you were giving to Mattie?'

'Not give, Inspector. I made her one or two small loans. The point is, my wife looks after our family accounts, and she does tend to notice unexplained outgoings. So – well that time in the park was the last time.'

Small loans? Enough to pay for a bathroom at her parents' cottage?

'Were you in love with her?' Thornhill asked.

'Good heavens, no. Whatever gave you that idea?'

'It does happen.'

'Not to us, not to Mattie and me. No, it was simply that I had a need, and she was willing to satisfy it. I like to think she had a bit of fun as well.' He smiled at Thornhill, inviting complicity. 'You're not shocked, are you? It's not that unusual.'

Pembridge was rapidly regaining his self-possession. In a moment he would be congratulating himself on his virility. But Thornhill was hardly in a position to condemn a married man for finding sex outside marriage. He stared grimly across the desk, until the other man averted his eyes. It was disturbing to accept that he had something in common with Gerald Pembridge.

'So when was the last time you saw Mattie Harris in private?' Thornhill rasped.

Pembridge's eyelids fluttered. 'I told you – near the end of April – that time in the park. I can give you the exact date, actually – it was the twenty-third, which is Edna's birthday. Very much a spur of the moment thing.'

'You're sure you had no meetings or private conversations after that?'

Pembridge shook his head. 'Of course I saw her at the Ruispidge Hall on several occasions. We didn't talk. I felt the thing had run its course, and I imagine she felt the same.' Suddenly he stood up, walked to the window and stared down at the road. When he next spoke, his voice shook slightly. 'Can you tell me who saw us in the park?'

'No.'

'It's just – well, my little fling with her can't have had anything to do with her getting herself drowned over a month after we last—'

'It's not for me to decide, sir.'

If Pembridge had been a dog, his hindquarters would have

been on the floor and he would have been wagging his tail. 'Don't get the wrong impression. I don't make a habit of this sort of thing. Never in Lydmouth, either. It won't happen again, I can promise you that.'

Thornhill let his eyes lose contact with Pembridge's. He picked up his hat and stood up. Something puzzled him, but he couldn't put his finger on it.

Pembridge fiddled with a cufflink. 'What happens now?'

'It depends.'

Like an obsequious waiter, Pembridge slipped round the desk and went to open the door. He put his hand on the handle and turned back. 'Did you ever meet Mattie Harris?'

'No. Not to speak to.'

'It's just that if you had, you'd understand why I made such a fool of myself. She wasn't a bad girl. Just a bit different from most of them. A free spirit. She made everything seem *fun*.'

Thornhill nodded and let his eyes stray down to the door handle.

'So sorry, I'm keeping you.' Pembridge opened the door and almost bowed Thornhill out of the room. 'You will let me know what happens, won't you?'

'We'll be in touch if there's anything we need,' Thornhill said ambiguously.

He ignored the hand that Pembridge was holding out to him and clattered down the stairs. It was not until he reached his car that he realised what had been puzzling him.

The Pembridges were great friends with the Williamsons. Gerald Pembridge and Ray Williamson belonged to the same Masonic lodge. They played golf together. Their wives shopped together. So why hadn't Pembridge reminded Thornhill of this significant fact? For that matter, why hadn't he insisted on dealing with Williamson instead?

Chapter Thirty-three

Before he left, Malcolm opened the top drawer of his dressing table and took out the leather case. He removed one of the razors and slipped it in his left-hand trouser pocket. If you were physically at a disadvantage, he reasoned, you had to find a way of redressing the balance. Not that this had anything to do with reason — he was hardly going to pull out the razor and use it as a weapon. It was as a talisman. He took it to bring him luck. He took it to give him courage.

He dragged himself into the centre of town. By the time he reached the bus stop in the High Street, he was sweating. Bill didn't know he was here, didn't know what he was doing. In a funny way, it was easier to be brave on Bill's behalf than on his own. Bill was at present at home, sleeping off the combined effects of yesterday's beating and today's liquid lunch.

Malcolm left the bus at the stop beyond the hospital. A woman old enough to be his mother helped him down. Malcolm thanked her, wondering why kindness should be almost as difficult to deal with as mockery. The rain had stopped. He shuffled down Broadwell Drive, swinging his weight from stick to stick. The air was muggy and he felt sticky and unclean.

What to say?

Anger bubbled inside him. He turned into the Broadwell Crescent. A tendril of smoke rose from the chimney of the Evanses' house, separating into lesser tendrils which waved like grey, ghostly fingers. He heard the clink of metal on stone and turned to look at the sound. Ted Evans was working with a couple of other men at the other end of the cul-de-sac. There was a trench running between two half-built houses, into which they were manoeuvring a length of pipe. Malcolm made his way slowly towards them, skirting a large puddle, stepping over a pile of bricks. The men ignored him. But he thought they had probably seen him because they moved stiffly, like bad actors.

He stopped at what would one day be the front gate of one of the houses. 'Mr Evans?'

Ted turned, his face expressionless. The other men ignored the interruption.

'Could I have a word?' Malcolm heard his voice rise on the last syllable and took a deep breath to steady himself. 'I won't keep you long.'

The builder walked slowly towards the roadway, his hands hanging loosely at his sides. He stared at Malcolm all the while. For once Malcolm was almost glad he was a cripple. If he'd had the full use of his legs, he thought he might well have run away.

'Yes?'

Malcolm took a step backwards and stood up as straight as he could. He hooked the left-hand stick over his right arm. He slipped his left hand in his trouser pocket, hoping he looked casual and relaxed, in full control of the situation.

'I'm Malcolm Sedbury.'

Ted's eyes flicked down to the sticks and the withered legs. 'I know.'

'I think it's time we had a little talk, Mr Evans.'

'Have you seen today's paper?'

Malcolm shook his head, feeling that control of the situation had been wrested away from him.

Ted took a copy of the *Gazette* from the pocket of his jacket. It was folded to show one of the headlines on the front page. ' "Drowned Waitress," ' he read slowly. ' "Inquest Adjourned." '

'They often do that,' Malcolm said loudly. 'The police need time to make enquiries. Just routine.'

'Really? So *that's* why it's adjourned. To give them time to make enquiries, eh?' The sarcasm stung like a whip. 'You live and learn, don't you? I've often wondered.'

Malcolm's fingers stroked the ivory handle of the razor in his pocket. 'I've not come to talk about that. I've come to talk about Bill Pembridge.'

'Oh aye?'

'You beat him up yesterday.'

The other man said nothing, just stared.

'You can't go around doing things like that,' Malcolm went on. 'Not in this country.'

Ted smiled.

'I'll go to the police,' Malcolm said shrilly.

'Be your age, son.'

'I mean it. I will.'

'You won't unless you're more stupid than I think you are.' Ted took a step towards Malcolm, and then another. 'No witnesses, were there? So it would be his word against mine. And everyone in town would find out why you assumed it was me. Because Bill bloody Pembridge put my daughter in the family way, that's why.'

'Listen, Mr Evans, I—'

'Can't he face up to what he's done? To everyone knowing? I don't reckon there'd be much sympathy for him, do you?' Ted jerked a thumb at the silent workmen behind him. 'Maybe some of my lads might want to finish the job. The job that someone else began, of course, I'm not saying it was me. Is that what you want?'

Malcolm felt tears burning his eyelids. 'You'd better watch it.' His fingers squeezed the razor. 'Do you hear me?'

Ted's smile grew broader. Malcolm was breathing heavily and trembling.

'Tell me,' Ted said. 'How well did *you* know Mattie Harris? You and your friend?'

Malcolm swung round, desperate to get away. But he had moved too abruptly. The tip of the stick plunged into a rut full of water. He tried to tug it free but the mud sucked it down. The resistance was enough to overbalance him and his weight slipped suddenly to his right. For an age he hung there knowing like a man who has leapt from a cliff that disaster would follow in the blink of an eye, and yet that blink of an eye seemed to last for ever.

The other stick, still dangling from his arm, tangled with his legs. He fell to one knee and then pitched forward into the mud. He was down on all fours. He had lost one stick completely and the other, still clenched in his hand, was half submerged in the rut. Both his blazer and trousers would probably be ruined.

Worse than the fall, far worse, was the kindness. Ted lifted him with insulting ease back to his feet. Both of the workmen came to help. One retrieved the sticks and the other gave him a rag to wipe himself down.

'Do you want to sit down for a bit, lad?' Ted asked. 'Get your breath back?'

Malcolm pulled away from Ted's grasp and took a couple of steps away, swaying on his sticks. 'No, thank you.'

'Is that yours?'

Malcolm followed the direction of Ted's pointing finger. The razor was lying beside the rut, the pale ivory bright against the deep brown of the earth. Ted picked it up, his face again devoid of expression.

'You'd best put that in your pocket.'

Malcolm juggled the sticks awkwardly, took the razor and slipped it in his blazer pocket.

'Mind what you do with it,' Ted went on. 'If you're not careful you'll cut yourself.'

Chapter Thirty-four

Elizabeth was keen to get home because she was in the middle of a complicated fantasy involving her doll's house, one teddy bear, and a Red Indian squaw that by rights belonged to David. She towed her mother into Victoria Road.

The first thing Edith saw was the Riley parked outside number sixty-eight. Behind the wheel was Uncle Bernie, his elbow resting on the sill and smoke billowing out of the driver's window. If there was one thing that Edith could have changed about Uncle Bernie, it was his habit of dropping in unexpectedly. She thought he cultivated the habit of these unannounced visits because part of his mind thought this was what people in families did.

'Hello, Edie,' he said. 'Have I timed it right for a cuppa?'

'Just about to put the kettle on.' Edith nudged her daughter. 'Say hello to Uncle Bernie, Elizabeth.'

The car door swung open and Bernie swept the little girl into a hug, which Elizabeth accepted with the detached amiability of a nurse in a mental hospital receiving a wilted daisy chain from a patient. His eyes met Edith's above Elizabeth's head.

'Richard told me the news,' she said. 'About the house.'

'Oh that.' He shrugged. 'Just an investment, really. By the way, have you seen the evening paper?'

'No, not yet. Why?'

'In the *Post* they're advising women to be careful about walking alone. People are talking about the Drowner.'

'That old story?' Edith glanced anxiously down at Elizabeth's head. 'Make sure that you wash your hands, dear, and get changed before you come down for tea.'

Elizabeth extracted herself tactfully from Bernie's embrace. The three of them went inside. Elizabeth slipped upstairs. Bernie made a beeline for the kitchen. ('The heart of the home, my old mam used to say.') Soon he was settled in the Windsor chair by the window.

'This stuff in the *Post*,' Edith said. 'It's because of the waitress, I suppose.'

'You've heard?'

'Richard's in charge of the investigation. But why are they bring the Drowner into it?'

'Funny thing, superstition,' Bernie said, patting his pockets in search of matches. 'Like an infection – like polio, for instance – once it starts, it's very hard to stop.'

'But it's just an old wives' tale.'

'The trouble with old wives' tales is that a lot of old wives believe them. Not just old wives, either.'

Edith went into the scullery to put the kettle on. When she came back to the kitchen to lay the table for tea, she found Bernie standing by the window staring at the garden.

He turned as she came into the room. 'So when's David due?'

'In about half an hour. There's a cricket practice after school on Tuesdays.'

Bernie nodded. 'He's turning into a useful little spin bowler. It'll stand him in good stead when he goes to Ashbridge.'

In September, David was going to the junior department of a public school a few miles outside Lydmouth. Edith was paying for this with the help of a small legacy from her mother, money which Richard had wanted to use as a deposit on the house.

'He'll fit in all right,' Bernie said, soothing a fear Edith had expressed to no one, not even Richard. 'Bright little chap like that would fit in anywhere.' He lit another match and watched her laying the table for a moment. 'How does Richard feel about me buying the house?'

'Pleased. Naturally.'

'That bit of land at the back has its own access from Chepstow Road. I was saying to Richard, it's just the place for a garage. And I reckon it would improve in value if I installed central heating.'

'There's – there's no need for that. Not from our point of view.' Edith's mind filled with a vision of evenly heated rooms free of coal dust on every horizontal surface. 'We manage.'

'*We* used to manage on bread and dripping,' Bernie said. 'With nine of us using one outside lav. With four of us kids in one bed. Can't say I enjoyed it, though.'

'That would be wonderful. But wouldn't all this cost a lot of money?'

Bernie beamed at her. 'I told you. It's an investment.'

'Richard was a little worried that people might talk.'

'Because we're related? There's nothing to worry about there, Edie. I'll make sure everyone knows it's above board.'

Edith made the tea in a happy daze. Central heating and a garage – it was better than she had dared hope. For an instant her mind strayed into an area of speculation she had always tried to avoid. Uncle Bernie was a very rich man. But Edith was only his first cousin once removed, and he had several closer relations.

'Thank you for the roses, by the way. They're beautiful.'

Soon David came home and Bernie talked to him about cricket, which was something Richard rarely did because Richard's interest in organised sport was so small as to be almost invisible. Elizabeth came downstairs and the four of them sat around the tea table.

Bernie did not outstay his welcome. He took David and Elizabeth for a ride in the new car before he left. Afterwards, the children came running into the house, their faces flushed, and Edith went out to say goodbye to Uncle Bernie.

He poked his great head out of the driver's window. 'Listen, Edie, I've been thinking. Might make more sense if I have them put the house in your name rather than mine.'

'But you can't do that!'

'Why not?' He grinned at her. 'Look after yourself, my dear.'

The car drew away and turned into Chepstow Road. Edith stood on the pavement, one hand on the gatepost, trying to take in what Uncle Bernie had said. She was still there five minutes later when Richard arrived in the Austin, jolting her back to the present.

'What's happened?' he said. 'You look as if you've been talking to the fairies.'

'Uncle Bernie dropped in. He's talking of putting the house in our name.'

'I'm not sure I like the idea of that.'

'There's nothing underhand about it. He is my uncle.'

'And he's also a member of the Standing Joint Committee.'

'Why do you always have to be so pernickety?' She touched his arm. 'Sorry. I didn't mean that.'

He kissed her cheek. 'Don't be sorry. Perhaps you're right. It's been a difficult day.'

'Why? Because of the waitress?'

'In a way. The *Post* is making a meal out of the fact we've adjourned the inquest on her. They're more or less hinting that we're treating this as a murder investigation. I think someone on the force has been talking to them.'

'Is it a murder investigation?' Edith asked, her voice rising.

Thornhill shrugged. 'No one really knows at this stage. Not really.'

'I do hope not, dear.'

She threaded her arm through his and they went into the house. The children swooped on Richard.

'Daddy,' Elizabeth said, using her wheedling tone. 'When are we going to get the kittens?'

'What kittens?'

'You remember – the ones from Miss Francis.'

'Oh, *those* kittens. I thought we were only going to get one.'

'No – two. One each.'

Edith squeezed Richard's arm. 'It seems fair, I suppose.'

'A boy and a girl,' Elizabeth demanded.

'Mine's called Buster,' David said.

'Mine's Alexandra,' Elizabeth announced.

He smiled at the three of them. 'We'll see.'

Gradually it turned into one of those evenings when everyone was on their best behaviour. The children had tea. Richard helped David with his homework. The children got ready for bed and then they played Beggar My Neighbour and Snap. While Edith made supper for Richard and herself, he read them their stories.

All the time, Edith felt as though she were walking on glass. For a few hours, they were a happy family. That was splendid, of course, except that it made her wonder what exactly they were for the rest of the time.

After supper, Richard followed her into the scullery and took control of the sink. The children were in bed. When he washed up, which was rarely, there was much foam and splashing but less attention to detail than Edith would have liked. But she didn't want to discourage him.

She waited until she'd finished drying up before she took the plunge. She draped the tea towel over the cooker and said casually, 'Is there something wrong? You seem a little on edge, dear.'

'No, everything's fine.' Richard turned away to put the kettle down on the hob. 'Just thinking about work.'

'You're not worried about Uncle Bernie and the house?'

'No. Not really.'

He stared at her for a moment, his face shadowed and intent.

She knew him well enough to realise that he was wondering whether to say something. But when he finally cleared his throat and opened his mouth, all that came out was, 'You go and put your feet up. I'll make the coffee.'

Chapter Thirty-five

Bill saw the dog first, darting across the field like a scrap of paper blown in the wind, turning and twisting, following the invisible logic of a scent. He crouched, safe behind the hawthorn hedge, and waited. Better safe than sorry. It might be Ma Evans or even Ted himself. He wouldn't put it past that old bastard to have locked Violet in her room and kept her on a diet of bread and water.

To his relief, he saw Violet climbing the stile into the field. Mindful of what had happened last time, he stayed where he was. She began to make a circuit of the hedgerow. The light glinted on her blonde hair. Still following the invisible rabbit, Rab dived into a little copse which stood at the further corner of the field. Violet switched course to follow him.

He limped along a parallel course behind the line of the hedge to the other side of the copse. His movements were stiff and slow. Ted's kick in the crotch was still causing him discomfort. He reached the trees before she did, and was standing in the green gloom when she appeared on the edge of the field.

'Rab?' she called. 'Rab?'

The dog saw Bill at that moment, gave a happy bark and rushed towards him.

'Violet, it's me.'

She said nothing but she came into the copse. To cover his confusion, Bill bent and scratched Rab's chest. He looked up at her when she was five yards away from him.

'I had to see you,' he said in a hoarse whisper.

She stared down at him. 'There's nothing to say, Bill. Not any more.'

'Of course there is.' He stood up, took a step towards her and watched her retreating. 'Listen, Vi, I keep—'

'What have you done to your face?'

His hand flew up to his swollen lip. 'I – I walked into a door.'

She shrugged, as if his injury was of no account to her.

'We have to talk about what we do,' he said.

'It's too late for that.' She raised her head and glared at him. 'Have you seen the paper?'

He shook his head.

'The inquest's been adjourned. The *Post* more or less says that Mattie was murdered.'

Bill swallowed. 'She can't have been.'

'That's what they were hinting. The police went back to see Mattie's parents and just about said it outright. So who killed her, Bill? Who killed her?'

'How do I know?' He ran his tongue over his swollen lip. 'In any case, it's nothing to do with us, do you hear? Nothing to do with us.'

'Isn't it?'

'Of course it bloody isn't.' He forced himself to speak more calmly. 'What are you going to do?'

'I'm going away.'

'Where?'

She shook her head. 'It's nothing to do with you. Not any more.'

'You can't mean that.' Suddenly he could hardly bear the thought of Violet not being there. He didn't want to marry her, but he didn't want her to go away, either. 'What will you do with the baby?'

'She's got a name. Grace.'

'You must at least let me help, then. What will you do for money?'

She ignored him. He might have evaporated before her eyes. She turned away, walked out of the copse and into the field. The dog glanced at her and then up at Bill, uncertain which way to go. Bill bent down and scratched the dog's chest, trying to work out what do for the best. The dog yelped suddenly, twisted up its head and bit Bill's hand. Then with a low snarl it ran off after Violet.

It was only then that Bill remembered Ted kicking the dog the last time he'd been in this field. Bill rubbed his injured hand. He must have touched a broken rib. He raised a hand and felt his swollen lips and the bruise just below his left eye. His testicles ached in sympathy.

Perhaps Violet would tell her father he was here. Bill hobbled away as fast as he could, keeping to the cover of the hedgerow, back to the security of the MG. The faster he walked, the worse the pain between his legs became. That kick on Sunday evening had bloody near crippled him.

Not a lot between him and Malcolm Sedbury now.

Chapter Thirty-six

Jill went to Gloucester to escape the empty cottage on Eastbury Hill and to give her restless mind something else to think about. She took the long road – first up through Ross and then eastwards to Gloucester. The same old thoughts swooped down from Eastbury Hill and followed her wherever she went.

She might well be pregnant. She did not want to be pregnant. She was not sure whether she could be pregnant. She did not want a baby. She did want a baby. She was not sure she would ever be capable of having a baby. If she had an abortion, which she wouldn't, where would she find someone to do it?

Last time she had been in London, and besides the father of the unwanted baby had been ready and willing to make the arrangements. Indeed, he had been almost indecently enthusiastic. Lydmouth wasn't Earls Court. She shied away from considering the possibility of a self-induced abortion.

That poor damned kid.

In Gloucester, Jill left the car on a piece of waste ground at the back of a small hotel off Westgate Street. She bought a newspaper and ate plaice and chips in the hotel's low-ceilinged dining room.

The *Citizen* had a small item about the adjourned inquest on Mattie Harris. The slant was much less sensational than that of the *Post*, but the story left behind the implication that no one seriously considered the death to have been accidental. Jill wondered whether Richard Thornhill was still at police headquarters or whether he'd gone back home to Edith and the children. He was probably at home by now. She imagined them celebrating the simple pleasure of being together again. A family. The clamour of her thoughts grew louder and uglier.

She ordered coffee and skimmed through the newspaper to the film advertisements. The new Larry Jordan film was on at the Gaumont. So she went to the cinema where she succeeded in forgetting both Richard Thornhill and the possibility she was pregnant for more time than she would have believed possible beforehand.

The film was set in the nineteenth century: Larry Jordan played an English gentleman who converted to Rome after the One He Loved married another, and in an astonishingly short space of time became a cardinal. Jill ate chocolates, smoked cigarettes and wept quietly and happily into her handkerchief.

All good things come to an end, in this case a tragic one. When the lights went up on an audience of snuffling women, Larry Jordan's celluloid perfections faded rapidly.

Jill made her way back to the car. It was almost dark now. The lighting was bad at the back of the hotel and she picked her way carefully across the uneven ground. Life would have been much simpler if Richard Thornhill had been safely tucked away in the higher echelons of the Roman Catholic Church, like Larry Jordan in *Higher Vocations*. A door opened on the far side of the car park, and there was a burst of beery laughter and the tinkle of a pub piano.

The most direct route to her car took her past one of the few other cars now parked on the waste ground. One of the windows must have been open a crack, because as Jill passed near by she heard a man's laugh, rapidly suppressed, and the sound of someone panting as though they had just run a race. No prizes for guessing what was going on in there. Part of her hoped the couple in there was taking sensible precautions, and part of her simply envied them. Now Edith was back, that was something she would have to grow used to doing without again.

Jill tightened her lips and hurried towards the safety of the Ford Anglia. She climbed inside and glanced back at the other car. Something about its lines was familiar. She snapped open her bag, took out her case and found another cigarette. She was smoking far too much at present – she would have to cut back; she simply couldn't afford to smoke at this rate.

She clicked the lighter and the flame seemed to light her memory as well as her cigarette. The car was a Riley RMF, like the one Bernie Broadbent was so proud of.

She drew hard on the cigarette. The RMF was a new model. There couldn't be many others in the area. She felt a sudden distaste for what was going on inside, and then remembered that she of all people had every reason to be tolerant about hurried, furtive sex.

Suddenly the front passenger door of the Riley swung open. As embarrassed as a voyeur, Jill held the glowing cigarette tip beneath the level of the window and hoped she wasn't visible inside the car.

Someone got out. Jill glimpsed Bernie leaning across from the driver's seat with a piece of paper, perhaps a bank note. She thought he looked grim-faced, even sad. A moment later, the door slammed and the Riley's engine burst into life.

The car swung in a wide, slow arc towards the road. For an instant, fluttering fingers and a pretty face were caught like an enemy bomber in the beams of the headlights. Then the car turned into the road and disappeared towards the centre of Gloucester.

Jill released a long, wavering breath. She watched the dark, elegant shape of the young man with the pretty face picking his way like a cat towards the lighted windows of the pub.

Chapter Thirty-seven

With hindsight Thornhill thought he should have guessed from the way Sergeant Fowles greeted him when he arrived at police headquarters on Wednesday morning. He was a little more offhand than was usual. Thornhill had his mind on other things, and paid no attention.

He went upstairs to the CID Office. No one looked up at him as he went into the room. No one except Brian Kirby. The rest of them gave the impression that their concentration on work was so absolute that only a bomb would have disturbed it.

Kirby, cup of tea in hand, sauntered over from the notice-board at the back of the room. There was nothing worth reading on the noticeboard, but it was near the window which over-looked the car park behind police headquarters where Thornhill had left the Austin a moment or two earlier.

'Morning, sir,' Kirby said.

'Morning, Brian. Anything new?'

'Yes and no.' Kirby leant forward and lowered his voice. 'Mr Williamson is back.'

'Come into my office,' Thornhill said in his normal voice. Once they were both inside, he closed the door and said, 'Well?'

Kirby spread his hands wide. 'He turned up a quarter of an hour ago, sir. Back from sick leave. Said he'd decided to take charge of the Harris case himself.' Kirby paused a fraction longer than necessary. 'Having discussed the matter with Mr Hendry. Oh, and he also asked if you'd come and see him as soon as you got in.'

Thornhill nodded and told Kirby he could go. He spent a moment flicking through his in-tray, partly in case anything important had come through during the night, and partly to give himself time to think. This was turning into the kind of investigation he'd come to dread. The kind which had ramifications stretching far beyond the case in hand. The kind that blurred the line dividing the guilty from the innocent.

He went into Williamson's big office overlooking the High Street. The superintendent was behind his desk, looking somehow smaller and more vulnerable than before.

'Change of plan, Thornhill. Did Kirby tell you?'

'I understand you're coming back to take over the Harris investigation, sir.'

'No reflection on you, of course,' Williamson said, looking as if he meant the opposite. 'Have you heard that Trotter's ill?'

Thornhill shook his head. Detective Chief Inspector Trotter was in charge of the CID in the Framington division, which was at the southern tip of the county.

'Glandular fever, they say. I want you down there as a caretaker until Trotter can see his way forward. Or not, as the case may be. And in the meantime, I'll keep an eye on things here.'

'Yes, sir,' said Thornhill, knowing better than to argue. Eastbury was in the Framington division.

'Now, you'd better brief me on what's been happening here before you go. According to Sergeant Kirby, the only thing of any significance on our plates at present is this business with the waitress.'

'Yes, sir. Have you —?'

Williamson tapped a file on his blotter. 'I've been through what we've got so far. It looks quite straightforward to me, and Sergeant Kirby agrees.'

'I'm sorry, sir – what looks quite straightforward?'

Williamson took his time lighting the pipe he was not at present supposed to smoke. On either side of him on the desk was a framed photograph – one of himself shaking hands with the Lord Lieutenant and the other of his wife Bunty. They faced out towards the door, so visitors rather than Williamson had to look at them.

'Oh – by the way, piece of good news.' The superintendent's pale blue eyes were moist and his lips looked as if there were made of crumpled pink tissue paper. 'When I saw Mr Hendry this morning, he said he thought the Standing Joint Committee would be willing to provide cars for us after all. That's an unmarked car for each divisional CID's exclusive use throughout the county. We've been trying to persuade them of that for years. In the meantime, of course, Lydmouth Division can keep the Hillman.' He lit the pipe and then coughed so hard he had to put it down in the ashtray. When he was able to go on, he said, 'Cyril George and Bernie Broadbent had a word with him last night.'

Thornhill had the familiar sensation of a man moving out of his depth. Broadbent and Cyril George were both on the Standing Joint Committee that controlled among other things the police force's finances. Hendry had been trying to get them to agree to authorise the purchase of cars for the divisional CIDs for months, if not years. Now, suddenly, they had. Cyril George and Bernie Broadbent were friendly with Gerald Pembridge, as was Williamson and indeed James Hendry himself.

Somewhere, somehow, a deal had been struck.

'Clearly that girl's death wasn't an accident,' Williamson said, reverting abruptly to the subject of Mattie Harris. 'Manslaughter or murder, that's my bet.' He waved at the file on his desk. 'And we don't have to look too far to find out who's responsible, do we? Simply a matter of marshalling the evidence.'

'I'm not sure I follow, sir.'

'Jimmy Leigh. It stands out a mile. We know he was obsessed with the girl. He was the last person known to have seen her.

He's got no alibi. There's a streak of violence in him, or I'm not much mistaken. And he even managed to *find* the body. Dear God, man — what more do we want?'

'It's all circumstantial, sir. And then, what about the bath water in Mattie's airways?'

'She was pregnant, wasn't she? Trying to get rid of the baby. Like all these stupid girls . . . perhaps he was helping her, and he got carried away. Perhaps he was even the father of the baby — thought of that?'

'Jimmy said he saw Mattie going into the drive of Councillor Broadbent's house the previous weekend.'

Williamson had another burst of coughing, and his face darkened to purple. 'For Christ's sake, Thornhill. I expected better than that from you. Has it not occurred to you that Leigh is not exactly a reliable witness? That boy probably said the first thing that came into his head when Brian Kirby was talking to him. Can you imagine what a jury would make of that? Let alone a prosecuting counsel?'

'Surely we have to bear in mind the—'

The superintendent rapped his pipe so firmly on the ashtray that ash and unsmoked tobacco sprayed over the polished surface of the desk. 'What really beggars belief is that you're prepared to believe that a man like Councillor Broadbent could have something to do with someone like Mattie Harris. The fact he's your wife's uncle makes it even more extraordinary.' Williamson paused, then added in a calmer voice, 'Of course, even if Leigh was telling the truth, he didn't see her go up to the house, did he? So she might have had another reason for nipping into that driveway. Call of nature, perhaps?'

There was a long uneasy silence. Thornhill examined his nails, which were clean. He wished he were anywhere but here. He looked up and saw Williamson staring at him. They were both waiting for Thornhill to choose. The trouble was, he was in a position where any choice would be the wrong one.

'There's one other problem,' he said slowly.

'Can't it wait?' Williamson said, meaning couldn't it wait forever.

'Gerald Pembridge admitted to me that he'd had an affair with Mattie Harris.'

Williamson leant back in his chair and took his time refilling his pipe. He gestured with the stem at the folder on his desk. 'There's nothing about that here.'

'No, sir. I haven't yet filed a report.'

'When did Mr Pembridge make this admission?'

'Yesterday morning, sir. Jimmy Leigh told me he'd seen Mr Pembridge kissing Mattie Harris in the park several weeks ago.'

'Ah – Jimmy Leigh. Keeps turning up like a bad penny, doesn't he? And you believed him?'

'Mr Pembridge did admit he had been having an affair.'

'Was there a third party present when you say he made this admission?'

'No, sir.'

'Then if I were you, Thornhill, if I didn't want to make a complete B.F. of myself, I'd be inclined to keep quiet about it. What I think probably happened is that Gerald Pembridge got a bit flustered when you talked to him – he's a nice man, but he does tend to panic – and just got confused. He probably thought you were asking him if he knew Mattie Harris, and of course he did – the girl used to go to those hops that he and Edna organise.'

'Sir, he admitted that they had had a sexual relationship. There was no doubt about it.'

Williamson nodded his head ponderously. 'That's as may be. I'm not convinced. But in any case, would it stand up in court? Is it relevant?'

Thornhill said nothing.

'Don't you worry, I'll have a word with Pembridge myself.' Williamson's voice was almost gentle now, the burr of the Lydmouth accent more evident than usual. 'And I really don't think we need pay too much attention to what Leigh's alleging.

He's desperate. He's trying to smear the reputations of the most respectable people in town. That's the way a jury will look at it, believe me. And that's what counts.'

Williamson pushed aside the file and picked up a letter from his in-tray, which he studied with the appearance of complete concentration. A moment later, he looked up at Thornhill, sitting in his chair and trying to contain his anger.

'What are you waiting for, man? You've got a job to do. Hadn't you better get down to Framington?'

Chapter Thirty-eight

Late on Wednesday morning, Violet told her mother she was going down to the library, which was true. She took the three romantic novels with her. They made her feel she still had a little bit of Mattie, the ghostly support of a friend.

The sun was out as she walked into town. Lydmouth looked different from usual, as though she were seeing it from a different perspective. This might have been any day in her life. She waved to one of her mother's friends on the other side of the road and had an intense discussion about the weather with the owner of the sweet shop, where she stopped to buy a quarter of toffee crunchies. But why did it no longer seem that this life belonged to her?

She decided to leave the library until last. With a crunchy in each cheek, she went up to Castle Street. At the last moment she lost her nerve. Mr Sedbury's car wasn't parked outside Sedbury & Son but that meant nothing because he often walked to the office, or Mrs Sedbury gave him and Malcolm a lift. Shadowy shapes of people moved like fish underwater in the front office. She imagined their faces if she went inside — saw the pity, the curiosity, the disapproval.

Her heart was thumping. Head averted, she walked quickly past the dark-green front door. The bag with the library books knocked against her thigh. Further up the street was a bench near a bus stop. She sat down, feeling in her bag for the toffee crunchies.

A door banged. She paused, a sweet half-way to her mouth. The footsteps coming along the pavement were slow, dragging and uneven. She pushed the crunchies back into the bag.

'Violet,' Malcolm Sedbury said.

She looked up at him. He was breathing hard too, just as she was, though not for the same reason. It had been an effort for him to come after her. He smiled and folded himself down onto the bench beside her.

'I saw you passing,' he went on. 'Couldn't let you go without having a word.'

'I was coming to collect my things.'

'I wish you weren't leaving us.'

'Well, your dad doesn't agree, and that's that.' She glanced at him. 'Sorry. Shouldn't take it out on you.'

'That's all right. You've had a lot to put up with.'

Violet picked a loose thread from her skirt. She didn't want Malcolm to see the tears in her eyes. It seemed a long time since anyone had actually said something sympathetic to her.

'Would it make things easier if I collected your things? You could tell me what you need.'

'Would you? It's only the stuff in the bottom drawer of my desk.' She glanced sideways at him. 'The desk I used to have. You'll have got someone else by now.'

'A temporary with a face like a pudding,' Malcolm said. 'She's no good at all. Even my father says so. Do you know what you're going to do?'

She shrugged.

'Bill said he was going to try and see you yesterday.'

'He did.' Violet turned to look at Malcolm. 'And I wish he hadn't. I wish I'd never bloody met him, and that's the truth.'

'I think in your position I'd feel the same.'

'Everything's gone wrong,' Violet said, feeling the tears breaking through again. 'And since Mattie's died, it's got even worse. It's *getting* worse.'

'Violet,' Malcolm said and then stopped.

'What?'

'It looks as if the police may think she didn't die by accident. The inquest was adjourned.'

'I know.'

The words hung in the air between them. Violet thought if she listened hard enough she would hear all the things she wasn't saying and Malcolm wasn't saying, all those ghostly conversations they must never have.

'So what will you do?' Malcolm asked.

'Perhaps it's best if I go away.'

'Do you need money?'

Violet shrugged. 'I've got five or six pounds. That's all I've got left. It's been expensive having Grace.'

'Would it help if I lent you some? I could manage fifteen pounds.'

She nodded. Mattie used to take money from men. Was this different?

'I'll give you a cheque made out to cash.'

'I – I'd better not,' she said mechanically. 'Wouldn't be right.'

'You can pay me back when you're settled.'

'I wish . . .'

'What?'

She shook her head. 'It doesn't matter.'

'Where will you go?'

'I don't know. Cardiff, maybe.'

He stared at her for a moment, his brown eyes full of sadness. 'I'll fetch your things, and a cheque. Will you wait here? I shan't be a moment.'

She watched him hauling himself along the pavement towards his father's office. Malcolm had always confused her and now the confusion had deepened. She couldn't imagine Bill ever being gentle and kind as Malcolm had been. She almost wished she had fallen in love with Malcolm, not with Bill. She wondered what he was like naked, whether the polio had crippled more than his legs.

Another crunchy found its way into her mouth. There was something unsettling about Malcolm, as well, and not just in the physical sense. Why was he being so kind? Why was he lending her money? He had never been like this before. He'd never been nasty to her, but he'd kept his distance. She'd thought of him as Bill's friend. At work he was Mr Malcolm, one of the bosses.

But now, for some reason, things had changed. And the most worrying thing of all was that she could date the change precisely.

Malcolm had started being nice to her on Saturday afternoon. Just before she heard the news of Mattie's death.

Chapter Thirty-nine

———=≫o◦o≪=———

'What are you doing here?' Jill said, squinting up at him through the sunlight.

'They've taken me off the Harris case.' Richard rubbed his forehead. 'Sorry to barge in like this.'

'You're not barging in anywhere. I'm glad to see you.' Jill put her marker in *The Vicar of Bullhampton* and extricated herself as gracefully as possible from the deckchair. 'Do you want some tea?'

'No, thanks. I should be getting back to Framington.'

'Framington?'

'Temporary transfer.' He sat down on the low wall of the little terrace. 'DCI Trotter's got glandular fever.'

She perched beside him. For a moment they sat side by side looking out over the estuary. Jill had spent all day outside. Everyone said the fine weather wouldn't last so she wanted to make the most of it. She was a little hurt that Richard hadn't mentioned her possible pregnancy. If he'd been a woman, it would have been the first thing on his mind.

'Are you going to tell me about it?' she said at last.

He smiled. 'There's no one else I can tell. What I think has happened is that Mattie Harris had friends in high places. Jimmy Leigh saw her kissing Gerald Pembridge a few weeks ago.

I talked to him, and he admitted he'd had an affair with Mattie. Not that he'd ever say so in public. And Jimmy also saw Mattie going into Netherfield the weekend before last.'

'Bernie Broadbent's place?'

He nodded. 'They'll both deny it. So it's Jimmy Leigh's words against theirs, and in any case no one's going to believe Jimmy.'

'But *Bernie* – I can hardly believe it.' She was about to say more, to mention what she had seen last night, but Richard gave her no opportunity.

'Bernie's on the Standing Joint Committee, and so's Cyril George, who's another great friend of Pembridge's. Williamson knows them all through the Masons, of course. Which is no doubt why he's come back from sick leave and taken over the case. He's made up his mind that Jimmy killed Mattie Harris if anyone did. And if he knew I was telling you all this, he'd probably assume I've got rabies and have me shot.'

'Surely the Chief Constable—'

'James Hendry won't cause them any problems,' Richard said harshly. 'He's been trying to persuade the Standing Joint Committee for years that the CID needs new cars, and for their own use only. The SJC didn't agree, but suddenly they seem to have changed their mind. He's not going to risk endangering that.'

'So the only fly in the ointment is you?'

'Bernie's threatening to put our house in Edie's name.'

'I don't understand.'

'I think it's partly a not-so subtle way of making sure I toe the line. It's not a bribe but it would look like one. And I'm not sure I can stop him doing it. They're sucking me in with them, Jill. It's like a quicksand. So if they go down, so do I.'

'What's this about Framington?'

'Luckily for them, Dick Trotter has gone off sick in the nick of time. Framington's a big divisional CID, a lot of men. So the temporary transfer seems quite natural. Especially as Williamson suddenly feels well enough to return to duty. What it all comes down to is that they're going to sweep Mattie Harris under the carpet. And probably make sure Leigh goes with her.'

'I saw Violet Evans yesterday,' Jill said. 'Down in the village. She'd just been to see Mattie's parents. I had quite a chat with her.'

'You didn't mention it.'

'I've not seen you since then.' She stared at him for a moment. 'Oh Richard, I wish things didn't have to be like this.'

He stretched out a hand and took one of hers. 'I'm sorry.'

'It's my fault as much as yours. Or it's no one's fault. Just one of those things.'

'What about your period? I should have asked before.'

'It hasn't come. But it may. It's not *that* late.'

He was still holding her hand. With his free hand, he began to stroke first the hand, then the wrist and then the arm above it. She shivered. He turned towards her. She felt his breath on her face.

'There's something else I ought to tell you,' she went on, rather hurriedly. 'Violet said that Mattie used to go with older men sometimes, for money. She was going to use some of it to pay for a bathroom at her parents' cottage. Violet wouldn't say who the men were. She claimed she didn't know.'

'But you think there's at least a chance that she knows the names of Mattie's lovers?'

Richard's hands were still moving over her, exploring other parts of her body. Jill stretched, languorously like a cat.

'I suppose it's possible. No more than that.'

She thought of something else that Violet said, that one of the old men hadn't in fact wanted to make love with Mattie, but had paid her to pretend that he had. Could that tie in with what she had seen in the car park near the cinema the previous evening?

Two things stopped her mentioning it right away. One was that she liked Bernie and couldn't see why the law should make an example of him, as it had done with Oscar Wilde. She needed at least to be sure that Richard would treat the information as confidential. The other reason was that Richard's hands were now roaming freely and pleasurably beneath her skirt. She felt ready to run any risk, to seize any happiness. They might not have another chance. She locked her hands around his neck and pulled him towards her.

'Come on,' she said. 'Let's do it now. Here. In the garden.'

Chapter Forty

Superintendent Williamson was squatting on the closed seat of the lavatory, thick forefinger pointing down like a vengeful god's at the floor. The wash basin was of the pedestal kind, with a gap of an inch between the pedestal and the wall behind. From this angle, you could just make out a small pile of pink powder, most of it lodged in the crack, vivid against the green linoleum.

With agonising slowness, he bent closer and closer to the powder. The tip of his finger touched the edge of the pile. Even more slowly, even more agonisingly, he sat up again and sniffed his finger with a rapt expression on his face.

'Looks like face powder to me.' He sniffed his finger once again. 'Bit like that stuff that was in Mattie Harris's compact. See if you can find young Sally the Sleuth. It's the sort of thing a girl would know.'

Kirby went to the door of the bathroom. He could hear Joan talking to Minnie Calder in the lounge. Two other constables were searching the house, one upstairs and the other downstairs. There was a third talking to the other inhabitants of River Gardens. There had been two other officers in the original party but they were now otherwise occupied – chasing Jimmy Leigh. The man-boy had taken fright when he saw the police cars drawing up outside the house and made a run for it. According to Minnie Calder, he'd gone through the back door like a rocket, down the garden and through the gate to the towpath along the Minnow.

Kirby went downstairs. Minnie Calder was sitting white and frightened in an armchair. She seemed to have shrunk since they arrived. Kirby beckoned Joan out of the lounge.

'We need your technical assistance, Constable,' he murmured on the stairs.

She stopped so sharply that he bumped into her thigh.

'Sorry,' Kirby said, and smiled at her.

'Why?' Joan said.

Kirby winked in what he hoped was an enigmatic yet attractive fashion and said nothing. Keep them guessing was always a good motto, in love as in a criminal investigation. He took her into the bathroom where Williamson was still enthroned on the lavatory pan.

'Ah, Sally the Sleuth!' Williamson beckoned her towards him and then pointed towards the base of the wash basin's pedestal. 'See that powder? What do you reckon it is?'

Joan shot Kirby a puzzled glance and knelt down. The two men watched her with an interest which in Kirby's case was not entirely professional.

'Just take a tiny bit from the edge,' Williamson commanded. 'And for Christ's sake, don't sneeze. That's evidence, that is.'

Joan gingerly touched the powder and then sat back on her heels. She sniffed her fingers. 'I'd say it was face powder, sir.' She smelled it again. 'In fact, it's almost certainly Fleur de Rose.'

Williamson beamed at her. 'Good girl. Now where have I come across that name before?'

'It's the name of the powder that Mattie Harris used, sir.' Joan looked up at him, frowning, trying to guess what he wanted. 'There was some in the compact we found, and a pot of the stuff in her bedroom.'

'This is a new house, right?' Williamson said. 'Minnie Calder is the only woman who's ever lived here, right?'

He looked from one to the other, until they both chorused, 'Yes, sir.'

'So we need to find out if she uses Fleur de Rose. Failing that, whether any woman who's likely to have used the bathroom could have used Fleur de Rose. And then we see if the lab will confirm the findings of your sensitive nose.' His mouth split into a smile. 'That's what a jury likes, hard evidence. Stuff you can see. And in this case smell.'

'So if it is Fleur de Rose, sir,' Kirby said slowly, 'and if we can't find anyone else who used it who came to the house, then it's reasonable to suppose it could have been Mattie Harris?'

Williamson nodded. 'I'm not one to speculate, of course, though I'd say the facts more or less speak for themselves. Jimmy Leigh runs away as soon as he sees us this afternoon. Lad's got a guilty conscience. Mattie Harris is in the pudding club. Wanted to try to get rid of it the traditional way. But she doesn't have a bathroom of her own, so she needs a pal to help, a pal with modern plumbing. Here's young Leigh, totally besotted with her, with a nice new bathroom in his house. And on Thursday nights, his auntie goes off to play housey-housey at the King's Head, so there's no risk of interruption. Do we know when Calder got back?'

'Neighbour thinks it was near midnight, sir,' Kirby said. 'But he's a long way from being sure.'

'All right. Mattie tells a few lies to her employee and her parents so she can recover on Friday. Then on Thursday evening, she comes here after that dance. She's probably already drunk by the time she gets in the bath, and she drops her handbag. Maybe that's when the mirror in the compact got cracked. Lid opens, and some of the powder spills out. Once she's in the bath, then Leigh gets carried away. Probably never seen a naked woman before.' Williamson's pale eyes flicked towards Joan Ailsmore. 'It's a sight that can do strange things to a man, especially one that's weak in the head like Leigh. Maybe they quarrelled. Who knows? Doesn't really matter *why* he did it.'

'But how did she get in the river afterwards, sir?' Kirby asked, sensing that this was what Williamson wanted him to say.

'Nothing easier. He's a big man. She was a little slip of a thing.' Williamson stood up and walked across the bathroom to the window. He pushed the casement wide and leaned out. 'He could have put her in that wheelbarrow down there. Which I notice has been left out in the rain, so there won't be any traces now. Just as easy, he could have carried her. Not got far to walk – just through that gate. Then he threw her in the Minnow there and then. The river was in full spate.'

'He must have got her dressed,' Joan pointed out.

'He's not a complete idiot, Constable.' Williamson glared at her. 'Besides, I can't help wondering if Auntie helped him tidy up afterwards. She's like a cat with one kitten, that one.'

It all sounded perfectly plausible, Kirby thought. Williamson sat down suddenly on his throne again. The expression of triumph was fading. A grey tinge haunted his high-coloured face.

'Are you all right, sir?' Kirby said, alarmed.

'Fine,' he mumbled. 'Carry on. See what else you can find. I'll just get my breath back, and then we'll have a little chat with Minnie Calder.'

But when they went downstairs, Miss Calder claimed she'd never even heard of a face powder called Fleur de Rose, and she didn't like foreign muck anyway. Certainly they found no more of it in the house. She stuck doggedly to the story about Thursday night. She wasn't sure when she got back from housey-housey, but she thought it must have been before ten thirty, and she had naturally assumed Jimmy was asleep. Yes, she had used the bathroom before going to bed, and no, she hadn't noticed that it had been in any way out of the ordinary.

Kirby knew that it wouldn't be easy to break this line of defence. By its very nature, there was little that could be disproved about her story, and she was not the sort of woman who would break down easily in an interview room or a witness box.

There was a ring on the doorbell. Jimmy was on the

doorstep, sandwiched between two constables. He was clasping a clockwork railway engine to his chest.

'We found him outside the old Fenner's yard up the river, Sarge,' one of the constables said. 'Trying to hide this under his jersey, and screamed when we tried to take it off him. If you ask me, he's completely off his rocker.'

Williamson, attracted by the sound of new voices, lumbered down the stairs and swept them all into the lounge. Minnie Calder shrank still further into her armchair. The room was overcrowded. Jimmy filled it with his smell, sour and sweaty, the scent of fear.

'Oh ho,' Williamson said. 'The wanderer returns, Miss Calder. And it looks like we've retrieved some stolen property, as well. It's never rains but it pours, does it?'

Jimmy Leigh moaned. He broke away from the two constables and collapsed on the carpet beside his aunt's chair. He buried his head in her lap. She stroked his hair, her fingers working their way down to the scalp. The engine lay on its side on the hearthrug.

There was a tap on the half-open door and Joan slipped into the room with an envelope in her hand. She glanced from Kirby to Williamson.

'Yes?' the superintendent said, his eyes still on Minnie Calder and Jimmy Leigh.

'I thought you should see this, sir.'

Williamson took the envelope and pulled out the folded sheet of paper it contained. Something else fluttered to the floor. Kirby saw the panic leap into Minnie Calder's face, then saw it instantly repressed. And only then did he look to see what had fallen. It was a lock of hair, tied with a blue ribbon.

Williamson unfolded the sheet of paper. 'Well, well. No wonder you're so fond of that young man, Miss Calder. After all, he's your son.'

Chapter Forty-one

Violet lifted the library books out of the bag, opened them out and slid them across the counter towards the assistant, a willowy young woman of about her own age. The assistant frowned when she saw the due date in the first book, and her frown deepened as she went down the pile.

'I'm afraid they're all a bit late,' Violet said, leaning on the high counter.

The willowy girl gave a nod. She flicked through the tickets on the trays until she found the first of Mattie's. 'It is Miss *Martha* Harris, isn't it? Not Mary J?'

'Yes, but—'

'Excuse me.' The girl wanted to pick up the second book and Violet's elbow was in the way. 'There's a reservation on this one.'

Another person had come into the library. Violet was vaguely aware of someone large and middle aged, who stacked her books forcefully on the counter as though reminding them of their place in life.

'Sorry.'

'*Love's Wild Dreamer*,' the assistant said, putting the book on a separate pile. 'And it's five pence each, Miss Harris, so the total fines are one and three.'

Violet thought about trying to explain that she wasn't Mattie

Harris, that Mattie Harris was dead and couldn't dream of anything any more, but it seemed too difficult and it would take too long. And everyone in the library would listen, and wonder who was that ugly fat girl making a fool of herself. Besides, she had cashed Malcolm's cheque and was feeling rich. Violet fished out her purse, which was rather greasy after the fish and chips she'd had at lunchtime, and took out the coins, one by one.

'Shan't be a moment, Mrs Wemyss-Brown,' the girl said, turning to put the other two books on the trolley behind her. A white envelope fluttered out of *My Kingdom For a Kiss*. She stooped, picked it up and put it on the counter. 'You left that in the book.'

A sixpence, a shilling and half-a-dozen coppers slipped through Violet's fingers, fell to the polished parquet floor where they danced, spun and scuttled away to hide in dark corners. The willowy assistant clucked and glanced piously in the direction of heaven. Mrs Wemyss-Brown, however, knelt down and helped Violet pick up the coins.

'This once happened to me in the middle of Harrods' Food Hall,' she said in a voice that must have been audible in the reference library upstairs. 'Luckily there was a frightfully handsome Indian playboy on hand who helped me pick them up. He took me out to tea afterwards.'

Violet put some of the coins on the counter, stuffed the envelope in her bag, and smiled her thanks. Everyone was looking at them. Wishing she were invisible, she left the library. She blundered into the door jamb and stumbled down the steps. She stood in the High Street, gulping breaths of fresh air and wondering why she always made such a fool of herself. She opened her handbag, and with trembling hands put the rest of coins back in the purse.

Only then did she take out the envelope. Small and white, it was addressed to Mattie Harris at Lower Slade Cottage in Eastbury. No surprises there.

But the address was in Bill Pembridge's handwriting.

Chapter Forty-two

'Mattie Harris?' Bernie Broadbent said. 'Why are you asking *me*?'

'As you know, we have a witness who saw her turning into your drive the previous weekend.'

'Some witness.' Bernie opened the door wider. 'You'd better come in, I suppose.'

He led the way not into the big sitting room but into a small office at the side of the house. The window looked out into the dank shrubbery. The furniture was scuffed and old, without being in any way being distinguished. It didn't belong with the affluent anonymity of the the rest of the house. Bernie sat in a swivel chair behind the desk and nodded to Thornhill to take a seat.

'Listen, Richard, I understand that the witness in question was Jimmy Leigh. I don't need to tell you that there are witnesses and witnesses. I've nothing against the lad, not personally, but the odds are he killed Mattie Harris, and most people in this town wouldn't give a brass farthing for what he says he saw.'

'We believe that Miss Harris was seeing at least one older man,' Thornhill said carefully. 'Almost certainly more.'

'She was putting herself about, was she? I don't like the way this conversation is going. Quite apart from anything, you're being bloody rude. If you weren't Edith's husband, you'd be out on your ear.'

Thornhill said, 'So you're saying that Mattie Harris never came here, that you didn't know her?'

'I told you – she served me at the Gardenia.'

'But you're sure she didn't come here?'

Bernie leaned back in his chair, resting his hands along the padded arms. 'A little bird told me that this investigation is no longer your concern.'

'If she was murdered, then it's everyone's concern to find out who did it.'

'Don't split hairs with me. Ray Williamson has taken over the case and you know it. What's he going to say if I tell him you've been poking your nose round here?'

Thornhill shrugged.

'Now, is there anything else you want to say?' Bernie stood up. 'Don't think I'm trying to get rid of you, but I am busy.'

Thornhill stood up too. 'Edith tells me you're thinking of putting the house in her name.'

Bernie nodded, and moved round the desk towards the door.

Thornhill stayed where he was. 'I'd rather you didn't.'

'Why not?'

'Because people will talk even more if it comes out. And of course it will come out.'

'I've nothing to hide,' Bernie said. 'Have you?'

Thornhill stared at him, riding both the anger and the fear he felt creeping around him like an invisible mist.

'In any case, you can't stop me.' Bernie smiled. 'There's no reason why I shouldn't give it to her. She's got a perfect right to accept the gift, without having to ask you. In one sense, it's nothing to do with you. For all I care you can pay her rent.'

Bernie held open the door. Thornhill preceded him into the hall. He nodded goodbye as he left; he didn't trust himself to speak.

He drove away, without looking back. Between them, the old men of Lydmouth had stitched up the case very neatly. Bernie was right – Thornhill no longer had official standing in this investigation. And if Bernie told Williamson he'd paid a call on him, there'd be hell to pay.

At the bottom of Narth Road, he waited at the junction for so long that the car behind him hooted. Then he made up his mind and turned right along the Chepstow Road rather than driving towards police headquarters in the town centre. No one was expecting him there and he knew he knew he wouldn't be welcome.

Nor would he be welcome at the Divisional CID Office at Framington. Trotter's deputy, a recently promoted detective inspector, was showing every sign that he could run Framington CID with rather more efficiency than DCI Trotter. Not unnaturally, he resented the arrival of Thornhill almost as much as Thornhill resented being sent there.

Might as well be hanged for a sheep as a lamb.

He turned into Broadwell Drive. The road had not yet been adopted by the Council and paved, so he drove with caution, because the Austin was his own car. Broadwell Crescent looked even worse, the muddy, rutted roadway littered with discarded planks and broken bricks. He left the car in Broadwell Drive and picked his way through the rubbish towards the Evanses' house. He rang the bell and eventually a plump middle-aged woman in a flowered housecoat came to the door. The sound of a baby's cries wafted down the stairs.

'Mrs Evans?' Thornhill removed his hat. 'I wonder if I could have a word with Miss Violet Evans.'

'She's not in.' The woman glanced behind her, up the stairs. 'Can I take a message?'

'I'm Detective Inspector Thornhill.' He tried the effect of a smile, and Mrs Evans's face twitched in response, giving a glimpse of how pretty she must have been when she was younger. 'I just wanted a word with Miss Evans.'

'About Mattie Harris's death, would it be?'

He nodded. 'When will she be back?'

'She should be back now. She was going to the library, and

she wanted to do a bit of shopping. But that was hours ago.' Her forehead corrugated into a frown. 'Baby's getting hungry again.'

Thornhill heard footsteps behind him, and the click of the latch on the gate. He turned. Ted Evans was walking down the path, bag on shoulder and pipe in mouth.

'Who's this then?' he demanded.

'It's Mr – from the police.'

'Detective Inspector Thornhill, sir. We've met.'

'Aye. What are you doing here?'

'I was hoping to have a word with your daughter about Mattie Harris, sir.'

Ted shrugged. 'She'll be back. We'll tell her you called.'

It was a dismissal, and Thornhill knew there was no point in arguing. But as he opened his mouth to say goodbye, a thought struck him.

'You must have known Mattie Harris yourselves. The family lived near you at one time, didn't they? What did you think of her?'

'No better than she should be,' Ted said. 'No point in pretending otherwise. She'd flirt with anything in trousers, young or old.'

'Oh, but she had a lovely nature, Ted,' Mrs Evans burst out. And she clapped her hand over her mouth, as though trying to hold back the words, and looked appealingly at her husband.

Thornhill said goodbye and drove home, hoping to catch sight of Violet Evans on the way. She was the only person who was likely to be able to confirm the existence of Mattie Harris's old men. She might even know their names. She might have seen Mattie with one or more of them.

When he reached Victoria Road, the children were making a tent out of the clothes line and an old sheet in the back garden, while Edith was in the kitchen, rearranging the roses.

'Hello, darling,' she said, inclining her cheek for a kiss. 'You're early. Good day?'

Perhaps she had been out in the sun, or perhaps it was simply the fact she was happy, but her face glowed. Edith had the promise of a house, of central heating. David was going to Ashbridge next term. She was even, God help her, back home with him in Lydmouth, after the weekend in Bournemouth which had involved too much family and too little enjoyment. He hadn't seen her looking like this for a long time. Why was that? For an instant, he had a glimpse of the monotony of her life, the round of dreary domestic tasks, and wondered how that could make anyone happy. But that's what she wants, he told himself, that's what most women want; and suddenly he wondered whether that were true.

'There's no reason why we shouldn't have a rose bed near the back of the lawn,' she said. 'It's nice and sunny there and it would draw the eye down the garden. What do you think?'

'Good idea.' He turned away, pretending to stare out of the window at the possible site of the rose bed. 'Next time I get a free day, I'll dig it out for you. Look at those clouds coming up. More rain's on its way.'

They took their tea out into the garden and stood watching the children play.

'They've been going on about the kittens all day,' Edith said. 'Do you think it would be all right if I phoned Miss Francis?'

Thornhill began to say that it wasn't worth trying to phone her until next week, then realised that Edith might wonder how he knew Jill was away, and pretended to choke on his tea. He cleared his throat. 'I'm sure she wouldn't mind.'

'I looked up her number in the book but it's not listed yet. Perhaps it would be better if I rang her at the *Gazette*.' Edith had looked up at him. 'Are you sure you don't mind the children having the kittens?'

'It's really a question of whether you do. I imagine you'll be doing most of the work of looking after them after the first day or two.'

'At least they shouldn't cost much to feed. I've had a word with the butcher. He's very obliging.'

Thornhill smiled and nodded, knowing that the butcher was obliging because CID had interviewed his son last year about his connection with a robbery at a tobacconist's. Charges hadn't been pressed, and the butcher was wrongly but usefully grateful.

'They'll be so sweet,' Edith went on, stirring her tea with great concentration. 'Sometimes I wonder if we should have another child. They're so lovely when they're young. And now money's getting a little easier . . .'

'Yes,' said Thornhill. 'Something to think about.'

He stared at his children. David was now tightly rolled in the sheet. His sister, making the most of her rare moment of physical superiority, was kicking him.

'Elizabeth, don't do that,' Edith called. She lowered her voice. 'If we do have another one, then the sooner the better.'

'Yes, you're right.'

They looked at each other, both half-smiling. Thornhill felt as though he'd crested a rise and found instead of a gentle slope beneath him, a sudden vertiginous drop. He wanted to say something – say anything to break the silence which was crowded with half-sensed possibilities. Then the doorbell rang, and the moment vanished.

'I'll see who it is,' he said.

'I'd better go and do something about David.'

Sergeant Kirby was standing in the porch with a mac slung over his shoulder and a wary expression on his face.

'Brian. What can I do for you?'

'I wondered if we could have a word, Guv.' He was standing at right angles to the doorway and he glanced down Victoria Road as if checking to see if he had been followed. 'If you can spare a moment, that is.'

'Come into the dining room. Do you want some beer? If the sun isn't over the yard arm, it damn well ought to be.'

Surprise fluttered across Kirby's face. Thornhill rarely swore, even mildly, and was usually a modest drinker.

The Thornhills ate in the dining room once or twice a year

when Edith felt that they should aspire to a station in life they did not belong to. Over half the floor was taken up with tea chests, homeless furniture, piles of unshelved books, the equipment of an amateur painter and decorator, and all the detritus that Edith had not yet found a place for. Now this was going to be her house, Thornhill guessed, she would want to settle into it. Wallpaper would have to be hung, shelves would have to be built, paint would have to be applied.

He left Kirby sitting at the table looking blankly at the tins of paint. He fetched beer and glasses from the pantry, told Edith who was there – did he imagine the expression of relief on her face? – and went back to the dining room. Kirby was still sitting where Thornhill had left him, looking as if he had not moved a muscle. Thornhill passed him a glass and an opened bottle. For a moment both men drank in silence.

Kirby took out his cigarettes. 'Do you mind?'

Thornhill shook his head and pushed an ashtray towards him. 'Has something happened?'

Kirby's eyes slid away from his, down to the packet in his hand. 'We went to Minnie Calder's this afternoon. Quite a lot of us.' He rolled a cigarette between finger and thumb and golden flecks of tobacco drifted down to the dark mahogany of the table. 'Including the superintendent.'

'And?'

'Leigh took one look at the police cars in River Gardens and did a bunk out the back. Gave them quite a run for their money. In the end they found him crying outside Fenner's – do you know it? – that old timber mill near the slaughterhouse?'

Thornhill nodded, sipping beer.

'He had the toy engine he nicked on Saturday. Cuddling it, like it was a teddy or something.' Kirby glanced at the cigarette between his fingers and frowned. He put it in his mouth and struck a match. 'Anyway, the search of the house had turned up a couple of things. One was his birth certificate. It turns out Minnie Calder isn't his aunt – she's his mum. Usual story – she was working up in the Smoke, had a fling with a bloke she'd met at the Hammersmith Palais and then persuaded her sister and brother-in-law to bring the boy up as their own.'

'Does Leigh know yet?'

'Mr Williamson came out with it in front of them both. Shock tactic, I suppose. I don't think Leigh's taken it in yet. He looks like someone's hit him over the head. Friend of mine at school was in the same boat, found out his big sister was his mum, just like that, out of the blue. He went off and joined up, lied about his age, and they—'

'Brian,' Thornhill interrupted. 'You said two things turned up in the search.'

He saw the flare of alarm in Kirby's eyes, and knew at once that this was the reason for his being here, this was the reason for his rambling on about Jimmy's parentage.

'Yes. Well, Guv, the other thing was, Mr Williamson found some face powder on the bathroom floor. Behind the basin. As if someone had dropped a compact and a little bit of the powder had fallen out. Joan reckons it's Fleur de Rose, which is the same stuff Mattie Harris used, the stuff that was in the compact we found on the riverbank.'

Kirby outlined Williamson's theory: that Mattie had asked Jimmy if she could have a bath at his house on Thursday evening in the hope of inducing an abortion, while Minnie Calder was down the King's Head; that Jimmy had got himself excited and ended up killing her; and that afterwards he'd put her clothes on and dumped her in the Minnow to make it look like she drowned.

'Perhaps Miss Calder helped,' Thornhill said. 'Her brain, his muscles.'

'That's what Mr Williamson thinks.'

Thornhill shrugged. 'It hangs together. But is there enough evidence to make a charge stick?'

'The super's got him down the station now. Trying to get a confession out of him. He tried with the Calder woman first, but he didn't get any change out of her. So now he's working on Leigh.' Kirby swallowed. 'Not that he's getting very far there, either. The lad's just sitting there, crying. Won't say a bloody word.'

'You can't argue with the evidence,' Thornhill said, wondering whether he'd ever learn to live with the humiliation of knowing that Williamson had been right all along.

'Well, that's just it, sir. You can.'

'What do you mean?'

'You remember me and Joan went to talk to Calder and Leigh on Saturday? I needed a pee while we were there.' Kirby inhaled deeply, his colour darkening. 'You know how it is. Sometimes a few drops go on the floor. Between the toilet and the basin. And Minnie Calder's like a textbook case of being house proud. There was a cloth behind the toilet, so I bent down to wipe it up.' He glanced at Thornhill. 'Christ, this sounds stupid.'

'Go on.'

'The thing is, from where I was, I could see behind the basin. If there'd been anything there, I'm sure I would have noticed it, because I was thinking how bloody spotless every surface was, how pernickety she must be. You see? I'd lay good money that she cleans that place from top to bottom at least twice a week. And if she knew Mattie Harris had died in her precious new bath, she'd be even more thorough than usual. Would *she* have missed the face powder too?'

'Brian, are you sure of this?'

'Yes, sir.'

'Sure enough to stand up in court if necessary?'

There was a long silence. Neither of them moved. Smoke drifted towards the ceiling. It was growing darker as clouds rolled slowly across the sky. In the garden, Elizabeth started howling.

Brian Kirby was one of the more observant officers in the force, and Thornhill would back him against most of his colleagues. He also had no reason to rock the boat. Which added up to two reasons for believing him. If the face powder hadn't been there on Saturday, it must have been planted since then. If the face powder was Fleur de Rose, it must have been planted by somebody who knew the face powder that Mattie Harris used, by someone who wanted to increase the weight of evidence against Jimmy Leigh. Williamson had found the face powder. Why had Williamson taken personal charge of the search of the house in River Gardens? He was a superintendent, for God's sake, not a sergeant.

Kirby took a long swallow of beer, put down the glass and wiped his mouth with the back of his hand. 'He's all but retired, Guv. He couldn't be so stupid. And anyway, why would he want to do a thing like that? It doesn't make any sort of sense at all.'

It made plenty of sense if the old men of Lydmouth wanted to keep quiet about their connections with Mattie Harris. It made perfect sense, too if one of them had been the father of that baby. And what if Williamson himself was one of the old men?

'Sir,' Kirby said urgently. 'What do—'

The phone on the end of the bookcase began to ring again, the sound slicing through the warm, smoky atmosphere of the room like a cheese wire. Thornhill snatched up the receiver.

'Lydmouth two one one four.'

'Inspector Thornhill?' Charlotte Wemyss-Brown's voice thundered down the wires like a well-bred avalanche. 'So sorry to ring you at home — I tried the police station first, but they said you weren't there. I could have left a message, of course, but I felt it's something *you* should know.'

'Why me, Mrs Wemyss-Brown?'

There was a muffled explosion at the other end of the line which Thornhill eventually identified as a snort of irritation. 'Because you're in charge of the Harris investigation. You should know that if anyone does.'

Thornhill often felt when he was dealing with Mrs Wemyss-

Brown, that she occupied a parallel universe, one in which she was able to suspend the normal social conventions at will. 'What did you want to tell me?'

No need to inform Mrs Wemyss-Brown that he wasn't in charge of the Harris investigation any longer. He watched Kirby shaking another cigarette from the packet and putting it between his lips.

'There was a young woman in the library this afternoon,' Charlotte trumpeted. 'Plump, fair haired, rather a sweet, pretty face. Which made it all the stranger.'

Thornhill bided his time.

'She seemed perfectly nice, you see. Which is what made it so odd. Why on earth would she want to pretend she was Mattie Harris?'

Chapter Forty-three

'A glass of sherry,' Jill said. 'Yes, I'd like that.'

At Bernie's suggestion, they took their drinks outside. The sky was inky-black to the south-west, but otherwise still clear. They sat in chairs on the paved area by the French windows. Jill sipped her sherry and watched him pouring beer into a glass with total concentration. She realised that under the shelter of the table, her left hand was stroking her belly, in case there might be someone in there who needed reassurance. She lit a cigarette to give the hand something else to do.

'You've just missed Richard Thornhill.' Bernie drank. 'He was on business. And what about you, Miss Francis? Work or social?'

Mock solemn, he looked at her over the rim of his glass. She couldn't help smiling at him.

'Neither, really. Or possibly both. It depends how you look at it.'

He chuckled. 'Typical woman's answer.'

'I've come about Mattie Harris.'

He raised his eyebrows. 'That's why Richard was here, as a matter of fact. Had some damned silly idea I might have known her.'

'And did you?'

'What is this?' The humour had left his face. 'Maybe you'd like to tell me what's going on. Why are you here?'

'Yesterday evening, I was in Gloucester. I went to see a film.'

'Very interesting, I'm sure.'

'If Mattie Harris was killed, then it seems that it would be very convenient for almost everyone if it turned out that Jimmy Leigh was responsible.'

Bernie frowned. He leant forward, resting his elbows on the table, both hands wrapped round the glass. He looked like a badger still, but an angry one. 'Is there supposed to be some sort of link between the two things you just said?'

'When the film was over, I went back to the car. Your car was there too – your new one.'

'My car? How can you be sure?'

'Because I saw you later. When the door opened. When the young man got out.'

'You were mistaken.'

'Mistaken about what?' She watched him for a moment, watched the gleam of sweat just below the hairline on the forehead, watched the knuckles whitening on the glass. 'Mistaken that it was you in the car? Or mistaken that it was some sort of homosexual encounter?' She saw him flinch at the last two words. 'No, there wasn't any room for a mistake. Not in either case. What I saw and heard made that quite clear.'

Bernie swallowed the rest of his beer. 'I still say you were mistaken. It's not as if you can prove anything.'

'Can't I? Who said I was alone?' She told the lie on impulse but once it was there she had no wish to withdraw it. 'And in any case proof need have nothing to do with it. A word here, a hint there – that's all it would take.'

'To blacken my name?' Bernie threw back his head and laughed. 'You've got some nerve, Miss Francis, I'll give you that. Threatening me in my own garden. Threatening me with a pack of lies, to boot. Why are you doing it? That's what I'd like to know.'

'Because of Jimmy Leigh. I think people are trying to frame him. Superintendent Williamson, and perhaps Gerald Pembridge. Not in so many words, most of the time. Just by making a series of minor adjustments to what really happened. Tinkering with history. And somehow you're involved. But if you came out and told the truth about Mattie Harris, then perhaps Jimmy would stand a better chance of having his side of the story heard. After all, what have you got to lose?'

Bernie chuckled. 'Quite a lot, by the sound of it. First you say I'm queer, next you say I'm having an affair with that little waitress. You can't have it both ways.'

'Why not?' She slowly stubbed out her cigarette. 'When I lived in London, I knew several people like that.'

Bernie stared at her, then laughed again, this time without any suggestion of mirth. Even the rumour of what he'd been up to would be enough to damn him for ever in Lydmouth. If there were any evidence against him, he could face prosecution under the Sexual Offences Act. Jill had covered a comparable case for the *Gazette* last year, and the defendant had ended up with an eighteen-month prison sentence.

He went into the house. A moment later, he returned with his tobacco pouch and more beer. He sat down and she watched him filling the pipe with stubby, powerful fingers.

'Are you sure that Leigh's being framed?'

'Yes — in so many words.'

'How do you know?'

'I'm a journalist. Finding things out is my job.'

Bernie lit the pipe. 'I wouldn't want the boy to suffer through my keeping my mouth shut. Mind you, Miss Francis, this has nothing to do with what you may or may not have seen last night. If you want me to do anything for Leigh, that stays out of the picture. Now and always.'

'Of course. It's nothing to do with me.'

'Nor's Jimmy Leigh, I would have thought — but there's no accounting for tastes.' He blew feathers of smoke into the evening air and watched them drift down the garden and disintegrate. 'Yes, Mattie Harris was a friend of Gerald Pembridge's. He had to stop seeing her – I think Mrs Pembridge got wind of it – but he thought that I might be interested in – well, taking over.'

'Were you?'

'A man in my position has to be very careful about the impression he creates,' Bernie said, picking his way carefully among the words he chose, as if they were a field full of stones. 'And of course, being a bachelor can have its inconveniences. Sometimes I have a little card party for a few friends. It's nice to have a hostess for that sort of occasion. But I don't want to give you the wrong idea. It's all—'

'Friends?'

'Their names are nothing to do with you,' he said, with the hint of a growl in his deep voice.

The old men? Ray Williamson, Jill thought, Gerald Pembridge, perhaps Cyril George.

'Card games?'

'Usually poker. Let's walk down the garden. I can't stand being cooped up.'

She followed him along the path down the lawn. The swallows and martins darted above them. She thought she saw a solitary swift nearer the river.

'We only did it a couple of times,' Bernie said over his shoulder. 'The last time was the Saturday before last. Mattie poured the drinks, made sure – made sure everyone was comfortable.'

He turned away, hurrying down the path, and Jill wondered what that euphemism covered. Perhaps they'd played for Mattie's favours. Or perhaps they'd taken her in turn. Bernie must have been the one Violet mentioned, the man who wanted to pretend they had done it when they hadn't, the man who gave her ten pounds for a little lie.

The thought of these middle-aged men prancing around Mattie Harris made her feel queasy. As far as they were concerned, she must have been like a toy, a sort of doll. And the obvious question was whether one of them had liked playing rough games, the sort of games that have unhappy endings for the dollies.

Bernie reached the riverbank. He sat down on the bench near the landing stage and waited for her to join him. Smoke billowed in the air above his head. Suddenly he leant forward, looking down at the water.

'What is it?' Jill said when she reached him.

He glanced up at her. 'You tell me.' He pointed with the stem of his pipe. 'See that over there? The branch caught between the two pillars of the jetty. Something's snagged on it. Something blue.'

Jill went on to the landing stage and peered over the edge. 'Yes,' she said. 'You're quite right – it is something blue.'

'Litter. You find it everywhere these days. Even up here. You'd think people could take it home with them.'

'It's not litter.' She looked back at him. 'I think it's something the police have been looking for.'

Chapter Forty-four

Robert Sedbury was beginning to wonder if he'd been rash. He had worked late at the office two evenings last week. He'd come in on Saturday. And now, here he was on Wednesday, working late again.

Could it have been avoided?

Malcolm was here too — Robert could hear the sound of agonisingly slow typing from his son's office. One of the farms on the Ruispidge estate was coming up for auction and he was typing out the details. It was a fiddly business — land, house, machinery, stock and furniture needing to be dealt with in separate categories, and fully particularised. He himself had been typing his own letters in the intervals of trying to track down wrongly filed correspondence.

Yes, he had to face it: without Violet Evans, the place was going to rack and ruin. He'd never before appreciated quite how much she had managed to do. She had dealt with callers, both in person and by telephone. She had typed letters and sales particulars. She managed the filing. She kept the keys on the right hooks and ordered stationery before it was actually needed. She prevented the clerks from wasting partners' time without good reason. She made tea and coffee promptly, and she knew which biscuits each of the partners favoured. She made sure the office was tidy. She had kept an eye on the women who came in to clean, and she made sure there was fresh milk on the premises.

Without her, it seemed to take twice as long to do everything half as efficiently. Had he perhaps made a mistake? Squeezed between his conscience and his comfort, he squirmed in his chair. Should he perhaps have been more understanding, more ready to forgive? After all, he had not actually been injured.

He stood up and stretched. The sky was darkening fast. He went next door to Malcolm's room. His son was typing with two fingers, one on each hand, while a cigarette dangled from the corner of his mouth.

'Let's call it a day. I'll buy you a drink.'

Malcolm stopped typing and took the cigarette out of his mouth. 'I'd better not, thanks. I'd like to get this finished tonight.'

'You look tired.'

'I'm fine, Dad.' There was a note of irritation in Malcolm's voice. 'Why don't you go by yourself? I'll lock up when I've finished.'

'You know what they say about all work and no play.'

'Please don't fuss. By the way, have you heard from Mr Christie?'

Robert nodded. 'There was a letter in the second post. They do want to make an offer for Wynstones. I think it was the fishing that clinched it. And have you heard the latest about sixty-eight Victoria Road?'

'Has Broadbent changed his mind?'

'Quite the reverse. He wants the sale to go through as soon as possible. But George Shipston tells me that he's planning to put the house in his niece's name. You know – Edith Thornhill. The sitting tenant. Lucky for her, don't you think?'

Malcolm rubbed his forehead with the hand holding the cigarette, as though trying to smooth away the lines. 'Some people seem to have everything handed to them on a plate.'

He jammed the cigarette back in his mouth and began to type, harder but not faster than before.

Robert watched his son's bent head for a moment. "I'll drive over later and collect you if you like.'

'It's OK, Dad. I'll phone Bill.'

Robert picked up his umbrella and briefcase and left the office. When he called goodbye, Malcolm did not reply.

More than half the sky was now dark. He had hardly gone a hundred yards when the rain started. First came a few scattered but heavy drops. He put on speed, hoping to reach the Bull before the worst of the downfall. Then came a sudden flurry, more than enough to make Robert raise his umbrella. Afterwards, for a few seconds, there was no rain at all as though the Rain God needed time to draw in his breath.

At last the deluge began.

The rain bounced on roadway, pavement and roofs, covering every surface with a grey sheen. Cars slowed to walking pace, wipers slashing vainly to and fro as sheets of water ran down their windscreens. The gullies separating roadway from pavement filled in moments and became rapidly widening torrents.

Robert hurried down to the High Street and ducked into the shelter of the entrance to an ironmonger's shop. The umbrella had kept his head and shoulders reasonably dry, but from his elbows downwards he varied from damp to wet. He swore under his breath.

At that precise moment, he realised he was not alone.

Standing at the back of the recess, pressed against the glass-fronted door to the shop, was Violet Evans. She had neither coat nor umbrella. Her summer skirt and blouse were soaked, the material plastered against her generous curves. She wore a tiny hat, now so saturated that it looked like a wet rag. Her perm was ruined.

'Miss Evans! Er – good evening. Frightful weather.'

Rain drummed on the pavement. Car tyres hissed along the roadway. Violet said nothing. It was hard to make out her face clearly – partly because she was right at the back of the entranceway, partly because the rain had bathed the town in premature twilight.

'How are you?' Robert said, trying to grapple with the awkwardness of the situation. 'We — we must find you a taxi.'

She muttered something he didn't catch.

'What was that?'

'Bloody men.'

He pretended he hadn't heard. 'Tell me, are you looking for another job?'

'I'm going away.'

'Really?' Robert was conscious of a feeling of disappointment. 'Where?'

'But maybe I'll say what I know first.' She took a step nearer to him, and he automatically recoiled. 'Bloody men,' she whispered. 'They're all bastards. All of them. You can't trust any of them.'

Robert wondered if she'd been drinking. 'Miss Evans, I—'

'Mattie knew that. She knew all about men. Found out the hard way, didn't she?'

So that was it. Violet was obviously distraught about the death of her friend. 'We were so sorry to hear about Miss Harris. She was quite a friend of yours, wasn't she?'

'*Friend*? Is that what you'd call it?'

Robert thought it best to ignore that. After a pause, he went on, 'We — we were also sorry to have to lose you. I'm sure you understand that it was not an easy decision.' He had been to the bank at lunchtime to draw some money, quite a sum because it included the week's housekeeping. 'There's no reason why we shouldn't perhaps reconsider the decision once a little time has elapsed. When — when we've all calmed down. One mustn't be too hasty.'

He slipped a hand inside his jacket pocket, looking for his wallet. Part of him thought he was being a fool. Part of him thought that sometimes it was better to act foolishly than to act cruelly. And the third part of him pointed out, with quiet insistence, that life in the office would be so much more pleasant in every way if only Violet Evans would come back and be her own sweet self once again.

'In a month or two, perhaps. And in the meantime, you must let me make a small contribution towards your expenses.'

'No.' She stared up at him. Despite the gloom, he saw the muscles of her face were working compulsively as if she were chewing sweets. 'No,' she repeated, this time drawing out the syllable until it was more like a howl than a word.

'No what?'

'I don't want your money. That's what men always do, they give girls money. They gave Mattie money, lots of money. Trying to keep her mouth shut. But you can't keep my mouth shut.'

He wished he could take back the offer of the job he'd just made, albeit tentatively. She was clearly unbalanced.

'Mattie wasn't my friend.' She came closer still to him. 'Do you know what she really was? She was a *cow*.'

'Miss Evans, you're overwrought. You need to go home—'

'Shut up.' She pushed past him, sending him reeling back against the plate glass of the shop window. 'But I'll tell you something. Mattie bloody Harris got what she deserved.'

Violet gave a ragged sob and ran out into the sheets of rain, lurching across the pavement. Robert watched her stagger across the road. A car braked just in time, its horn wailing. He let out his breath in a long, wavering sigh. Then, regardless of the weather, he ran up the High Street to the porch of the Bull Hotel.

Here normality reasserted itself. Old Quale mumbled sympathetically and found him a towel. Robert was so relieved that he overtipped the man, which led to the offer of a dry pair of trousers. Ten minutes later, warmer, drier and much happier, he reached the saloon bar. Gerald Pembridge was draped elegantly over one end of the counter with a whisky and soda at his elbow.

'What can I get you, Robert?'

'I might have a brandy, actually. I got thoroughly soaked.'

'You don't want to catch a chill. Better make it a large one.' Gerald relayed the order to the barman and turned back to Robert. 'Have you heard the news?'

'No.'

'The police have arrested someone for the murder of that little waitress.'

'Really? Mattie Harris?'

'With luck that'll be the end of this silly Drowner business. Not before time, either.'

'Who've they arrested?'

'Someone called Jimmy Leigh. You must've seen him around. Looks quite normal, if a bit gormless, but there's quite a lot missing in the upper storey. Seems he had a – what do you call it? – a sort of unhealthy attraction for the waitress. Must have got carried away.'

'I'm glad they've caught him, at any rate.'

'So am I. Edna wouldn't go out by herself the other evening. Too scared.'

The barman placed Robert's brandy on the counter and turned away to refill Pembridge's glass.

'Mind you,' Pembridge went on, 'we wouldn't have had to wait so long for an arrest if Ray Williamson had been there from the start. Did you hear they had to bring him back from sick leave to take charge of the case? They had some other chap at first, man called Thornhill.'

'Oh yes? He's married to Bernie Broadbent's niece, isn't he?'

'That's the one. He came and had a word with me. The Harris girl used to come to the Ruispidge Hall dances occasionally. Can't say I thought much of him. Rather an insignificant type. He's not a local man, either, which doesn't help.'

Pembridge stared at his reflection in the mirror beside the bar and adjusted the silk handkerchief in his top pocket. The brandy ran down Robert's throat and spread its warmth deep into his stomach. He was surprised to find the glass was empty and, suddenly reckless, ordered another. He was not used to spirits, especially on an empty stomach, and it seemed to him that he had somehow become a little larger than life. He remembered that Dr Johnson had said brandy was a drink for heroes. Having survived a trying day at the office, the rain, and last but not least that difficult encounter with Violet Evans, he felt quietly heroic.

'Talking of Mattie Harris,' he said, 'I met a friend of hers on my way here. Girl who used to work in my office. You probably remember her? Violet Evans. She and Mattie Harris used to be great chums.'

'Violet? Old Ted's daughter? She came to one of Edna's dances once or twice, I think. Curvy blonde, eh? You old dog.' Pembridge nudged Robert in the ribs. 'Never realised she worked for you.'

'She doesn't any more.' Robert swallowed more brandy. 'Fact is, I had to give her the sack. She got herself pregnant, you see. I felt a bit guilty about it at the time.'

'Nonsense, old chap. Such a terribly bad example. Think of the effect it would have had on other girls if you'd kept her on. You couldn't have Sedbury & Son paying the wages of sin.' Pembridge threw back his head and laughed.

'Well, there is that, I suppose. Though in a way she wasn't the only one who was responsible.'

'If you ask me, the good God made us differently, men and women, gave us different responsibilities. No, you were right to give her the push.'

'I bumped into her on the way here. She was sheltering in a shop doorway. Acting in a most peculiar way.'

'There you are.'

'I tried to say something sympathetic about Mattie Harris – I knew they'd been friends – but she practically bit my head off.' He finished the brandy and, when the barman raised his eyebrows, pushed the glass towards him for another refill without making a conscious decision. 'Perhaps she'd been drowning her sorrows, I don't know. But what surprised me was that she practically said Mattie Harris was — well, not to put to fine a point on it — she more or less said she was a tart.'

'She *what*?'

'It's true. Said she went with men for money. Mattie Harris did, I mean. Miss Evans said she was going to tell the world about it.'

'What did she mean by that?'

Robert shrugged. 'Reveal the names of her *clients*, I suppose. Or whatever they call them.'

'Where did you say you saw her?'

'Don't think I actually mentioned it. She was sheltering in Mutlack's doorway. Then she nearly got herself killed running across the road, and went off down Lyd Street.'

'Women! God knows why they do what they do. If you ask me, each and every one of them is a complete mystery.' Pembridge laughed again for what seemed like a very long time. 'And talking of mysteries, what did you think of our perform-ance on Saturday? Bernie was saying the last time we let Ashbridge run-up a score like that was in nineteen thirty-two.'

The talk turned to cricket, and drew in the barman and a couple of other drinkers. Five minutes later, Robert went out to the lavatory. He swayed slightly as he urinated, and wondered why he didn't do this more often — coming out for a drink at the Bull with a few friends. He thought he would suggest to Gerald Pembridge that they had another one. Or even two. He could ring home and let them know he'd be a little late.

But when he got back to the bar the only sign of Pembridge was an empty whisky glass and an overflowing ashtray.

'Mr Pembridge had to go home, sir,' the barman told him. 'Asked me to say goodbye. Same again?'

Chapter Forty-five

When the doorbell rang again, Edith went to answer it because Richard and Brian Kirby were still talking in the dining room, with the door closed. She was not entirely surprised to find Uncle Bernie on the doorstep. But what she hadn't expected was his companion.

'How nice to see you.' She stepped back, wondering whether she'd ever be able to prepare supper let alone eat it. 'Won't you come in? Let me take your coat.'

Her first thought was that something had happened that would affect the house. Perhaps the Chief Constable had said that Bernie couldn't give it to her after all. Perhaps the sale had fallen through. Simultaneously, she was helping Jill off with her raincoat, which was rather a nice Burberry. Jill was carrying a large, oval shopping basket covered with a cloth.

'Sorry to come at this time,' Jill said. 'And without any warning. You must be very busy.'

'Is Richard in, Edie?' Bernie said, closing the front door. 'We need a word.'

'He's in the dining room with Sergeant Kirby.'

'That's all right.' Bernie tossed his raincoat on the hall chair. 'This is police business.'

'Would you like me to take your basket?' Edith said to Jill.

Jill smiled at her. 'No thank you.'

Then Richard opened the dining-room door. 'Good evening.'

His face showed no change of expression. But Edith knew him well enough to guess what he was feeling. Poor boy, she thought, this must seem like an invasion, especially when he and Brian are working.

'Me and Miss Francis have got something that you ought to see,' Bernie said.

Edith saw Richard throwing a glance at Miss Francis. That was natural enough in the circumstances. Nevertheless, she felt a twinge of jealousy, so small as to be almost unnoticeable, but not quite. Jill knew how to dress, there was no denying that, but it was more than that, of course – she had the money to do it properly. She wasn't that much younger than Edith, but not having children meant she had a more youthful figure. Still, that wouldn't last for ever, and it couldn't be much fun being a dried up old spinster.

Richard said, 'What is it?'

Jill twitched away the tea towel that was covering the basket. 'We've found a handbag.'

'In the river at the bottom of my garden,' Bernie said. 'Snagged on a branch near the mooring.'

'We haven't opened it. We thought we better not.'

They seemed to have forgotten about her. Edith peered into the basket. It was a blue imitation patent-leather handbag, rather ostentatious. Not something she'd ever consider buying herself. She noticed also, with irritation, that there were several little puddles of rainwater forming on the linoleum.

'But it's the wrong river,' Richard said as if talking to himself. 'And the wrong time.'

Brian Kirby appeared behind him in the doorway of the dining room, his eyes darting from one face to another. When his eyes met Edith's, he smiled.

Jill said to Richard, 'There's something else. Mr Broadbent has something he would like to tell you.'

Chapter Forty-six

'He's asleep, I'm afraid, he always has a little nap after his tea.'

'I'm sorry, Mrs Williamson,' Thornhill said. 'I need to have a word with him.'

Bunty Williamson smiled warily. She was in her sixties, with a thin, rosy-cheeked face and a powerful smell of peppermints on her breath. 'Perhaps I could take a message? And you've driven all this way out to see him, too. Couldn't you have phoned?'

'No. I need to see him. It's important.'

'Then I'd better wake him.' For an instant she winced as though he'd hit her and the face aged ten years as lines appeared, cutting channels across her forehead and radiating from her eyes. 'Would you like to wait in here?'

She opened one of the doors in the large, square hall and showed him into the dining room. It was a far cry from the Thornhills'. For a start, it was properly furnished. Everything was modern. The chairs, the table, the sideboard and the book-case matched. On the bookcase were photographs of Ray and Bunty and the little Williamsons at various stages of their exis-tence. The old man had done well for himself over the years, and Thornhill wondered how he'd managed it on a police officer's salary.

He had no enthusiasm for the coming meeting. He stood by

the window and watched the rain sheeting down on the drive and drumming on the roof of his car. The little Austin wasn't water-tight, so there would soon be puddles on the floor and on the seats again. Perhaps they would be able to afford a new car if Bernie really did give Edith the house.

What was Bernie playing at? He had asked Jill out to dinner. Thornhill couldn't understand it. Why had she said yes? The dark part of him wondered if she were contemplating having an affair with Bernie, who at least had the merit of being single. And rich. Thinking of dinner reminded him that he had missed his own meal.

Bunty poked her head into the room. 'Sorry to keep you waiting. He won't be a moment – just washing his hands. He had a couple of phone calls before we ate, so everything's been behind this evening. Can I get you a drink?'

Thornhill declined. She left him alone again, left him pacing to and fro in front of the window. He knew who would have phoned Williamson. Broadbent and Hendry. He thought he'd smelled a layer of alcohol on Bunty's breath, only partly masked by the peppermint. There was a rumour that she drank more than was good for her. Who wouldn't, if they were married to Ray Williamson? Had she guessed what was going on? More likely Williamson never talked about his work with her.

Feet shuffled in the hall. The door opened and Williamson came in. He wore a green cardigan with little leather buttons, cavalry twill trousers and slippers, and around his neck was a bright blue cravat studded with silver horseshoes. In this setting, in those clothes, he looked smaller and more vulnerable than he did at the station.

'Ah, Thornhill.' Pipe in mouth, he stared outside. 'Still raining, I see. Terrible weather.'

'Yes, sir.'

Williamson took an ashtray from the tiled mantelpiece and put it on the table. He pulled out a chair and sat down, motioning for Thornhill to do the same. 'So you and Bernie have been talking?'

Thornhill nodded.

'Christ knows why he felt he had to.'

Thornhill himself had wondered why Bernie had talked so freely. Jill might know. The thought that she might be concealing something from him twisted inside him like barbed wire.

'But there it is, eh? No use crying over spilt milk. The fact is, could have happened to anyone. But to be honest, I really can't see why I had to be dragged into it.' Williamson's words were aggressive but he mumbled them, turning the pipe in his hands as he spoke. 'Something that Bernie cooked up with Gerald Pembridge. Nothing to do with me.'

'Was it just the once, sir?'

Williamson looked up, an ugly flush staining his face. 'Of course it was. Not the poker evenings, mind. Some of us would meet every month or two. Could be here – could be at Gerald Pembridge's or Bernie's or Cyril George's. Just a few games of cards, couple of drinks, bit of chat.' He put down the pipe very slowly in the ashtray as though lives depended on his not making the slightest sound. 'I wouldn't want Bunty to hear about this. It'd kill her.'

'So what exactly happened on the Saturday before last?'

'You already know, Thornhill. Bernie's told you.'

'It would be useful to hear from you, too, sir.'

Williamson glared across the table, then dropped his eyes. 'As far as I was concerned, it was just going to be a normal evening. Must've been about half-past eight by the time I got to Netherfield. Bernie answered the door and said it was going to be just the three of us – him and me, and Gerald. Then he said he thought he'd liven things up a little this time.' Williamson looked up again, and this time his eyes were full of pleading. 'That was the first I knew about it.'

Thornhill nodded. Bernie's story was that he'd told Williamson about the plan a couple of days before.

'He took me into the lounge, and there was Gerald – and this young woman. She was sitting on the arm of the sofa, he was standing over her. First thing I noticed was she wasn't wearing very much. Came as a bit of a shock, I don't mind telling you. I'd always thought Bernie was a bit shy with the opposite sex. Girlfriends and things. Used to tease him about it.'

'The woman was Mattie Harris?'

'Yes – he introduced her as Mattie. Said she was going to be our hostess for the evening. Then – then it all got a bit silly. The idea was, when you were winning, she'd come and pour you a drink, give you a kiss—' Williamson swallowed compulsively '– and then you had to remove an article of her clothing. That was Gerald's idea. He seemed to know her rather well, I thought, maybe better than Bernie.'

'And?'

'Well, when we finish playing poker, we usually add up who's won what, and settle up. And this time, Bernie said, there'd be a special prize for the winner. He could take Mattie upstairs to one of the bedrooms. You know, have a bit of fun by themselves.' He ran his tongue across cracked lips. 'She was certainly keen. Practically begging for it.'

'Who won?'

'Bernie. Personally, I played to lose, of course. Not Gerald, though. God, he looked furious when Bernie won. If looks could kill—' He broke off and ran a finger between the jaunty cravat and the sagging skin of the neck. 'I heard her laughing and giggling on the stairs. Oh, she was enjoying it all right.' He glanced at Thornhill with the ghost of old lusts flickering in his eyes. 'She was a damned attractive girl, you know. Especially when she wasn't wearing most of her clothes.'

Thornhill looked away, out of the window at the silver curtain of rain and the dark swaying mass of the bushes that lined the boundary with the road. *Who am I to judge?* If Williamson was telling the truth, he'd only contemplated adultery, whereas Thornhill had not only contemplated it but committed it, and would like to do so again as soon as possible. For an instant he stared inside himself and did not like what he saw. Was this the effect of Lydmouth? A slow-acting contagion in the air? In time, would he become like Williamson, playing poker with cronies and leering drunkenly at a girl in her underclothes?

'As I understand it, sir, Mr Hendry thinks that in view of your health it would be better if I took over operational charge of the case again. Framington can manage without me. Trotter's number two is very competent.'

Williamson gave the slightest possible nod.

'Naturally I'll report back to you as usual,' Thornhill went on. 'Perhaps you'd like me to summarise the case so far?'

Another, barely perceptible nod. Williamson produced his tobacco pouch and began to fill the pipe.

'The autopsy suggested that Mattie Harris was drowned in the bath while she was drunk. She was pregnant at the time. So someone must have dressed her afterwards and presumably dumped her in the river to make it look like an accident. The discovery of her powder compact on the riverbank near the Ferryman suggests she may have gone into the river somewhere round there. We have witnesses who heard her laughing with a man on the Thursday evening. Young Sedbury and Bill Pembridge.'

Williamson's eyelids flickered at their names.

'Then there's the handbag. Miss Francis and Mr Broadbent found it in the river at the bottom of his garden late this afternoon. Nothing revealing about the contents, nothing odd about them either. Lipstick, matches, a packet of contraceptives, her ration book, a purse containing change, a bus ticket and so on. The problem is when and where it was found.'

'Get on with it, man.' For an instant Williamson looked like his old self. 'No point in making this longer than it need be.'

One moment Thornhill was in perfect control of himself. The next he'd lost his temper and he was on his feet. 'If everyone had told the truth about Mattie Harris from the start, this investigation would have taken a lot less time than it has so far.' He watched Williamson flinch away from his anger. 'Sir.'

The anger left him as quickly as it had come, leaving him with a sense of unease, almost shame. He sat down again and went on his normal voice, 'The trouble is, the handbag was found in the Minnow, whereas the powder compact was found beside the Lyd. There's another problem. Sergeant Kirby and I visited Mr Broadbent on Sunday and we actually had a look at the river down there. I suppose we could have missed the handbag. But it's more likely that it's appeared since then. So did someone plant it in an attempt to incriminate Mr Broadbent? The other possibility is that it floated downstream from somewhere. The bag was more or less airtight, and there was a lot of air trapped inside so that's perfectly possible. There's another point – you'd think Mattie Harris would keep her powder compact inside her handbag. How did the two come to be separated?' Thornhill paused, watching Williamson light his pipe. 'Then there's the matter of Jimmy Leigh.'

The match burnt down to Williamson's fingers and he swore. Still burning, the match fell to the polished surface of the table. He swatted it with his hands, sending it smouldering down to the carpet. He swore once more, stood up and ground it out. 'Bloody thing,' he growled, resuming his seat and lighting another match. 'Now, what were we talking about?'

'Jimmy Leigh, sir.' Thornhill leant back in his chair. 'As far as I can see, there's very little evidence linking him with Mattie Harris's disappearance on Thursday night. Most of it's circumstantial.'

'He was seen talking to her at the dance,' Williamson pointed out. 'Outside the Ruispidge Hall.'

'But she disappeared *after* that, sir. The only real evidence is the face powder that turned up in his bathroom. And Sergeant Kirby is pretty sure that it wasn't in the bathroom on Saturday, when he and WPC Ailsmore first interviewed the lad.'

Williamson puffed furiously, as though trying to create such a fog of smoke that he would be invisible. 'Fleur de Rose, wasn't it? As it happens, there may be the possibility of a mistake in that department. Just a moment.' He scraped back his chair and opened the door. 'Bunty!' he yelled as though summoning a dog. 'Bunty!'

Her feet pattered in the hall. She came into the room, wiping her hands on her apron. Her face was pinched. 'Yes, dear?'

'Didn't I give you a present this evening?'

'Oh, yes.' Her face relaxed into a smile. 'Such a nice thought.'

'Never mind about that now. Tell Mr Thornhill what it was.'

'Some face powder. Really lovely. I shudder to think what it cost.' She looked at Thornhill. 'It's our wedding anniversary next week.'

'And what's the powder called?' Williamson said with the relentless impatience of a prosecuting counsel.

'Fleur de Rose, dear.'

'But there was a little problem, wasn't there?'

'The top had come off in your jacket pocket, and some of the powder had fallen out. But not very much. We were able to get most of it back.' She smiled up at her husband. 'It really didn't matter, Ray.'

'No,' he agreed. 'It didn't matter. Why don't you put the kettle on? We could all do with some tea.' He waited until she had left the room. 'I mentioned all this to Mr Hendry when he phoned just now. I bought the powder this morning.' He lit another match and held it over the pipe bowl, though the tobacco was still glowing red. 'Quite a coincidence. So when I was having a look at that bathroom, it is just possible that some of the powder fell out.'

'Yes, sir.'

The two men stared at each other. The whites of Williamson's eyes were covered with what looked like tiny red cobwebs. It was a thin story, Thornhill thought, practically transparent, but it would serve. This, in so many words, had been the deal between Williamson, Hendry and Broadbent. Williamson had agreed to co-operate, to tell the truth and leave the investigation to Thornhill. And in return no one was going to ask any awkward questions, not least about the Fleur de Rose in Miss Calder's bathroom.

'Well, there you have it,' Williamson said. 'Simple enough, eh?'

What they had, Thornhill thought, was a murky little compromise, designed to save face all round. He was going to accept it. Was that another effect Lydmouth had had on him – made him more willing to compromise? He wasn't sure that the change was for the better.

'So if we assume the powder found in the bathroom had nothing to do with Mattie Harris, do you think we still have enough grounds to hold Jimmy?'

Williamson pursed his lips and pretended to think. Then he shook his head slowly. 'I'm not sure we do.'

'So if we're not going to charge him, sir, I suppose we should let him go.'

'Looks like we'll have to.' Williamson sucked on his pipe. 'Though my gut feeling is that he's as guilty as hell. Still, that's neither here nor there. But he remains in the frame – you agree?'

'Yes, sir.' Thornhill thought the conversation was like a ritual dance. The words they were saying had little to do with its real meaning. 'Will you ring the station and tell them to let him out? Or would you like me to do it for you?'

Williamson scowled at him. Phoning through the order for Jimmy Leigh's release himself might be construed as a climbdown. On the other hand, it would also send a signal that he was still in charge, that Thornhill was reporting to him.

'I think I'll do it,' Williamson said. 'No time like the present.'

He got up again and went into the hall, leaving the door open. Thornhill listened to him phoning headquarters. The superintendent asked for Kirby, and made him confirm that he hadn't seen the powder when he was in the bathroom the previous Saturday.

'Shame you didn't mention it at the time, Sergeant,' Williamson said, and Thornhill felt unwilling admiration for the old devil. 'Anyway, you'd better let Leigh go. Mr Thornhill and I have discussed it, and I can't see any reason why we should continue to hold him. Just as well you remembered before we charged him, eh?'

He came back to the dining room, his face flushed, this time with triumph. His wife followed him in, carrying the tea tray. She poured two cups. She began an explanation about the whereabouts of sugar and hot water, but her husband waved her out of the room and shut the door after her.

'You've still got to explain that bath water in her airways,' Williamson said softly.

'Yes, sir. Given the amount of alcohol she'd had, it's perfectly possible that she was trying to induce an abortion. The bruising on her shoulder suggests that she was killed, that someone held her under the water, but I suppose she might have died by accident. But the one thing we know for certain is that someone tried to cover up her death, tried to make it look as if she drowned in the river. If you ask me, we have to look very carefully at Malcolm Sedbury.'

'The boy's a cripple. Are you saying that he was having an affair with Mattie Harris? Surely she wouldn't –?'

Is a boy with withered legs somehow a less attractive proposition than a procession of prurient old men?

'It might not have been him who was having the affair. He might have lied about the compact, lied about overhearing the conversation near the Ferryman, to protect someone else. His friend Bill Pembridge, for example, or even Bill's father.'

'Ah. Yes. Gerald. I suppose we have to bear him in mind.'

'He'd had an affair with Mattie. As you know, he told me so himself. He could have been the father of that baby. The point is, the only evidence we have connecting Mattie Harris with the Ferryman and the Lyd on the night of her death comes from Malcolm Sedbury and Bill Pembridge.'

Williamson turned the words over in his mind. His face had become grey and haggard. Then he put down his pipe in the ashtray and cleared his throat.

'What about Wynstones?'

'I'm sorry, sir?'

'Wynstones,' Williamson barked, as though Thornhill's ignorance was an offence against regulations. 'It's a house just outside town. You'll have passed the turning on the way here. It's been on the market for a while – husband of the last owner hanged himself there. Large garden running down to the river at the back. The Minnow, that is.'

'How does this link up with the case, sir?'

'Christ knows, Thornhill.' Williamson stared gloomily across the table. 'All I know is when I was driving home from the Bull on Sunday lunchtime, there was a car in front of me. A little two-seater. Turned right into the lane that leads to Wynstones. Doesn't go anywhere else. And when it turned off, I saw who was in it. Bill Pembridge was driving, and young Sedbury was sitting beside him.'

Chapter Forty-seven

'Oh dear,' said Mrs Sedbury when the phone rang as they were eating peaches and cream, 'I do wish people wouldn't telephone when one's having dinner. So inconsiderate.'

Her husband was already on his feet, dabbing his mouth with his napkin.

Malcolm said, 'They can't know we're eating.'

'That's not the point, dear. The point is, it upsets your father's digestion.'

The ringing stopped. The telephone was in the study. Malcolm and his mother continued to swallow bright slimy sections of tinned peach. His mother was the first to finish.

'I'll put the kettle on for coffee.'

At that moment, Robert came back into the room. 'Not for me, thanks. I've got to go out.'

'Now? But why?'

'I'm not exactly sure.'

'Darling, don't be so mysterious.'

Her husband bent down and kissed his wife's crisp grey hair. 'It's not me who's being mysterious. It's that chap Thornhill. The inspector Malcolm saw the other day. He wants to know about Wynstones.'

Malcolm laid down his spoon and fork. 'What sort of things was he asking?'

'Whether anyone had been there recently. I told him about you showing the Christies round on Sunday. But I must go. He wants to have a look round now. We're meeting at the office, so I can pick up the keys.'

'Surely it can wait?'

'Apparently not.'

'But you're not feeling well.'

'I'm much better now.'

Robert had returned from the Bull half-soaked, uncertain on his feet and with a headache. But a bath, several aspirin and a nap before dinner had mitigated some of his symptoms, which he had blamed on the weather and on a glass of brandy on an empty stomach.

'What about the rest of your peaches?'

'I've had enough.' Robert paused, his hand on the door handle. 'I'm not sure when I'll be back. There was another odd thing.'

Malcolm pushed his bowl towards his mother. 'What?'

'Damned odd – the fellow asked if the gas was still connected.'

He left the room. A few minutes later, they heard the whine of the car's starter motor.

'I think it's most peculiar,' Mrs Sedbury said, gathering the bowls together. 'Still, I expect the police have their reasons. Now where shall we have our coffee?'

He looked up at her. 'Don't make any for me, thanks, Mother. I'm going out.'

'Really? But it's such a dreadful night. I hope your father has his wellingtons in the car.'

'A bit of rain won't harm me. I said I'd pop round to Bill's. But I'll give you a hand with the washing-up first.'

His mother washed, and Malcolm dried. The delay chafed his nerves. But he instinctively felt it would be better to act normally, which meant helping with the washing-up. And it gave him time to digest the news.

'You'll wrap up properly, won't you?' his mother said. 'With all this rain it would be so easy to get wet. You wouldn't want to catch a chill.'

He knew he could phone Bill instead, but he wasn't sure whether it would be safe. An overheard conversation would be worse than no conversation at all.

His mother made him wear a heavy waterproof that came down to his knees and a sou'wester. He moved stiffly and felt a complete fool. She kissed him goodbye. Because of the rain it was gloomy in the hall. Shapes and colours were indistinct, as though seen through mist.

Perhaps it was a trick of the light but when he was pulling away from her it seemed for an instant that her features dissolved and reformed, not just once but twice. He glimpsed the faces of his sisters, one after the other. The girls were older than he was. One was married to a solicitor, the other to an RAF officer. They both had children. When he was young, it had been like having three mothers.

He walked slowly up to the wrought-iron gates of Jubilee Park. The stiff clothes gave him the illusion he was enclosed, armoured against what the world had to throw against him. The sou'wester came down over his ears, which increased his sense of isolation from the rest of the world.

He cut through the park to the top of Albert Road, partly because there was less risk of meeting people. At least the weather kept people indoors, kept them from watching him. He'd found a word in an old novel that described the way he walked – *hirple*. It meant to walk lamely, dragging a limb, hobbling. Guessing what it meant from the context, he had looked it up in the big dictionary at the public library, driven by a furtive need to see the definition in print, to confirm that there was a vocabulary for people like him.

He reached Albert Road, and hirpled along the darker of the

two pavements, the one that was overhung by trees. The sooner he talked to Bill the better. He forced himself to move faster and faster, and his muscles ached in protest. The Pembridges' house loomed in its bare garden, as grimly utilitarian as a small factory with an outdoor tennis court for the workers. The lights were on in some of the downstairs rooms.

There was a police car outside the front door.

I shouldn't have helped with the washing-up.

Malcolm paused on the other side of the road, leaning on his sticks and panting. He shrank back into the shelter of the trees and waited. Drops of water rustled through the leaves and pattered on the sou'wester. All he could hear was the rain. The wet roadway shone like a river of metal.

Four minutes later, Malcolm's patience was rewarded. A police officer came out of the front door, followed by Bill, who was followed in turn by another police officer. They ushered Bill into the back of the police car. Malcolm scuttled through the open gate of the nearest garden and ducked behind a slatted fence.

He peered through it, watching the car nosing down the drive of the Pembridges' house. The beams of its headlights danced momentarily through the fence, slicing his waterproof with bright stripes. It turned right towards the town centre.

Slowly the darkness settled around him again. He shivered.

Chapter Forty-eight

They took him home in a police car. There was a time when Jimmy would have liked that. It wasn't very often that he rode in a car, and a police car with a bell on the roof and a uniformed driver was obviously much more exciting than most.

Except that it wasn't exciting any longer. It never would be again. During the last few days he'd ridden in several police cars and now he thought of them as dark blue coffins on wheels. The police wanted to hang him for killing Mattie Harris.

When the nasty sergeant came down to the cell and told him he could go home, Jimmy wasn't sure whether to believe him or not. It might be a trick. He didn't know what the trick might be designed to achieve, but he did know the police played tricks on you. When in doubt, he had learned over the years, it was always best to say nothing.

They took him upstairs, gave him a cup of tea and a chocolate biscuit, and then returned his braces and his tie. Jimmy didn't know why they had taken the braces and tie. He thought it was probably another trick. Either that or they were trying to make him look silly.

He stared through the window, ignoring the driver's attempt to make conversation. *Just trying to trap me.* The wipers were going full tilt but the windscreen was still a blur. Perhaps he'd die in a car crash, and then everything would be over. He had had enough of it. Since Mattie had gone away, everything had gone wrong and he thought there was no longer any possibility that it could go right.

'Here we are, son,' the driver said as he pulled up outside the house in River Gardens. 'I expect you'll be glad to be home again.'

Say nothing. It's safer.

He sat motionless in the passenger seat. The driver came round the car and opened the door for him.

'Come on, lad. Auntie's waiting for you.'

The front door was open. Minnie Calder was standing in the doorway, silhouetted by the light behind her. The policeman held an umbrella over him, just as if he were royalty, as they walked quickly up the path to the door.

'I shall be writing to my MP, young man,' Minnie Calder told the policeman. 'You tell your superintendent that. I think it's disgraceful what you've done.'

The driver muttered something and beat a retreat back to the car. Minnie put her hand on Jimmy's arm and drew him into the hall. She stood on tiptoe and kissed his cheek.

'Are you all right? Have they hurt you?'

Say nothing. It's safer.

'There's a nice bit of tinned salmon for your tea. And I daresay we can find a slice of cake for you.'

She sniffed suddenly and turned away. 'It's nice to have you back.'

They went into the kitchen and he sat down at the table. She busied herself with preparing a meal for him.

'Why don't you say something?' she said as she hacked at the tin with the blade of a tin opener.

He caught the fear in her voice. He was good at knowing if people were scared or not.

'You're not my auntie.' He stared at her. 'You told me a story. You told me a story all my life. You told *everyone* a story.'

She abandoned the tin and sat down beside him. She took one of his hands in hers. 'Jimmy, love, it was for the best. Yes, I'm your mother, but I wasn't married to your daddy. It was just one of those silly grown-up things that sometimes happen.'

He pulled away from her, went into the lounge and picked up the photograph of the man in the tight suit and the woman in the white wedding dress. Minnie followed him into the little room.

'You said they were my mam and dad.'

'Well, they were in a manner of speaking. They adopted you when you were a little baby because I wasn't able to have you with me. Then there was the war and I came back to Lydmouth, and they died, so it was like it was always meant to be, you and me together. Nothing's changed, Jimmy.'

He stared at her, slowly shaking his head from side to side. 'But it has.'

Then, with all his force, he threw the photograph. It spun in the air, the chromium-plated frame catching the light. It crashed into the window. There was a sudden, shocking sound of breaking glass.

'Jimmy – Jimmy—?'

Damp fresh air flowed into the room. The tears were running down his face. He turned towards her, brushing a shard of glass from his sleeve. She barely came up to his collarbone. He couldn't hear what she was saying. She was just a silly, red-faced, old woman whose mouth was moving to and fro, up and down. Playing tricks on him. He wanted to stop her doing whatever she was doing more than he'd ever wanted anything else in his life.

He lobbed a blow at her with his right arm, the hand had clenched into a fist. The swing caught her on the left cheekbone. Her body collided with the edge of the doorframe. Her mouth had stopped moving but it hung open as though waiting for someone to drop a worm in it. She looked like a stranger. She'd turned into someone else.

Playing tricks again.

Leaning against the jamb, she slid slowly down to a sitting position. She looked up at him. Still she said nothing. The only sounds Jimmy could hear were the hissing and tapping of the rain and his own snuffling. He wasn't sure where the one began and the other ended. He didn't think it mattered.

Someone hammered on the front door.

The new noise galvanised him. He pushed past Minnie and ran down the hall, through the kitchen and out of the back door. The rain hit him, sluicing him down, washing him clean. The faster he ran, the cleaner he would get.

He went down the garden, unbolted the gate and slipped onto the path by the river. Now the only sound was the rain. He stretched out his hands to it. He liked water. As he ran through the twilight, the words danced round and round his head.

Wash me clean. Wash me clean. Wash me clean.

Chapter Forty-nine

'The turning's up there,' Sedbury said. 'See the gap in the hedge?'

'I know,' Kirby said. 'I've been here before.'

There were four of them in the police car. Kirby was driving with Joan Ailsmore beside him. The rain forced him to keep the speed down. Robert Sedbury and Thornhill were sitting in the back. As the car swung sharply right into the mouth of the lane, the four passengers swung equally sharply to the left. Sedbury's shoulder jarred against Thornhill's.

'Sorry,' he muttered.

Two stone pillars marked the opening to Wynstones' drive. The white five-bar gate was standing open. Kirby had been here before when the retired bank manager topped himself. Before Thornhill's time. Not a lucky house. Thornhill wasn't superstitious, but he knew that some places attracted trouble.

'You mentioned a cleaner,' he said to Sedbury. 'When does she come in?'

'Once a week. Thursdays. Just for an hour or two — enough to keep the house aired and looking reasonably tidy.'

'So it's not empty?'

'Generally a house is easier to sell if it's furnished. Looks more attractive.'

'So apart from your son showing the Christies round on Sunday, no one's been in since last Thursday?'

'That's correct. Why do you ask?'

No one answered him. The car drew up outside the front of the house. The four of them got out. Kirby and Thornhill raised umbrellas and they made a rush for the shelter of the porch. Sedbury fumbled for the keys. At last the door opened. Sedbury opened his mouth, then closed it again. No doubt he was used to showing people round houses, and knew exactly what to say to them, but this wasn't a normal occasion. He didn't have the right words.

'I'd like you to turn the electricity on,' Thornhill said. 'Sergeant Kirby has a torch if you need one.'

The mains switch was under the stairs. Sedbury flipped the lever. Then he took the police officers on a quick tour of the house, turning on the lights as they went.

'It might help if I knew what you were looking for,' he said.

Thornhill threw a glance at him over his shoulder. 'Hard to tell at this point, sir. Just bear with us, will you?'

They were in the morning room at the back of the house, casting like hounds for a scent.

Thornhill sniffed. 'Can you smell something?'

'Nothing you'd notice,' Kirby said.

'Someone's been smoking in here recently.' He guessed he was the only person in the room who didn't smoke. 'The cleaner?'

'It's possible,' Sedbury said. 'Or it might have been the Christies or Malcolm on Sunday. Can't smell it myself. I'll ask Malcolm, if you like.'

Kirby walked over to the window and examined the catch. 'Locked.'

Like all the other windows so far. Thornhill stared at the window and saw only the dark reflections of the four of them in the room. He told Joan to turn out the light. The garden came into view at once, grey and ghostly. Thornhill put his face close to the glass. A paved area ran along the back of the house.

Somewhere a drain must be blocked because the slabs were covered with a sheet of water, a shifting pattern of ripples and dents. The remaining light was rapidly fading.

'I want to have a look at the garden while we can still see something.' He glanced at Joan and caught her exchanging glances with Kirby. 'You stay here – see what you can find.'

'Inspector,' Sedbury said, his voice trembling slightly. 'What exactly are you looking for?'

'Hard to know until we've found it, sir. You lead the way.' He looked at Kirby. 'You'd better fetch the umbrellas, Sergeant.'

'Yes, sir.'

There was a hint of reluctance in his voice, almost insolence. Kirby thought they were on a wild-goose chase here, Thornhill realised, and that they would be better waiting for the morning, for more light and less rain. He followed Sedbury into a kitchen that needed modernising. Huddled under the umbrellas like black beetles, they hurried down the sodden garden. Thornhill wished he knew what he was looking for.

The footprints of a six-foot navvy with a limp and an unusual pattern on the soles of his boots? The butt of a hand-made cigarette? A bloodstained handkerchief with the murderer's monogram embroidered on one corner? It wasn't so simple. In a criminal investigation, as in life, you generally knew what you were looking for only when you found it.

'What's that?' He pointed towards a roof by the river.

'A boathouse,' Sedbury said. 'There's a rowing boat. Quite a draw for the fishermen. There's an outboard motor, too.' He gave a little laugh and smiled at them, as though hoping he had disarmed Thornhill and Kirby with a mild witticism.

They reached the river. The muddy waters of the Minnow glided from left to right, moving endlessly down to the Lyd. Thornhill and Kirby walked along the riverbank. The lawn beside the path had been neatly trimmed but apart from that there was nothing to show that anyone had been down here for months.

Sedbury went on ahead and wrestled with the door of the boathouse. 'It – it tends to stick,' he gasped over his shoulder. 'But only in damp weather. Couldn't get much damper than this, eh?'

He laughed again and, as if the sound had been a password, the door jerked open. He flew back and would have fallen if Kirby had not steadied him. The three of them crowded round the doorway.

'No power down here, I'm afraid,' Sedbury said. 'The boat's over there.'

'Sergeant,' Thornhill said.

Kirby produced a torch from the pocket of his raincoat. The beam danced round the boathouse. Two sets of oars were slung on racks on the right-hand wall. The motor hung from a sling suspended from one of the pillars supporting the roof. Water dripped softly near the far end, by the double doors leading to the little slipway.

Thornhill ran a hand along the blade of an oar.

'We try to take the boat out occasionally,' Sedbury said. 'Just to turn the engine over.'

'Who actually does it?' Thornhill asked.

'My son. With a friend of his.'

'Bill Pembridge?'

'Yes.'

'When was it last used?'

'I'm afraid I've no idea. It might even have been on Sunday.' He looked from one face to another. 'My – my son would know.'

They walked quickly back to the house and hung their dripping raincoats in the hall. Sedbury was silent now. Thornhill could almost smell the man's growing uneasiness. Everything was leading back to Malcolm.

Joan came downstairs. She shook her head when Thornhill raised his eyebrows at her.

'Nothing obvious, sir.' She hesitated. 'There's a pile of towels in the airing cupboard upstairs, though. I thought the top ones were a little damper than the others. Hard to be sure. And it could be just the house, being so near the river.'

'Perhaps you'd like to wait down here, sir,' Thornhill suggested to Sedbury. 'We'll have a look upstairs.'

There were five bedrooms, four of them spacious and one with a dressing room attached, and a bathroom. Thornhill glanced at the banisters along the landing, wondering if it was from one of these that the retired bank manager had hanged himself. Down in the hall, the estate agent was standing near the hat-stand. His shoulders were bowed and his hands were rolling and unrolling a large white handkerchief.

The three police officers moved from room to room, pulling out drawers, opening doors, folding back carpets, checking windows, looking under the beds. Like the building itself, the furnishings were as devoid of character as a blank sheet of paper. Most houses are bursting to the seams with secrets, Thornhill thought, and everywhere you look you find crumbs of information about their owners' lives. Not at Wynstones, though. It was a house that no longer belonged to anybody.

The airing cupboard was on the landing. Thornhill felt the towels. Joan was right – those on top seemed very slightly damp. He and Kirby opened them out, one by one. The three of them stood under the landing light and examined them.

Thornhill saved the bathroom until last. They went over every inch of it and found nothing. The window looked over the back garden and was locked. The bath was spotless. Kirby lit the pilot light on the Ascot, turned on the hot tap and held his hand under the stream of water. The Ascot fired and Kirby snatched his hand away.

'Christ, it's hot.' He turned off the tap. 'Looks like that's it, Guv. Unless you want to look in the loft?'

'The trap under the plug hole.'

Kirby stared at him, his face unnaturally blank.

'There's a bag of tools in the boot of the car,' Thornhill said. 'Bring them up, will you? We might as well try it now.'

Kirby clattered down the stairs, making more noise than was necessary. Thornhill heard the murmur of voices in the hall below and the slam of the front door. A moment later, Kirby was back, his head and shoulders gleaming with rain.

The bath had been boxed in but there was a panel for access, held in place with screws at the back. To reach it, Kirby had to lie on his side on the floor, which didn't do his suit or his temper much good. The panel was easy enough to remove. But unscrewing the trap beneath the drain took him longer. At one point, the spanner slipped, grazing Kirby's hand, drawing blood. When at last he passed the trap to Thornhill, he was sweating. All the while, Joan stood by the door, hands folded in front of her, a demure expression on her face.

Thornhill carried the trap to the basin, which was underneath the light. He opened his penknife and scooped out the contents. Soon there was a mound of grey sludge laced with hairs on the white porcelain. He scraped the inside of the pipe, drawing out more. Using the tip of the blade, he dissected the sludge, drawing to one side the strands of hair.

No longer sulking, Kirby breathed heavily at his shoulder. Joan joined them by the basin.

Most of the hairs were grey, almost indistinguishable from the sludge in which they were embedded. They varied considerably in length, though the longest of them was no more than two inches.

'The retired bank manager?' Thornhill said, tapping the pile with the tip of his knife. 'And the longer ones are probably the wife who died last year.' The tip of the knife scraped across the porcelain to three other hairs, longer and much darker than the rest. 'But what about these?'

No one answered.

Thornhill took out his handkerchief and transferred one of the longer, darker hairs on to it. He wrapped all but one end of the hair in the linen, held it tight and drew it free, squeezing the moisture from it. Finally he held it under the bulb of the light and squinted up at it.

Hard to be sure, not until they got it under a microscope in the lab. But he was almost certain that the hair was tinged with red.

Chapter Fifty

Dinner had been part of the bargain.

After they had talked to Thornhill and Kirby at Victoria Road, Bernie drove Jill back to Church Cottage and left her there to change. Forty-five minutes later he returned, looking almost distinguished in a dark suit. He took them to the restaurant of a small hotel outside Elmbury where the staff treated them with servility.

'I'm thinking of buying a garage a little way down the road,' Bernie said almost apologetically. 'It's owned by the manager's dad.'

Jill wasn't quite sure why Bernie had asked her to dinner but after a couple of glasses of very good sherry she began not to care. He was at the mercy of a muddle of motives, just like everyone else, and some of them showed him in a better light than others. She had struck a deal with him at Netherfield earlier today and she had yet to discover what all its ramifications were.

So when he had agreed to talk to Richard, to tell him at least part of the truth about that Saturday evening, Jill had felt almost at a disadvantage as if he were actually doing her a favour. He had invited her to dinner while they were driving to the Thornhills' house. It would have been churlish to refuse.

Jill had other, less creditable reasons to accept the invitation.

She deserved at least one evening of pampering after enduring the primitive pleasures of Walnut Tree Cottage and *The Vicar of Bullhampton* for the better part of a week. There was also an obscure but powerful feeling that Richard Thornhill needed to be reminded that she had a life which did not include him. Left to herself, moreover, she would spend the time brooding on whether or not she was pregnant.

During the meal Bernie stuck to bottled beer, Thorogood and Nephew's India Pale Ale. He noticed Jill looking at the label.

'Never got a taste for wine,' he said. 'Much rather drink this. Might even buy a share in the brewery.' He stuffed a forkful of plaice into his mouth and said with his mouth full, 'Mattie liked it, as a matter of fact. That's what she drank, the evening she was at Netherfield. She could hold her beer, that girl, for all she was just a slip of a thing.'

'The police found a Thorogood's bottle on the riverbank near her body.'

'Did they? How did you find that out?'

Jill pinched her thigh under the table. She knew because Richard had mentioned it to her when they were in bed together. 'Philip Wemyss-Brown has got very good contacts with the police. Best not to inquire too closely about them. The point is, Thorogood's isn't a Lydmouth beer.'

Bernie nodded his heavy head. 'No. So the odds are that if the bottle floated down to New Bridge, it was one of mine. Could have been that evening. We went out for a breather in the garden halfway through. Ray threw an empty bottle in the river. You know how sometimes they fill up part way and then that's enough to give them ballast so they float with the neck upwards? It's what happened to this one. Mattie said we ought to put a message in it.'

'Saying what?'

'That's what I asked her. Know what she said? *Cheers! Make mine a Thorogood's IPA.* Funny to think where that bottle landed up.'

He smiled, spearing another forkful of plaice. 'No message in it, I suppose?'

'Not as far as I know. But in a way the bottle itself was a message. What it said was that something could float all the way down the Minnow and end up at New Bridge.'

'All the way down from my garden.'

'Yes,' Jill said. 'That's what I mean.'

'The police will have thought of that.' In went another mouthful of plaice. 'You seem to know the Thornhills quite well.'

The words formed a statement, not a question. *But he can't know about us.*

'I meet Richard Thornhill regularly through work. And I've seen a certain amount of Edith lately. My cat's had kittens, and they may take a couple of them off my hands.'

'Edie's a local girl for all she's lived away from here for most of her adult life. Fits in easily enough. Richard's another kettle of fish, though. He doesn't know how we do things. He's a bit stiff-backed, too. Did you know that I'm buying their house?'

Jill's shook her head and mimed mild surprise. For an instant she wondered whether Bernie were trying to trap her.

'So you didn't, eh? No reason why you should. I'll probably put it in Edie's name. Richard's a bit upset because he thinks that folks will see it as an attempt to bribe a police officer. What do you think?'

To mask her relief she took a mouthful of water. Bernie was asking her advice, perhaps because she worked for the *Gazette*, or, less flatteringly, he wasn't asking her advice but he was setting out to prepare the ground for the news becoming public. But either way it meant that he was not hinting that he knew about herself and Richard.

'I can't see that anyone's going to object.'

'I've talked to Mr Hendry.'

'If the Chief Constable isn't worried, I can't see who else would be.'

'That's what I think.' Bernie split a matchstick and excavated a piece of fish from between his teeth. 'But you can't be too careful. Talking of which, you said you were with someone last night. In Gloucester. Who?'

'It was a lie,' Jill said.

'Sure?'

'Yes. I just wanted to make you tell the truth about Mattie.'

'It worked.' He smiled. 'I underestimated you.'

As the meal continued they talked of other things. But when he was driving her home, he reverted without warning to the subject of Mattie Harris.

'Nice kid and all that. But if you ask me she was riding for a fall.'

Jill glanced at his darkened profile. 'Why?'

'Too free with her favours. Not many girls like that in Lydmouth.' Suddenly he jabbed his foot on the accelerator and the car surged forwards. 'Too independent. Made her dangerous, you see. We're used to men who bend the rules but when you get a woman who acts as if they don't exist, that gets people's backs up. Causes problems.'

'But people liked her. Have you noticed that? Almost every-one liked her.'

'True enough. But still she didn't fit. No more do I, in a way.' His head swung towards her. 'Nor you, Jill, but for a different reason.'

'I'm not sure I understand.'

'Simple enough to my way of thinking. Me, I belong here in every way but one. And that one thing makes me an outsider, and always will. But you *are* an outsider. You come from London.'

'You make it sound like Ultima Thule.'

'Where? Don't get me wrong, folks like you. Though they think it's odd you've got a job, that you live on your own. Good-looking lady like you ought to have a husband.'

'That's up to me.'

By now they were driving through the northern outskirts of

Lydmouth. Neither of them spoke again until they reached the High Street, until they were only a few hundred yards from Jill's cottage. It was still raining, though a little less heavily than earlier in the evening. There was little traffic about and fewer pedestrians.

'Maybe this isn't the time,' Bernie said. 'But I'd like to make you a little business proposal. No need to answer it now. Maybe it's the sort of thing we should both think on. But will you hear me out?'

'Of course I will. But I can't imagine – look out!'

She wasn't sure if Bernie hit the brake before or after she shouted. She was thrown towards the windscreen. Just in time she cushioned the impact with her arm. The jolt jarred through her body.

'Christ!' muttered Bernie, hauling on the wheel.

The Riley had gone into a skid. It fish-tailed through 45 degrees, coming to a halt only when the nearside rear tyre collided with the kerb. Jill was aware of sounds beyond the car, of the clatter of metal and a dull thud. Bernie opened the car door and scrambled out. Jill followed. She was trembling, and for a moment she leaned against the car, wondering if she were going to be sick.

A bicycle lay on its side, half on the pavement, half on the road. A man in a flat cap was sitting in a puddle beside the kerb.

'You all right?' Bernie bent over him. 'Give me your hand. God, what a foul night.'

Jill reached the other side of the man. She took one arm and Bernie the other. Together they helped him to his feet. He was small but strongly built, surprisingly heavy. He wasn't wearing a coat and his jacket was soaked.

'Can't see a thing on a night like this,' Bernie said. 'You weren't using lights, either, were you?'

'Nothing to do with you.' It was the first time the man had spoken. 'You were driving like a bloody maniac.'

'Ted,' Bernie said. 'It's you, isn't it, Ted?'

'Mr Broadbent,' Ted said without enthusiasm.

'What are you doing out on a night like this?'

Ted pulled his arms away from them and stood up by himself, swaying gently. 'Violet's not come back home. Came out to look for her.'

'Maybe she's gone to the cinema, or met a friend or—'

'The baby's missed a feed.'

'Is there anything we can do?' Jill asked.

'Send her home if you see her, Miss. Do you know what she looks like?'

'Yes — we have met.'

He peered at her through the rain but she wasn't sure whether he recognised her. Bernie lifted the bicycle. Ted snatched it from him and tried turning the wheels.

'You must let me know if there's any damage,' Bernie said. 'And any damage to your clothes, as well. One of those accidents, eh? Nobody's fault but I wouldn't want you to be out of pocket because of it.'

It was a typical speech for the man, Jill thought: not ungenerous, superficially at least, but canny.

'Bugger that, Bernie Broadbent. If you've damaged me or my bike, you'll pay for it. You can be sure of that.'

Ted wheeled his bicycle down the High Street without a backward glance. Bernie started after him, but Jill laid a hand on his arm, restraining him.

'Let it wait,' she said.

'But I want to help the fool.'

'He doesn't want help. He wants his daughter.'

They returned to the car in silence. Bernie drove on to Church Cottage.

'Come and have a drink, if you like,' Jill said, feeling reasonably certain that she would not have to defend her virtue from Bernie's attentions.

'Thanks. Might have killed him.'

'But you didn't.'

They got out of the car. Jill unlocked her front door. There were people in Lydmouth who left their houses unlocked but she retained London habits. She twisted the handle and pushed. The door went back a few inches, then snagged on something.

'I reckon there's a scrape on the near side,' Bernie said behind her. 'And I've had that damn car less than a week.'

Jill had bent down to pick up what was obstructing the door. An envelope had managed to fold itself over. It was wedged between the bottom rail of the door and the mat beneath. She pulled it out and pushed the door fully open.

Somewhere in the darkened house came a miaow. Alice was in residence and like most nursing mothers was hungry.

Jill switched on the lights and went into the hall with Bernie behind her. While he was closing the door, she unfolded the envelope and glanced at the superscription. She sucked in a breath.

'What is it?' Bernie asked, closing the door behind them. 'Bad news?'

She did not reply. She stared at the envelope, reading the words on it once again.

Miss M Harris, Lower Slade Cottage, Eastbury, Lydmouth.

The address was written in blue ink. Here and there the words were smudged, as if drops of rain or perhaps tears had fallen on them at some point in the recent past. There was one other alteration. Someone had used a pencil to scratch out *Miss M Harris*. Just above Mattie's name they had scrawled a new word.

Bitch.

Chapter Fifty-one

———◆◆◆◆———

Brian Kirby was only human. That's what he told himself. He didn't like Bill Pembridge and he didn't mind if it showed.

They were sitting opposite each other, with nothing to keep them apart but the scarred metal table and the ashtray on top of it. The only other person in the interview room was Joan, sitting by the door taking notes. Bill had his elbows on the table, head bowed between his shoulders, cigarette cupped between the fingers of his right hand. His face was pink and the skin around the eyes was puffy. The blue eyes were moist, but he hadn't actually broken down. Not yet.

Kirby preferred to have him sitting down. Bill was a good three inches taller than he was, and he didn't like men who made him feel small.

'We'll take it again,' Kirby said. 'From the beginning. Something makes me think I'm not quite getting through to you.'

'But I didn't know Mattie Harris.'

'Of course you did.' Kirby flicked back the pages of his notebook. 'Here we are. You seemed to know all about her when you claimed to have heard her near the Ferryman on Thursday evening. Lost your memory, have you?'

'You're — you're twisting my words. I knew who she was. But I didn't know her well. She wasn't a friend.'

'Whose idea was it — yours or Malcolm Sedbury's?'

'What idea?'

'To use Wynstones.' He saw the flicker of fear in Bill's eyes. 'You know all about Wynstones, don't you?'

'I've never been inside it. I drove Malcolm up there on Sunday. He had to show some people over it. But I didn't even go inside the house. I stayed in the car.'

'Didn't you even have a walk in the garden?'

Bill shrugged. 'I might have done. I don't remember.'

Kirby sighed. He let his eyes linger on Bill. Then he turned to Joan. 'I don't know about you, love, but I'm parched. Why don't you get us some tea?' He winked at her, knowing Bill couldn't see his face.

'Yes, Sarge.' She stood up, straightening her skirt. Kirby watched her leave the room. Nice arse, he thought, something for a man to get hold of. He turned back to Bill, this time with something like a smile on his face.

'Listen, I know this isn't easy.' He closed his notebook and tossed it on the table between them. 'But we could make it less hard. Much less hard.'

'I don't know what you mean.'

'This is off the record now. That's why I sent the girl away. You and I know Mattie was a bit of a goer. Trouble with girls who are hot stuff is that someone tends to get burnt. She was pregnant. My bet is she was trying to get rid of it the traditional way. She was a — well, let's say a friend of yours. So she came to you. You had a word with young Sedbury, and you decided the best thing to do would be to let her use the bathroom at Wynstones. Wouldn't do anyone any harm. No one would know. Problem solved. Now I don't know what happened next. Do you?'

Bill was still staring at the pitted surface of the table. The cigarette was burning lower and lower and as Kirby watched, a cylinder of ash fell on to the table and disintegrated.

'Then maybe there was an accident,' he went on. 'Maybe she drank herself unconscious and drowned. So then you had another problem. You panicked. Nothing strange in that – God knows what I'd have done in your shoes. But—'

The door opened, cutting him off just as he was getting into his stride. Joan slipped into the room, without any tea. He scowled at her.

'Can I have a word, Sarge? Outside.'

He followed her into the corridor.

'The Guv'nor wants you,' she said. 'He's in his office.'

'Christ, what timing. I was just getting that little bastard where I want him.'

'What do you want me to do while you're gone?'

'Keep an eye on him but don't ask him any more questions until I come back.' He jerked a thumb upwards, in the general direction of Thornhill's office. 'What's going on?'

'Don't ask me. When he gave me the message he was talking to that reporter in reception. You know, the lady one. Miss Francis.'

Kirby nodded. *So that was the way the wind was blowing.* He went up to the ground floor. Thornhill's voice was audible in reception. He slipped through the glass door leading to the public part of the building. No one was behind the reception counter. The hall beyond was empty except for Thornhill and Jill Francis. Instinctively he stepped back, so he could not see them.

But he could hear them.

'I think there's a real possibility that Violet's in danger.' It was Jill's crisp, officer-class voice. 'Shouldn't you be searching for her?'

'I don't agree. Anyway, I can't justify the manpower. Not on what we know at present. We're very stretched.'

'It's not a question of *justifying*, it's—'

'We'll let the beat officers know we're looking for her.'

There were hob-nailed footsteps on the stairs. Kirby retreated behind the glass door, then advanced again, timing his official arrival in reception to coincide with that of Sergeant Fowles.

Fowles was carrying a lady's umbrella, which he handed to Jill. She thanked him and smiled at Kirby. She was a good-looking woman, all right, made Joan look a little clumsy. Something, maybe anger, had put a bit of colour into her cheeks. She said goodbye to Thornhill and left the building.

'Brian, come up to my office.'

They walked up to the first floor without speaking. Thornhill waved Kirby to the one visitor's chair in the little room and sat down behind the desk. The blind was down over the window but Kirby heard the rain spattering against the glass.

'Have you got anything out of Pembridge yet?'

'No, sir. Saying nothing and practically crying – that's him. But he'll crack.'

'You sound as if you haven't taken to him.'

'You could say that.'

'This won't change your mind.' Thornhill pushed his blotter across the desk. Resting on it was an envelope and a sheet of paper. 'Better not touch it.'

Kirby leant forward in his chair. The name of Mattie Harris was the first thing to catch his eye. Then the scrawled word beside it. *Bitch.* The paper was headed with an address which he recognised.

'Read the letter.'

The Beeches
Albert Road
Lydmouth
29th April

Dear Mattie

Malcolm's lent me the key so we could go to Wynstones again. Just one more time? I've got you a little present. I'll bring some beer and the portable gramophone, and we can have a little party, just us two. I'll be waiting on Thursday evening at seven o'clock in the lane near your parents' cottage. I'll run you back home afterwards, of course. Do come, can't wait to see you again.

    Bill xxx

'Bill?' Kirby blinked. 'She was sleeping with *Bill* Pembridge as well as his dad?'

'Not at the same time. Not quite.'

'And neither of them knew about the other.' He shook his head slowly, half shocked, half admiring. 'She must have split her sides.'

'What if one of them found out?'

'Where did the letter turn up, sir?'

'Someone put it through Miss Francis's letterbox. Must have been this evening, when she was out to dinner. Presumably the same person who made the alteration to the envelope.'

'There's only one person that's likely to be.'

Thornhill nodded. 'Trouble is, she's missing. Miss Francis and Councillor Broadbent met Ted Evans looking for Violet in the High Street three-quarters of an hour ago. I've had a constable round the house but she's not back yet. We'll pick her up, of course, probably sooner rather than later.'

'You don't think—'

'There's nothing to suggest she's suicidal, Brian, if that's what you mean.'

'But it adds up to one hell of a motive. Especially as she's just had a baby.' Kirby's right hand made an undulating motion like a choppy sea. 'Women act funny then, sometimes, they say. Emotional, eh? Easy for them to get things out of proportion.'

'We'll go and talk to Bill Pembridge.' Thornhill stood up. 'You ask the questions for the time being. I'll just sit and watch.'

They were going down the stairs when a uniformed sergeant came along the landing behind them at the next best thing to a run.

'Sir,' he called down to Thornhill. 'Bit of news you ought to hear.'

Thornhill and Kirby stopped, looking upwards at the sallow face craning over the banisters.

'Call from PC Hemlett, sir. His beat includes River Gardens.'

Thornhill went back up the stairs. 'What is it?'

'There's a broken ground-floor window in number nine, Miss Calder's house. He rang the bell but no one answered. Then the neighbour came out, said Miss Calder was with her. Hemlett went to see her. She'd obviously had a bit of a shock, and there was a bruise on her cheek. Said she'd tripped and fallen against the window, somehow broke it. Just an accident, she kept saying, just an accident.'

'What about the nephew, Jimmy Leigh?'

'That's just it, sir. He's done a bunk. And Hemlett said it looks like blood on the lounge carpet.'

Chapter Fifty-two

It was a bad dream. This couldn't be happening. Not to him. He was the lucky one.

The minutes dawdled more and more slowly. Bill had run out of cigarettes. The policewoman had left with the sergeant, and they'd slammed the bolt home. There was a Judas hole in the door, and now and then he saw a face looking at him. Once he tried to talk to the face, but there had been no answer. He shredded the empty cigarette packet into strips of cardboard and arranged the pieces into the letter M.

He had asked the sergeant, earlier, much earlier, whether he could have a solicitor, but the sergeant had laughed and said there was no need for that because no one had charged him.

Not yet.

He'd had such rotten luck. His father would have known how to handle the police – Superintendent Williamson was one of his friends. But his father hadn't been in the house when the police arrived, and his mother had been worse than useless. He screwed himself up to the point when he thought that anything would be better than being left alone in this room with only his thoughts for company.

The bolt rattled. The door opened and the sergeant returned with Inspector Thornhill. Neither of them said anything to him.

The inspector sat down where the woman had been. Kirby went back to his chair on the other side of the table and lit a cigarette.

Bill cleared his throat. 'Can I have one, please?'

Kirby blew out smoke. 'That depends.'

'On what?'

'On whether you tell me the truth this time.'

'But – but I have told you the truth.'

Kirby sat back in his chair and yawned. 'You've told me a pack of lies. You've wasted police time. We could charge you for that alone.'

Bill swallowed, looked at the inspector, hoping to find help there. But Thornhill was jotting something down in his notebook.

'We've found out something very interesting, Mr Pembridge.' Kirby leant across the table and blew out smoke again, this time so it went into Bill's face. 'While Violet Evans was having your baby, you were having a little fling with her friend Mattie Harris.'

'That's not true.' Bill's voice squeaked like air rushing from a tyre. 'I swear it's not.'

'Don't bother. We've got a letter you wrote. Leaves no room for doubt. You were going to take her along to Wynstones, weren't you, along with some beer. Not to mention the portable gramophone.'

When that horrible man mentioned the gramophone, Bill knew that it was all up with him. If they hadn't found the letter, there was no way they could have known about that. Mattie loved to dance. On two occasions he had danced her into bed. Except they hadn't bothered with a bed. She liked to show off, to dance while he watched her. She wanted to dance and he wanted to make love to her. And in the end they had come to the same thing.

'I – I didn't kill her. I swear it.' Bill stared wildly from the sergeant to the inspector. 'You must believe me.'

'Then tell us the truth.'

Bill slumped in his chair. How could you tell anyone the

truth about Mattie? She was as hard to hold on to as a handful of air. He remembered her kicking up her legs when they played Fats Waller's 'Your Feet's Too Big' on the gramophone, each kick a little higher until at last he could see right up her legs, only to discover that she wasn't wearing any knickers. He remembered her sitting astride him and telling him that he really should be a good boy and marry Violet. Just a little earlier, her eyes had widened like a happy child's when he gave her the powder compact.

'I've – I've been seeing Violet for about a year,' he said. 'Sometimes we'd go out with Mattie. Make a foursome.'

'A foursome?' Kirby said.

'With Malcolm Sedbury.'

There was a short silence.

'Did you know of any other lovers she had?'

Bill shook his head. 'I asked her once. She said it was better not to talk about it.'

They had been kissing at the time, sitting side by side on the sofa in the morning room at Wynstones. He'd lit a candle, and her dark red hair had glinted with mysterious lights. She'd smelt of smoke and sherry, spices and Fleur de Rose.

'What the eye doesn't see,' she'd said, 'the heart won't grieve over. It's nothing to do with you or me. Nothing to do with *now*.'

'And what about me?' Bill had replied. 'Would you tell others about me?'

'Of course I wouldn't, you silly boy.'

'But you do like me best, don't you?'

Then she stopped him talking with a kiss. Soon the kiss turned into something else.

'How long did you go on seeing her?'

'When Vi came out of hospital with the baby, Mattie wouldn't do it any more.' He realised that what he'd just said might give the policeman the wrong sort of impression about him and hastily added, 'Not that I wanted to, of course. It was just a fling. We got a bit carried away. But it couldn't go on.'

Yet he wished it could have done. At one time Violet's smooth, pale body could make him quite desperate with lust. But when she found out she was pregnant, everything changed. She'd rather talk about nappies than have sex.

What could a man do? Once Mattie was under your skin, you could never get rid of her. She would never talk about nappies, Bill had been sure of that. He hadn't been sure of much else about her, because that was part of her charm. You never knew which way she was going to jump. Nor, perhaps, did she.

Kirby pushed the cigarette packet across the table. 'When did Mattie find out she was pregnant?'

Bill shook out a cigarette. 'Must have been about three weeks ago.' He leant across the table, so Kirby could give him a light. 'She said it must've been me, that first time. That was early in April. So we had a meeting – Violet, Mattie, me and Malcolm. Of course we couldn't tell Violet it was me who got Mattie up the spout.'

'Was Malcolm one of her lovers too?'

'You must be joking.' The cigarette was making him feel stronger, more in control. 'Poor old Malcolm. Anyway, Mattie said she wasn't going to have the baby, come what may. Said a friend of hers had got drunk and had a very hot bath, and that had done the trick. She was going to do the same. She wanted Malcolm and me to make the arrangements. Get the key for Wynstones again, get some gin, take her home afterwards in the car. There was nowhere else she could do it, you see. Her parents hadn't got a bath, and anyway, it's not the sort of thing you can do at home, is it? We thought about going to a hotel or something, but someone would be bound to notice. Cost a lot of money, too. No, she was right – Wynstones was the best bet.'

He had hoped – not something he need mention here – that perhaps she might like to make love, too. Well, why not? She'd wanted to go dancing beforehand at the Ruispidge Hall, because she said the exercise might help get rid of it. If she wanted exercise, he could give her exercise.

'We had it all planned out,' Bill went on, feeling aggrieved because the plan was good, even if it hadn't worked. 'You know the Ruispidge Hall? There's a lane at the back, just a little path, really, goes round the back of the playing fields of the girls' school and comes out on Narth Road. Brings you out about a hundred yards before the turning to Wynstones. Malcolm said it would be better not to risk being seen together. Just in case.'

Mattie had already had quite a few drinks by the time she got to Wynstones. Not enough to make her unsteady – that came later. But Bill had watched her coming up the drive, seen the spring in her step, sensed her excitement. That's what alcohol used to do to Mattie, at least in the early stages. She glowed, as though someone had lit a candle deep inside her.

She'd reached Wynstones at about a quarter-past nine. Bill and Malcolm had taken her into the morning room at the back of the house, where the three of them sat smoking and drinking for a few minutes, watching the light leaving the garden. Malcolm said it would be wiser not to turn on the electric light, just in case. Bill had wanted to find a way of suggesting to Mattie that now might be a good time for a little exercise in the big bedroom. But she hadn't given him an opening, and he'd lacked the courage to make one. She'd sat on the sofa with Malcolm, squirming like a little girl at a party, telling stories about people she'd known in London with Gary, stories without beginning or end. Then suddenly she'd stood up and drained her glass, as if in a toast.

'Time for my bath,' she'd said. 'Be a sweetie, Bill, go and run it for me.' She held out her glass to Malcolm and said, 'Give us a top up. Let's drink to a happy killing.'

She collapsed back on the sofa, giggling and crying at the same time. Glad to be away from her, Bill went upstairs and ran the bath. When he came downstairs again, he found her holding Malcolm's hand, swaying from side to side on the sofa, humming 'Auld Lang Syne' very slowly.

She continued to hum 'Auld Lang Syne' while they helped her

upstairs and into the bathroom. She sent them away then, saying she didn't want a pair of peeping Toms watching her get undressed, but telling them to stay in earshot in case she wanted them.

She'd treated them like a pair of servants, Bill said. She'd called down for more gin. She'd shouted for cigarettes, for matches, for an ashtray. Mostly it was Bill who took them up, because Malcolm didn't find it easy to manage strange stairs.

By then Bill couldn't see much, because the twilight was so far advanced. Mattie was a spectral presence in the bath, issuing commands in that husky voice. When she ordered him to put the hot water on, the flames danced in the Ascot, painting the bath and Mattie in a flickering, orange glow. Not that there was much to see, because most of her was underwater. He had been pretty drunk himself by then, no longer excited but sullen, and he couldn't imagine how he'd ever found her attractive.

A little later, Mattie's wail had drifted down the stairs. 'For God's sake!' she shrieked. 'I've dropped the bloody cigarettes in the bath.'

Malcolm and Bill looked at each other. Malcolm had forgotten his own cigarettes. They had just finished Bill's.

'Bring me a fag, will you?' she shouted.

'We'll go and buy some,' Malcolm said.

Bill stood up. 'I'll go.'

Mattie had started singing 'Auld Lang Syne' once again.

Malcolm had said, 'We'll both go.' He hauled himself upright. 'All right,' he said, answering Bill's silent plea. 'I'll go and tell her.'

The interview room was silent. Bill felt the memories swirling like flood water around him. You could drown in memories. Sergeant Kirby lit another cigarette. The two of them might have been alone in the room.

'So Malcolm went upstairs to tell her where you were going?' he prompted.

'No. In the end we both did. She wanted another drink, and he couldn't manage the bottle as well as the banisters.'

'You weren't worried about leaving her by herself?'

'Why should we be? She was quite safe. A bit tight, maybe, but that's all. No one could get in.'

'No one?'

Bill ignored the question and rushed on. 'I was glad to get out, to be honest. The whole thing was giving me the creeps. That bloody singing. Sounded like a funeral dirge.' He hesitated, wishing he knew what to reveal, what to invent, what to conceal. 'She wasn't always gloomy, though. Last thing I heard of her she was laughing at something Malcolm said.'

'So he was alone with her?'

Bill nodded. 'Yes, I went down first. She asked him something, and they stayed talking for a while. Then she laughed.'

He would have known Mattie's laugh anywhere. It was the sort of laugh that ran down your spine and made you think of guilty pleasures, that drew you into a delicious conspiracy with her.

'I went outside to bring the car round,' Bill went on. 'We'd put it round the side of the house just so it was out of sight if anyone came up the drive. Malcolm came out a few minutes later, after he'd got himself downstairs and locked up.'

'So he was by himself with Mattie?'

'Yes,' Bill said eagerly. 'That's right.'

They had driven to the Ferryman because Malcolm thought it would be safer. They had both had quite a lot to drink, and there was more chance of their being stopped if they drove into Lydmouth. They bought the cigarettes and had a drink as well. Neither of them had wanted to rush back.

'How long were you away from the house?'

Bill shrugged. 'I don't know. Maybe forty-five minutes.'

'And when did you get back to Wynstones?'

'I didn't look at my watch. It must've been between half-past ten and eleven, I suppose.'

He and Malcolm had gone into the house together. The hall seemed much darker than when they'd left it. Bill had thought fleetingly of the ghost of the retired bank manager, the man who'd hanged himself. For an instant he wondered if there was something up there in the darkness above his head, some greater darkness, swinging gently in the draught from the front door.

'Mattie, we're back,' Malcolm had called. 'Mattie!'

The house was silent. His words rose like unanswered prayers up the stairwell and were sucked into the darkness above their heads. It would have been a relief to hear her laugh, even to hear 'Auld Lang Syne'.

He and Malcolm went up the stairs together, Malcolm leaning on Bill with one hand and on the banister rail with the other. The bathroom was almost completely dark. Just the tiny blue flame of the Ascot's pilot light. Malcolm swore under his breath and brushed his hand down the wall until he found the light switch.

Suddenly everything had been unbearably bright. There was the bath, at least two-thirds full of water. And there was Mattie, suspended beneath the surface, the dark-red hair like a cloud of seaweed around the pale triangle of her face.

The scene was frozen in Bill's mind with Arctic clarity. Her clothes had been draped over a wooden towel rail. The gin bottle, the glass and the ashtray stood on a chair beside the bath. The ashtray was full of cigarette ends, and the glass was half full, the rim smudged with lipstick.

'The floor was wet,' Bill said, staring across the table at Brian Kirby. 'Can I have another cigarette?'

Kirby took one out of the packet and gave it to him. He held out a match. Bill scratched his chin. The smoke burnt his throat. Why did one always think a cigarette would make things better?

'How wet?' Kirby said.

'Looked like some water had slopped out around the bath. There were footprints, too. She must have gone down for the gin bottle, then brought it back up again. Probably splashed a bit while she was getting out of the bath.' He squinted through the smoke at Kirby. 'That's what Malcolm thought, anyway.'

'You're sure she was dead?'

'Of course I'm sure—' Bill broke off, and tried to smile. 'I'm sorry. Malcolm checked her pulse. Besides, you – you could tell.'

'What did you think had happened?'

'It was obvious. She'd fallen asleep, and drowned. Poor old Mattie.' He bit his lower lip.

'Tell me what happened next,' Kirby said.

'I wanted to call the police,' Bill said, 'but Malcolm said we couldn't let her be found here. He said if we did, it would all come out about her and me, and that his father would probably have a heart attack.' He screwed up his face. 'The way he said it, it didn't seem wrong. She drowned by accident, didn't she? So we were going to put her in the river to make it look like she drowned there. You know, had a few drinks and fallen in. Came to the same thing in the end. Wouldn't have harmed anyone, either.'

He looked for sympathy in Kirby's face but found nothing there but mild curiosity.

Gradually the details stumbled out of him. It was lucky that Mattie had been so small and light, though death had made her heavier. Bill lifted her out of the bath, successfully resisting the urge to be sick, and laid her on one of the big towels from the airing cupboard. Her arms and legs flopped awkwardly and unnaturally. Malcolm had knelt and straightened them, so her arms were by her side and her legs were together. Her little breasts poked out of her body like a pair of pomegranates. He'd noticed Malcolm staring at the dark triangle of hair at the top of the legs, and wondered whether this was the first time he had seen a naked woman.

Dead meat. Enough to put a chap off sex for life.

'Take the torch and get the boat out,' Malcolm had said. 'And a pair of oars. We'll take her downstream a little way, and put her over the side in the middle of the river. Get the boat in the water and then come back.'

'What are you going to do?'

Malcolm had stared up at him, his mouth twisting. 'Get her dressed, of course. Unless you want to do it.'

Bill had gone downstairs. He was trembling. Nevertheless, the fresh air helped, so did having a job to do, a job that did not involve Mattie. When he got back to the bathroom, she was still lying on the towel, but now she was fully clothed. Her eyes, cloudy brown, stared at the ceiling.

'We'll roll her in the towel,' Malcolm said. 'It'll be easier to move her that way. I'll fetch another one from the airing cupboard.'

Not a person. Just an awkward weight. That's the way to think of it. Carrying a mattress or a roll of carpet.

Bill had slung her over his shoulder and taken her downstairs with Malcolm dragging himself behind them. He kept his eyes half closed, because that lessened the risk of seeing something upsetting. Down the garden they went. He dumped her in the boat. The towel fell open and for the last time he'd seen her face.

Except she hadn't looked like Mattie any more.

Malcolm rowed. He was good with oars – his shoulders and arms were very well muscled, and the withered legs hardly mattered in a boat. They slid silently downstream for several hundred yards and then, where the river widened out, Bill rolled Mattie into the water while Malcolm leant over the opposite gunwale as a counterbalance.

Mattie had gone into the Minnow with scarcely a splash, but the boat rocked and swayed, and Bill had to grab Malcolm's hand to prevent him from falling in the water.

They rowed back to Wynstones to tidy up. They were still drunk at that time, but the shock and the night air had gone a long way towards sobering them, at least temporarily. Luckily they had used only two rooms, the bathroom and the morning room. They dried the bathroom floor as best they could with a blanket from the car and scoured the bath.

Malcolm had polished the taps and the door handles. He

made Bill wash the ashtrays and take away the cigarette ends. 'He even made me brush the upholstery, brush the carpet.' Bill rubbed his eyes. 'It was a nightmare, I tell you. A bloody nightmare.'

'So all this was Malcolm's idea?'

'Yes.' Bill shook his head slowly from side to side as though trying to shake out a memory. 'Things kept going wrong. We didn't leave until well after midnight.'

That night he had taken two of his mother's sleeping pills, but had slept badly. He had spent most of Friday in a daze induced by barbiturates and hangover. He knew he should try to get in touch with Violet, tell her that Mattie hadn't turned up at Wynstones, which he and Malcolm had agreed was the simplest story. It was only on Friday evening that fear brought his energy back. When he remembered the letter. The one letter he had written to Mattie.

'She might have thrown it away,' Kirby said.

'That's what Malcolm said,' Bill replied. 'But we couldn't be sure. And her body could turn up at any time. Once that happened, someone would search her room. So I had to make sure it wasn't there.'

He had been in Mattie's room before – he'd spent most of the night in her bed after bringing her home one evening. Then, by arrangement, he'd gone round to the back of the cottage and climbed up the roof of the outhouse to Mattie's room, where she was waiting for him at the window, unbuttoning her dress.

He'd taken the same route on Friday night and slipped the catch of the window with his penknife. But it was no use. No sign of the letter. But the sight of her room had reminded him that there were other possessions that hadn't turned up, notably the gold powder compact he'd given her. It was then he realised what else was missing. Mattie's handbag.

'A fellow doesn't think of handbags,' he said to Kirby. 'They're a girl's sort of thing.'

So he had rung Malcolm the following morning and found

him in the office. They'd agreed the bag must still be somewhere at Wynstones. The trouble was, Robert Sedbury now had the keys for the place. They had to wait till Sunday, when Malcolm was taking the Christies round.

'Malcolm took them into the garden first, so I could have a look for the bag. You'll never believe it – she'd left it on the hook on the back of the bathroom door – we'd missed it. It was there in front of our eyes all the time. Trouble was, it was so big that I couldn't hide it anywhere. And the Christies were coming back to the house and they got between me and the car. So in the end I had to take it down the garden. Finally I – well, I suppose I panicked. Threw it in the river. I'd already had a look inside. No letter, worse luck. But I did take out the powder compact.'

'The one you planted near the Ferryman?' Kirby said. 'Whose bright idea was that?'

'Malcolm's. Trying to be clever again. We thought that as the body had come out at New Bridge, the handbag probably would as well. Malcolm said it was important to draw your attention away from Wynstones, away from the Minnow. We'd been seen at the Ferryman on Thursday evening, so that gave us an alibi. We left the compact in the meadow nearby and made up this story about seeing Mattie with a man in the field. We weren't doing any harm.' He stared at Kirby's unreadable face and blurted out once again, 'It was all *Malcolm's* idea, I promise. Listen, she drowned by accident, that's what counts. You've got to believe me.'

A chair scraped on the floor. Bill swung round towards the sound. Thornhill was now on his feet. Kirby looked at him too, and between the two policemen there passed a message that Bill couldn't read.

Thornhill put his hands in his trouser pockets. 'The trouble is, Mr Pembridge, we can't be sure it was an accident.'

Bill's stomach lurched. 'But it must have been.'

'By your own account, there was a lot of splashing on the bathroom floor. There's another thing – there was very recent bruising on Mattie Harris's shoulders. Could well have occurred at the time of her death. Symmetrical bruising, too. Four little bruises along the collarbone on either side of her neck. Then two little bruises at the back. One on each shoulder blade. What does that suggest to you, Mr Pembridge?'

'I don't know. Why are you asking me?'

'The most likely explanation for those bruises is that someone was standing, or perhaps kneeling, behind Mattie Harris and had his hands on her shoulders. Judging by the extent of the bruising, he was pressing very hard indeed. Pressing downwards.'

Bill stared up at the inspector, trying to think of something – think of anything – he could say. 'Someone – someone must have broken in while we were out and—'

'Not very likely, Mr Pembridge. No sign of a break-in, was there? You say you locked up when you went out. Someone could leave the house once they were inside – there's only a Yale lock on the front door. But they couldn't get in, could they, not without leaving a trace. Not unless someone let them in or they had a key. Even if someone came to the door, Mattie wouldn't have let them in, not in the state she was in. Besides, she was upstairs in the bath.'

'Malcolm.' Bill croaked, relief breaking over him like a shower of warm water. 'Then it must have been *Malcolm*. Well, I'm damned.'

He paused, but neither of the policemen said anything. He looked wildly from one to the other. Calm-faced, they stared back.

'He always had the hots for Mattie,' Bill said in a voice little louder than a whisper. 'You could tell, the way he looked at her. He – he must have tried something on while she was in the bath. Or maybe earlier. You know I told you I heard her laugh? Perhaps she was laughing at him. Perhaps he killed her to shut her up, to stop her telling me what he'd done.' Bill looked imploringly from one blank face to the other. 'He's very strong, Malcolm is. And there's always been something — well, something strange about him. He's carrying around a razor in his pocket at present. He showed me it. This bloody great cut-throat razor.'

Still the policemen said nothing.

Bill felt tears pressing at his eyelids. He laid his head on his arms and wept.

Chapter Fifty-three

If the police wouldn't look for Violet Evans, then she would.

The rain had slackened a little. Jill wore wellingtons, a long raincoat, a headscarf and carried an umbrella. There were few people around, which made the job easier. She thought of going back for the car then remembered that she had left it at Netherfield. In any case, a car would restrict where she could go.

She decided that the best thing to do would be to quarter the centre of Lydmouth. She began with the area near her own home, working on the assumption that it must have been Violet herself who delivered the letter at Church Cottage. She spent nearly half an hour walking up and down streets, delving into cul-de-sac, peering into alleys, calling Violet's name. In Nutholt Lane, she met a policeman who looked at her suspiciously. She asked him if he'd seen Violet but he hadn't.

Next, she investigated the part of town that lay east of the High Street, sloping gently down to the river. No luck there, either, though she encountered Ted Evans at the bus station. Jill offered to find a taxi to take him back to Broadwell Crescent to see if she'd returned.

'No need, Miss.' Barriers which had slipped for a moment were now firmly back in place. 'I can manage all right on my own, thank you.'

'Are you feeling all right? After the accident?'

'I'm all right. No thanks to Bernie Broadbent.'

'I'm worried about Violet,' Jill said.

'Why?' He took a step nearer to her, water dripping from the brim of his cap, his compact body suddenly something to be wary of. 'What's it to *you*?'

'Because it's a bad night to be out. She's upset. She needs help.'

Ted brushed water from his face. 'She'll have all the help she needs from her family. Nothing to do with anyone else.'

'That's the point. She hasn't had the help she needs from her family, has she?'

For an instant she thought he might hit her. Then Ted sighed, and his eyes drifted passed her, staring up the road to the High Street.

'None of your business.' He spoke mechanically now, as one repeating a formula prescribed by protocol while the mind was elsewhere. 'But you can come along with me if you want. Then I won't waste time looking where you've already been. I suppose two heads are better than one.'

'Thank you,' Jill said. 'Have you tried the ladies' lavatory on the corner of Bull Lane?'

Chapter Fifty-four

Much harder to hit a moving target.

The razor was in his left-hand trouser pocket. Sometimes Malcolm stopped to make sure it was still there. His raincoat had slits in the pockets so you could put your hands through to the clothing beneath. He wasn't sure why he found it reassuring to touch what was, after all, just an object made of steel, silver and ivory. But he liked the way the razor had grown steadily warmer until it had reached the same temperature as his body. The shared warmth made them part of each other.

Bill's going to talk. Not a matter of if. Just a matter of when.

He wasn't sure how long he'd been walking. The rain hadn't stopped, though at least it had slackened a little. He kept away from the centre of town, zigzagging slowly through Temple-fields instead. Sometimes he sheltered in doorways, and he spent half an hour sitting in the dry shell of a half-built house, smoking his last two cigarettes, until the old, restless fear drove him on again.

Much harder to hit a moving target.

By now, he was more wet than dry. The rain had soaked into the mackintosh, and now the dampness of the lining was beginning to penetrate the jacket beneath. Matters were much worse below the hem of the raincoat. The bottoms of his trousers were soaked, and the water had long since penetrated his brogues.

Twice he saw policemen, both times in Templefields. The

first time the man had his back to him. The rain was streaming off his long cape and he was pacing slowly up the cobbled roadway. Malcolm ducked into the alley he had emerged from, and the danger passed. The second occasion was when he saw a patrol car in Mincing Lane. He thought it possible they were looking for him.

Time passes very slowly when you're afraid and looking for somewhere to hide. Malcolm allowed gravity to draw him back down the hill towards the river. He needed to make a decision. There was no doubt that the worst had happened, or was about to happen. The police had turned their attention to Wynstones. He wondered if they'd charged Bill yet. Now his teeth were chattering, though whether from cold or fear he wasn't sure. He wanted to go home.

That was just what he couldn't do. The police would be waiting for him there. Worse than that was the thought of his mother and father.

In his mind he saw their faces, pale and worried, so close to each other they were touching. The sight was familiar. Then the memory slotted into place. He'd seen them looking like that in reality, not imagination.

Peering in at me through the round window like a ship's port hole in the door of the isolation ward. Oh Christ.

The unexpected confluence of past and present was too much for him to bear. He left the shadows of Templefields and staggered in to the main road down to the station. Opposite him, the windows of the Station Hotel shimmered with light, a mirage of dry warmth.

He dragged himself over the road, stumbling and nearly falling as he stepped on to the opposite pavement. A moment later, he was standing in the hallway that separated the hotel's public bar from the saloon. Rivulets of water ran down his mackintosh to the linoleum. The lobby was stuffed with wet coats, wet hats and umbrellas. He found a peg for his own hat and coat and shuffled into the lounge.

The room was full of heat, light and smoke. Malcolm made his way to the counter. Most of the other customers were men. He recognised none of them. They stood in a ragged line along the counter and round the gas fire, laughing at a joke one of them had made. *Arf-arf. Arf-arf.* The sound belonged to another species. They might have been seals barking in a zoo. *Arf-arf. Arf-arf.*

Malcolm reached the counter. The barmaid was flirting with a large man in tweeds who was leaning towards her, canting like the figurehead of a ship. *Arf-arf. Arf-arf.* He tapped half a crown against an ashtray until at last she condescended to notice him. He ordered a large brandy and ten Senior Service. He put the cigarettes in his pocket and carried the drink to the table near the door. On the way he stumbled, because he could use only one stick while carrying the glass, and spilled a few drops on his hand. *Arf-arf. Arf-arf.* He knew they were all looking at him. He wished, not for the first time, that he was invisible.

But the advantage with the Station Hotel was that most of the people in the lounge bar would be commercial travellers. They didn't know him and he didn't know them. He was as nearly anonymous here as he could be in any pub in Lydmouth.

He sipped the brandy, making it last, and smoked two cigarettes. The future remained as murky and unhappy as ever, but at least the present was a little warmer. His parents' faces swam in memory like pale, bloated fish behind the port hole of the isolation ward.

They'd be better off without me.

What about Bill? How would he manage?

The brandy cleared his mind. The best thing to do would be to go up to London. He had a school friend who lived in Pimlico, a man who owed him money. He could sleep on Jack's sofa.

Not tonight, though. The last of the through trains had already gone. He didn't want to end up at Paddington Station in the early hours. He would do better to find somewhere to spend the night here and then go up early. There was a through train at six-thirty. He wondered briefly if they would watch the station. He pushed the thought away from him. Something to deal with later.

He resisted the temptation to have another brandy and left the warmth and shelter of the hotel. He was standing in the porch, settling the sou'wester on his head, when a saloon car drew up beside him. His heart lurched. It was the Pembridges' Vauxhall. For a blissful moment, he thought everything had miraculously sorted itself out. Bill had been released. He'd come to look for him. Everything was going to be all right.

But when he opened the passenger door, he saw Gerald Pembridge behind the wheel.

For an instant they stared at each other, as though both had lost the faculty of speech. Pembridge was the first to break the silence.

'Foul night to be out, Malcolm. Do you want a lift?'

'No, thank you. I'm – I'm meeting someone.'

'Righty ho.' Pembridge gave a gasp which might have been a laugh. 'The night is young, eh? No doubt you and Bill have plans.'

Either he hadn't heard that Bill was at the police station or Bill must have been released and there was nothing to worry about.

'You know that girl who used to work for you?' Pembridge went on. 'Violet Evans?'

Malcolm stared at him. 'Yes. What about her?'

'She's not in there, is she?'

'Not in the saloon bar.'

Pembridge chewed his lip. 'She wouldn't be in the public bar. No – it was a long shot.' And there was another half gasp, half laugh. 'I – I happened to find her purse in the High Street. Just wondered if you'd seen her.'

Malcolm shook his head. 'She lives in Broadwell Crescent.' He hesitated. 'Or you could hand it in at the police station.'

'Yes, yes I suppose I could do that. Sure you don't want a lift? Well, I'd better say goodbye. Edna will be waiting for me.'

Malcolm slammed the door. Pembridge revved the engine and let out the clutch. His timing was poor, and the car jerked forward, its nearside tyres spraying water over Malcolm's legs.

The glow from the brandy still enveloped him. He watched the dwindling tail lights of the Vauxhall for a moment and then staggered across the road to Templefields. Here among the maze of alleys and building sites and derelict buildings he would be safe. There was little street lighting in Templefields, which was part of its attraction. He stumbled uphill, the sticks and his feet slipping on wet, barely visible cobbles. The further he walked into Templefields, he told himself, the safer he would be.

No one else was about, or if they were, he couldn't see them. But the rain, the wind and the poor lighting made it impossible to be sure. The sou'wester acted as an acoustic hood, distorting the sounds.

Sometimes, though, when he stopped to draw breath, he thought he heard hesitant footsteps continuing into the darkness.

Chapter Fifty-five

Time no longer seemed to mean very much. Violet stared through the window of the buffet. A stretch of grey asphalt ended abruptly. A million pins and needles of rain fell into the darkness above the tracks. Platform four was a dimly lit outline, a foreign country for trains serving unknown destinations.

'We're closing in a couple of minutes,' called the woman behind the counter.

Violet gave no sign that she'd heard. She sneezed, licked her finger and dabbed at a stray crumb on the plate that had held her third currant bun. As well as the buns, she had had four cups of tea, two bars of chocolate from the machine on the platform, and a stale cheese sandwich that the lady behind the counter had let her have at half price, because she was going to throw it away. Her clothes were still damp but she was much warmer now.

Two trains to London had come and gone since she had been in the buffet. She opened her handbag again and took out her purse. She didn't want to count her money again. She was going to look at the lock of Grace's hair.

'I'm afraid I shall have to ask you to leave.' The lady behind the counter wasn't behind the counter any more, but looming over Violet. 'Some of us have got beds to go to, you know.'

The door opened and one of the porters came in. He eyed Violet and said to the woman, 'You OK, Ena?'

'Soon will be, when I can lock up.'

'Come along, please,' the porter said to Violet. 'Where you going, anyway?'

Violet took out her purse again and removed a platform ticket. The porter examined it.

'I'm meeting someone,' Violet said. She'd bought the platform ticket because she hadn't known whether she was staying or going. She still didn't know. Grace pulled her here, Grace pushed her away.

'You'd better come back tomorrow,' the porter said. 'You heard what the lady said, the buffet's closing now.'

Without looking at them Violet stood up, put on her coat, picked up her handbag and left the warm room. She heard them whispering as she closed the door. She wished she were slim, beautiful and able to make cutting, witty remarks when the occasion demanded them. Too late for all that now.

She tried the door of the ladies' waiting room but it was locked. She sat down heavily on one of the benches along the platform. The porter reappeared and told her that she had to go home now.

'Why?' she said, suddenly defiant. 'I've got a platform ticket.'

The porter went away. Somebody else came and talked to her, perhaps the station master. Then he went away too. They would have acted very differently if she had been Mattie Harris. She would have acted differently, too. Mattie had taken no nonsense from anyone, even her friends. Least of all her friends. Mattie would have laughed in their faces, would have made them laugh, too.

Damn Mattie. None of this would have happened if it hadn't been for Mattie. None of this would have happened if Mattie hadn't made people love her.

More footsteps were approaching briskly along the platform,. Perhaps it was a policeman. She didn't care.

'Violet?' The voice was smooth and familiar. 'Violet, my dear.'

She looked up and saw Gerald Pembridge. He was bending over her, smiling. No one else was in sight. Panic rose inside her. There was a soft, continuous noise like distant thunder.

'Violet, you remember me? Gerald Pembridge. A friend of the Sedburys. Now, I wanted to have a little chat with you. A little chat about Mattie.'

She was on her feet now, backing away from him. 'Don't come near me. You dirty old man, it was you.'

'Violet, calm down, please. There's nothing to worry about.'

She backed away, further down the platform, closer to its edge, too.

'Tell me, dear, did Mattie ever mention me to you?'

The distant thunder had come closer and resolved itself into the sound of a train pulling slowly into the station. It was a goods train, couplings clanking, wheels rumbling, the smoke and steam hissing and billowing along the wooden frills on the edge of the platform roof. Pembridge was coming closer and closer.

He's going to kill me because I know about him and Mattie.

There were other people on the platform now, rushing towards them. Not rescuers, Violet thought, but people to help Pembridge. They were all against her.

She saw her father first, his face twisted with hate, his mouth opening as if he was shouting something but the train drowned his words. Behind him was Jill Francis – surely that couldn't be right? – and last of all came a pair of constables, first walking quickly, then breaking into a run.

All the time, the noise of the train grew louder and louder. All the time, it became harder and harder to think.

Pembridge turned to face the newcomers, his arms outstretched as if welcoming them. The engine flashed past Violet and the long train of goods trucks pulled thorough the station, heading north for Gloucester.

Ted's fist was a pale blur. She heard a *smack*.

Now Pembridge was lying on his back, his hands clamped

over his face. The hands were bloody. Ted kicked him in the ribs. Once, twice. The police officers seized him, one to each arm, and he wrestled with them, forcing them to turn this way and that.

Jill Francis ran towards Violet.

'No,' Violet screamed, though she wasn't sure what she was refusing.

Ted flung off one of the policemen. The man cannoned into Jill. She staggered, lost her balance and fell back on the bench where Violet had been sitting.

Drops of red spotted the grey asphalt.. Gerald Pembridge scrambled to his feet. His raincoat was filthy. He had lost his hat. Blood was streaming from his nose and mouth. He looked wildly round, first at the struggling men, then at Violet.

This can't be happening, Violet thought, everyone's gone mad.

Pembridge staggered towards her, one hand out, his face a bloody mask.

Violet screamed again. She turned and ran. She ran along the platform, down the slope at the end and on to the permanent way beyond.

Chapter Fifty-six

'Thought it was you,' Jimmy Leigh said. 'Can't walk proper, can you?'

The towpath was full of shadows. This was one of the darker ones, the one that talked.

'Sounds funny, look, not like anyone else. So I knew it was you, even though I couldn't see you. It's the way you walk.'

Malcolm rested his back against a wall that ran down the landward side of the towpath. 'What — what are you doing here?'

'This is where I come.' The voice was sharp, with an edge of fear. 'See, I know everywhere round here. That's Fenner's behind you. The slaughterhouse is up there. Just upstream.'

'You're Jimmy Leigh, aren't you?'

'I remember you in hospital. You cried and cried. Cry baby.'

'You cried too.'

'I didn't! That's a lie!'

Malcolm put his hand deep into his pocket. 'You ought to go home now. It's getting late. And it's raining.'

'I don't mind the rain. Don't care how wet I get. And I don't care that it's late, either. Saw *you* out late the other night, didn't I?' Suddenly the voice trembled. 'Saw you at Wynstones.'

'Oh did you?' Malcolm's fingers curled round the handle of the razor. 'You know what that means.'

'It's all your fault,' Jimmy said quickly. 'It's all your fault, what happened to Mattie. You're dirty, aren't you? You made her do dirty things with you. You made her. I hate you.'

Malcolm drew the razor out of his pocket. Jimmy was a blurred silhouette on the other side of the towpath. Behind him was the Minnow, flowing down to New Bridge. Blood in the Minnow, Malcolm thought, blood from the slaughterhouse. He drew out the razor and lifted it to his lips. He pulled out the blade with his teeth. As he did so, he felt the rain on his upturned face.

Threats are dark prayers.

'Jimmy Leigh,' he said, so softly only he could hear. 'Jimmy Leigh, I'll kill you, Jimmy Leigh.'

Chapter Fifty-seven

'May we come in, Mrs Sedbury?' Thornhill said gently.

'But I told you, Inspector. Malcolm isn't here.'

'We'd also like to speak to you and your husband.'

Frowning slightly, she held open the door to allow Thornhill and Joan into the hall. He guessed she was wondering whether or not to offer to take their coats and hats. She wouldn't want to make it seem like a social call; nor would she like to encourage them to stay for a long time. On the other hand, rainwater was running off their coats and forming small puddles around them on the shining parquet floor. The instincts of the housekeeper triumphed.

'Shall I take your coats?'

Once they were stripped of their outer coverings, she showed them into a drawing room overlooking the front garden and went to fetch her husband. It was a large, airy room with modern furniture, including a radiogram, a television and a cocktail cabinet. Joan stared at herself in the mirror over the mantelpiece, patting her hair. Thornhill looked at the photographs standing on the windowsill.

One showed the Ashbridge School Under-13 cricket team — eleven very small and very earnest boys. One of the boys sitting in the middle row was instantly recognisable as a younger version of Malcolm Sedbury. Another photograph showed him at the crease, hunched over his bat, scowling with concentration. He had batted left-handed.

Mrs Sedbury returned with her husband.

'You say Malcolm isn't at the Pembridges', he said, without wasting any time.

Thornhill put down the photograph. 'He's not been there all evening.'

'Then where is he?'

Mrs Sedbury's hand flew to her throat. 'He's had an accident?'

'Not as far as we know.'

'Thank God for that.' She sank on to the sofa.

'Bill Pembridge is at the station now, by the way,' Thornhill went on. 'He's been helping us with our inquiries this evening.'

'Inquiries?' Sedbury said, still standing by the door, a miserable expression on his dark face. 'Inquiries into what? Something to do with Wynstones?'

'We're investigating the death of Mattie Harris.'

Sedbury went to sit on the sofa by his wife. 'You think that Malcolm and Bill were somehow involved, don't you?'

Mrs Sedbury gave a little squeal.

'Yes, sir. I think it's very likely.'

'You can't think that Malcolm's—' Mrs Sedbury began.

'That's enough, dear,' her husband interrupted. 'We must keep cool. I'm sure there's a perfectly reasonable explanation.'

'But, Robert, he can't have even known the girl.'

Thornhill said, 'Tell me, sir, what sort of razor does your son use?'

'A safety razor, of course.'

'Does he have a cut throat as well?'

'Yes, as a matter of fact he has. I gave him a pair that were my father's the other day. Why?'

'May we see them?'

Sedbury stood up, his face a mask of wrinkles. 'They'll be in his room, I expect.'

'May I come with you, sir? WPC Ailsmore has a few things she would like to ask Mrs Sedbury.'

Mrs Sedbury began to cry. 'I wish he was at home with us.' She produced a handkerchief from the pocket of her cardigan and began to dab her eyes. 'He's so easily hurt.'

Joan sat down beside her on the sofa. 'We'll find him, Mrs Sedbury, don't you fret.'

She might have been talking to a toddler who had mislaid his mother. Thornhill followed Sedbury out of the room and up the stairs. Neither of them spoke until they were in Malcolm's bedroom and Sedbury had closed the door.

'Listen, Inspector, I didn't like to say this downstairs, but you think this is a very serious business, don't you?'

'I think it may be, sir.'

Sedbury swallowed. 'I – I just don't know what to say or do. This isn't the sort of situation . . .'

'Do you have a solicitor, sir?'

'What? Yes. George Shipston.'

'If I were you, I'd telephone him.'

'You can't think – you can't seriously think . . .'

Sedbury fell silent, groping for a handkerchief.

'Judging by the photos downstairs, your son's left-handed?'

'What? Yes, yes he is. Would have made a damned good bowler if – if that wretched polio hadn't happened. Not a bad little batsman, either.'

'Must have been a terrible blow for you all.'

Sedbury blew his nose. 'One gets over it. But there's no denying that – that . . .'

He broke off and walked over to the chest of drawers. He took out a slim leather-covered case from the top drawer, flipped up the catch and opened it. Wordlessly, he handed the case to Thornhill. There was one ivory-handled razor inside. Beside it was the indentation where its twin had lain in its blue silk bed.

'Perhaps he put it somewhere else, Inspector – meaning to try it out.'

'Would you mind if I had a look around his room while we're here, sir? If you'd prefer I could get a warrant but that would take time.'

Sedbury sat down heavily. The bedsprings creaked. He waved a hand. 'Go ahead. What does it matter?'

Thornhill went quickly round the room. There were two guides to London and several textbooks on surveying on top of the bureau. In one of the pigeon holes inside was a bundle of letters from Bill, written when he was away on National Service. Thornhill found a hip flask and a packet of condoms, never opened, in the top drawer beneath the socks. Tucked in an old jacket in the back of the wardrobe was a brown envelope containing twelve black-and-white photographs, a sequence showing a young woman with a bored face undressing herself and lying on a bed. Thornhill returned them where he'd found them.

Sedbury gave no sign he'd noticed. He was still sitting on the bed, staring at the door as though he saw something strange and monstrous standing there.

'That's all I need here, thank you. Shall we go back down-stairs?'

Sedbury stood up, balancing uncertainly on his feet. 'You know, I'm sure there's some simple explanation. Malcolm would never – he knows how important our reputation is.'

'Your *reputation*?' Thornhill blinked. The word collided with a recent memory, a painful one at that. '*Your* reputation?'

'Our *reputation*,' Sedbury said with a touch of petulance. 'We've been here for well over a hundred years. We're one of those old-fashioned firms. Reputation is everything. We depend on it. You see, if people don't trust us, they simply won't come to us. Nowadays we have plenty of rivals, I'm afraid.'

Thornhill frowned. He had hardly taken in what Sedbury was saying. He felt as if he'd been winded. Somehow he'd failed to ask a glaringly obvious question. He had been distracted, yes, but –

'Reputation,' he murmured. 'Sorry, sir – something's just occurred to me.'

The question he hadn't asked had been handed to him on a plate. It couldn't have been made more obvious if it had stood up and shouted at him.

He smiled at Sedbury. 'Yes, I can see how important reputation must be in your line of work. Would you mind if I made a phone call?'

'Of course not. The phone's in the study.'

The two men went downstairs. The drawing-room door was partly open. Mrs Sedbury's low voice rose and fell. Thornhill couldn't make out the words. Just as Sedbury was opening the study door, the phone inside began to ring. He muttered under his breath and picked up the receiver.

'It's for you, Inspector.'

Thornhill took the telephone and waited for Sedbury to leave the room. 'Thornhill here.'

'Kirby, sir. There's been a bit of a barney at the railway station. Uniformed gave us a call when they found out who was involved.'

'What's been happening?'

'Seems that Violet Evans had been hanging around there for an hour or two. No coat, soaked right through – the station staff thought she was a bit mental. Then Gerald Pembridge turned up and started to talk to her. Closely followed by Ted Evans and' – Kirby coughed – 'and Miss Francis. Evans went for Pembridge, landed him a real facer. Luckily they'd sent for a couple of constables to deal with Violet, and they managed to stop Evans doing much more damage. That took a bit of doing, apparently. In the confusion Violet Evans ran off along the permanent way.'

'Have they found her yet?'

'No, sir. The chap in the signal box saw her at the level crossing. The gates were still closed because a goods train had only just gone through. But she went out through the side gate. He said he saw her run across the road and go into Angel Lane. And there was something else, sir. Pembridge says he talked to Malcolm Sedbury this evening.'

'Where?'

'Just outside the Station Hotel. Pembridge assumed he'd just had a drink there. I've got Hemlett checking.'

'When did Pembridge meet him?'

'About thirty-five minutes ago. We've got independent confirmation of that, too. The man in the signal box saw him. You could hardly miss him, he said, the way the lad drags himself around on those sticks. He saw him coming out of Templefields, crossing the road and then vanishing, presumably into the Station Hotel. Later he saw him going across the road again and into Angel Lane. It all fits with what Pembridge said.'

'So they're all there?'

'Beg pardon, sir?'

'They're all there except Bill Pembridge. Almost certainly. Jimmy Leigh, Violet Evans and Malcolm Sedbury. All somewhere in Templefields. We need to find them, Brian.'

'Not just them. Apparently Miss Francis went after Violet.'

There was a moment's silence. *Did Brian know? Or had he guessed?*

'All the more reason we need to find them soon,' Thornhill said crisply. 'I want as many men as possible down there. You'd better call in a dog-handler as well.'

A moment later he broke the connection. Then, despite the need to get to Templefields as quickly as possible, he dialled the operator and asked to be connected to Troy House. While the phone rang, he shifted his weight from foot to foot. Philip Wemyss-Brown answered.

'Good evening, sir. This is Richard Thornhill.'

'My dear fellow! What can I—'

'May I have a word with Mrs Wemyss-Brown?'

'You want the boss? Nothing simpler.'

Then Charlotte herself was on the line. He asked the question he should have asked before and received the answer that made everything clear.

'But I thought you *knew*, Mr Thornhill.'

'There was some uncertainty about the facts of the case,' he heard himself saying.

'You must have had your mind on something else,' Charlotte told him. 'A personal matter, perhaps. One should never allow oneself to be distracted from the business in hand, don't you agree? In my experience it's always a mistake. Once you allow yourself to be distracted, you never know what's going to happen.'

Chapter Fifty-eight

The only sounds were her footsteps on the cobbles, her own breathing and the rustle of water. Jill knew that only a hundred yards behind her, at the other end of Angel Lane, was New Bridge, with the lights of the railway station just beyond. She had left them all there – Ted Evans struggling between two police officers, Gerald Pembridge holding his bloody face and moaning, two porters, one with a cup of tea in his hand, standing with dazed expressions on their faces, watching events unfold.

Jill had followed Violet. She hadn't wanted to but no one else was going to do it so it had to be her. There was some light from the station behind and from the level crossing ahead. What looked like a rat scuttled across the tracks in front of her. She stumbled from sleeper to sleeper, closing her mind resolutely to the knowledge that the area between the rails on a line regularly used by passenger trains was little better than an open sewer.

The level-crossing gates were opening. She looked up and saw the bald, bowed head of the man in the signal box. He was hauling the wheel which operated the gates and did not look up. The side gate on the town side of the crossing was still swinging on its hinges. Jill went through and looked up the hill. No one was in sight. There hadn't been time for Violet to reach the Station Hotel. Logically, if logic had anything to do with it, she must have crossed the road and gone into Angel Lane.

Into Templefields.

Jill crossed the road. Angel Lane curved away into the distance. There were a few street lights along its length so light and darkness alternated. Darkness was winning. In the patches of light Jill saw cobbles, brick façades and the wire-thin lines of rain. At the far end of the lane, passing through the last bubble of light, was Violet Evans.

Jill shouted but the girl carried on running. There was nothing for it but to run after her.

But following someone in Templefields was not like following them somewhere else in town. Templefields was a place in transition, a place which was only partially connected to the stone and brick, tarmac and concrete, flesh and blood of the rest of Lydmouth and its inhabitants. Here and there were pockets of new council housing, some inhabited and some only half built. A few people still lived in the older buildings, clinging to the courts and tenements they'd known all their lives. There was also a sprinkling of shops, of small factories and warehouses. But many of the buildings were derelict, waiting for the arrival of the demolition men, and in the meantime the temporary domain of cats and rats. It was bad enough to find your way through Templefields in daylight, but the darkness and the rain made it much worse. So did the sense of fear that crept slowly over her.

She met no one. At the end of Angel Lane, she thought she heard footsteps in the small alley going off on her left. She called out but there was no reply. She followed the footsteps. Buildings closed in on her on every side. The alley swung round through ninety degrees and suddenly everything was dark. Water plopped noisily nearby, a steady dripping like a hurrying clock.

Jill moved a few yards on, feeling her way over the cobbles, step by step. There was a light on her left. She was at the mouth of an entry. She was just in time to see a figure hurrying round the corner.

'Violet!'

Jill swore and walked through the entry as fast as she dared. Just as she reached the other end, the thought occurred to her that she did not know it was Violet. She had glimpsed only a moving shape, roughly Violet's height, which had whisked round a corner as soon as Jill had set eyes on it.

The entry came out on another, wider road, where the darkness was relieved by a few street lamps. Jill turned right, as the figure ahead had done. No sign of her — *or him?* — now. She walked on, wishing she'd left Violet to her own devices.

The rain and the darkness sealed her off still further from the rest of the normal world. She began to feel she could wander here forever, trapped like Templefields between past and future, waiting for a dawn that might never come.

Jill's headscarf and the upturned collar of her raincoat muffled and distorted the sounds which reached her ears. The area itself, the network of lanes, alleys and passageways running between the buildings, created its own backdrop of noises, sometimes amplifying, sometimes diminishing them, sometimes creating echoes. Then there was the rain, always the rain, rustling and dropping and splashing, constructing a vocabulary of what Jill hoped were auditory illusions — pursuing footsteps, rustling leaves, whispering voices and, once, what sounded like a gunshot.

Suddenly everything changed. The road she was on curved sharply left and sloped downwards. It narrowed to a path, which almost immediately ran into a sloping T-junction with another path. On the far side of it was a broad strip of darkness. Beyond that was a greyer darkness, speckled with lights. The sounds of Templefields receded.

The sense of relief, of liberation, came before understanding.

She had reached the towpath along the river. The band of darkness immediately in front of her was the Minnow. She was no longer lost, not that she had admitted to herself earlier that she had been lost. If she turned right, she would come down to the Lyd, just a few minutes' walk away from New Bridge and the railway station. She wasn't sure where she would come out if she went left. But eventually the river must cross under the main road north.

Turning right was the sensible choice. Jill had no idea where Violet was, and there was no point in getting lost unnecessarily.

She was within a second of moving off down the path when a new sound stopped her. Midway between a grunt and a sigh, it was barely audible through the deep murmur of the river and the spitting and pattering of the rain. She turned round. There was a noise as if a stone had landed in a deep puddle.

'Who is it? Who's there?'

Her eyes adjusted to the shades of grey, picking out a paler huddle against the wall on the other side of the towpath. She took a step towards it.

'Violet?'

There was no answer. She took another step towards the wall. Someone was there, she was sure.

Metal chinked on stone.

'Who's there? Violet? Is that you?'

Out of the darkness came a man's laugh. Not quite a man's.

'Hello-ello,' said Jimmy Leigh.

Chapter Fifty-nine

'Hello-ello,' said Jimmy, wondering if this was another trick that someone was trying to play on him. 'Who are you?'

'I'm Miss Francis. I work for the *Lydmouth Gazette*. Have you got Violet there? Violet Evans?'

'Oh yes.'

He was standing behind her now. His left arm was across Violet's face, the crook of his elbow covering her mouth. He had Malcolm Sedbury's razor in his other hand, the one that was bleeding, and he'd lifted it up so the blade was resting lightly against Violet's throat. She was breathing very fast and raggedly. There was a funny smell which must come from the slaughter-house. His face and the front of his clothes felt wet, slippery with something which wasn't rainwater.

'Can she talk to me?'

Jimmy considered the request. He liked the sound of Miss Francis's voice and didn't think it was the sort of voice whose owner would play tricks. Besides, his left arm was getting uncomfortable. He doubted Violet would do anything silly if he took the arm away. Not while the razor was nudging her throat.

'You be a good girl, mind,' he murmured, releasing the left arm but fractionally increasing the pressure of the blade on her throat, just for an instant. 'Don't get up to no tricks. This one here, he might slip if you're a bad girl.'

'Miss Francis, I—'

'You be quiet now,' Jimmy ordered, enjoying the novelty of power. He edged the razor just a little closer. 'You be a good girl now. You wouldn't want to be like that Malcolm Sedbury. Dirty boy. He made a mess in bed in hospital.'

'Malcolm?' Miss Francis said. 'Has he been down here too?'

'He's bad,' Jimmy said. 'So I sent him away.' He felt Violet tensing herself against him. He pushed his crotch against her. He enjoyed the sensation so he pressed harder.

'How was Malcolm bad?'

'He did nasty tricks to Mattie. Mattie Harris.' Jimmy felt his excitement diminish and pulled himself a little away from Violet. 'Then he tried to hurt me, this evening, with this razor. But I took it off him. He cut me, so I cut him. Fair dos. Yes, he cut me, so I cut him.'

'So where is he now, Jimmy?'

'I put him in the river. Where Mattie was. That'll learn him. Won't be bad again, will he?'

'No,' said Miss Francis. 'I don't suppose he will.'

There was a moment's silence. Jimmy nuzzled against Violet's thigh and felt the excitement returning. She was so nice and soft and big. And she didn't say much. Not like Mattie. He remembered her in the bath. Her shoulders had felt like skinned rabbits. He'd felt the bones moving underneath the skin. She'd said dirty words to him, wanted him to do dirty things.

All Malcolm Sedbury's fault.

So Jimmy had to stop her talking, he had to stop her saying those dirty things, stop her making him feel funny. Aunt Minnie would wash her mouth out with soap if she'd heard. And his for listening. For wanting.

Not Aunt Minnie, not now. Cow. Ladies were all the same. You couldn't trust them.

But none of them were as bad as Malcolm bloody Sedbury

with his la-di-da parents and his big, expensive toys. Jimmy remembered when they were little, in the hospital, when he'd poked Malcolm in the eye one night and Malcolm had cried and cried. Aunt Minnie had known, Aunt Minnie who wasn't really Aunt Minnie, but she must have thought it was all right because she gave Jimmy a humbug and told Malcolm Sedbury to stop blubbing like a little baby.

'Mattie was nice to me,' he said to that darker part of the darkness where the lady's voice came from. 'So I looked after her. I kept an eye on her. She needed me to look after her.'

Then she spoiled it by saying dirty things, playing dirty tricks.

'And you looked after her on Thursday?'

Jimmy said, 'She asked me to. Asked me to walk with her. She said she was scared of going alone.'

'Going where?'

'Going from Ruispidge Hall up to Wynstones. On the footpath round the back of the girls' school – part of it goes through a field, and sometimes there's a bull in it. I'd have fought a bull for Mattie, I'd have fought anyone.'

'I'm sure you would.'

Jimmy slipped his right arm round Violet's waist so he could pull her against himself. He rotated his hips. 'She hadn't any clothes on, Miss. That Malcolm Sedbury made her take off all her clothes. She saw me outside and let me in. But she took me up to the bathroom. She wanted me to do dirty things with her. She shouldn't have done that, should she, Miss? She kept talking about things like that, dirty things, so I had to stop her, didn't I? And when she stopped I let go. Didn't really hurt her, Miss. I wouldn't do that.'

She'd waved her legs around an awful lot, Jimmy remembered, and splashed not just the bathroom floor but himself. She'd clawed at his hands and wrists with her fingers. She couldn't use her nails to scratch because they were bitten down to the quick.

But once her head had reared above the water. 'Fuck off,' she'd gasped. 'What do –?'

Dirty, dirty word. Had to stop her. Wash her mouth out with soap.

He'd been too strong for her. Then she was quiet and he could go away, let himself out through the front door and run home and lie with his head under the blankets.

'Drowner took her and put her in the river,' he went on. 'Drowner killed her.' His voice shook. 'Poor Mattie. Looked so funny in the river. Not like Mattie at all.'

'Why don't we go somewhere dry?' Miss Francis suggested. 'It's rather wet outside.'

Jimmy had an idea which shone like a bulb in his mind. They could go into Fenner's. The key was still under the stone outside the gates. The policeman had caught him just after he left Fenner's the other day, so they hadn't seen him hide it. Fenner's was his place, his and Mattie's and Violet's. Violet was here, so was he. The Drowner had Mattie now, but this Miss Francis lady would do. She could be Mattie instead.

There was a candle and a box of matches in the loft where he had hidden the engine. He could see what they looked like. Miss Francis, especially. Perhaps she looked like Mattie. Perhaps her body would be like Mattie's, as well as her face. The idea was so nice, that he'd found Mattie again, that he found himself grinding away, faster and faster against Violet's thigh. Violet's head jerked against his nose. The razor blade had slipped.

'Mattie,' Jimmy said breathlessly. 'I know somewhere dry. It's very near.'

'Let's go there, then,' said the nice Miss Francis. Not Mattie. 'You show us where to go, Jimmy.'

Jimmy liked having the razor. People did whatever he wanted. He thought he would always have a razor from now on. He guessed, though, because he was clever, that they might try and take it away from him. Then they wouldn't have to do what he liked any more.

So he kept tight hold of Violet, and tight hold of the razor which wasn't easy because the handle was so slippery. He nudged her towards the opening of the alley leading up to the gates into

Fenner's yard. There was some light here, filtering down from a street lamp on the corner of Mincing Lane. Not much, but enough to see the stone which covered the key.

He was finding it harder to breathe. His thing – what Aunt Minnie used to call his little man – felt big and hot. As they shuffled towards the gate, it rubbed against his trousers as though trying to burst the fly buttons and pop out into the open air. What would they do if that happened, he wondered? What would Violet do, what would the Miss Francis lady who was now Mattie do?

He heard a car engine in Mincing Lane. He prodded Violet to make her hurry. A moment later, they reached the big gates.

'Get the key,' Jimmy said to the Mattie woman. 'It's under that stone.'

The woman bent down and pulled at the stone. Jimmy hardly noticed. He rubbed his little man, which was not now so little, against Violet. He moved faster, pressed harder.

'Yes, yes, yes.'

Nothing mattered except the sensation welling out of what seemed to be the very centre of his body. Part pain, part pleasure, it surged out of him like an unfolding flower. He wanted it to stop and he wanted it to go on. He wanted it to last forever.

He arched his neck, raising his face to the sky. Drops of water fell on the skin, somehow complementing and increasing the pleasure below.

'Now, Mattie, *now.*'

It was at that moment that Mattie put her hand on his little man. Through half-shut eyes he saw her, the red hair so dark it looked black.

Dirty? Dirty?

She didn't speak this time, she didn't say anything dirty so it was all right. In a fraction of a second the hand slid down the stalk of the flower to the roots. The fingers curled and squeezed. Exquisite pain poured into him.

Jimmy was not aware of a car door slamming, of running

footsteps from Mincing Lane, of a man shouting. *Jimmy! Jimmy Leigh!* He was not aware of the Mattie lady wrapping her hands round his right wrist and the razor slipping through his bloody fingers and clattering on the cobbles below. He was not even aware he was screaming.

Chapter Sixty

Richard Thornhill drove slowly up Church Street and pulled over beside the lych gate. He glanced over his shoulder, across the road at Church Cottage. The light was on in the left-hand of the two upstairs windows.

There were always choices. Some were more noticeable than others, that was all.

He had phoned Edith more than an hour ago, telling her he would be late, telling her not to wait up for him. He had heard with a pang of guilt the relief in her voice when she heard that Mattie Harris's killer was now under lock and key. She always hated it when he was involved in a murder case. She was a good woman, and she loved him. She was the mother of his children.

Nothing was simple any more, and sometimes he doubted whether it had ever been. Jill Francis wasn't the woman he had thought she was just five days earlier.

He drove on a little way and tucked the Austin discreetly behind a big van parked in Nutholt Lane. He walked back to Church Cottage and rang the doorbell. There was a street lamp on the other side of the road and he felt like an actor under a spotlight. He stepped away from the front door, guessing she would look down from the window to see who it was.

The curtain twitched. He waited.

Time dragged by. Nothing happened. Perhaps, he thought, slipping into despair, she had seen him and decided not to answer the door. Perhaps she felt that enough was enough. Perhaps she felt, as he had sometimes felt during the last few days, that all this had been a mistake. One of those mistakes you find it hard to regret making, but a mistake, nevertheless.

God said, take what you want, and pay for it.

He wasn't the only one who had paid.

The bolts rattled back. The door opened a few inches. He slipped inside the house. Jill was wearing the Shantung silk dressing gown, cream with a faded blue and green pattern.

She looked up at him and the first thing she said was, 'My period's come.'

For a split second he did not know what she was talking about. His mind was full to the brim with Jimmy Leigh and Mattie Harris, with Edith and Jill herself.

What a heel I am. He had not thought of the delayed period for hours.

'I'm so glad,' he said and held out his hands.

She took them in hers. She looked years younger than when he had last seen her. 'I think it must have been that beastly business down by the river. The relief or something.' She winced. 'It's very painful.'

'Should I go?'

'There's no need. I was about to come down and make myself a drink. Would you like something?'

The boundaries were laid out early on. For this visit, at least, he was staying downstairs. Jill had a cup of cocoa and a couple of aspirin, while he mixed himself a large whisky and soda. There was a slight hesitation when they went into the sitting room. Two armchairs faced each other across the empty fireplace with a sofa further back between them. If Jill chose the sofa, she might be saying one thing. And if she chose an armchair, she might be saying another. She sat down at one corner of the sofa. But she did not make it clear whether or not she wanted

Thornhill to sit with her. So he postponed the decision, standing in front of the fireplace and sipping whisky.

'You knew it was Jimmy,' she said, looking up at him. 'You were expecting it to be him. You shouted his name as you came down the alley.'

'Yes.' He tried not to remember how he'd felt at that moment.

'But I thought you were sure that Williamson was wrong.'

'Williamson was right, I'm afraid. But for the wrong reasons. Damn him.' Thornhill had rung Williamson with the news, and the superintendent's jubilation had been barely decent. 'But I should have known much earlier. Your friend Charlotte said something when I bumped into her at the hospital on Tuesday morning. It should have put me on the trail right away.' He swallowed. 'Something distracted me.'

'Richard, you look *embarrassed*.'

'No, I'm not. Well, all right.' He jettisoned what was left of his dignity and smiled at her. 'I'll tell you later. The thing was, when I talked to Charlotte, we were still assuming that Mattie Harris had gone into the water near the Ferryman. Because of the compact and the story that young Sedbury and Pembridge made up. So we thought she'd floated down the Lyd, not the Minnow. And we thought whoever had been there with her, at about half-past ten was the man responsible. But Charlotte said it couldn't have been Jimmy because he was nowhere near the Ferryman at half-past ten. *In other words, she'd seen him somewhere else.* The trouble was, I wasn't listening to what she was saying.'

'But why not?'

'Because her real reason for buttonholing me had nothing to do with Leigh. What she was really wanted was to warn me to stay away from you. To tell me that I was damaging your *reputation*.'

They looked at each other for a moment. Then Jill patted the sofa beside her, and he sat down. She put her hand on top of his.

'She's warned me, too. I told you.'

'So she knows about us,' he said. 'We have to assume that. Or if she doesn't know, she's got very strong suspicions.'

Jill released his hand and sat back. 'But there's nothing we can do about it now. But what did she say about Jimmy? Where *had* she seen him?'

'When she was at the High School on Thursday evening.'

Jill nodded. 'The Governors' Meeting. That must've been it.'

'She'd parked the car near the old library at the back of the school. When she turned on the headlights, the beam shone right through the fence. And there he was. Jimmy. He was walking towards the Ruispidge Hall. There's a footpath that runs all the way from Narth Road. As soon as the lights came on, he bolted, of course. There was something a little odd about his appearance, she said this evening, and she'd only just realised what it must have been. He was wet. Dripping wet. Dripping wet, on a dry evening.'

'But why?'

'Because Mattie must have struggled. Perhaps she even pulled him down towards the bath. And if I hadn't been so stupid—'

'Stop it, Richard. What's done, is done.'

'If I hadn't been so stupid, Malcolm Sedbury might still be alive.' He swallowed the rest of his whisky. 'His poor bloody parents. I had to tell them the news.'

God said, take what you want, and pay for it.

'Have they found the body?'

Thornhill nodded. 'Down by New Bridge. Very near where Mattie's was. It looks like he took the razor out with him to protect himself. Ted Evans said he had it in his pocket the other day. Jimmy had slashes on the palm of his left hand so we think Malcolm pulled out the razor, then Jimmy grabbed it and turned it on Malcolm. There's a slab they use for sharpening knives outside the slaughterhouse. One of the coping stones of the parapet just above the river. Jimmy got him there. Sliced through the carotid artery. He was covered in Malcolm's blood. But you know that. You saw him.'

'Not in the light.'

'Puddles of the stuff on the path and the parapet. So much that the rain couldn't wash it away.'

'It will.'

He turned his head to look at her. 'I'm sorry. Talking about myself again. You must be feeling terrible. When I think how near you came to——'

'The relief helps to make up for it. Sounds very selfish, I'm afraid, but it does.'

'Relief?'

'That I'm not pregnant.'

'Yes,' said Thornhill, irrationally disappointed. 'Yes, I can see that.'

'What will happen to Evans?'

'Not very much. I had a quiet word with Williamson. He's going to have a quiet word with Pembridge. All the quiet words. I'm learning.'

'What do you mean?'

'That it's the way business is done in this town. People have quiet words with other people. Pembridge will leave Ted Evans alone because otherwise I shall raise awkward questions in public about the nature of his relationship with Mattie Harris.'

'And Violet?'

'She's going back to live with her parents. With her daughter, too. Williamson tells me that Pembridge may be able to provide her with a small allowance.' He laughed, and the sound came out more harshly than he expected. 'Would you mind if I had some more whisky?'

When he came back into the room, Jill said softly, 'We all assumed that Jimmy Leigh couldn't hurt a fly, just because he's retarded.'

'He's not had a pleasant life. It makes you want to pass it on to other people. At least he won't hang.'

'How did you know where to come this evening?'

'I didn't. We went down to Mincing Lane because it was near

his house, and because when Jimmy ran off, he was found outside Fenner's. So it seemed a good place to start. Violet says the three of them used to go there with Mattie when she worked at the slaughterhouse. Mattie treated Jimmy like a sort of mascot. A pet.'

'People like Mattie are dangerous in Lydmouth,' Jill said. 'They disrupt things. When people aren't sexually conventional, you never quite know what's going to happen.'

'There's a price for everything.'

'But you know, it wasn't her fault. In a way they were all guilty.'

Bewildered, Thornhill stared at her.

'All the men who wanted to go to bed with Mattie.' She avoided his eyes. 'All the men who did. The young men, the old men. The only difference between them was that the old men could be cleverer about covering their tracks. You could just as well say that the *men* are the guilty ones. And that girls like Mattie sooner or later turn into their victims. Because they bear the burden of the guilt and the men don't.' She paused for a moment and then went on in a quieter voice: 'Talking of conformity, talking of guilt, reminds me of Bernie. He—'

'I don't want to talk about Bernie.' Thornhill put down the whisky glass on the side table. He turned towards Jill and placed his hands on her shoulders. 'You think you're like Mattie, don't you?'

'A victim? Sexually unconventional?'

'Both.'

'Well? Don't *you*?'

'No,' he said. 'No, I don't.'

'Perhaps I want to be. Both.' She nibbled her lower lip. 'Just a bit. God knows.'

The more he knew Jill, the more there was to know. He looked at her, thinking that perhaps he was seeing her now more clearly than he'd ever done. He noticed how pale she was, the fine lines around her eyes, the faint blueness of her eyelids, the shining blackness of her pupils.

What had really happened in the alley with the screaming man-boy? What effects would it have on her, on him?

He slid his arm round her shoulders. She leant towards him, her body fitting snugly against his. He wished he could save her from her past and her future. He wished there could be no today, no tomorrow, no yesterday.

Just now.

'Jill?' he murmured into her hair. 'Jill darling, what the hell are we going to do?'

ANDREW TAYLOR

THE SUFFOCATING NIGHT

When squatters move into a disused military camp near Lydmouth, public opinion is divided: do they have a genuine and desperate need of shelter or are they merely unpatriotic scroungers and Communist sympathisers? The controversy attracts the attention of Cameron Rowse, a right-wing London journalist.

There are other strangers in Lydmouth too, and each has his secret agenda. When a man is found murdered in the Bathurst Arms, Detective Inspector Richard Thornhill has no shortage of suspects. One of them is Philip Wemyss-Brown, editor of the Lydmouth Gazette – the friend and employer of Jill Francis.

Once again, Jill and Richard Thornhill pursue the same answers for conflicting reasons. This time, however, there is a difference. Thornhill and Jill have a second problem to solve. And this one is even harder, and far more personal.

HODDER AND STOUGHTON PAPERBACKS

ANDREW TAYLOR

THE LOVER OF THE GRAVE

After the coldest night of the year, they find the man's body. He is dangling from the Hanging Tree on the outskirts of a village near Lydmouth, with his trousers round his ankles. Is it suicide, murder, or accidental death resulting from some bizarre sexual practice?

Journalist Jill Francis and Detective Inspector Thornhill become involved in the case in separate ways. Jill is also drawn unwillingly into the affairs of the small public school where the dead man taught. Meanwhile a Peeping Tom is preying upon Lydmouth; Jill has just moved into her own house an is afraid she is being watched. And there are more distractions, on a personal level, for both policeman and reporter.

HODDER AND STOUGHTON PAPERBACKS

ANDREW TAYLOR

THE MORTAL SICKNESS

When a spinster of the parish is found bludgeoned to death in St John's, and the church's most valuable possession, the Lydmouth chalice, is missing, the finger of suspicion points at the new vicar, who is already beset with problems.

The glare of the police investigation reveals shabby secrets and private griefs. Jill Francis, struggling to find her feet in her new life, stumbles into the case at the beginning. But even a journalist cannot always watch from the sidelines. Soon she is inextricably involved in the Suttons' affairs. Despite the electric antagonsim between her and Inspector Richard Thornhill, she has instincts that she can't ignore.

HODDER AND STOUGHTON PAPERBACKS